M.A.G.I. HUNTERS 2

D. LEVESQUE

By D. Levesque

Don't forget to leave a review here after you are done
reading the book
And also, please sign up for my newsletter at
http://dlevesqueauthor.com/
You can also join my fan group on Facebook here
https://www.facebook.com/groups/975722739547373

CHAPTER ONE

I glance down at the form of my beautiful wife of three months, and I can't help but grin. To say that the last three months have been a whirlwind would be an understatement. What with my new job as a M.A.G.I. Hunter, and also the deals we were doing with Mike and his parents, things have been quite busy.

One thing that had shocked me, though, was when Mike's parents—Leo and Linda—had made it a point that no deal was going forward unless I got ten percent of the profits on both sides. So technically, I was making ten percent on both ends of every deal. Based on the numbers that Mike was throwing around, it wasn't going to be just a couple of coins, either.

According to Tallen, who had wholeheartedly agreed to the deal, I might be the richest M.A.G.I. agent ever. While Marissa's father was powerful and wealthy, that didn't mean she was. But, since technically we were married, mi casa es su casa, or did that fall more into 'what's yours is yours and what's mine is also yours'?

I had told Leo and Linda that they didn't need to do that, but apparently, according to Mike, it was their way of showing me their love and how proud they were of me. They didn't know all the details of my new job, but they knew I was now technically in law enforcement, just of a supernatural kind.

I hear a soft female voice whisper, "What?"

And I jerk in surprise, as I had been so focused on my thoughts, that I had apparently zoned out. With a small laugh, I tell Marissa, "Nothing. I was daydreaming... Or trying to process what has been happening to me these last four months."

With a wry grin, she replies, "Yeah, a lot has happened." Scooting over, she rests her chin on my chest and, peering up at me, she asks, "What's the plan for today?"

I reach over to grab my phone. Yes, I finally broke down and bought a cell phone—since the conversion rate of Galactic Credits, or GCs, to the US dollar was pretty sweet. With my new pay of almost 60,000 GCs a month, I converted some of it to dollars and joined the 21st century. While I was on Vraka, though, it didn't work, as there were no cell towers here. But I was still able to use its calendar feature offline.

"Let's see," I say, sliding open my phone. "We have a meeting at noon with your Dad for something, but before that we have to go see Mike. He said he had something amazing to show me that came out of his R&D lab." I roll my eyes. "Something that Jim cooked up."

Shaking her head ruefully, Marissa snorts. "That man scares me just how smart he is."

"Yeah," I tell her with a chuckle. "Jim is smart as hell. Let's see. Then, we need to see Pathy later for our new assignment." I frown. "I guess we will need to have someone watch over our new place since we're starting our official assignment on Earth. God, it feels weird saying that."

"Actually, Mavin offered to watch our place for us."

"I bet he did," I say, laughing at her. "How many packages of Oreos will that cost us?"

With her own chuckle, Marissa tells me, "As if you care. How many packages do you have socked away in the kitchen cupboard?"

"Hey, I like Oreos, too!" I tell her defensively, which makes her giggle.

"Well, I'm sure you can sacrifice a package or two a week to Mavin. Oh," she utters, suddenly leaning up. "Did you hear that Mavin is engaged?"

"He is?" The idea of Mavin, our carefree, Oreo cookie-eating fairy getting engaged, is hard to take.

"He's a Royal, so I'm not surprised. Maybe we will meet her?"

"That would be nice," I tell her with a smile. "Is she a cookie monster too?"

"Kevin," Marissa replies, rolling her eyes. "She's a fairy."

"Right. So that's a yes." I snort, turning off my phone. "Well, that's our day."

With a sigh, Marissa slumps back down on my chest. "I guess that means we should get out of bed."

I put my phone down, grab Marrisa by her arms, and flip her over, so that now I am loom over her while leaning on my arms.

"Or..." I tell her with a grin.

"Or?" she repeats, her grin even bigger.

"Or we take our time and arrive fashionably late."

With a laugh, Marissa raises up to kiss me on the lips. "I like that idea!"

* * *

"Glad you decided to join us," Mike tells me with a knowing grin.

I can't help but laugh at him. "Sorry... not sorry."

"Leave the poor man alone," Jim tells him, slapping Mike on the shoulder. "They're newlyweds."

Looking over at Marissa with a smile, he says, "Not that you can blame the man, having such a beautiful wife."

Marrisa smiles at Jim, but she's beaming and blushing at the same time.

"So," I say, changing the subject from my sex life to the reason they wanted to see me. "What do you have to show me?"

Mike looks at me with a big grin. "Oh, you're going to love what Jim came up with."

"Only because you asked some what-ifs," Jim says, blushing.

Jim always took praise from Mike seriously. One thing about Jim, he was so smart, he didn't need to suck up to anyone. I'm one hundred percent sure that, if Jim had been on his own, he would have been a millionaire himself by now. He was that smart. The fact that he prefers to work for Mike, knowing he could succeed on his own, tells you a little about the high regard Jim has for Mike.

We have been best friends for so long, that the number of times we have overheard people say that Jim was Mike's sycophant, was laughable. Jim called Mike out on his bullshit —or even called him an idiot—so many times, that I would need multiple hands to hold up that many fingers. Then again, I've called Mike an idiot my fair share of time, too.

"I'll let Jim explain."

"Thanks, Mike. So, what Mike thought, after looking at that Portal stone of yours…"

"It's my PDA, or Porting Device Assistant," I interrupt.

"Right," Jim continues, "when Mike looked at your PDA, as you call it, he noted how it lacked certain features."

I lift an eyebrow at him. "It's a rock."

"He's got you there, Jim!" Mike says.

"Ah," Jim says with a grin, "but it's a rock with an energy signal."

Marrisa chimes in, her tone confused. "It does?"

"It does. One that is even quantifiable by our equipment. Though," Jim continues, getting into lecturer mode, "if we had used standard equipment to check for normal energies, we would have just found out that your PDA rock was just that—a rock. But imagine our surprise when we used…"

"Jim," Mike interrupts him.

"Sorry," he says, blushing. "Anyhow, we found that we can track the energy inside the stone. Thanks for letting me use it for the past 48 hours," he says, handing me back my PDA.

I see that he does so almost reluctantly, not that I can blame the man. I mean, technically, I'd just let him borrow my rock. My magical rock.

"So, from what you told me, you have... what? Three locations tagged to that PDA?"

"Yeah." I nod. "I have my house on Vraka..."

"Which is still freaky to hear about," Mike mumbles.

"I also have one for M.A.G.I. HQ, and also here... at Mike's place."

"Right, that's what you said. Looking at the signatures, I was able to isolate those three signatures." He squinted at me. "And then we found a fourth signature."

"A fourth?" I ask, puzzled. Then it dawns on me. "Oh, crap. That would be the training facility they sent me to." I rub the back of my neck. "My bad. So... uh... yeah, there are four locations in my PDA."

Jim nods. "Then that make a lot more sense."

"Ok," Marissa asks him, "You can see how many locations are in a PDA based on their signatures? But what does that mean?"

"Yes, we can identify the stored signatures," Jim tells her excitedly, "but, not only that. We can do other things to it."

I stare at him, not understanding. "Other things to it?"

He nods with a big grin. "We can add locations to it, too. You now have five locations in your PDA. Come on, you'll want to see this."

He waves for us to follow him, and we head into the next room, which I see is a lab of some kind, with equipment I can't make heads or tails of.

"Now," Jim says, pointing to a low table with a pedestal on it, "Can you put your PDA on there? Align it so that it points to the middle of the room." He walks over a few steps to stand in the middle of the room. "Right here."

"Sure," I tell him hesitantly.

I take my PDA out of my pocket and place the black portal stone on it, and, as he requested, I point it, so the focal point aligns to where he had just been standing.

"Perfect," Jim says, jumping over to the strange rack of equipment to fiddle with one of the machines, turning dials and flipping buttons. He then sits down in a chair in front of a laptop and begins typing in a series of numbers.

Suddenly, there is a loud hum of power in the room, and without warning, a black portal appears in the middle of it. I immediately notice that this portal shows signs of instability. Whereas a typical portal was black as midnight, with a glossy sheen to it, and round, like the entrance to one of those cozy homes in a hill you might expect a rather short person with hairy feet to live in, this one was a tall oval—and erratic. It had shots of gray static in it now and then. And the edges, instead of being crisp and sharp, were fuzzy and seemed to throw out static bursts of white and black motes.

Marissa was looking at the unstable portal dubiously. "I would not walk through that. But, my gods... you were able to activate it without using any magic?"

"Yes! I have not totally isolated the necessary signal, but as I only had 48 hours with your PDA, Kevin, I was limited in what tests I could run. Even so, we came up with... this!"

"Jesus H. Christ," I mutter, my jaw still on the floor. "You took a magical device and, without any magic of your own, you were able to activate it!"

Suddenly, with a loud bang, the less than subtle hum of power in the room disappears.

"Yes, but there is also that," he says with a sour expression. "I used up so much power doing so, it seems I blew another capacitor."

"Do you even know what this means?" Marrisa murmurs looking at Jim with new respect.

"That a non-magic user can one day use a PDA?" Mike replies with a shit-eating grin.

"Yes." She frowns. "Mike, don't take this the wrong way, but having humans being able to access a PDA without magic, and being able to add locations to it like you said you could..." My wife trails off, her eyes wide.

"Speaking of which," I say, pointing to the location where the portal had just been, "where did that portal go to?"

"Outside in the garden," Mike tells me.

"But I already had your place programmed into it."

"Yes, but you had it set to outside the front gates. Jim here was able to input a new location. We know it works, since when we did it earlier, Jim kept an eye on the portal here in this room while I checked on the one out in the garden."

I look at Marissa, and her mouth is open. In either shock or awe, or both.

She turns and whispers. "Do you know what that means?"

"That Mike and Jim came up with something amazing?"

"Not exactly," she says numbly. "It means that if this works, those magical folk who can't do enough magic to use a PDA, suddenly can!"

"Damn," Mike whispers in awe. "I never even thought of that! We were only thinking about how a human could use one to travel."

Ah, hell. That would really turn the galaxy on its head. Then I have another thought, one that sends a chill down my spine.

"Mike?" I ask him slowly, looking around the room. "Who else knows about this?"

"No one—yet," he replies, confused. "Why?"

Sighing, because I seem to be the only one who sees the implication of this, I stare at my two friends. "I think you need to keep this close to your vest, while we," I point to my wife and myself, "go talk to Marissa's Dad, Targun. Because something tells me that if the Council finds out what you two did, they won't think this is amazing—it'll scare the crap out of them."

"Why?"

"Think about it. You are telling me that humans can now use, or are learning to use, a PDA without magic—which will enable them to travel, not just to locations on Earth, but to any location in the galaxy that the PDA has a setting for?"

Mike, Marrisa, and Jim all stare at me with wide eyes. Marrisa is the one to utter the words we are all thinking.

"Oh, shit!"

CHAPTER TWO

Marrisa asks me for the fifth time this morning. "Are you sure you want to tell my Dad this?"

"Yeah," I say, giving a deep sigh. "If I don't, I'm afraid that it will get out to the other members of the Council." I pinch the bridge of my nose. "And I don't want my friends hurt or killed if this gets out."

"Well, I don't think they would necessarily be..." she begins to say, but then closes her mouth at my raised eyebrows.

"Fine," she says with a sour expression. "They would."

"Which is why we need to talk to your Dad. I'm glad we already had a meeting set up. By the way, when is Carmen supposed to meet us?"

Her sour expression gets more pronounced. "She is meeting us at M.A.G.I. H.Q."

Knowing some of the history between those two, I understand that Carmen isn't my wife's favorite person—though the two had once been lovers. The reason for Marissa's attitude revolved around a bizarre unrequited love triangle with Marissa's mentor and trainer. Marrisa had loved her first M.A.G.I. partner, but those feelings did not seem to be returned. Unable to act on that relationship, she met and had gotten close with Carmen.

When her partner died five years ago while on Earth, killed by humans in a crossfire of bullets masterminded by a thief they were chasing, Marissa found out that Carmen and her recently deceased had once been an item. It seemed that the main issue wasn't so much Carmen, but the fact that Marissa's love for her partner had been unrequited, and that she had only found out after her partner had lied about their previous relationship. When she'd found out, she was hurt that neither Carmen nor Marissa's partner had told her they had once been intimate, which had let to a big fight and their split.

I think it was most likely a combination of jealousy, as Carmen once had what she had wanted, and being left in the dark, that infuriated my wife. So while that phase of her life with Carmen was over, ever since then, there had been bad blood between the two women. It seems Marissa was the type who held a grudge.

Hell, she'd hated me when we first met, just for being human. Because humans had killed her partner. Things between us had gotten off to a rocky start when it became necessary for the two of us to wed—even though this kept me out of the Galactic Council's hands and Marissa out of jail—given her prejudice. Getting past the high and strong walls she'd put up, was a significant achievement I was rather proud of.

Though Marissa had softened enough to admit that humans might not all be bad, and she liked to point out that I wasn't completely human anymore, her attitude towards Carmen had not improved. I explained to Marissa that she was asking a lot. Was I required to give her a list of names and reference for all the lovers and partners I'd had before we had been forced together? Once it was said out loud, she slowly agreed that no, she didn't need me to give her a list of names. Only then, did Marissa realize that her distrust of Carmen was just as silly as it sounded. But my beautiful wife could teach mules a thing or two about being stubborn.

A shrill voice pulls me from my thoughts, "What you doing here?!"

Turning with a smile, I tell the little goblin. "Hey, Preeka! I have a meeting with your master."

The goblin gazes at me suspiciously, but then slowly nods, her mouth making chewing movements. Preeka was, as odd as it sounded, an excellent specimen of a goblin. She was smart, but she was ugly... like damn ugly, almost on the verge of being fugly. She was about three feet tall, with loose green skin, and skinny to the point of being scrawny. On top of that, she has no hair to speak of, and her eyes are black and twice the size of a human's. And they're bloodshot—which seems to be a thing for her.

Goblins, I'd learned, got smarter by working for someone—it had something to do with them working and doing something well. Magic was somehow involved, which made them smarter. Unfortunately, it didn't make them any cuter. Having met a few other goblins recently, I had to admit that the bug-eyed, scrawny, snaggle-toothed goblin was prettier than most of her kin. The last one I'd met, was much uglier than Preeka.

A goblin's indenture usually lasted twenty years or so, but it was something they got a measurable benefit from. It seems that goblins were what kept the Magical worlds going; they were the common workforce on many magical worlds. It even got to the point, that when the majority of Magical Folk left earth for their own worlds, and goblins had asked all the races for help moving to their own world, they'd gotten the help. That's how important goblins were.

So there were nine worlds, including Earth, which was the mother world. Then there was Vamir, the Vampire world; Gotro, the Beast world; and Vraka, the Changeling world. Then there was Lotri, the world of the Fairies; Kratar, the Werewolves' world; and Rima the Dwarven world. Finally, there was Ilia, the Elven world; and, last but not least, was Grog—the world that the Goblins were given. Vraka is where Marissa was from, and the current world we were on.

"You sure?"

With a disarming smile, I tell her, "Yes. But, I brought you a surprise."

"Oh?" she perks up.

Out of my pocket, I take out one of those small packs of Oreo cookies that contains only four cookies. Preeka's eyes widen in joy, and she sticks out both her small stick arms towards me, claws grasping. Both Marrisa and I laugh at her, and I toss her the pack of Oreos.

Preeka catches the package without any effort, and screams, "I tells master you's here!" Then she is gone in a displacement of air.

"You know you'll need to keep bringing her cookies now," Marrisa says, shaking her head. But she's smiling, which is a good—if uncommon—look for her, and nice to see.

When we'd first met, I didn't like her. Or rather, I didn't like her attitude. She was bitchy, snarky, and downright mean to me. But now that things between us were better, she was a joy to be around. It helped that she was also a hot as fuck catgirl!

I turn to Marissa and grin at her. "All good. I bought a box of those snack pack ones."

"You're going to spoil her," I hear a deep voice rumble from the doorway.

Turning, I see that it's Marissa's Dad, Magus Targun. Sorry, I suppose it would be best to introduce him by his full title: Sir Magus Targun Lalouton. He was not only the strongest and most powerful Magus in all the nine worlds, at least until I was fully tested, but he was also the Lead Councillor on the Council of Galactic Folk.

Technically, he was also my boss, as I now worked for M.A.G.I.—the Magical Agency for Galactic Investigation. We were a small group of maybe twenty-five or so senior mages, and we served the Galactic Council to enforce its edicts, but on a galactic scale. As we worked on all the worlds, we were not beholden to the authority of a world—even the one on which we were stationed—but to the Council itself. And with Marissa's father being the Galactic Council's lead member, and me M.A.G.I.'s most powerful mage, I worked directly for him.

I laugh at his quip. "If it means I can get on her good side," I explain, "I'm willing to spend a couple of dollars to bribe her with cookies."

"Well, just don't overdo it. Otherwise, she will start asking for it as part of her employment with me," he growls, but he's smiling as he says it. "You're early for our meeting, aren't you?"

I rub the back of my neck nervously. "Yeah. I wanted to talk to you about something before it got out."

Targun looks at me with a raised eyebrow. "What can that be?"

"So, my friends Mike and Jim might have figured out a way to, hmm..." I take a deep breath and then blow it all out at once. "They figured out how to access and use Portal stones without magic."

At first, Targun doesn't answer me or reply, but his face had suddenly shut down. He had lost the smile he had, and he was gazing at me hard.

"Please, tell me everything," he instructs.

So I do. For the next five minutes, I explain as much as I can about what Jim had said, and about the demonstration they'd given us—with Marissa chiming in now and then to correct me, or to add her own observations on a point that she'd heard.

Marrisa's Dad, throughout the entire, long-winded explanation, remained quiet and didn't interrupt. Finally, once we are done talking, he sighs and waves for us to follow him out of the foyer to a door that I had never before seen on the second floor of his home. He opens the door and walks in, beckoning the two of us to follow him.

Inside is a large office, with a desk and shelves loaded with tons of books. But, these aren't just any old books, like you might find in some bookstore. These books are incredibly old, but it is also clear that they were not printed or bound by a machine. They give off the comforting smell of old paper that I've learned to associate with knowledge. They are all excellent examples of what on Earth is the lost art of bookbinding. All are leather-bound works of art.

Once inside, Targun points us to the seats in front of his desk, while he sits down in the large chair behind that massive piece of oak.

After staring at the ceiling for an uncomfortably long time, he asks, "You're sure about this?"

"Yes." Marrisa is the one to answer. "We saw the Portal open, even though it was unstable."

Sighing and pinching the bridge of his nose, Targun mutters with his eyes still closed. "Well... shit."

"Yeah," I tell him. "I figured we 'd tell you right away—hence why we are early. I don't want my two friends suddenly to disappear on me."

"No, I don't want that either," Targun nods and tells me, opening his eyes. "Preeka!" he suddenly shouts.

I have gotten used to him doing that, but this time he caught me by surprise. Though, I am happy to say, that Marissa jumped as well. It made me feel better, knowing I wasn't the only one that he'd made jump out of their own skin.

"Yes, master?" she suddenly appears on his desk, looking expectantly up at him.

How the hell do Goblins do that? With all that information I'd downloaded—or that had been shoved into my head, really—not once had it ever mentioned how Goblins can appear and disappear like that.

"I need form 34 and form LA4... actually I will need two of each of those. Can you go get them for me? And a pen!" he blurts out quickly, before she can disappear.

"What forms are those?" I ask him after Preeka is gone.

"Form 34 is to make it so that both of your friends work directly under me. Form LA4 is a Leave Alone level 4, meaning they can't be touched—and if they are, there will be dire consequences. LA4's are only given to those working on high-profile, galactic security projects. And with this, your friends just become part of my team." He heaved a massive sigh. "If this was to get out, Kevin... Your two friends would be killed for the knowledge they possess, or in this case, for what they figured out."

"Is it that bad, Dad?"

Targun turns to his daughter and nods. "Yes. This is the first time I have ever heard of a human being able to even make a Portal stone do anything more than serve as a decent paper-weight. Though, from what you are telling me, they were able to open a Portal to an unregistered location, which is even worse." He stroked his chin. "But damn, the idea of being able to use a Portal without Magic? Do you know what Magical folks who can't do enough magic to operate a Portal stone would pay for that? Being able to skip going to a Porter portal?"

"Are they that expensive? I thought Portals were cheap... something like 30 dollars, or only 25 credits?"

"Yes. But add that up for every single trip, and it gets costly. Now, imagine you can buy a device that will replace the tedium of waiting in line for you and paying for rides left and right?" He grunted. "Damn, I need to go see those two, and see what they have puzzled out so far. I might even be able to help them a bit."

"Does that mean they can get a patent for this?"

"No." Shaking his head, Targun explains. "There is no such thing as a patent in the Magical worlds. Earth is the only one that has something like that. But, your friends will get rich off of their invention—though, it will have to be through an intermediary. They're human, after all." He finishes with a shrug.

"Can we use me as their intermediary? Since I'm technically human, but can do Magic?"

Targun looks at me thoughtfully. "Hmmm."

"It might just work, Dad."

Suddenly Preeka is on the desk once more, and hands Targun some forms. Targun smiles at her, taking the forms, and the offered pen.

"Can you also get me a form 3, Preeka?"

Without a word, Preeka disappears again, and Targun lines the forms up on his desk and begins to fill them out. By the time he is on the last form, Preeka has reappeared to offer him another form. Absently, Targun sets this one down next to the others and continues writing.

Once he is done, having filled out the last form, he offers me the final paper. "This is a Form 3. This makes you the sole owner of that technology. How you decide to pay your friends, though, is up to you."

In surprise, I ask him. "Wait. You're saying that any money from the sale of this technology will come to me? I thought they were going to be working under you?"

"They are," he says with a nod. "But while we magical folk have no patents, there is still a rule that whoever creates something, that person owns it. No one would try to do so without your permission."

"Damn, that would never work on Earth," I say with a whistle.

"No, it would not. But, these are Magical folk we are talking about. They know, understand, and abide by rules."

Under her breath, I hear Marissa mutter, "For the most part..."

"Now that this interesting news is taken care of," Targun sits back in his chair, "shall we get to primary reason I wanted to see you today?"

My wife frowns. "You never did tell me why you wanted to see us, Dad. Is something wrong?"

This time, Targun's sigh is even deeper and more pronounced.

"Yes. About that..."

CHAPTER THREE

Half an hour later, I say to Marissa in a shocked tone for about the third time, "Your Dad can't be serious!"

Now it's her turn to sigh deeply. "It seems my Dad is quite serious."

"But what he is asking is impossible!"

"He would not ask it of us if he thought we couldn't do it."

"But, he wants to remove all other M.A.G.I. Agents from Earth, and make it so that only, you and I work there," I sputtered.

"And Carmen," she adds with a sour expression—which I can't tell if it is because it feels like we have been given an impossible task, or because it's Carmen.

"But that means that the twelve agents working there now will be removed. How does he expect just the three of us to watch over the entire Earth?"

"That, I'm not sure about." She pursed her lips, pinching the bridge of her nose. "Maybe Carmen will have some ideas?"

"God, I sure hope so." I press the heels of my palms to my eyes. "I know she worked on Earth for a while, before she was demoted to a desk job. Though, now that she's partnered with us, it seems that she is back on the active roster."

"Did she mention why she was benched?" Marissa asks.

"Yeah. Apparently, Carmen got into too many Council members' faces and caused too much of an uproar… though I'm not sure about any of the details."

With another sour expression, Marissa asks, "Well, shall we get going? We are supposed to meet her at M.A.G.I. HQ."

Nodding, I take out my P.D.A.—my Portal Device Assistant—and call up a Portal. Within seconds, the black Portal appears before us—black and circular. Thankfully, it is stable, not like the one that Mike and Jim had tried to call up. This one was rock solid and not at all fuzzy.

Without hesitation, Marissa walks towards it and, within seconds, disappears. Blowing out a heavy sigh, I follow her. Once on the other side, after feeling an uncomfortable icy sensation wash over my skin, I look around.

We come out in front of the M.A.G.I. H.Q. building. The Portal wouldn't allow us to go directly into the building itself; special permits were required for that. But, we needed to get to the top floor in order to see Pathy, the administrator who runs M.A.G.I. HQ. And one thing I'd learned about using Portals, was that you always did so at ground level—unless you could fly. It seems that, if you are on, say, the fifth floor and call up a Portal to somewhere... you will come out of your portal five stories up in the air.

Can you say *SPLAT*? Unless you can fly, that is. It's a doozy of a first step.

And while flying is possible, it uses an extreme—like beyond stupid—amount of power to do so. I had seen Marissa do it once. She had floated down the side of a building after throwing the criminal she was pursuing out of the warehouse's top floor window. Thinking back, I realize now why she had been fatigued and out of breath. At the time, I'd been too mesmerized by her heaving chest to wonder if flying like that was difficult.

M.A.G.I. HQ was six stories high, and the admin officers were on the top floor. It had never occurred to me to ask what else might be on the other floors. Marissa had said M.A.G.I only occupied the top floor. Of course, that means that once we are in the building, we head on up the stairs. At least this time, when we get to the sixth floor, I am not out of breath—much.

Once upstairs, I look down the hall and see Bower walking towards us. To call him a big man is a gross understatement —the guy is enormous. He's what I know now to be a Beast. He is what we call an Enforcer, and he is huge. If a grizzly bear had human features, it would look like Bower.

"Kevin!" growls the man, a big grin on his face.

At least there are no hard feelings for what happened last time we met. I am thrilled not to see anger flare up in his brown eyes this time, but friendship.

"Hey, Bower," I tell him, returning his grin and sticking a hand out, which he takes in a firm grip.

The first time we'd met, he'd tried to attack me. Though she thought it would be a good prank, Marissa did kind of give him permission. Fortunately for me, at the time, I'd been wearing a collar that Targun had placed on me—partly to make sure I didn't run away, but it also provided the additional benefit of protecting me.

Which Bower found out the hard way, when he'd tried to grab me. He'd obviously been trying to hurt the human who showed up where he had no business being—maybe he'd even intended to kill me—but thanks to the collar's protection, he'd been blown across the room, through the wall, and into his wife's office. He literally pancaked her desk, landing on her. To say Pathy had been angry, would be like saying a Canadian goose isn't nice. It was an understatement.

The big man bends down to my ear and growls what I supposed he thought of as 'softly', "Carmen is already in the office with Pathy."

Rolling her eyes with a sour expression, Marrisa tells him. "You know I'm not deaf, right?"

The big man has the grace to blush. His idea of a whisper was a growl that I'm sure anyone in the offices to either side of us, if there is anyone in there, can hear.

"Thanks, Bower." I clap him on the back—or rather, I try to. I end up slapping my hand on his side.

"No problem, Kevin. I'm about to go get lunch for Pathy and myself. Did you all want something?"

I look at Marissa, and she shakes her head.

"No. We are only picking up Carmen and getting our assignment from Pathy. Thanks, though."

Bower looks at both of us with a look I can't place and finally nods. "Good luck." With that, he heads down the stairs, his footsteps echoing in the stairwell. I mean, the man is immense. I don't think he could tiptoe, even if he wanted to.

"What was that about?" I ask Marissa with a raised eyebrow.

"I think he knows something about our first assignment, but can't say anything. Shall we go see Pathy?"

At Pathy's door, I knock on the doorframe.

"Come in!" I hear her voice shout through the door.

I open the door, walk in, and hold it open for Marissa.

Pathy isn't alone. A blonde in a short skirt with an impressive bust has one leg crossed over the other in a chair before Pathy's desk. Carmen gets up at our entrance with a big grin.

"And now the big man himself arrives!" she says, coming over and giving me a hug and a peck on the cheek.

Marissa glares at her the entire time.

"Oh, stop it," Carmen tells Marissa with a smile. "I promise I'm not going to eat him—yet."

"Carmen!" I warn her.

She laughs at my outburst, but walks back to her seat, which I now see is one of three in front of Pathy's desk.

"Sit, you two," Pathy says in a serious tone.

I take the middle seat and turn to look first at Marissa and then at Carmen, who flank me on either side of me. Both are beautiful women. Carmen is wearing her signature outfit of a brown beret on her head, which matches her short brown skirt, with a white blouse. The blouse is thin, though, and I can see that the bra she is wearing underneath it could be described as more like a bikini top. She also has on a short red cape that covers her shoulders.

I don't see her Focus, which looks like a sniper rifle. One thing I was surprised to learn about Carmen, she is the top sniper in the Magical worlds.

"What's up, Pathy?" Marissa asks the tiny woman facing us from behind the desk.

While she might be small, I know Pathy is tough. She's a Beast, like her husband, Bower. She isn't a bear like him; she's of the weasel family. Even Bower is afraid of her, though, which tells me all I want to know about staying on her good side.

Pathy doesn't answer, but instead reaches into her desk drawer and pulls out a blue manila folder, tossing it across the desk to Marissa.

Marissa looks confused, but reaches for the folder. She opens it, and inside are images and papers.

"Oh fuck me sideways, you've got to be kidding, right?" Carmen blurts out suddenly, her tone shocked.

I look down at the folder in Marissa's hands. She's scowling at the images and skimming the text.

"I don't understand."

Sighing, Pathy explains, pointing to the folder in Marissa's hand. "It seems that you three are now the newest—and soon to be the only task force on Earth. The council wants M.A.G.I. to start enforcing the rules there. What happened with Gordo, demonstrated that maybe there are many others fugitives hiding on Earth. Your job—and by 'your', I mean all three of you—will be to find them, arrest them, or deal with them."

Carmen is the first to respond. "Pathy, asking only the three of us to watch over the entire planet by ourselves is asinine! How the hell do they expect us to do it?"

Pathy sniffs, and then points to me.

"Me?!"

"You," she agrees with a nod. "You may be untested, but currently are at least a level ten Magus, according to Sir Targun. He thinks, once you are tested, you will be even be higher than him."

"What?! But he's level fifteen!" I blurt out in shock.

"Precisely. That is why the Council, or I guess it would primarily be Sir Targun, feels that you will be up to the task. I have worked with that man for over twenty years, and if he says you can do it, then you can do it." She rubbed her temples, as if fighting an oncoming headache. "But even I was shocked when he said he expects you will test out at level seventeen... or even level twenty."

The petite beast woman is shaking her head, as if she'd just said something that was unheard of. Which, technically, she wasn't wrong. With the download of all that information from my two weeks of training into my normally empty noggin', I know that the last time there was someone even close to level twenty was more than three thousand years ago. Unfortunately, there is no name associated with this information. I only know that, several thousand years ago, there once was a level nineteen Magus who was incredibly powerful and strong.

Marrisa still had not said anything but closes the manila folder with a snap of annoyance. "Pathy, that's nuts. I get that Kevin is powerful, but I have very little information on Earth!"

"That's where Carmen will come in handy," Pathy nods. "She will be quite an asset to your team."

"But, the targets they are asking us to go after," Marissa throws her hands up in the air, "are worse than even Gordo was!"

"Yes. I know. Which is why they are sending in the big guns." Pathy winked at Carmen. "I think you three will get the job done."

"Pathy," I ask her slowly. "Isn't that a whole lot of responsibility for someone so new to the M.A.G.I? Even if they are human, whatever their level of power?"

"The fact that you ARE human, is partly why it was decided you were the best fit for a posting there. But also, a new Council member felt that you were the best man for the job, and Sir Targun agreed." She shrugged. "When the Council voted, they mostly voted in favor. Though, for some, I think it was more to get you off the Magical worlds, and back onto Earth where they think you belong."

With a look of confusion on my face, I ask, "New Council member?"

"You already know him," she says, suddenly grinning from ear to ear.

"Oh, fuck me. William!"

William—William Tonlia, that is—was a Vampire who we had rescued, in the process of rescuing Marissa. She'd gone chasing after Gordo, a man who had killed her partner over five years ago, who was hiding on Earth. She went after him, leaving me—her partner—behind. In the process, she got captured.

The reason she found out about it all in the first place, was because William was a Vampire who wanted to learn in Earth's universities. William was a Vampire Count, which is, for all intents and purposes the same as being royalty—he was a King, though the Vampire court didn't use that term. He'd been captured by Gordo. At the time, we didn't know that Gordo had done so on purpose, to draw Marissa out.

During the rescue, I was bitten by Tallen—another Vampire —and was given what Vampires call the full Transformation. Except it didn't go as planned; I'm not a Vampire. But that doesn't mean I didn't get anything out of it—I can heal faster, can move more quickly, but am also a lot stronger, as well. Only thing I didn't get, really, is that I can't change into a Vampire.

Tallen had done it at the time, thinking to gain the upper hand in his plan to bring Magical folk into the world of the humans. He thinks that the Magical folks can learn a lot from humans. Or at least our technology.

There are some instances of technology being used, but it's small and not really that much. That's why William's plan was so bold—he was going to schools on Earth to learn technology, in order to bring it back to the Magical masses. Magicals knew of technology, but refused to adopt it simply because it came from a race they hated—humans. William figured that if he can say it came from him, and not from some Earth-born human, then magicals would snap it up.

"What was the other reason? You said that was partly the reason."

Pathy shrugs. "The other reason is that the Council members fear you. A human who can do Magic?" She paused. "No, not just do Magic, but whose magic surpasses the level of the current head of the Council, Sir Targun? People are scared shitless of what you can or will do. They want you gone, away from here and back on Earth—so that any damage you do happens there and not on anyone's home world."

"Why are they afraid of me?"

Carmen leans towards me, laying a hand on my arm. "Remember how Marissa treated you when you first met? Well, most magical folk are even worse. Marrisas' prejudices, despite what happened to her partner Prita, was mild compared to some of the hate that is out there."

I look over at Marissa, and find she's nodding.

"Now," Pathy says, opening up her drawer once more and taking something else out. It's another folder, but this time, it's red. "Your first case," she says.

Before I can grab it, Carmen snatches it off the desk and opens it. Suddenly she's grinning, looking from Marissa to me, and back again.

"What?" Marissa asks her hesitantly.

"Looks like we are going after the mafia."

I stare at her, as if she had said a foreign word. She can't mean what I think she means. My mouth hanging open, I ask her, "As in the mafia, mobsters and gangsters?"

"Yes! But most of the mafia on Earth is run by Changelings. Unfortunately, they aren't nearly as nice as we are," Marissa says with a raucous laugh. "Most of these Changelings are rotten apples, but damn, they are going to be a straightforward assignment."

CHAPTER FOUR

With a jerk that I am surprised doesn't give Marissa whiplash, I yank her back. Just in time, too, as suddenly from around the corner she had been standing next to, trying to peek down the alley, a gunshot rings out. The wall where her head had just been is shattered by a bullet.

"Fucking hells!" Marissa growls in annoyance.

"Easy assignment?" I ask her, giving her a raised eyebrow and a grin.

"What the fuck?! Why are they so powerful?"

"Because," Carmen says, through our communication stones. "They are much more organized here than on Vraka. Here on Earth, they are powerful. They have their hands in a lot of human things."

"Just like the Vampires?" I ask.

"Yes, like the Vampires," Carmen answers me.

We were using the communication stones like walkie-talkies. There was no such thing as telepathic speech, well, not for Magical folk, though the information that had been downloaded into my head told me that there were some monsters who communicated that way. Unable to speak into each others' minds, we used the communication stones to talk over distances. Carmen, for example, was up on the roof somewhere, providing overwatch, as our sniper.

Suddenly there is a shout of pain, and just as quickly, it cuts off.

"Got one," Carmen says gleefully.

We were on Earth. Specifically, we were in New York city, on our first assignment. We were searching for our contact. That's whose picture had been in the red folder Pathy had given us. It included the name, information, and a picture of our contact in the underworld's mafia.

The fact that we walked right into a turf war wasn't helpful. Carmen said that the mafia—though it still surprised me to learn that the Italian mafia were mostly all Changelings—was freaky as shit. The turf war we'd stumbled onto, was between the mafia and a group comprised of renegade Vampires, who called themselves the Bloods.

"What can you see?" I ask Carmen.

"Well, right now, they are learning to keep their heads down. There are two groups. One composed of roughly twenty or so Changelings, with the other about the same number of Vampires."

"I thought all Vampires came under William's authority?"

"Not on Earth," Marissa supplies. "On Earth, authority depends on whoever is the most powerful. But don't forget, gangs are much more prevalent on Earth. Mostly composed of rogue elements of their races." She turned around to give me a cheeky grin. "Think of Earth as the wild west of the Magical worlds."

Carmen adds, "While every race is still here on Earth, many don't follow their Counts, Kings or Queens, of their respective Magical races. William Tonlia might be powerful and strong, but he has to deal with this all the time. Though, over time, the gangs have learned to stay out of his domain and jurisdiction."

"Which is where?"

"For William Tonlia, that would be Florida, southern Georgia, Nashville, and New York state—except for New York City, which is an open city, as are California and Texas in the USA."

"Wait. William controls other cities all over the world?"

Marrisa next to me snorts. "Yes. He has places in Canada, the UK, and even one or two in Mexico—though, Mexico is mainly owned by Beasts. The entirety of Earth has been cut up and divided by us Magical folk. We live all over the world." She frowns. "Though we try to stay out of war-torn countries."

I glance at Marrisa. "I thought you'd never been assigned to Earth, and didn't know much about it?"

"I still learned things in school and also catch the news whenever I can." She rolls her eyes. "I also like to read the reports as they come in."

Shaking my head in wonder, I say, "Wow... just, wow."

Again, I hear another shout of pain, but this time it doesn't cut off as quick, since I hear the screams go on for a while. Suddenly, it's quiet once more.

Carmen's voice says in my ear, thanks to the comm stone, "Got another one. He was trying to sneak towards you. We can't just sit around, we need to do something."

I shuffle until I am near the wall, and quickly, thanks to my vampire quick speed, I take a peek at the scene around the corner. In milliseconds, I've withdrawn my head back around the brick wall. And just in time, too, as the corner of the wall gets riddle by bullets for my curiosity, sending chips flying. Fortunately, I had moved back far enough that I wasn't hit by any of them. But, I know now what is out there.

There were two groups on either side of the long alleyway. It seems they were more interested in going after us, for some reason, than going after each other. I guess when they had a common enemy, they were willing to bury the hatchet until we were taken care of.

But, that gave me an idea. "I have an idea," I tell Marissa and to Carmen through the stone.

"Kevin…" Marissa says in warning.

"No, listen. I do. Right now, we are pinned down; but so are they, thanks to Carmen. We can't stay here for hours. Someone is bound to call the NYPD."

Carmen is the one who gives me a vote of confidence. "What's your idea?"

As best as I can, I describe what I want to do. Once I'm done, Carmen is laughing, and Marissa, though she still looks nervous, has a grin on her face.

"Gods, you humans are sneaky as fuck!" she blurts out.

* * *

"READY?" I ask Carmen.

"As ready as I will be, hon."

I nod nervously, even though I know she can't see me. Taking a deep breath, I use the power inside me and call up a shield. This is not a normal shield, though. Most Magical shields are meant to stop attacks from the front. This time, I use it to call up a shield behind me, instead.

This is part of the plan. Let's hope it works. Taking a deep breath, I dart out from cover and, turning away from the two gangs down the alleyway, I haul ass. I get maybe ten feet, before I feel an impact, which throws me forward. I land flat on my face. Thank god I had that shield! The bullets that had hit my shield so hit it so hard that it had thrown knocked me off my feet.

The shield did its job, though. To the goons who shot me, it hopefully looks like I had been shot in the back and fell down, dead. But I'd taken no damage. It still hurt, don't get me wrong, getting thrown hard to the ground like that. Pretty sure I scraped my knee up something fierce; I can feel it stinging. Shit, I guess I will need to replace these jeans.

"I got him!" I hear a shout behind me.

"Get ready, Marissa," Carmen says.

"I'm ready," she says, annoyed.

Then, after lying there for what I know is seconds, but feels like minutes, I hear the shuffling of several pairs of feet and shouts of joy from behind me.

"Now!" Carmen shouts.

As soon as she gives the command, Marissa comes around the corner, with her revolver out, and she starts shooting. I can't hear Carmen's shots, on the other hand. But I don't worry, as it shoots Magical shots. As soon as I'm back up on my feet, I call up my Focus. Normally my focus appears as a set of daggers, but an interesting thing about a Focus, is that I can change its shape to suit my needs. In this case, I change its form to that of a shotgun. If I am going to take on a crowd, I want something that is meant to take down a crowd.

I do so just in time, too, as not even ten feet from me is a man who was walking toward me, with a handgun aimed my way. But he doesn't get a chance to shoot at me, as my shotgun goes off first, throwing the man backward.

One thing that I have to thank Tallen for, when next I see him, is the speed his full transformation gave me. I was able to move incredibly fast—which let me dodge around things, including bullets. The man who had been behind the one I'd just shot had lifts his gun, which I see was a hunting rifle, and shoots at me. Fortunately for me, we were so close that it was harder for him to aim the long rifle. This gave me a chance to dodge, which I do by throwing myself to the ground. Rolling onto my side, I point my shotgun up at his center of mass and pull the trigger.

For the next half a minute, which feels a hell of a lot longer than that, there is a chaotic gun battle. Carmen's shooting is dead on, though. Men, and some women, go down left and right with headshots. Marrisa, on the other hand, is all over the place. She blasted shots from the hip, before darting forward, ducking when she needed to.

Ever see that movie the Matrix, where Neo's girlfriend, Trinity, runs along the wall? Well, Marissa did the same thing, sprinting around the alley's wall. Then, it's over. I'm breathing hard, but I know it's not from running—just the adrenaline, and knowing that I just killed at least nine people, two of them women.

"There are two left, but they are running—one from each faction."

Marrisa growls, "So news will get out?"

"Which is fine," Carmen tells her. "They already know that we are here. There is no way that the news that Kevin, you, and me were coming did not reach Earth already."

"Will that be an issue?" I ask, concerned.

"Not really," she replies. "They just know that a powerful group was assigned to Earth from M.A.G.I., and now they've met us. This will just make the stories about us more intense. It might give us the street cred, as they say, that we'll need."

"Damn," I say, shaking my head, looking at the bloodbath the alley had become.

Marissa goes from body to body, making sure they were dead. Her handgun didn't go off, so I assume no one needed to be put out of their misery. Once she is done, she comes back our way, but she is throwing small black disks onto each body, tossing them on their chests, backs, or sides. Within seconds, there are dozens of black clouds covering the bodies. Once the clouds disperse, the bodies are gone.

I know the Magic behind that now. What Marissa was using was a form of Magic that dissolved the bodies, so that no evidence is left behind. When I'd asked her if we could use that as a weapon, she'd explained that it only worked on dead bodies and their immediate surroundings. It could not be used on a live person or creature.

Having knowledge simply stuffed into my brain and having the experience to understand how to use it, are two different things, as I am finding out.

Once Marissa is done, Carmen appears next to me as if by Magic. She has a big grin on her face. "Damn, that was a good first battle!"

"It could have gone terribly wrong," Marissa begins, but snaps her mouth shut. "Sorry. I know I should be glad it went so well, but we aren't done. We still need to find our contact."

"Was it any of them?" I ask, pointing to where the bodies had been.

"No. I checked."

Carmen growls. "Shit, guess we need to go find them. The question is, though, why were these clowns here, where we are supposed to meet our contact?"

"Do you think someone found out?" I ask.

Marissa is shaking her head. "I seriously doubt it. Unlike here on Earth, there is no way to hack a computer and get information. The only people who would have known specifically where we were going would have been my Dad, Pathy, and... maybe Bower? And of course, us."

She arches an eyebrow, looking at me and then Carmen. "And I doubt any of us would have given our location away, knowing it would land us in a crossfire between the mafia and the Bloods."

I shake my head to indicate it wasn't me, and Carmen shakes her head as well.

"We still need to find our contact then, since he has the information we need," Carmen says with a sour expression.

Hearing a noise, I look up, but thank god that I wasn't alone. Next to me, Carmen's rifle is suddenly in her hands, and it goes off. Marissa's focus, which is shaped like a badass looking .357 Magnum goes off, too. Without warning, a body falls down next to me from the top of the roof, with a wet *splat*.

Carmen spits on the body and growls. "Hmm… Oops. Missed one."

"Come on," Marissa says, looking around to make sure no one else is around. "Let's head the way they all came from."

"Sounds good to me," Carmen tells her, taking point, with her rifle out and sweeping side to side in front of her, in case something jumps out of us.

We go past where our welcome committee had all been hiding, on both sides of the alley, and eventually turn down first one, and then another alleyway, Carmen holds up her hand for us to stop.

"Body," she says softly, pointing her rifle towards a large green garbage bin, the kind that only a massive municipal trash truck can pick up.

Marrisa puts a hand on my chest to stop me from going forward to check it out. "Cover me."

I nod to her, and shoulder my shotgun as Marissa slowly makes her way to the body on the ground.

Kneeling down next to it, she mutters, "Shit!" She looks up at the two of us. "This was our contact."

"Fuck," I swear.

Marissa's head suddenly whips up and she looks around, though I'm not sure for what. Finally, she cries. "Over there!"

I look to where she's pointing. Roughly ten feet away from where we stand, I see another body that's almost hidden amongst a number of smaller aluminum garbage cans. I can see two legs sticking out from between them.

CHAPTER FIVE

J ust in case it's a trap, we take it slow, with Carmen covering Marissa and me. Once closer to the body, I see what looks like it's a small child.

"Crap, it's a Brownie!" cries Marrisa, rushing forward to the body.

A Brownie? I thought it was a child? Looking closer as I get nearer the body and can see the rest of it around the garbage cans, I see that I was mistaken. Rather than a child, I see what is a little person—or a person of small stature.

A Brownie, as far as I know, are a race of small statured people who can do Magic. Frequently described as pranksters, they were considered to be mischievous. Though, that information is thousands of years ago. The more recent information I have, is that Brownies are considered second-class citizens on the fringes of Magical folk society. They didn't have a planet of their own, as they were not powerful enough, so tended to live on most of the planets, alongside other races. Though, that same information told me that they lived mostly on Earth, since they were closely linked with nature spirits on Earth.

Once I get a closer look, I see that if this person had been standing, they would have been a little less than five feet tall. This person's long white hair covers most of their face; I can't tell if it's a male or a female.

When Marissa turns the body over onto its back, she sighs a sigh of relief. "She's alive. But she's been shot," she says, pointing to the bullet holes in her clothing. Marrisa places her hands on the body and closes her eyes.

I don't see anything, but I assume she's healing the bullet wounds. It won't seal up the bullet holes in the petite woman's clothing, though.

After several seconds, she sits back with a sigh. "I think I got to her in time. I'm not sure, though, healing was always my worst spell. What about you Carmen?"

"I sucked at it, too," the blonde replies with a sour expression. "I barely passed the requirement for my badge."

"Just like me, then." Marissa sighs.

They both turn to me.

"What?"

"Can you heal?" Marissa asks me.

"I'm... not sure?" I say cautiously. "I know the spell," I tap the side of my head, "and I know what to do, but I have never cast it."

"Come give it a try," Marissa says, waving me down beside her and the Brownie's small body. "I suck at it. Even your inexperienced casting should help."

"Sure," I say, unsure I will cast it any better than two experience M.A.G.I. who have probably cast the spell dozens of times. I kneel down next to the small Brownie and finally get a better look at her.

She's tiny. I'd thought she might be around five feet tall, but now I realize I was being much too optimistic. She is probably only a little over four feet—hence why I had mistaken her for a child initially. She is so small. Her long white hair still covers much of her face, so I can only see that her eyes are closed. Her skin is really pale—almost white—which I think can't be good. Peeking through her hair, I see a tip of an ear sticking out, which is longer and more pointed than a normal human ear.

Placing my hand on her stomach, I do what my downloaded knowledge tells me I should be doing; I call up the power inside me and push it into the Brownie, focusing on my healing intent. Magic really is nothing more than using your imagination and your will to push what you want to do out into the outside world.

Think of it like this. You want to heal? You grab a hold of your power, focus your energies and your thoughts on healing, and—like that old British guy who played Captain Picard used to say—you 'Make it so'.

Fortunately, you don't need to know the internal structures of whoever you are healing, or even what specifically needs fixing. You simply need to imagine them healing and will it to be so. That's a good thing, really, since I'd sucked at biology. And now—never mind the biology of humans, I was clueless about the biology of Brownies.

I feel power drain from somewhere deep inside me, and suddenly, without warning, the body under my hand jerks upright—as if she'd had a bucket of cold water thrown over her. That's when I first get a look at her eyes. They are a piercing blue, like the color of the ocean. Her delicate features are beautiful. I can't place her age, though, and those piercing blue eyes are wide in fear.

"It's all right," I tell her softly. "You're safe."

"Where's Malroy!" she cries suddenly, looking past me.

"If that was Malroy," Marrisa tells her softly, pointing to the body next to the large dumpster. "He's dead."

"No!" she cries, burying her face in her two small hands. Abruptly, she pulls her hands away from her face, jerking her head up quickly, she stares at the three of us. "Who are you?"

"We're M.A.G.I.," Carmen tells her just as softly. "We came to meet Malroy," she says, pointing to the dead body, "he was our contact."

Bitterly, the Brownie says, "And of course, you're too late."

"Sorry," I tell her, patting her leg awkwardly. "We didn't expect to walk into a firefight."

The Brownie sighs and nods. "That's okay. We didn't expect it, either. We were simply told to come here to meet up with someone special. When we got here, though, there was already a pitched battle going on." She winced. "We got a Circle up just in time."

A Circle is a spell that most Magical folk, at least those who can do Magic, can cast. It's a spell that, when cast, create a circle—the size of which is based on the power of the person casting it—that keeps humans out. It doesn't work against other Magical folk, and is primarily used to keep humans noses out of Magical folk business. It couldn't keep away those whose curiosity was particularly strong, though. It was more like a gentle persuasion, encouraging humans to ignore everything inside the circle.

It wasn't like casting a Border. That was something that no human, and even some weaker Magical Folks can't walk through. A Circle was easier, and used a lot less power. But, it worked to keep all but the most inquisitive humans out of wherever it was cast.

"Well, you might have saved several lives—except those who tried to ambush us, of course. Two of them got away."

"One," I point out, reminding her of the body she and Carmen had shot on the roofline.

"One got away," Carmen nods. "Though I'm fairly certain one that ran and didn't double back was a Blood."

"Shit!" says the Brownie vehemently.

That's when I notice that her voice is very light, and fairly high in pitch—as if she had been sucking on helium.

"Do you have somewhere safe we can go?" Marissa asks her.

The Brownie looks around the area and nods. She starts to get up, but I have to reach out and grab her, as she'd stumbled and been about to fall over. She nods to me gratefully and, instead of slapping my hand away, she holds onto my arm to keep herself upright.

"Wait, I need to get rid of Malroy's body, first." She shakes her head sadly. "Man, his wife is going to be upset… but they knew the risks."

With my aid, she walks over to Malroy's body. Looking down at him sadly, she mutters, "Damn, you bastard. I'm going to miss you."

Once done speaking, she pulls out a dark disk like the ones Marissa had used earlier, and tosses it on Malroy's body. Within seconds, there is no indication that someone had died here—even the blood that had pooled on the asphalt is gone.

Turning, the Brownie points down the alleyway, opposite the way we had come, and says, "That way."

I'm still holding her up—or rather, she was still holding my hand.

"What are your names?" the Brownie asks suddenly, looking up at me.

"I'm Kevin. This is Carmen," I nod to the blonde, "and that's Marissa."

The Brownie nods. "I'm Liia." She sighs. "And that was Malroy." She shakes her head.

"Well, Liia," I tell her. "Let's get somewhere safe, first, and then we can talk some more."

Liia nods and, for the next ten minutes or so, leads us down alleyway after alleyway. Just how many fucking alleys are there in New York City?

As if reading my mind, Carmen laughs. "It's how New York City was built. It was built by Magical folk, so there are alleyways like this all over. Trust me. Unless you were born here, or have lived here for a very long time, you'll get lost. Most New Yorkers—the humans, I mean—never come here. There are sigils all around to ensure they get turned around."

Right. Sigils. Like I had seen at Tallen's Club 58. The guy who'd tried to give me a full transformation just so happened to be another Vampire Count. The fact that I know two Counts, still makes my head spin. Tallen was royalty, just like

William. Though, William shared that power with his twin sister on planet Vamir, the Vampire home world.

She had tried to get him killed—or at least arrested, by saying that he was going feral. But when Marissa and I investigated, we found that was about as far from the truth as could be. The power-hungry sister just wanted to get rid of him, so she could assume the only open seat on the Galactic Council. That plan really backfired on her. Now, William was studying mechanical engineering here on Earth, while his twin sister was now being investigated by Targun, Marrisa's father. I wouldn't want to be in her shoes.

Sigils were handy, though. They can be set and then forgotten. They can make someone not feel like going into a particular location or convince them they got turned around somehow. They can also be used to trap someone, though, as we'd found out when going down the steps into Club 58.

I look around as if to see if I can see one of these Sigils, but I don't see one, which makes sense. Unless I was extremely close to it, I can't sense its Magic. I'd been able to identify the one in the club, since it was so close. In the end, that kept Carmen and me from getting caught in the trap.

"In here," Liia says, pointing to a non-descript metal door on the back wall of some building.

Placing her hand against it, she closes her eyes. Only because I had been looking for it, do I see a flash of red around the edges of the door after a few seconds, and then it opens. Good thing we had not tried to open the door ourselves. It had been trapped with a rather nasty bit of Magic that would have burned us to a crisp. The ward had been a powerful one.

Looking down at Liia, I wonder how powerful she is.

Marissa leans against me and whispers in my ear. "That was a powerful ward. It couldn't have been cast by Liia, as she isn't powerful enough. Whoever set that, was a strong Magus."

Liia must have overheard my wife, since she turns around and nods. In a sad voice, she says, "that was a ward Malroy had cast; he was a level six Magus."

"What level are you?" I ask.

"I'm only level four; I was still learning that spell," she replies with another squeak of a sigh.

"Makes sense," I say, looking at the information in my head. "That was a level five spell."

"What level are you?" Liia asks me.

"Let's just say he's powerful," Carmen interrupts, before I can answer the Brownie.

Liia looks at Carmen, but Carmen gives her nothing further, simply looking back down at her. Liia slowly nods and enters the open doorway and we all follow her.

Once inside, my eyebrows climb up my forehead. It's a restaurant—more specifically, a restaurant's kitchen. Right now, though, it's empty. I guess they weren't open yet. Looking down at my watch, I see that it's just only just past nine in the morning. We'd arrived early in the morning from Vraka.

That is still hard to get used to—walking into a portal in a place where it was almost midnight, then instantly stepping out somewhere it was already morning. Talk about jet lag!

We walk out of the kitchen through large, double doors that swing both directions, and enter the restaurant itself. But instead of going further into the dining room, Liia takes a sharp right up a set of stairs to the second floor. Once there, she leads us down a hallway to a plain door, where she once more places her palm against it.

As she closes her eyes, I once again see a flash of red around the edges of the door. Good thing I was paying attention, because it's so fast, that if I had not been looking for it, I would have missed it. Once the door opens, the little Brownie walks right in, and we follow behind her.

As soon as we are all inside, the door closes on its own.

Surprised by the door, we all turn to see it lock behind us. When I turn back around, Liia is facing us and has a gun pointed at me. And I don't mean a Focus. I mean an actual, human gun.

"Now, just who the fuck are you?"

"We are M.A.G.I." I tell her, looking at the gun worriedly. Can you blame me, given how short she is, it is practically pointed at my crotch.

"No fucking way. You're human. Now... these two? I can smell that they are Changelings. But, you? You stink of human."

Sighing, I nod, and then, using the speed I got from being bitten by a Vampire, I snatch her gun out of her hand quicker than she can react. Once I have her gun secured, I pass it over to Carmen, who takes it from me, removes the clip, and empties the chambered round before tucking the gun in the waistband of her skirt.

"Like I said," I tell Liia softly. "We are all M.A.G.I.—I'm the human who got Magic."

"Holy shit!" Liia looks at me in surprise. "You mean the stories of a human gaining Magic were real?"

"One hundred percent," Marissa tells her with a chuckle. "Now, care to tell us what the fuck is going on?"

Liia finally removes her gaze from me and looks at my wife, slowly nodding. "We have an issue. People are disappearing."

I frown at that, but Carmen is the one who replies. "People disappear all the time."

"Yes. But they don't turn up dead, pinned to the ground with silver spikes, their innards exposed on a busy street, with humans all around."

All three of us look at each other as if to ask. What the hell? That wasn't in the reports.

CHAPTER SIX

"Start from the beginning," Carmen tells Liia. "We came here to stop a turf war, according to the reports. Malroy was our contact."

"No. There's no turf war," Liia says bitterly, shaking her head, which makes her white hair fly. "That's what the other gangs have been saying, since they have no clue who is doing the killings or why."

She snorts. "Do you honestly think they would ask M.A.G.I. for help?"

"What's a Brownie doing getting involved with the gangs?" Carmen asks her.

Liia turns to the blonde and glares at her. "What do you expect us to do? We aren't powerful like you Changelings. I do what I have to do, to survive."

"I'm not dissing you, hon," Carmen tells her softly. "We are just gathering information. We have always known the

Brownies, and even most of the Fae, to be on the sidelines for battles like this."

"Yeah," she replies, blowing out a heavy breath from her small frame. "But, we are getting pushed from the sidelines into being involved. Like I said earlier, someone is going around killing us Magical folk, and they are using silver spikes."

"You mentioned that before when you said that this wasn't a turf war."

Liia looks at me at first, but finally, almost reluctantly, she replies. "This isn't a fight between the mafia and the Bloods. This is a battle against time—we have lost people on both sides."

"What side are you on?" Marissa asks her with a raised eyebrow.

She looks at Marissa, and nods. "I'm not on either side. I was investigating with Malloy's help, because of his high level. He was the one who sent a request to M.A.G.I. for investigative powers, but it was denied because we didn't have enough evidence. As if," she continues bitterly, shaking her head. "Apparently, showing them images of the dead bodies wasn't enough."

I look over at Marissa and Carmen, and they are both frowning.

"That makes no sense." Carmen is the one who replies. "If there was any indication of this, there is no way that we would not have gotten involved sooner. Who was your contact at M.A.G.I.?"

"We didn't go directly to M.A.G.I.," Liia admits. "We went through the Council."

Carmen snorts.

"What?" I ask her.

"If they went through a Council member, then he—or she—probably felt it wasn't worth their time." Carmen turns back to Liia. "How long ago was that?"

I hear the bitterness again in the Brownie's tone. "Last year?"

"Fucking hell," Marissa curses.

I ask the obvious question. "These deaths have been going on for over a year?"

"Well… it wasn't until after maybe the fifth or sixth body that we started looking into it? So maybe fourteen months?"

"You mentioned that the bodies had silver daggers in them."

"Sort of," she replies with a frown. "Are you sure you're human?"

"Like I said," I tell her with a smile, "I got Magic."

Shaking her tiny head, making her white hair fly all over the place, she mutters, "still hard to believe that the stories were true. But, yes. The bodies we have found had been killed with magic, but the daggers were used to pin their victims in place."

"What were the races of the deceased?" Marissa asks her.

"So far, of the victims that we know of, there were two Elves, one Changeling, one Beast, and a Fairy." She taps her finger against her chin. "Oh, the most recent one was a Werewolf, but he managed to get away—though he was so injured that he died hours after being found. He had too much silver inside him to be saved." She shrugged. "There might be others that we haven't found."

"Was this Werewolf able to identify his assailant?"

"No. He said that he was walking home, when he was jumped from behind. When he came to, he was tied to the ground with wooden stakes and strong rope. He only got away, he said because the person," she held up a hand to stop me from interrupting, "and before you asked, he was not able to identify what race they were, got distracted by a phone call. He said this person had no scent to speak of, so identification that way was out."

"So all we know about the perp is that this person was not only able to surprise, but also able to take down a Werewolf, uses a cell phone, and has no scent?" Marissa sums up what we have learned.

Liia give an angry snot. "Yeah. It sounds just as dumb as you think it does. But that is all we have to go on."

"What happened to you guys, today?"

The Brownie scrubs her face with her small hands. "What happened today was a mistake. We tried to check out the meet up before you were expected to arrive. But in the process, we ran into the shootout, and someone shot Malroy —and in the process, shot me as well."

"Well, at least it wasn't silver bullets," Carmen tells her.

I ask her, "Do you think it was this perp?"

She frowns at me. "Perp?"

"Sorry, perpetrator."

"We aren't sure. We'd had a tip that a suspicious person was seen roaming around the area you found me. It was close by, so Malroy and I went to check it out." Her head drooped. "We should have waited for back up. It seems that the Mafia and the Bloods heard the same tip—that must be why they were where you showed up."

"Now what?" I ask my two partners.

"Normally, I would say we needed to file this, and call for backup," Carmen growls, "but since we are on our own here, I'm afraid we are the back up."

"Liia," Marissa asks her softly. "Is there any more information you can provide us? Anything at all?"

Liia gets a thoughtful look on her face. "There isn't much else. That was why we sent a request for a M.A.G.I. investigator. We were operating well outside our expertise."

"Well, I guess we need to figure what the hell is going on. Carmen, have you ever heard of anything like this, from your time on Earth before?" Marissa asks her.

"Not really. This is a first for me," she replies her with a shake of her head, causing the tall blonde's braid to sling around her head. "The issue is, that this has been going on for over a year. This person probably feels safe, since they haven't been caught yet. So I'd expect more victims." She frowns. "Though, if they shot Malroy and Liia, that might be a first."

Carmen turned to the Brownie. "Have any other victims been shot, or had gunshot wounds?"

"No. Only the daggers."

"Any idea how their victims are caught?"

"That's the odd part. Most of them don't have anything that really stands out. Most of them were done with their shifts at work, and were taken on their way home."

I ask the next question. "Hmm… all in New York City?"

Liia turns to me and nods. "Yes, so we know they must be from here."

"Or, they come here for their victims," I add.

"You don't think they are from here, Kevin?" Marissa asks.

"I am just thinking out loud, here. I used to read a lot of books on stuff like this." I turn back to Liia. "How long between the killings?"

Liia doesn't answer me right away, but walks over to a table and opens the folder that is on it. She has to climb up on a chair to reach it, because of her diminutive stature. "Let's see. According to this, the time between the first one we found and the second victim was almost a month. Just slightly over that... by two days. The next two were over roughly three weeks apart... and this last one was four weeks apart, or roughly a month."

"So, this person kills a victim just about once a month." I pause. "Question is, do they do it that way because they aren't from here, coming into the city every month or so, or are they from here and they hide out for a month after each attack? Hmmm."

"Idea?" Carmen asks me.

"Well..." I say slowly, "what kind of job would make someone only come to New York City, or any city, really, only once a month?"

All three of them look at each other confused, but finally Carmen snaps her fingers. "A business man here for work!"

"Precisely. Now, I might be totally off with this hypothesis , but it makes sense. Hell, it could be someone coming to New

York City to visit a lover—but I doubt someone in love would do this."

"So, that means they would be flying or driving into New York?"

With a sour expression, I reply to Marissa's comment. "Yeah. That's the part I'm not sure about. Damn," I groan, "we need more information. That's not a lot to go on. Are you sure there isn't anything else?" I ask the diminutive woman.

She shakes her head, but then suddenly stops and grabs the folder, looking through it quickly again. "Wait. I thought there was something else. So, the victim who got away before they died, mentioned something about their clothing. He said," and she has her finger on the paper she is reading from, *"they had no scent, but wore an outfit that looked like a uniform. They could not tell if it was a human, Changeling, Beast, Vampire, or any other race, since there was no distinctive feature, or scent. But, they did mention that this person's phone kept going off, and so they kept walking away to take the calls. That was the reason they were able to escape, as it happened after they got angry and left to answer the phone."*

"They must have had no choice about to the calls, then," I point out. "So it might be they work for someone and had to take this call. So... maybe they are a business man working for some company?"

"Damn, that's reaching," Carmen tells me.

"I know," I reply with a sigh. "But we have nothing else."

"I guess we need to do some more investigating. What about you, Liia?"

"I'm done here," she growls. "I'm taking the first Portal to Lotri. I have family there I can stay with."

"She means Lotri, the home world of the Fairies." Carmen turns to Marissa. "I have a contact here in town I can talk to."

"Will they have information that we can use?"

"Only one way to find out." Carmen grins. "He's a human, so fair warning. But trust me, he might prove useful."

With a snort, Marrisa rolls her eyes. "You expect a human to be useful?"

"Oh trust me," Carmen tells her with a big grin as she pinches my cheek, "this human is quite useful."

I feel a tugging on my pants. I look down and see it is Liia. She had been so quiet, I had not heard her get off her chair. I kneel down next to her so I am at eye level with her.

"Are you really a human?"

"As human as I can be. Except, thanks to drinking that elixir, I can do Magic."

She nods at that. "Well, please be careful. You don't act like a human."

"I don't? What does a human act like?"

"Entitled."

I laugh. "Oh trust me, I am just about the least entitled person you might ever meet. I work for what I want."

"Well," she says, tapping my forehead with a little finger. "Don't let it get to you here. I know plenty of humans, and you seem cool."

"I like to think I'm cool," I tell her with a smile. "But I promise not to let this new power go to my head."

"Good," she replies with a firm nod to me. Then she looks up at Carmen and Marissa. "Are you two married to him?"

"No, just her," Carmen replies before Marissa can, then shoots me a wink. "For now."

Liia grins at Carmen. "You go girl. All right. I'm going to grab some stuff and get the hell out of here. If you need me, here is my stone."

With that, she takes out a communication stone, waits for Carmen to take hers out, and then touches her comm stone to Carmen's. Both close their eyes and open them again.

"There. If you need me for anything, you can contact me."

"I guess we should get going. We will need to take an uber to get to the person I want to see," Carmen tells Marissa and I.

"An Uber?" I ask her, with a raised eyebrow.

"We can't always be zipping around opening Portals," she says with a laugh. "While on Earth, I use all the local resources I can, including an Uber driver."

I don't reply, just give a rueful shake of my head. When in Rome...

CHAPTER SEVEN

"In here," Carmen says, pointing to the building where the Uber had dropped us off.

To say that the Uber driver hardly kept his eyes on the road, would be an understatement—though I can't really blame him. He had two drop-dead gorgeous women slide into his back seat. Hopping into the passenger seat, I was ignored.

The building in question was in downtown Manhattan—some business or another. Or make that multiple businesses. Once in the lobby, I see that there is a guard there, who Carmen heads directly towards.

The guard looks up at us at our approach. The man behind the desk is wearing your typical security guard blue uniform. The guard is a white, older gentleman, probably in his sixties, with plenty of gray in his hair and beard.

"Good day. How can I help you?" he asks us politely.

"We are here to see a friend. He's on the nineteenth floor."

"Very well," he says, nodding.

He turns the book around that's in front of him and opens it. "Please sign in here. Do you know the office number?"

"Yes. It's office 1919."

"Ah," he says with a grin. "You're here to see Pete. I saw him head up earlier with a coffee."

"That's right." Carmen returns his grin.

She takes the proffered pen and writes in the book. Once done, she gives the pen back to the security guard.

"Go ahead and take the elevators up."

"Thank you for your time," Marrisa tells him with her own smile.

"For two beautiful women? Any day," he winks as he returns her smile.

Once in the elevator, Carmen turns to Marissa. "See, not all humans are bad."

"I never said they were," the brunette growls back, not deigning to look at her but staring straight ahead. "I just said that I hated *most* humans."

"You kind of did say all humans are bad," I say, reminding her about when we'd first met.

Turning, she glares at me. "Fine, I might have pigeonholed all humans in the same barrel. Can you blame me, though? I didn't grow up on Earth like Carmen here."

"And hon, that's why I'm glad you got assigned here. You need to understand that, just as in the Magical worlds, there are rotten apples everywhere. I grew up here on Earth and have many human friends and acquaintances, but will be the first to admit that there are bad humans, just as there are bad Magical folk. You've just got to seek out the good ones."

"And this Pete we are going to see?" I ask her, to stop Marrisa from answering and hopefully heading off another fight before it starts between the two of them.

"Pete is a good one."

"What does Pete do, exactly?"

"You will see," she replies with a grin, wagging her eyebrows at me.

The elevator dings to tell us we are on our floor—the nineteenth. We step out and, without pause, Carmen turns left and heads down the hallway until she gets to a door that has a plaque on it that reads 'Technology Lord'. She knocks on the door twice and waits.

We hear noises on the other side, but no one comes to answer the door. Carmen growls and knocks on the door again, harder, a good four times.

Suddenly there is a screech of static, and a small grill I had missed beside to the door blares, "What do you want!"

"Now, now, Pete. Is that any way to talk to me?" Carmen purrs into the grill.

The voice on the other end is male, English-speaking, and sounds surprised. "Carmen?

"The one and only," she tells the speaker.

Suddenly the door buzzes, and with a click, the door opens slightly. Carmen pushes it open and enters the office. Inside, I see a small office, with a desk, but there is no one at it. Behind the desk, there is a second door. That one abruptly opens, and out of it comes a short, dark complexioned man, likely of Mediterranean descent.

"Carmen!" he shouts, suddenly rushing forward and hugging Carmen, who hugs him back. He holds her at arm's length. "Damn, it's been a long time, babe!" he tells her, looking her up and down.

Only then does he turn to Marrisa and me. He looks at Marissa and nods, but when he looks at me, he eyes me up and down before frowning.

"Another boyfriend?" he asks her, turning to Carmen.

"Pete, are you still not over me?"

"No one can be over you, babe," he replies with a grin. "Come in. Come in. I assume you being here is for work? What does the FBI's special projects division want my help with this time?" he asks, waving us through the other door.

Once inside, I look around and, I have to say I was impressed. The long room had desk after desk with dual monitors hooked up to large desktop computers, and they were all on. But there was no one else here.

I frown at all the empty seats. There were, after I do a quick count, twelve desks full of active monitors. But no one was sitting at them.

Pete must have seen my frown since he laughs. "No, there is no one else here. I run the shop myself."

"What exactly is Technology Lord?" I ask him, flipping a thumb over my shoulder back the way we had come, and the plaque at his front door that had the company name on it.

"Technology Lord is me," he replies with a grin. "I'm the best gray hacker around."

"Pete works alone," Carmen says with a laugh. "He hates people."

"Hey!" he replies, offended.

With another laugh, she allows, "Okay, he hates most people, but he loves me."

"But you won't come back to me?" he asks her, with a raised eyebrow.

"But, I won't come back to you." She nods. "We had a good time, but the past is the past."

"That it is. And you working for the FBI also had something to do with our breakup. But that's also in the past. As for the here and now, though, to what do I owe the pleasure of seeing your beautiful face again? And who are your friends?" he asks Carmen, but he is looking directly at Marissa.

Even though he does that, there is no creepiness in his look, only curiosity.

"This is Agent Kevin, and this is Agent Marrisa," Carmen points first to me, and then to my wife.

"Badges, please?" he asks us.

Without a pause, Marissa takes hers out and flashes it to him. He nods and looks my way. I frown, but take out my M.A.G.I. badge and show it to him.

One thing about these amazing badges, is that they too, are Magical in nature. They will show a person—at least if they are human—exactly what they want to see. Pushing a little Magic into my badge as I show it to him, I know it will appear to him exactly like what one might expect an FBI agent to show, when flashing their credentials.

Pete nods and looks at Carmen. "So, what do you need?"

"We are investigating a series of murders. But, as usual when we need to come to you, we don't know much about who the murderer might be. Only that the murders happen roughly once a month. Agent Kevin feels that it might be a businessman coming to New York City, and killing when they are here."

"Fucking hell, another serial killer?" he growls. "The last one I helped you with ended up killing how many before you guys caught him?"

"Nine," Carmen replies. "But the FBI finally got him in Sacramento. Which, by the way, if I remember correctly was due to your help—for which you got paid quite handsomely."

"That I did," he says with a hard nod. "but I would have done it for free. That man had been killing women." He frowns. "And you want my help again?"

"Yes. The usual rate?"

He shakes his head. "Nope. You get a discount, babe. Now. Let's see. Once a month, you said? Do you have the dates of those murders?"

"Give me a second."

Carmen steps away and takes out her communication stone. The good thing about Magic, is that you can easily change things. Carmen had, on the sly, cast an illusion spell that made it so that her communication stone looked like the latest hi-end cell phone.

"Hey, it's me, Carmen," she says, pretending to *talk* on the phone. "Do you have the dates of those murders?" Then she nods, so I know she is talking to Liia on the other end.

Pete gives Carmen a pad and pen, for which she smiles gratefully and mouths 'Thank you', then begins to write down a series of dates that Liia gives her.

"Good. Thanks, Liia." Carmen puts her *cell phone* away before giving the pad and pen back to Pete.

Taking it from her, he looks at down at the dates. "All right. So… let's see. February twelfth, last year. I don't remember reading about that." He looks up. "Were any of these in the news?"

"Nope. They have all been kept silent."

"Makes sense, if you are after a serial killer," he nods absently, looking back down at the dates.

Going to one of the desks, he sits down, and begins to type away furiously. I might be a tech guy, but this was outside my league. I don't even know what operating system he's using, since it doesn't look like your typical Windows' user interface.

Every now and then, he glances at the dates on the pad, and then looks back at his screen, tap tap tapping away the whole time.

I grab a chair and sit down. Something tells me this won't be quick. Carmen does the same. Marissa is the only holdout, and stays standing. And I'm soon glad that I did. After forty minutes, according to my watch, Marissa throws in the towel, and grabs her own chair.

Absently, Pete points over his shoulder at the back of the room. "there's beer in there."

Smiling, Carmen tells him, "We're on duty."

"There should be pop in there, too, and I think there's even some leftover pizza in the fridge."

I look at where he had pointed to, and see there's a large, double-door aluminum fridge. "Anyone want anything?" I ask around.

"I'll take a pop. What kind of pizza?" Marissa asks.

"Just cheese," Pete answers her distractedly, still tapping away.

"I'll take a slice then."

Carmen grins up at me, "Make that two."

Nodding, I head to the fridge and open the door. Inside are cans of pop and a box of pizza. Opening the box, I see that, just as stated, there was three quarters of a cheese pizza in it. I look around, and I see on the counter next to the fridge is a stack of paper plates. Grabbing two plates, I put two slices of pizza on each and pop them in the microwave. Snagging two random cans from out of the fridge, I bring them over to the girls while their food reheats.

Once they have their pizza, I head back to get myself some. When was the last time I ate? I've noticed that another benefit to being bitten by Tallen, is that I don't get hungry nearly as often. That doesn't mean I don't eat, but where before I would be hungry just about all the time and want to snack, I barely eat two meals a day.

I grab an extra can from the fridge and head back to the girls. I set the can of pop next to Pete, who turns to me quickly with a grin and nods, opens it, and takes a sip, immediately going back to his screens and his tap tap tap.

I don't bother reheating my slice before taking a bite. The logo on the box wasn't from a chain, but from most likely a mom and pop place, and I taste it. Even cold, the pizza was damn good. Once done, I grab everyone's empty plates to clean up and sit back down.

And we wait.

After what feels like hours, Pete suddenly shouts. "Got it!"

"What do you have?" Marissa asks him quickly.

I had fallen asleep, so at his yell, I jerk awake, looking around in confusion.

"So, taking the dates Carmen gave me and looking at flights coming in. I think I've found your perp."

Carmen looks at him, and I can tell she's impressed. Jesus, so am I, if he figured who our murderer was from just that!

She asks him, "You did?"

"Yep, though, you're shit out of luck, though," Pete says, shaking his head.

"Why is that?" Marissa asks him slowly.

"Because it looks like your perp keeled over two weeks ago; he died of a heart attack. Here is a clip of his obit."

On his screen, suddenly pops up an online newspaper obituary page. On it is an image of a male, in his forties, white. His name is John Smith.

"John Smith? Seriously?" I ask.

"Fake name?" Carmen asks him.

Pete shakes his head. "That's what I thought, too. That was why it took me a bit longer. I thought he had been using a fake name, so I had to go back and research him. Nope, that's his honest to goodness real name."

Marissa is the one to ask. "And he's dead?"

"Yes. He died in his sleep, according to this. He's from Halifax."

"A Canadian?" I say incredulously.

"Seems he worked for a company that had an office here. He was their financial officer, or something like it—he kept their books straight. He was good at his job, according to the company's records. They had no issues with him. He came to the head office once a month, to verify their accounting was correct."

"And he's dead?" I repeat the question.

"Dead," Pete says, then shrugs. "Sorry, it was a dead end."

"I guess that means we are heading to Halifax," Carmen sighs.

Pete chuckles at her. "The FBI works in Canada? I thought they only worked here in the States."

"We work where we are needed. We will contact the local RCMP to help," she tells him with a shrug.

"The alphabet-soup, who?" he asks.

Carmen flashes him a grin. "The Royal Canadian Mounted Police... RCMP."

We are? Wait, will that work for us when working in other countries? I know when we flew to Casablanca, Carmen had told the hacker we met there, Houmad, that she was CIA. I guess we pick the alphabet soup that makes the most sense.

"Well, here is his home address," Pete continues, writing something down and handing it to Carmen.

"Thanks, Pete," she tells him, bending down and kissing him on the forehead.

"Thanks… but not thanks enough to date me again?" he asks her with a grin.

She laughs and slaps his shoulder. "Stop. We have a good thing."

"True," he says with a dramatic sigh, but then suddenly grins. "But my fee is my usual."

"See?" Carmen laughs at him, "I told them it's all about money! Here you go," she says, reaching into her pocket and bringing out a small bar of gold.

Pete's eyes widen at seeing it, but so does his grin. "Always a pleasure doing business with the Special Project's Division."

CHAPTER EIGHT

"So you dated Pete?" I ask Carmen with a raised eyebrow as we get into the elevator, heading down to the lobby.

She turns to me and laughs. "No. He thinks we used to date. I worked with him, what… ten years ago? And we worked on one case, or I had him work on a case that involved us being in the same room for weeks, hours at a time. He thought of that as dating. I like the man, but he isn't my type."

"Oh?" I ask her, "what is your type?"

She looks me up and down and grins.

"Right," I tell her with a laugh.

"You know I'm right here, right?" Marissa growls.

Carmen doesn't say anything at her, but her grin grows wider.

Marissa's mouth goes into a thin line, but when she turns to me, her face softens. "I guess we need to catch a flight to this Halifax place."

"Yes. That's going to be a little difficult," Carmen says hesitantly.

"Why?" Marrisa asks her sharply, turning back to the blonde, her glare reigniting.

"I might, or might not, have been kicked out of Canada."

We both stare at her in some surprise.

"You got kicked out of Canada?" My tone might have been very skeptical. "But Canadians are so... nice. How the hell do you get kicked out of an entire country?!"

In an annoyed voice, she replies, "It wasn't my fault!"

"What did you do?"

Coiling a blonde lock around two fingers, she frowns, "I might... or might not... have had sex with one of their Prime Ministers."

Raising one eyebrow, I ask her. "Which one?"

"Hmm. Yes?"

"Jesus, more than one?" I ask, my grin growing.

"Hey, they were cute. One of them was very charismatic. I heard his son is into politics there now. He's kind of cute, too."

"We aren't gonna be there for you to clean the dust off your vagina," Marrisa growls at her in annoyance.

I put my hand on Marrisa's shoulder to calm her down, as I don't want them fighting all the time. She puts her hand on mine, blows out a breath, and nods slightly to show she knows what I am doing.

"How about we buy a private jet? Or do you have a Portal location on your stone?"

Carmen stops giving Marissa the evil eye and nods in response to my question. "I have one for Ottawa, but not Halifax. Though," she says thoughtfully, "it might prove easier to catch a plane from Ottawa within Canada. If we don't have to go through customs, I should be good."

"Lead on," I tell her, waving my hand ahead of us.

We are on back in the lobby, but had yet to leave the building. The security guard looks over at us and nods. After nodding back at him, I whisper. "Maybe in the alleyway next to the building?"

Carmen looks around and suddenly grins. "Follow me."

With that, she heads towards the far side of the room, and I see she's heading towards the restrooms sign—public restrooms. Without hesitating, she heads right into the men's restroom. We follow behind her, Marissa and I looking at each other worriedly.

Once inside, I ask Carmen, "Why the Men's room?"

With a laugh, she replies, "Because I always like to see what you men do to your restrooms."

I roll my eyes. "We need to hurry. I'm sure I saw the guard look our way."

Nodding, Carmen takes out her PDA, and suddenly, there's a black Portal in front of the bathroom sinks. She waves us through. Nodding, I walk into the Portal without hesitation, hoping that Marissa doesn't cause any trouble and follows suit. But, I need not have worried, as she follows right on my heels, and then Carmen joins us.

I look around, and I see that we are inside a warehouse of some sort. It's also nighttime outside.

Carmen looks around. "Ok, so we are in the east end of what is the city of Ottawa. Let's see," she says, walking towards the doorway of an office building on the side of the warehouse's main large floor. She grabs the handle for the door and turns it, and it opens. At least it wasn't locked.

The blonde walks in, grabs one of the black-colored corded phones from one of the desks and, even from here, I can hear the dial tone. She punches a bunch of numbers and waits. "Hey Susie!" she tells the person on the other end, with a big grin on her face.

Even from where I am, a good ten feet or so, I hear the scream of a female on the other end of the line. Fortunately, it's a scream of excitement.

"Yes! I'm in town. Listen. Can you pick me up at the Donbury Warehouse?" Carmen nods when she looks at me. "Yes. I'm not alone. So don't come on your Harley." Suddenly, she's shaking her head. "I know," she says soothingly, "Next time, I promise I will come alone and you can give me that ride. See you in... what?" There is a pause. "Thirty minutes works for me. We will be outside the back alleyway."

Carmen hangs up the phone and smiles at us.

Marissa is looking at her suspiciously.

With a wink, she tells me, ignoring Marissa's look, "always make friends wherever you go. Come on. Let's go wait outside."

"So, who is Susie?" I ask as I walk with the blonde as she heads back out of the office, turning towards the back of the warehouse and the loading dock.

"Susie is a contact I found here when I was assigned to Earth. I worked with her on a couple of assignments."

"What race is she?" I ask her, curious.

"Human," she tells me with a big grin.

"Wait," Marissa says, suddenly stopping behind us. "You're trusting a human, again?"

"Of course," Carmen says, stopping and turning towards her. "She thinks I'm part of the DHS, working with the RCMP. She's actually a good kid. She's an excellent contact to have, as she works for CSIS."

"DHS? CSIS?" Marissa asks her at the unfamiliar acronyms.

"DHS is the Department of Homeland Security in the United States, and the CSIS is the Canadian's version of the FBI. CSIS stands for Canadian Security Intelligence Service. It's not as big as any of the Americans' intelligence services, but they still do good analysis—at times."

"Does the CSIS know about Magical folk?"

Carmen shakes her head. "Not really. Most governments across the world have an idea, but it's more a rumor than anything concrete. Article 1 makes it very hard for people to pin us down. Think of it as all those stories you heard growing up as a human. They're based on truth, for the most part, to varying degrees."

"I still find it hard to believe that even with Article 1, that we Earthlings... err, humans... don't know about all the Magical folk out there."

"Because we work hard at keeping it hidden," Marissa growls.

"That, and we do trust some people—though the list is short, and very selective."

Marissa gasps, eyes going wide.

"While Article 1 is good at keeping us hidden, there are times we need to trust humans," Carmen tells her with a shrug. "But overall, it's rare to bring in a human into our fold. Unlike the planets, Earth runs on its own special set of rules. Don't forget, the Council has limited control here."

"But what about Tallen and his Court?"

"Tallen is special," Marissa snorts.

"How so?"

"He has the soldiers to make it hard for the Council to send anyone after him. Most Magical races might have our own planets, but we aren't very populous. Earth, on the other hand, has a hell of a lot more people." She sighs. "You saw his soldiers?"

"Yeah, those big fuckers?"

"Yes. Well. They're allowed—under the rules—and Tallen has taken full advantage of a rather lenient interpretation of those rules. It would not shock me to learn he has his own standing army of modified soldiers."

I stare at her with wide eyes, thinking of an army of all those big beefed-up fuckers. Jesus!

Once outside, I look up at the night sky. We must be in a busy part of town, because although the sun went down an hour or so ago, the stars are hidden because of all the light pollution from the surrounding buildings. I had never been to Ottawa, but I knew it was the Canadian capital—sort of their version of Washington, DC.

We lean against the wall, each of us keeping to our own thoughts as we wait for this Susie character. Looking around, I see a number of security cameras. "What about those?" I ask, pointing to the cameras.

Carmen looks up and smiles. "All good. I already cast a spell on them to hide us."

Nodding, I close my eyes, trying to sense the energies around me. One thing I've noticed since being able to do Magic, is that I can also feel it, too. It's almost like a slight tingle, a feeling of warmth, when I am near it. Like closing your eyes and feeling the sun's rays on your face—just not as intense.

Then, I feel it. The Magic that surrounds the cameras. With my eyes still closed, I look up at the cameras, and detect a slight gray—at least to my mind's eye—haze surrounding them. That would be the Hidden spell, except Carmen had reversed it so that it hides us from the cameras, not hiding the cameras from sight.

I have all this knowledge in my head, but it still amazes me that it is real. Magic, I mean.

"Here she comes," Carmen says suddenly, about ten minutes later.

"That was quick," I quip.

With a laugh, she says, "Looks like she might have broken some speed limits getting here."

Looking down the main road, I watch as a car pulls up to us. The car in question is a candy-apple red freaking Mustang GT with heavily tinted windows.

Coming to a stop, the driver's door opens, and out pops a tiny woman. She can't be taller than five feet three, if that, in high heels. "Carmen!" she squeals, coming around the vehicle, leaving her Mustang running and the door open. She hugs Carmen to her tightly, and looks up at the blonde, with what I can only say is adoration in her eyes.

The woman, Susie, looks to be of Eurasian descent, with tanned skin and long, shiny black hair. And while she might be short, she packs a number of gorgeous curves onto that small frame; nice tits, too.

"Hey Susie," Carmen tells her with a laugh, hugging her back just as hard. "It's been too long, girl."

"It has! You took off three years ago, with not a word or anything since!" the petite bombshell pouts up at Carmen.

"Yeah. I'm sorry about that. I tried to message you, but the DHS sent me on an assignment where technology was limited, and I couldn't really do much in the way of contact."

"Ohhh!! More counterintelligence spy shit?"

"Yeah, more spy shit," Carmen replies with a loud laugh. "These are my associates. That's Kevin, and that's Marrisa."

Susie turns to us and looks us up and down. I see her gaze lingers on me for a bit before looking up at Carmen with an enormous grin.

"So, how 'associated' are you with Kevin there?"

Carmen rolls her eyes. Pointing to Marissa, she explains, "Well, that's his wife."

Susie gets a sour expression on her face. "Why is it whenever you bring around cute guys, they are always taken?"

"Story of my life, Susie. Story of my life," she replies in a dramatic voice, lifting the back of her hand to her forehead

Susie laughs but steps back. "So, where to?"

"Well we need to catch a flight to Halifax," she starts to say, but Susie is already shaking her head.

"Good luck with that. There is something big going on in Halifax, so flights there are hard to come by. If you are expecting to find a flight tonight, forget it."

"Something big?" I ask.

She turns to me with a grin. "Yes. There is some large demonstration happening there, because of the world summit for something or other to do with trade and shit." She shrugs. "Not my bailiwick, but hey, if you need to get there. I would suggest your best bet is to get your Homeland Security agency on the horn to lease a private jet."

"Yeah, I don't have the budget for that," Carmen lies to her.

"What about Tallen?" I suggest.

"Tallen?" Susie asks, puzzled.

"Hmm. Kevin here has some powerful contacts. Do you have his number?" she asks me with a raised eyebrow.

"Yep," I tell her with a grin. "he gave it to me after the incident."

"The 'incident'..." Suzie mouths to Carmen, eyebrows climbing her forehead.

"Then call the man!"

"I don't think that's such a good..." Marissa starts to say, but stops when I lay a hand on her shoulder.

"We need help, and if he can help, why not?"

Marissa looks pointedly at Susie, then looks back at me. I turn to stare at Susie as well, who stares back at me with a curious gaze.

Bending down to whisper in Marissa's ear, I say, "We need help, Marissa. I know you don't trust humans, but Tallen isn't human."

"No," she hisses back, "he's a Vampire who currently lives on Earth, but he is also royalty."

"Well, technically, so am I then, aren't I?" I ask her with a raised eyebrow.

"What do you mean?" she asks me, pulling back with a puzzled look on her face.

I take out of my pocket the medallion Tallen had given me after biting me. He'd said at the time, that technically—because of the full Transformation—I was a Vampire of his family, now. Which, William had later explained meant that Tallen was, for all intents, my adopted father—though, in the Magical, metaphorical way.

Her eyes widen at the medallion. "Is that why you can do what you can?"

"Pretty much."

"I knew it!" she cries out, poking me in the chest accusatorily. "There was no way you could have jumped into that hole like you did without breaking your legs!" The brunette throws her hands up in the air. "Fine! Call him. But don't count on him helping."

"Why not?"

She leans in close again, adding quietly, "he's a Vampire."

CHAPTER NINE

Calling Tallen was easier than I thought. Or getting a hold of him was. I'd expected when I called the number he gave me, that I would get some secretary. Nope, I got the man himself. He answered on the first ring, too, and the first words out of his mouth were, "are you in trouble?"

When I told him no, I wasn't in trouble, but that I was in Ottawa and needed a private jet to take us to Halifax because there were no flights tonight, or even tomorrow, he put me on hold. Not more than five minutes later, he was back. When he got back on the line, he said there would be a private plane landing at the Ottawa Airport to pick us up just before two in the morning. Tallen promised he would get us to Halifax, no matter what. He even gave me the name of a contact to check in with when we got to the airport, after explaining how to reach the private section at the airport.

Leaning back as best I could in the back seat, which in a Mustang was not conducive to sleep, I close my eyes and smile. Leave it to Tallen, to make sure I was taken care of. Ever since we'd saved William, his counterpart on the planet

Vamir—meaning he was Vampire royalty with a capital R—Tallen had tried to reward me. I kept telling him he didn't need to. That the power he'd given me after biting me was more than enough.

It seems that in helping save William from Gordo, it had stopped an intergalactic, which was still odd saying, catastrophe. Having a royal, a Vampire to boot, die on Earth under Tallen's watch would have been bad. I don't mean just bad PR, I mean rally bad—as in Tallen would have needed to make restitution to William's living relatives. Which would have been William's conniving bitch of a twin sister, the one who had wanted William dead so that she could take over the seat on the Galactic Council the Count, or Countess, of Vamir, was entitled to.

But, after saving him and uncovering the plot where his twin had tried to have him killed, Willian was now a student in an Ivy League University here on Earth, while his sister was on the hot seat. She was being investigated by Marissa's Dad for her role in the mess that had happened several months ago.

"Can you tell me what's going on?" Susie asks as we pull out from the industrial sector, turning to glance at Carmen, who sits next to her up in the passenger seat.

"Sorry, hon. Not this time. But, I promise to make it worth your time for coming to get us."

Susie snorts at that. "Please. I still have money in the bank from the last time I helped you out. You don't owe me a thing. Thanks to the reward I got for helping you three years ago, I was able to go back to school. I am in my last year of university!"

"Oh, wonderful!" Carmen cries in joy. "What did you end up majoring in?"

Susie smiles at her. "I took your suggestion, and am studying Historical Pagan Religions. I'm loving it!"

"You encouraged her to take what?" Marissa, next to me, cries in disbelief.

"I did." Carmen turns around in her seat, grinning back at us. "I wanted Susie to have a well-balanced education."

Marissa looks at Carmen suspiciously. I have to admit I did as well. Why would she tell the girl to study Pagan Religions? I mean, I now know Magic is real, but before that, I didn't have a clue about what really went bump in the dark. Why would encourage Susie to take a course of study like that?

As if reading my mind, Carmen explains. "The teacher here is a *good* friend of mine."

The fact that she put emphasis on the word 'good' makes me raise my eyebrow. Is she saying that her friend, this teacher, is one of the Magical folk? She nods at my raised eyebrow, and her grin grows more prominent.

Damn! Is she prepping Susie for an introduction to the Magical world? I know on Earth that Article 1 is circumvented every now and again... but, damn. I hope her introduction to it is not as intense as mine was.

"Here we are," Susie says, pulling onto a road that runs along the rear of the airport. "You said your contact was at one of the private hangers?"

I nod to her in the mirror. "Yes. We are supposed to meet someone by the name of Jimmy. Building thirteen he said."

"OK, that would be that building, then... the large blue one, with the big 13 on it," Susie says with a chuckle. With that, she turns down a side road towards the large building in question.

As we get closer, I see that in front of it, on the tarmac, is a large black private jet.

Susie pulls up to the gate, and there's a man there, smoking a cigarette. As she pulls up, the man throws his cigarette away and walks towards the car. Susie opens her window.

He's very nondescript. Tall, slim with a mustache, dark hair. He's wearing a pilot's uniform, composed of dark blue slacks and a light blue shirt, with a plastic set of wings on his chest over one breast. He nods to Susie in a friendly manner. "Kevin?" he asks in a deep voice.

Susie points to me in the back seat. "That would be him."

The man looks in the back seat and sees Marissa and me sitting there. "Kevin?"

I nod to him and say, "Yep, that's me."

"Well, Sir, your ride is here. I was told to take you where ever you wanted to go. I already put in a flight plan for Halifax. Do you have any bags?"

While he spoke with me, Carmen had gotten out, and Marissa had climbed out on her side. Opening her door, Susie lets me out.

"None," I tell him. "We are traveling light."

He looks at me and grins, and nods. "Gotcha. Well, come on. We can probably take off in about twenty minutes."

"Okay. We will be right there," Carmen tells him. "We just want to say goodbye."

"Sounds good." He smiles. "Just close the gate after your ride leaves, and make sure that it's locked behind you. I'll go prep the plane for take-off."

"Thanks...?"

Blushing hard enough that I even see it in the dim light above the gate, he coughs into his hand. "Oh. Sorry. Where are my manners? I'm Jimmy."

Damn. I never even thought to ask who he was; I had just assumed this was our contact. Leave it to Carmen to verify.

"Well, Jimmy," Carmen says with a smile, "give us five, and we will be right there."

"Sounds good," he replies, giving her a lazy salute.

Once he's gone, Carmen comes around the car and hugs Susie, looking down at her. "I'm glad you're doing so well. Unfortunately, I probably won't see you again for a while." She pulls back. "Are you sure you don't want payment for the ride?"

Susie shakes her head. "Gods, no."

"Gods?" Carmen asks, with a bark of laughter.

Susie grins up at her. "Of course! You don't think I would take Historical Pagan Religions and not become Pagan myself, did you? I believe in many gods, now. Though my parents went ape shit the first time I gave the prayer at one of their Sunday suppers."

"You didn't?" Carmen says, her mouth open in surprise.

"I did! I even had my brother, Bill, afterward ask me a ton of questions. He's always been into Dungeons & Dragons and stuff, so he was happy to hear about it."

We can't help but all laugh at that, even Marissa. Once the goodbyes have been said, we all head towards the plane, ensuring the gate we came back through was closed and well locked up. Once up the small steps and into the plane, I notice the pilot's cockpit door is open.

"Make yourself comfortable," Jimmy says, flipping switches, then looking down at some checklist. "We should be good to go in about ten minutes or so. There's a small bar fridge in the back, filled with drinks and sandwiches. My boss said you might be hungry."

"Sweet! Thanks!" Carmen says, heading to the back of the plane.

I do the same, but take a seat instead. Marissa, hesitant and nervous, follows me and sits down in the seat next to mine, against the window. Within seconds, Carmen is back, and her arms are full. She has three drinks and three sandwiches.

"Here you go," she says, passing out a drink and a sandwich to Marissa and me.

I look down at mine and see that it's a chuck wagon. Shit, I haven't had one of those in ages! When I was in college, I lived on ramen and these things. You would think I'd be sick of them, but not a chance. They are still my favorite go-to snack, especially after the gym. I'm sure if I had eaten a proper post-workout meal, I would have packed more muscle on me.

With a grin, I have to thank this Magical shit, because I finally had a six-pack—or it might have come after Tallen bit me. I'm not sure when it happened, but I will take it. I'd never had a six-pack before. Opening the wrapper, I take a big bite, inhaling half of it in one go.

"Fucking hell," Marissa tells me in shock, looking at me. "Hungry?"

"Starving," I tell her with a grin, my mouth full. "I don't seem to get hungry very often, but give me some food, and my body reminds me I still need to eat."

"What is this, anyhow?" Marissa asks me, nervously eyeing the sandwich.

"Oh, this?" I hold up my sandwich. "It's a sandwich, called a chuck wagon. It's just meat, cheese, and bread."

"That's it? What kind of meat?"

"Hmm…" I frown. "Not sure. I think pork? Beef?" I tell her with a laugh. "Who cares; it's good. I lived on these during college."

With a sceptical frown, she looks down at the sandwich in her hand and then looks back up at me. "Why?"

"Why? Because it was cheap and readily available. I even lived on ramen noodles."

"What are these ramen noodles?"

I stare at her. Is she's fucking with me? But she has an honest to goodness confused look on her face.

I turn to Carmen. "Are you telling me that they don't have ramen noodles on the other worlds?"

She laughs at my look of disbelief, and says, "Nope. Those are an Earth thing. Personally, I love them—the spicier, the better!"

"You go, girl!" I cry, giving her a high five as she sits down in the seat across from front, facing towards the rear of the plane. "Spice is the variety of life!"

Marissa cautiously opens the package and takes a small bite, but then her eyes widen. "Oh my gods, this is so good!"

"Man," I chuckle, sitting back and looking over at her chowing down on her Chuck Wagon. "We need to get you some good ramen. Though, I think for your first time, we'll need to get you the real thing."

I look over at Carmen. "Any chance you have Japan in your PDA?"

"Maybe," she tells me with a grin.

I'm about to crack a joke in reply, but Jimmy comes over the overhead speaker. "Thanks for flying with us tonight, folks. We'll be taking off in a couple of minutes. I've got our flight plan, and it looks like we will get to Halifax in just under two hours. Sit back and enjoy the ride."

"Nice," I say about the flight time.

I take out my phone, and I see it's later... err, earlier, than I thought, almost three in the morning. That means we will get to Halifax around five.

"Remember, there is a time change in Halifax. They are..." and here Carmen takes out a cell phone and looks something up, "one hour ahead of us."

"Okay, so we will get there around 6 am, local time," I tell her with a nod.

"Do we have a ride from the airport to this John Smith?" Marissa asks me, taking a sip of her pop.

That's when I notice that her Chuck Wagon is gone, the only evidence left of the large sandwich an empty wrapper in her lap. I also see how she's eyeing the other half of mine. With a snort, I pass it over to her.

Grinning at me, she takes it, and it's gone within seconds.

Carmen tells her, "No, but I'm sure we can use Uber again."

"What is Uber anyhow?"

"Well, it's a ride-sharing program on Earth. Most cities have them, just not all," I explain to her. "But they aren't all over the world. So, there might be times where we might need to hail a cab or something."

"Or ride a horse," Carmen says with a straight face.

I look at her, wondering if *she* was shitting me now, but she's just looking at me. And I see Marissa in the corner of my eye, nodding her head.

Almost stunned, I blurt out, looking at the two of them. "Seriously? Horses?"

"If we are lucky. And if not, we walk."

"Damn," I mutter, "guess that means I'll need to learn how to ride."

CHAPTER TEN

I feel a hand tap on my shoulder and, with a jerk, I startle awake and look around, disoriented.

"We're about to land," Marissa says quietly.

Jimmy had turned down the lights once we were up in the air, and the darkness showed me just how tired I was. I am not one of those military types who can fall sleep whenever they get a chance. I was exhausted, though. We hadn't got much sleep these past thirty-six hours.

Rubbing my eyes, I look around. Carmen is across from us, fast asleep as well. I nudge her with my foot slightly. She jerks awake as well, just as disoriented as I had been, until she sees Marissa and me.

She nods at me and smiles. "We're landing?"

"Yes. Jimmy came over the overhead speakers a minute ago to tell us to use the restroom or grab breakfast, then we need to buckle our seatbelts before landing. But you were both still out of it."

Rubbing her eyes and fixing her hair back into place, Carmen says, "Damn, guess Kevin and I were more tired than we thought." She yawns. "I know I was."

She looks up and, seeing that the light for the seatbelt sign is still off, she gets up and heads back towards the small kitchen area with the fridge. She comes back with her arms full, passing each of us a water bottle and a muffin in a plastic package. Sweet! Chocolate chip muffins.

"Thanks," Marissa says, taking the offered food.

"Anytime," she says with a nod, sitting back down and buckling herself back in. "No clue when we will have our next meal, and well, it's free, on Tallen's dime." she finishes with a grin.

"Did you get any sleep?" I ask Marissa, finishing my muffin.

"I tried to sleep, but I'm still not used to these things," she waves around herself to indicate the plane.

"Well, now that we are all assigned to Earth, you will get plenty of chance to get used to it. I looked at the budget we have, and I have to say, someone up high must really like you, Kevin," Carmen tells me with a grin.

"Can't we just create our own money, like you did with that gold?"

"Sure," she replies with a shrug of her shoulder. "But we try not to use Magic for stuff like that. It would unbalance this world's economic stability."

"But," I say with a frown, "didn't you create that gold bar with magic the first time I met you?"

"Yes, but I had to mark it down in the report."

"What's stopping from anyone from just... I don't know, creating tons of it and selling it, telling no one?'

"Oh, that does happen," Marissa smirks. "But we are M.A.G.I., so we keep tabs on stuff like that. When people from other worlds come to Earth, they are required to sign a binding Magical agreement that says they will limit their doing such actions. But, also if someone comes to Earth, they have to demonstrate that they already have sufficient funds for their projected stay."

I look at her oddly, never having heard about the term she just used. "A 'binding' Magical agreement?"

"Yes," Marissa says, finishing her own muffin. I may or may not have scarfed mine down in all of two bites.

"When someone signs it, they are under a geas while on their visit to Earth. When I came to Earth for those concerts when I was younger, I had to show proof of the money I already on Vraka. Usually, credits are acceptable, which are converted to gold, which are then converted into cash for whichever country on Earth we want to visit."

"That's nuts. How come I wasn't required to sign anything like that?"

"Because you're M.A.G.I. We hold ourselves to a higher standard. If you were a civilian, you would have been required to."

I stare at Carmen and shake my head. I still have so much to learn. Just then, I feel the plane start to dip down towards the ground, indicating we are about to land. After the plane has landed, and parked at the gate, Jimmy opens the cockpit door.

Smiling at us, he tells us, "Thanks for flying with me. Sir Tallen said that if you needed me, I should stick around and wait for you."

"I'm not sure," I tell him, looking at Carmen and Marissa for some help here.

"I would say stick around for six hours, in case we need you," Marissa tells him with a nod. "We might need to leave quickly."

"Sounds good. Well," he smirks, "flight plans don't allow for *leaving quickly*, but it won't take all that long to file one. Just don't come in, guns blazing behind you," he tells her with a chuckle.

With a laugh of her own, Carmen tells him, "We can't promise that."

He nods, opens the door, and pushes the stairs down, so that they hit the tarmac. "Welcome to Halifax," he says, moving out of the way, so we can go down the stairs.

"Do we need passports or such?" I ask him warily.

"Nope," he tells me with a big grin. "You have those freaky badges of yours for that."

"Freaky badges?" I ask him, puzzled.

"Yes," Carmen says from behind me. "The badges that we show people?"

"Ah!" I say, clueing in on what he means.

He is talking about how our M.A.G.I. badges are made, so that if you push Magic into it, it will show whoever you are showing it what they want to see. It's a special sort of illusion Magic.

"Anyhow, you've got six hours before I take off. I'll file a flight plane for noon, unless I hear from you before then."

"Thanks, Jimmy," Carmen tells the man, giving him a friendly shoulder bump as we head down the stairs.

Jimmy's grin gets even bigger. "Anytime."

* * *

Once we got to the airport's exit gate closest to the plane's parking spot, we had to call an Uber again. When our ride got here, we headed to the address of this John Smith.

It was on the other side of Halifax, the east side. This was my first time in Canada, so I had no idea where I was going. But, Carmen and Marissa admitted that they had never been to Halifax before, either. Before we left, we all added the Halifax airport to our PDA's memory, if you wanted to call it that. I had done the same back in New York City and Ottawa.

I look at the house where we had been dropped off at. It was one older home, probably built back in the 1960s. It was a bungalow, with overgrown grass. Since it was so early in the morning, there was not much traffic. I mean, we'd landed just past six in the morning, and by the time our ride got there, it was almost seven.

"Thanks for the ride," I tell the Uber driver.

Once out on the sidewalk, we all three take a moment to look around, but the street is empty. It is still pretty early. Carmen heads to the front door, with Marissa and I following. Just as we are about to get to the front door's entry, though, I feel something.

"Stop!" I cry out.

Carmen stops, turning back to give me a questioning look.

"I feel something," I tell her, confused at what I was sensing. "It almost feels like what I felt the time we were in Tallen's club, when I sensed that Sigil. It felt Magical."

Carmen turns back to look at the front door, but doesn't move from her spot. She looks around, and I notice that Marissa is doing the same thing.

"There!" Marissa says, pointing to the side of the door.

We all look where Marissa is pointing. Suddenly, Carmen waves her hand and, on the doorjamb, there's a Sigil. It's one I haven't seen before, but thanks to all that knowledge inside my head, I know what it is.

It's an explosion Sigil. Technically, it's a bomb—a Magical IED, or Improvised Explosive Device. If we had tried to open the door, or passed over the door's threshold, actually, it would have exploded. From the power I could sense, it would most likely have taken the entire house with it, and probably the neighbor's, as well.

Carmen whistled. "Things just got interesting."

"So that means the killer is a Magus?"

"Not sure how that would be possible," Marissa tells me with a puzzled look. "How can they handle silver?"

"Care to remove the Sigil?" Carmen asks me.

I nod and step forward. The Sigil is safe to walk around, and even to touch, as long as you don't pass over the threshold. I walk up to it and take a closer look. It looks sort of like an inverted U, with a line through it that curves slightly off to the left.

Putting my finger below it, I push Magic into the tip of my finger and slowly let the Magic build up until I feel there's enough to smash through the Sigil's defenses. Then, I push all that Magic out of the tip of my finger. It fires off like a bullet into the Sigil, causing it to explode into a thousand tiny motes of light. When the fireworks fade, the Sigil is gone.

"Damn," Marissa says, shaking her head and looking at me. "I still can't believe you have all that power inside you. It would have taken me ten minutes of focusing, to gather that much Magic together."

In surprise, I turn to look at her. "Really?"

"Really," Carmen tells me with a chuckle. "It would have taken me a good seven or eight minutes, myself." She shakes her head. "Kevin, you did it in about thirty seconds."

I stare at both of them in shock. Am I that strong? Is that the difference between a level twelve or higher Magus, and level six? Holy shit.

"We should check for more Sigils or traps," Marissa says, turning back to the door.

For the next ten minutes, we study the entirety of the door-frame, the door, and the doorknob. For shits and giggles, I said we should even check the mail slot. And it's a good thing we did, since we find another explosive Sigil underneath it.

"OK, that's two Sigils," Marissa mutters. "We are dealing with a Magus for sure—or our John Smith is getting help from someone Magical. We should be safe to go in, but take it slow."

"Right," I say and, putting my hand on the doorknob, I cast Unlock. The door opens easily under my hand. I love Magic.

Once just inside the doorway, I stop and close my eyes, trying to sense the feel of Magic, but I don't feel anything. I step in, still with my eyes closed, to let the girls come in behind me and close the door, so that the neighbors don't call the cops on a bunch of strangers hanging around next door.

Inside the house, it's quiet. The furniture is modern but cheap.

Carmen looks around, and says out loud, "At least we know John Smith isn't home. But we should hurry, in case someone comes. I would say that in a day or two, this place will become unavailable."

"OK, let's each take a room. I'll take the bedroom," I tell her.

"I'll take the kitchen," Marissa says, pointing to the back of the house down the hallway.

"And I'll take the living room," Carmen nods.

And for the next twenty minutes, we search the house. I check the bathroom, the closets, and even the linen closet in the hallway. And find… nothing.

Nothing odd, nothing Magical.

I head to the living room, to see Marissa helping Carmen finish up there. At my entrance, they look up at me. "Anything?" I ask them.

"Nope," Carmen growls. "This place is clean—and not clean, because it was cleared. There's nothing here."

"What about the basement?" I ask.

"Oh right," Carmen says, slapping her forehead. "This isn't Florida, where it's rare to have a basement. This is Canada, where that seems to be the norm."

We head to a door that must lead down to the basement, since it is the only door that we have yet to check. It was in the kitchen. Opening the door, I see that it's pitch black down there. When I try flicking on the light switch, though, nothing happens.

"Of course, it doesn't work," Carmen says with a scowl. "Who's first?"

I take a deep breath, "I've got it."

I cast Light, and a small ball of light hovers above the palm of my right hand. Holding my hand out in front of me, I head down the steps, the spell lighting my way. Once at the bottom of the stairs, I stop dead in my tracks.

"What in the actual fuck?" I whisper in awe. What I'm staring at should not be here—there is a forest inside the basement.

"Oh shit," Carmen whispers in shock, pointing.

I look at what she's pointing at, and I can't believe I missed it. On the basement floor, which is a thick carpet of tall grass, is a body that appears to be chained up, but it isn't a human body; the female form in the grass is hard to see because of the color of her skin. It is green.

Is that a dryad?

Marissa echoes my thoughts out loud. "Is that a Dryad?" Her tone is one of shock and awe.

CHAPTER ELEVEN

I go to rush to help the dryad, but Carmen stops me with a hand on my chest. She reminds me that we need to make sure there are no traps, first.

"Right," I tell her with a grateful nod.

I close my eyes and try to sense Magic, and I feel it alright—but it's all over the room. How did I miss this upstairs? It's so strong.

As if reading my mind, Marissa points to the ceiling. Looking up, I see the Sigil there—one for hiding Magic. That's how I missed it. Someone hid the Magic in the basement behind a Sigil.

"All right, that's a powerful Sigil. You need to be at least level ten to even cast it." Carmen says, frowning up at the Sigil. "That's why we couldn't feel the dryad's Magic."

"How did a dryad even get in here?" I ask.

"I'm not sure, but that chain tells me it wasn't by choice."

I look around, but I don't see any other Sigils. The girls had been checking as well.

"Nothing," Marissa says.

"Yeah. I don't see anything either," Carmen says out loud.

They both turn to me, eyebrows raised.

"Nothing... except that one," I say, pointing to the Sigil to hide Magic.

"Let's be careful."

I nod at Carmen, and we slowly step towards the dryad, who is lying in the thick grass on her side. She is tiny, slim, and—as we get closer, I can see—she is naked. She's also got green hair, a shade or three lighter than her skin. Her skin is more of a dark forest green, but her hair is a light foam green.

As we get closer, there's still no reaction from her. "Shit," I ask, "is she dead?"

Carmen kneels next to the green woman and puts a hand on her neck. "No, there's a pulse, but it's slow... she's asleep. But I daresay it's not a natural sleep."

"Drugged?" I wonder.

"Or Magically induced," she says. Setting a hand on the dryad's head, she closes her eyes.

Suddenly, the dryad's eyes snap open, and much faster than I expected she could move, she's up and has scooted away from Carmen, her chains rattling, until her back is pressed against some sort of tree that fills much of the basement, its upper branches running along the ceiling.

"Who are you?" the dryad yells out in fear.

"It's all right," Carmen tells her, both hands up, palms out, to show that she had no weapons.

Marissa and I do the same, showing the dryad that we, too, have no weapons.

"I'm Carmen. This is Kevin and Marissa."

The dryad's head whips towards the stairs, and there's terror in her eyes.

"It's all right," I tell her. "The man who lived here is dead."

"He is?" she says, and her head snaps towards me.

"He is. How did you end up down here?" I ask her softly.

The dryad sighs and slumps back against her tree. Well, I assume it is hers, since she's a dryad. You know, trees and shit?

"I'm not sure," she says, confused. "I was in my forest one night, and then just woke up one morning down in this basement. I was chained and could not escape."

"Here, let's get that chain off of you," I tell her, reaching for it with a soft smile.

She looks at me suspiciously, sniffs my approaching hand, and suddenly hisses. "You're human!"

"Yeah," I say, rubbing the back of my neck. "I am, but I can do Magic."

"Liar," she growls. "Humans can't do Magic."

I hold up my hand and cast the Light spell again, since I'd canceled it when we got to the bottom of the stairs, as there was some sort of ambient light down here. Not any that could be seen from the top of the stairs, though, which might have been because of the Sigil—since this light seemed Magical in nature.

Her eyes open wide in surprise.

"How?" she breathes.

"Long story," I tell her. "But the short of it is, I got Magic accidentally, but now I'm part of M.A.G.I. These are my partners." I point to Marissa and Carmen.

"The question I have, is why are you down here?" Marissa asks her.

Sighing, she nods. "I have been down here for what feels like half a year or so. By the way, my name is Jina."

"Hi, Jina. What dryad branch are you from?"

At the question from Carmen, Jina sits up proudly. "I am of the Oak family."

"Damn!" Marissa whistles appreciatively.

I look at her inquisitively.

"Look in your head for that," she tells me with a smile.

I do, and it comes to me. Dryads come in many forms—as many as there are types of trees. There's Oak, Birch, Ash, Elm, Pine, Walnut, Maple, and Spruce, just to name the most common. The most powerful of them are Oak dryads. The weakest of these are Pine dryads.

Dryads are Magical creatures only found on Earth. Part of the reason for that, is because they are spirit bound to the trees of this planet. And while there are other trees on other planets—even trees and plants that have been transplanted to other worlds—the spirits were not in them. They were just normal trees. On Earth, only some of the older trees had spirits in them, though it wasn't so much a spirit, as it was an ethereal entity bound to the Earth itself.

Dryads were solid creatures, even though they were Magical. They had long been worshipped as the oldest living creatures on Earth. According to my information, Dryads had been around when the Magical races such as the Elves, Vampires, Werewolves were just starting to be recognized as races.

Hell, they were around long before humans were using fire.

"What's an Oak dryad doing down in a basement?"

"I obviously was captured and brought here," Jina says, waving a green arm around the basement.

"Why, though?" I ask the obvious question.

"For my sap," she says with a sigh.

"Your sap?"

"It has special properties," she says, hesitantly, almost reluctantly, as if she is giving up some big secret.

I look at Marissa and Carmen, but they have just as a confused a look on their faces as I do. "What kind of special properties," I ask her, frowning.

She doesn't answer me right away but simply stares hard at the three of us, as if judging us. "Let me see your badges," she suddenly blurts out.

I nod and take out my badge to show it to her, but I don't push Magic into it. That way, she sees what I want her to see, since my M.A.G.I. badge is actually just that—a M.A.G.I. badge.

She slowly crawls forward and gingerly takes my badge, looking down at it. She closes her eyes as she traces her fingertips over the seal and sigils on it. Opening them again, she nods as if satisfied.

"You're the real thing," she breathes in a sigh of relief.

"Now, can we get these chains off you?"

"They are enchanted with powerful Magic," she tells me with a wistful sigh. "You would need to be a powerful Magus to remove them."

"Well," I tell her with a soft smile, "I guess it's a good thing that I am one."

She looks at me, as if gauging my power, and her eyes widen in shock. "You're above level twelve!"

"Yep," I tell her with a grin.

"But... how? You're a human!"

"Let's just say that I drank something that gave me powerful Magic," I tell her with a chuckle, "which tasted like shit."

She looks puzzled at that, but suddenly her eyes open even wider in shock. Looking at Carmen and Marissa, she whispers, "He drank the last vial?" Her voice sounded rather... incredulous.

"Jesus. Does everyone know about this vial?"

"Yes," all three of them say, turning to me.

Carmen is the one to explain. "That vial was considered a Galactic treasure, worth unknown riches. Everyone who wasn't able to rise above the lower Magical levels—especially those who could not do Magic at all—dreamed of drinking that vial."

"Wait... the vial that that guy stole when I first met you, stole something that valuable?"

Nodding, Carmen says. "Why do you think the Council wants your ass so badly? If it wasn't for her Dad," she says, pointing to Marissa, "you would be on a table—probably more than one table, actually—and dissected, already."

"Christ," I say, shaking my head. "I'm glad you're Dad found me first then."

"Same here," she says with a soft smile.

"Now, let's let Kevin get those chains off of you, and you can explain to me what has been going on," Carmen tells Jina.

Jina nods as I walk slowly up to the dryad. Smiling, I grab the chain and I focus my Magic until just like I'd done with the Sigil, I push a large amount of power into the chains, breaking their Magical bonds.

Suddenly, the chains which had been bolted to the floor and attached to a band of metal around her neck, explode into a thousand motes of lights.

Jina's hands fly up to her neck, and she looks at me in awe.

"Does that feel better?" I ask her.

"Yes!" she cries, suddenly throwing herself at me and hugging me hard around the neck, causing me to squeak in surprise. Without thinking, I'd put my hands around her waist. She felt soft, but also very light—much lighter than a body her size should feel. It felt like I was lifting balsa wood.

Once she's done hugging me, she stands on her own, hand running back and forth across her neck, as if she still can't believe the chain and collar are gone.

"Now, what's this special property of your sap?" I ask her.

"You promise not to tell anyone?" she says, hesitantly.

"Su…" I start to say, but Carmen stops me with a hand on my arm. I look at her.

"Careful. If you promise a dryad something, you are bound by your promise." Carmen turns to Jina. "Can we promise not to share it with anyone else, unless it is required? Say, by the lead Council member, who also happens to be her Dad?"

"Your Dad is Sir Targun?" the dryad says, her eyes wide.

"Yeah," she says, with a wry grin.

Jina slowly nods and says, "Promise me that you will tell no one this secret unless it's required."

We all three promise her that we will do precisely that.

The dryad looks up at me and says, "My sap can make it so that someone who is normally affected by silver, can handle it safely."

"Holy shit!" Carmen says, and there is awe in her voice.

"Wait," Marissa says, confused. "You're saying that dryad sap can stop the effects of silver?"

Jina nods to her. "But only if you are touching it. You can't ingest the sap and be protected from silver on the inside."

I look at the two girls. "So it seems our killer is—or was—a Magus."

"Sure sounds like it." Carmen nods thoughtfully. "It makes sense."

"So maybe that's how someone could take down Vampires, Werewolves, and other Magical folk—because they were a powerful Magus, who was able to handle the silver daggers, because of Jina's sap," Marissa explains.

"Damn," I whistle in appreciation for the evident preparation behind such a diabolical plan.

"But he's dead now, so we should be fine," Marissa says out loud.

"He is?" Jina says, her eyes opening wide, and she has a grin on her face.

"Yep. We were told he died in his sleep. This was him, right?" I ask her, taking my phone out and showing her a picture of John Smith that we got from the online obituary.

She looks at my phone and she gasps.

"No, that's not him!"

"It's not?" I ask her, frowning.

"No!" she cries, suddenly hunching down, as if expecting a blow. "The man who trapped me was tall and smelled like nothing—but he wasn't human. I can tell that much, since he was affected by silver."

I look at the two girls, and they have the same look on their faces. It's an 'oh… shit!' look. It looks like our killer is still out there on the loose.

Carmen looks at the dryad. "Jina, you need to leave—now! While you can. We will take care of things from here. You don't have a picture of the man who chained you here, do you?"

"No," she says, shaking her head. "but I can describe him.

"Oh, that will help!" Marissa tells her.

Jina nods. "He's tall, about six feet or so, and has long dark hair. He also has a scar on his chin, and a slight limp when he walks. He is also really strong in Magic. Though," and here she looks at me, "not as strong as you. But close, I think." She pauses. "Oh, and he also talks like he has rocks in his mouth."

I look at Jina, confused. "Rocks in his mouth?"

She gets a frustrated look on her green face. "As if he had something in his mouth and was talking around it. I... I can't explain it."

"It's all right," Marissa tells her soothingly. "That's a lot more than what we had to go on before. Thank you, Jina, of the Oak dryads."

Marissa bows to her, and Carmen and I follow her example.

"Well, I want to thank you for saving me. If ever you need me, come and find me. I live in what the humans call the Long Lake Provincial Park. Come there if you need me."

I ask, "And how will we find you in the park?"

"Easy," she says with a impish grin. "I will find you."

"All right. Thanks, Jina."

"No, thank you."

With that, she places one hand on her tree while waving to us with the other. With a ground-shaking rumble, her tree slowly disappears into the ground. Within a minute, her entire tree—with all of its branches, and even the long grass that carpeted the basement floor—is gone. All that is left in the basement, is a massive hole in the ground, with the cracked concrete foundation pushed out to the sides.

Turning to the girls, I ask, "so... what now?'

Marissa sighs and looks at the two of us. "Now, we have to find this Magus, before anyone else dies."

CHAPTER TWELVE

And it wasn't long before we learned about another death. Actually, we found out about it just as we exited the basement and regrouped in the living room. Carmen had stopped halfway to the front door, and held up her hand for us to stop as she pulled out her communication stone.

Nodding, a frown flickers across her pretty face. She nods again and puts her stone away. "That was Liia. It seems there has been another death."

"So our perp is still alive, then?" Marissa growls.

"Yep."

"Where did it happen?"

"This one was in a small town in Texas."

"I guess that means we are heading to Texas?" I ask her.

"Yep. Care to call our pilot Jimmy and tell him?"

"Yeah," I tell her, taking my phone out. Before we'd left the plane, Jimmy had given me his personal number. I called him up from my new contacts. "Hey Jimmy, it's Kevin. We need to get to Texas. Hmm. Give me a sec. Do you know what town?" I ask Carmen.

"Someplace called Rollingwood," she supplies.

"Did you get that?" I ask Jimmy.

I pull my phone down and do a quick search to answer his obvious question. "Yeah" I tell him, "Looks like the closest airport is the Austin-Bergstrom International Airport... Oh, all right. Yeah, we should be there in a couple of minutes."

Putting my phone away, I turn to the girls. "It seems Rollingwood, Texas, is a suburb of Austin. He's putting in a flight plan for Austin, departing in just over half-an-hour."

"All right, let's get going. Hopefully we'll get there before they disturb the area too much around the body."

I nod as Marissa takes out her PDA, and a Portal appears in front of us in the living room. Without pause, I walk into it, with Carmen following me, with Marissa last. Once through, I look around, and see we are near the gate where our Uber picked us up. One neat thing about Portal Magic, is that humans won't see it unless they are dangerously close to where one opens.

To them, if anyone happened to be looking right at where it opens, we just suddenly appear. Fortunately, the other thing a PDA does, is if there are any eyes that should not be watching, it creates the same effect as a Circle spell, effectively encouraging someone to look the other way—almost like an aversion to looking at something.

No one is nearby, and the mechanics in the next hangar over don't notice our arrival. The only reason I can see the black

Portals now, is thanks to the Magic inside me. Walking up to the gate, we get there just as Jimmy arrives.

He looks at us in surprise. "Damn," he swears. "I didn't see you get out of your taxi."

"Yeah, it just left before you got here," I lamely tell him.

"Well," he says, unlocking the gate—as it can only be opened from the inside—"the flight plan is in. We can take off in about twenty-five minutes. I wasn't sure how long it would take you to get back, but I got fresh coffee and donuts."

"Damn," Carmen says with a big grin. "Are you flirting with me, Jimmy?"

He looks at her and laughs. "With the ladies? Always."

I bend down to Marissa and with a grin, whisper into her ear. "See? Not all humans are bad."

"Oh, if humans bring me donuts and coffee," Marissa answers with her own smile, "I'm sure I could get to like them."

Once we are all on the plane, Jimmy closes the door and points to the back of the cabin. "It's all back there. Enjoy."

"You want any?" I ask him.

He laughs and shakes his head. "I already had my large coffee and an apple fritter."

"Wait, there are apple fritters?" Carmen says, her eyes glazing over.

"Yep," Jimmy tells her with another grin. "I got two dozen, since I wasn't sure what you all liked. There's cream in the fridge, and sugar in the brown bag next to the coffee box."

With enthusiasm, I say, "Damn, a man after my own heart."

"You're cute and all, Kevin, but you're not my type," he replies with a laugh as the girls both snicker, before heading to the cockpit and sitting down in the pilot's seat and going through his checklists.

Within minutes, we all have donuts and coffees. Marissa and Carmen had each opted for the apple fritters, but I went with the holy grail of donuts—Boston cream. Taking a sip of my coffee, I sigh, content. Damn, coffee is wonderful.

Once we are all sitting down, Marissa is the first to ask. "What do you think we will find in Texas?"

Carmen says in a contemplative voice, "Based on what Liia said, I would expect the victim is a Magical folk, though what race, we don't know... well, Liia wasn't sure. She'd only found out through some informants because the local police were going to get involved. But I guess someone at M.A.G.I. called the police off, telling them that the FBI would send a team from a special Task Force working these cases." She shrugs. "That would be us."

"All right, folks," Jimmy comes over the overhead speakers. "This flight is going to be much longer than our last— roughly ten hours. I'm glad I refueled here, just in case. We should be good. It will be dark when we get there. If you want to catch some shut-eye, I would suggest you go ahead and do that. Like before, the restroom is in the back, and more food is in the fridge. I refilled the sandwiches and snacks."

I frown at the large coffee in my hand, which is almost a quarter gone.

"Now he tells us," I say.

Both girls laugh at me. "Well, coffee doesn't affect us Magical folks. Except that it tastes awesome."

"Wait," I say, turning to Carmen, who is now sitting next to me, with Marissa across from me. "Caffeine doesn't affect me anymore?"

"No clue about how it will affect you, but for Magic folk—and we can probably assume you now fit in the same category, since you have magic—caffeine doesn't really do much for us." She shrugs, but I can tell she isn't one hundred percent sure.

"Well, I'm not about to give up coffee just because of that," I tell her with a grin, taking a large gulp of my cream laced black nectar. Another thought occurs to me. "What about booze?" I suddenly ask.

"Oh, that we still get affected by," Marissa says. "Trust me, I can vouch for that. There are some concerts I can barely remember, I got so drunk."

With a raised eyebrow, I ask her. "You? Drunk?"

"Hey, I was young once," she says with a grin. "And stupid. You never got drunk off your rocker?"

"Hmm," I tell her awkwardly. "Maybe."

And I had. Mike, Jim, and I used to get drunk all the time. Though if it had been up to Mike, it would have been more often than it had been. During college, he'd once claimed that to be a proper university man, it was required. I'd asked him about those of us who didn't finish college? He told me to shut up and pass him the bottle.

Feeling a tug, I look down, and see that Carmen moved the arm between us up and was now snuggling against me. I give her a questioning look.

"I'm tired," she says with a grin, "and I want something to lean on,"

I look over questioningly at Marissa, but she simply looks at us and sips her coffee. There's no anger on her face. Was my fiery wife finally warming up a bit to Carmen?

"Fine," I tell her, putting a wounded look on my face, "If I'm nothing more than a pillow, I will try to be useful."

"Oh, hush you," Carmen says with a laugh. "You love the attention."

"Who doesn't love the attention of a beautiful woman?"

Carmen smiles and turns to look at Marrisa. "I'm truly sorry, Marissa. That I never told you about dating Prita. She was the one who wanted to keep our previous relationship quiet, as she didn't want to hurt you."

"No prob—" she starts, but suddenly stops. "Wait. She did it on purpose?"

"Yes. Prita knew how you felt about her. But, never could return the feelings, or at least she felt she couldn't."

With a confused look on her face, Marissa asks. "Why not?"

"To put it in simple terms, Prita was afraid of your Dad—and of losing her job if ever the two of you would have a falling out."

"My Dad?" Marissa growls threateningly.

Carmen puts both hands up. "Now, hold up. I said she was afraid of your Dad—not that your Dad told her to stay away.

It was her choice, and her request. I wasn't happy with it, but I stupidly allowed myself to be swayed by her, since she was your partner, and we had used to date."

"Wait, so all this anger I have is because Prita didn't want to date me..." She pauses, face clouding up with anger, "because she was afraid of my Dad? But she was the strongest hunter in the M.A.G.I.!"

"Well, yes. But she was afraid of your Dad. Prita spoke to me about it when you first got assigned to her. She was finding it hard, because she was falling for you, but was afraid of your Dad."

"Gods! How could she have been so stupid? My Dad would have done nothing! He married me off to a human, for the gods' sakes!" she blurts out quickly. "No offense, Kevin."

"None taken," I tell her with a soft smile.

"Well, I knew her longer than you," Carmen tells Marrisa softly. "And I have to admit, how obtuse she could get was part of the reason we broke up. She was pigheaded and stubborn, but also viewed things differently than I did."

Sighing, Marissa nods. "For that, I can vouch. She was a great partner, but Gods, if you were anyone she didn't like, she went out of her way to make your life hell." My wife buries her head in her hands, before pulling them down with a growl. "I guess I owe you an apology, Carmen. I thought it was you who'd hid it from me."

"I wanted to tell you, but I promised her that I would not. Which, looking back," she says with a sour expression, "might not have been the smartest thing."

I look between the two girls and wonder, does that mean they are friends again?

Carmen reaches across with a hand. "Friends again?"

"Friends again," Marissa tells her with a smile.

Suddenly, Carmen, who still has Marissa's hand, pulls her across the space between the seats, and my wife falls on top of Carmen and me, laughing.

"What are you doing!" Marissa laughs.

"I'm making your husband more comfortable," Carmen says with a grin.

"How is me flopping onto Kevin making him more comfortable?" Marissa asks, looking up at Carmen and me.

"Easy," Carmen tells her with a big smile. "You fall asleep in his lap, and he will be happy."

With a puzzled look, she asks, "He will?"

"Yep, I will," I tell her with a laugh. "I mean. Who doesn't love having a beautiful catgirl fall asleep in his lap?"

"But, I'm not in my Changeling form," she says, looking up at me again.

"No, but in my head, you are," I tell her with an even bigger grin.

"Men," she complains, rolling her eyes, but she snuggles into my chest.

She looks over at Carmen. "What about you?"

"Oh, I'm good," she tells her, leaning her head against my shoulder and places her hands more comfortably on Marissa's legs, which are draped across hers.

We put our seats back, and that's how we fall asleep—with Carmen leaning against my shoulder, and Marissa curled up in my lap. I fall asleep with a smile on my face. And that was how I flew across the country, snuggled up with two beautiful women, who were friends again.

CHAPTER THIRTEEN

"Over here," Carmen calls out.

As Marissa and I head towards her, you can't miss the terrible smell. My stomach clenches up, and I almost hurl. The body that is spread across a small patch of ground is hardly recognizable as non-human—or a body, for that matter. It had been attacked by animals.

While the local cops, or whoever it was, had stayed away from the body—feral dogs and other animals don't understand procedures and shit—like keeping a crime scene clean. The body had been gnawed on and torn apart. The area around it was far from clean.

"How are we supposed to tell what race it is?" I ask, doing my best to breathe through my mouth.

"Good question," Marissa says, squatting down next to the body.

Gods, doesn't the smell affect her? Maybe she's used to it? Carmen does the same thing, squatting next to Marissa and studying the body. I go over as well, but let's be honest, I am not used to this.

The smell is terrible—nothing smells quite like a mangled pile of spoiled meat left out in the Texas sun for days. It seems that Tallen biting me, has given me a heightened sense of smell, as well. With my arm over my mouth and nose, I look down at the mangled mess that was once a person. I can't even tell if it was male or female.

"Female," Carmen offers, without me asking out loud.

"Yep," Marissa says, nodding as well. She grabs a stick close by, and pushes some mangled, ripped-up clothing aside.

"Can you tell what race?" I ask her.

Shaking her head, she frowns at me. "Can you cast Identify? It's a level twelve spell."

With hesitation, I shrug. "Hmm. Not sure?"

"With all that knowledge inside your noggin'," Carmen says, throwing a wry grin my way, "you should have a ton of spells we don't know. Hell, you're also a much higher level than either of us, so you must be able to cast something useful."

I scan through the information in my head and, as I dig through it all, a spell does come to mind. I cringe, though. In order to do the spell, I'll have to place my hands on the body in question—meaning I need skin-to-skin contact with that gory mess.

I will freely admit, that I had to swallow the bile that threatened to erupt from the back of my throat. And... I might have squeaked like a girl. Gods, I hate Magic! Reluctantly, I shuffle closer and reach my hands out.

With what I'm sure is absolute disgust on my face, I place my hands on the cleanest part of the body I see. I can't even describe what the cold, gelid flesh feels like under my fingertips. With my eyes squeezed tightly shut, I cast Identify. In my mind's eye, I see the image of a Changeling—a girl who is half-human, half fox.

I never understood, until now, the differences between Changelings and Beasts. Beasts, while they had a hybrid form like Changelings, have an animal form, too. Beasts were categorized as either Bear, of which there were multiple types such as Grizzly, or Black Bear, Badger, Wolverine, Buffalo, and Hippos—though the last was rare. Then, there were Changelings, which could assume a completely human appearance, in addition to their hybrid form. Changelings included most cats—from domesticated cats to lions—and dogs, of which there are too many breeds to name. And, as odd as it may sound, bears. Then, of course, there were uncommon Changeling varieties, like this fox girl.

It seems there was some mixing back and forth between the two magical races. There really wasn't all that much of a difference between the two. But also, Beasts were much stronger, though Changelings were much faster.

With bile still clawing at the back of my throat, I say, "Changeling girl. Half fox. The name that comes to mind with the Identify spell is Julinia Malgrantor, age 33."

"Damn," Carmen swears.

"You knew her?" Marissa asks.

"Yes. She used to be a cadet in the Vamir Police Force. Last I heard, she was working for a private security force here on Earth."

"Okay," Marissa says, "we know who our victim was, but not why they were killed." She squints up at me. "Did you get anything else from the spell?"

"Nothing else," I tell her with a shake of my head. "Just what I said, that she was a Changeling, a fox girl, age 33, and her name."

"Damn," Carmen says with a sigh. "I guess it was to much to hope, that the spell would reveal to us the killer and everything."

"Here," I say, thinking it over. "Let me try something." I move away from the body and place my hands on the ground. Casting Identify again, I try to see if I can get any impression from the area. The Identify spell is used to do exactly what it says—to identify something or someone—but maybe I can get an impression of the area?

Suddenly, to my mind's eye comes a very fuzzy image, almost as if I'm looking at brief flashes of an image that appears through otherwise constant static, like you would get sometimes with old televisions and trying to watch porn on locked adult channels... not that I ever tried to do that.

It's not so much an image, though, as it is a feeling.

"Evil," I say out loud.

"Evil?" both girls ask me in stereo, each in the same questioning tone.

I tilt my head sideways, still staring at the ground where my hand is half-buried in the dirt and leaves. "Evil," I repeat, nodding. "Whoever this person is, they have evil in their hearts. They want to hurt people... they want to change things."

Carmen asks me, "Change what?"

Sighing, I stand up and brush my hands on my pants. "That's just it. I don't know. It's just a vague impression."

"Well, we got more information from this than we thought we might." Marissa stares sadly down at the mangled body. "Care to remove the daggers?"

I look back at the body, and search for the daggers, which I hadn't noticed before. When I look closer at the body, I finally see them. I was so preoccupied with not getting sick when placing my hand on it, that I had completely missed the five daggers that pinned the body down to the ground. Two were in her hands, two more in her chest, and another pierced her throat.

Changelings were affected by silver, just as much as Vampires, Werewolves, or other Magical folk. Other races were affected by it as well—it seems most Magical creatures were.

"It won't affect me?"

Both girls exchange worried glances with each other, before turning back to me. Carmen is the one to answer. "We aren't sure. You are still, technically at least, human."

"So, you aren't sure?"

"No," Marissa admits hesitantly. "Just touch one lightly, to see if you feel a burning sensation."

I nod and bend down, stretching my hand towards the first dagger. When my hand hovers over the sullied metal, I slowly lower my hand until my finger brushes the hilt, ready to snatch my hand back quickly. But when my hand touches it, I don't feel anything more than the cold chill of the metal.

I look up at both girls, who each have worried looks on their faces. "Nothing," I tell them.

"Phewf," Marissa says, blowing out a breath she'd apparently been holding. "We weren't sure. Can you wrap your hand around it and pull the dagger out?"

I nod and do exactly that. I grab one of the daggers and pull it out with a wet *squelch*. Standing, I back up a few steps from the corpse and look down at it. The dagger is about a foot long and of pure silver—but I notice that the handle, while silver, has etchings on it. The symbols look similar to Sigils, but, I don't recognize any of them.

"Shit," Carmen swears.

"What?" I ask, looking up from the dagger.

"Those symbols. They are Magical in nature."

"They are?"

"What do you think?" Marissa asks us both. "Should we take it to my Dad?"

"It's not Elvish, but it has flowing characters similar to that script," I say, frowning at the characters.

"Shit," Carmen repeats. "I'm not one hundred percent sure, but I definitely think we should get Marrisa's Dad to look at the daggers."

Nodding, I start to pull the rest of the daggers out of the mangled body. Once done, I have spread out on the ground five seemingly identical silver daggers.

"How will we move them?" I ask, looking up at the two girls.

"Well, I can't carry one," Marissa says, looking at the daggers as if they were vipers.

"Ditto," Carmen adds.

"Can't you… I don't know… stuff them into your pockets or something?"

"Hmm. I have jeans on," I tell her, pointing to said piece of clothing.

"Take your shirt off," Carmen supplies.

"Oh, I guess I can do that," I say, and I remove my shirt, and place it on the ground next to the daggers. I then place the daggers into them, and fold the shirt over and tuck here and there, until I have a makeshift container.

Once ready, I stand up and nod to the girls.

"Ready."

Marissa nods and takes her PDA out, and there's suddenly in the forest with us, a black Portal.

"What about the body?" I ask. But just as I say it, Carmen throws a black disc onto the body.

"Right," I say lamely with a laugh.

Knowing the body is taken care of, I walk into the Portal.

Once through, I hear a screech.

"Why you bring silver here!!!!!"

I look over, and see Preeka cowering over to one side of the room we step out into. We are in the entryway of Targun's mansion. The goblin is pointing a long crooked finger—one with a large wart on it—at me.

"It's all right, Preeka," Carmen says from behind me. "We are in the middle of an investigation, and we need to see Marissa's Dad right away."

"Go fetch my Dad, Preeka. Please," Marissa adds.

Preeka looks between the three of us. Okay, fine, she glares from one of us to the others, before finally nodding. With a displacement of air, is gone.

Within half a minute, I hear footsteps approaching, and shouting. "It's all right, Preeka! I will take care of this!"

Just then, Targun walks into the room, his staff in his hand. On seeing the three of us, he stops in shock.

"Oh," he says. "Preeka said we were being attacked by someone with silver."

"Well, we aren't attacking, Dad. But we do have silver. Silver daggers, to be more precise. "

"Why in the hell would you bring silver here?!" he asks her in a horrified voice. "And why are you naked from the waist up?" my father-in-law demands.

"We brought them for you to see, because of what's on them —and bundled up in his shirt was the best way for Kevin carry them," Marissa tells her Dad.

With a puzzled look, he asks, "What's on them?"

"Let's go to your lab," I tell him, holding up my shirt, "and we'll show you."

Targun nods slowly and then leads us out of the room and towards his lab. Once in the lab, I find a clear space, which really means just unrolling my shirt on top of things that are already there, since there was no open space, per se. Once I open the shirt and expose the daggers, Targun slowly makes his way closer to where he can see them.

When he sees the symbols on the hilts of the silver blades, he gasps in dismay. Head whipping up, he glares at the three of us and barks out, "Where in the hells did you get these?"

"We retrieved them from the body of a dead Changeling on Earth. We were investigating reports of bodies that are turning up with silver daggers in them," Marissa tells him, shock on her face at his reaction.

Targun places his hand just over the daggers, but doesn't touch them. He's shaking his head.

"Dad?"

Sighing, he turns to her. "We have a problem."

"We do?" I ask.

"Those," he says, pointing down to the daggers, "are a major concern; they should not exist anymore."

"Dad, what are they?"

"Those are a Dark Elf assassin's daggers."

"What?" With a frown, Carmen asks, "But, I thought the Dark Elves died off eons ago?"

"They did," he says with his own frown. "Or at least we thought they had. The characters are Dark Elvish Sigils," he says, his finger pointing to the alien flowing script, but not touching the daggers. "These daggers are something extraordinary, but also terrible, and dangerous."

He looks up at the three of us—four, if you include Preeka who had come in quietly, or had silently appeared.

"They leach Magic out of a person, transferring it to whoever uses the dagger."

"Wait, so Dark Elves can touch silver?" Marissa asks incredulously.

Her Dad shakes his head. "No, they aren't immune to silver. They are, or at least were, just as much affected by it as we are."

"That's why they had the dryad!" I blurt out.

"What?" Targun's head whips around to face me so quickly, I am sure his neck popped.

"We found a dryad who had been captured and was being kept in a basement. She said that they kept her…" I lick my lips, "for her sap?"

"Fucking hell," he breathes, his eyes widening.

"Dad?" Marissa asks him again.

Targun places his hands on the table, on either side of the daggers on my shirt. He doesn't answer her, but stares at the daggers, as if they were vipers.

Marissa gives her Dad more information. "Also, when Kevin did the Identify spell, he said he sensed evil."

Targun looks over at me, arching an eyebrow.

"Yeah, it was odd. I used Identify by placing my hand on the ground in the area they had been, and I got a vague sense of evil."

"Gods," he mutters, "don't tell me the Dark Elves are back."

CHAPTER FOURTEEN

"But, Dad," Marissa continues, "all of the history books say that they were wiped out eons ago, because they tried to destroy the mother world."

Targun nods, still staring down at the daggers as if they might come alive. "And we thought they had been," he says. "The last known Dark Elves were destroyed over 9,000 years ago. The battle was only won, because of the combined might of all the races. We even had the help of some human allies at the time." He shakes his head. "It was the last time humanity ever cooperated openly with us, instead of trying to hunt us down, or kill us."

I interrupt his musings. "I'm sorry, but the information in my head doesn't talk about any of that."

He glances at me. "No, and it won't. Dark Elf history is just that—ancient history. We only learn about it as a side note in school. But, I know a bit more about them, since when I was young, I was fascinated by it all." He shakes himself, pulling his thoughts out of whatever pit they'd fallen into. "Come. Let's go sit, and we can talk."

"Preeka," he shouts suddenly, making us all jump.

"Master?" she appears next to him, standing on the same table as the daggers—though I notice she is on the edge of it, as far away from them as she can be.

"Gather up these daggers, and place them under lock and key." He frowns. "Hmm… Put them in that large black box in the basement. And then bring back the shirt, so that Kevin here has a shirt to wear again."

He glances down at the garment in question. "Actually, can you clean off the blood and whatever else is on it, before returning it to Kevin?"

"Yes, Master," she nods.

The little goblin takes the shirt up slowly, folding it over the daggers once, and then once again, with Targun's help. And then, without warning, she, the daggers, and shirt, are gone.

Targun nods for us to follow him. We do, and we eventually get to a larger room, that he uses as a living room. Just imagine your typical living room, except that this one has nine couches, five sitting chairs, and lots of tables. With no television.

I take a seat on a large couch, and the girls flank me on either side. Targun takes the sofa facing us. I can see that he is gathering his thoughts, so I keep quiet. The girls don't say a thing, either.

"Now," he says, finally looking up at us. "Dark Elves… Where do I start?"

"From the start?" Carmen offers. "I don't know much about them."

"Ah, right. You were born on Earth," he nods to her in understanding. "Well, even what Marissa would have learned in school was fairly basic." Targun turns to his daughter. "Can you tell me what you remember from school?"

"Hmm. Let's see," Marissa says, scooting over until she is sitting forward on the edge of her seat. "The Dark Elves got destroyed… they were destroyed as an entire race, supposedly because they followed false gods." She frowned, as if remembering something. "But that wasn't the issue. The real issue, was that their false gods told them to destroy and enslave all the other races, as they were supposedly the 'Chosen' ones… according to their holy scriptures."

"Good so far," Targun tells her, nodding encouragingly.

"They wanted to kill all humans, Elves, Dwarves, and Changelings. The Beasts, Vampires, and other races, they wished to enslave. And they tried to do so for thousands of years. It was a time of brutality beyond understanding. From what I can remember, while for thousands of years, humans hunted or killed us, they didn't torture us or enslave us as a species. They just wanted our Magic."

"A good start, my dear," he says. Targun's smile makes his daughter sit up a bit straighter.

"The Dark Elves were evil; they even killed their own people indiscriminately. They didn't care for the sanctity of life. They cared for nothing more than sacrificing the 'weak' to their false gods, to make them more powerful."

"Their deities weren't really gods?" I ask.

Targun nods at my question. "They were not gods. They were what you would call Demons. Ages ago, a powerful Demon had been summoned, but the summoner failed—not because the demon was not summoned, but because he failed to properly contain it."

Targun's lip curls in disgust. "How do you think a Demon gets stronger?"

I frown at the question, racking my brain to see if there's any pertinent information in there, but come up empty. Finally, I shake my head, and admit, "I don't know."

"Life force—others' lives... that is how they get stronger. They feed on the life force of others. A Demon had been summoned and got loose somehow. We aren't sure of all the details, as that was well over 12,000 years ago, but those in power at the time thought little of it. It wasn't the first time a Demon had gotten loose and lived on Earth."

He sighed. "But, this Demon was different. It gained power by killing many of the races then on the Earth. And, in the process, it got stronger. That's where the Dark Elves come in. They had always felt superior to the other 'lesser' races—that they should be the top race—the race that should reign as overseers above all the others."

Carmen shuddered next to me, and I lay my hand over top hers. On my other side, Marissa's hand found mine, clutching it tight.

"The legend goes—and this is a myth, so I'm not sure how much truth there is to it—this Demon approached the Dark Elves, and offered them the Earth as their playground... but at a price."

"Lives," Carmen hisses.

"Lives," Targun nods. "But, not just a couple. It wanted sacrifices... in the thousands."

With a frown, I ask, "I don't get it. How is it that you called up your gods to help you against humanity, but not against these Dark Elves?"

"It was a different time," Targun explains. "We thought we would be powerful enough, and in some way, it was the height of our vanity. We did not want to ask for help, since we thought we could do it on our own." He sighs. "And we did. But, it was a battle unlike any other today. We, the multiple races, that is, rose up against the Dark Elves and brought them low... but not before millions of Magical folk were sacrificed to this Demon—who got stronger and stronger with every sacrificial death."

"The Magical races destroyed this demon, too?"

Targun shakes his head. "In that, the gods took action without our asking for the aid. On the same night that the Magical races rose up against the Dark Elves, the gods took out this Demon." He leans back on the sofa, staring unseeing at the ceiling.

"My understanding," he continues, "was that some of the gods took extensive damage. But, in the end, they got rid of the Demon, so that we mortals would not have to deal with it. But, the combined races had more than enough trouble dealing with the Dark Elves, themselves."

"But didn't the combined races vastly outnumber the Dark Elves?" Marissa asks.

Her father nods. "Once we took the battle to them, we had the numbers. We'd always had the numbers in truth, but never the organization. We lacked cohesion and unity. But this, if anything, brought us all together. We were dying at a terrible rate. And though there were more Dark Elves than, say, any one population of any one of the Magical races… combined, we outnumbered them."

Targun closes his eyes. "The war lasted for decades. We knew that the Dark Elves could not be allowed to continue to exist, since it would only be a matter of time before they would try to do something like this again." The older Changeling opens his eyes to fix me with a hard look. "You have to understand, the Dark Elves were an arrogant people who felt they were Chosen to rule over the Earth and all other races, including monsters."

He shook his head. "Their conceit knew no bounds, but was ultimately what brought them to an end. They felt nothing could hurt them."

"What happened to them?"

"In the end, every single Dark Elf was hunted down and killed. The combined races had to show no mercy, or all other races might be hurt again. About 9,000 years ago, on the plains that you now call Scotland, was where the massive final battle happened. The last cluster of the Dark Elves, numbering over 3,000, faced off against all the races they had tried to destroy or enslave—numbering in the tens of thousands. The number that our records indicate we numbered over 400,000 strong."

"Overkill?" Carmen tells him.

"Overkill, yes, but the Dark Elves were powerful Mages. In the end, though we won, we lost over half our combined host." He shrugs. "After that, there was more than a thousand years of posted bounties, when all of the combined races chased down any word of Dark Elves and exterminated them. We—the combined Magical races—who value life, hated doing this. But we knew it needed to be done. It was mostly done by the Elves, as they had borne the brunt of the Dark Elves' hatred. Light Elves, were an endangered species for centuries following the Dark Elf War."

"Wow," I say, sitting back. "And now you think one might be still alive?"

"Either a Dark Elf, or someone who knew about them. Those daggers you brought me had inscriptions in the hilts in the Dark Elf language." He fixes me with a heavy gaze. "And Kevin? Those daggers were newly forged. They aren't old daggers that someone found and has been using. The style is different and something newer than what the Dark Elves were said to use."

Carmen frowns, turning to me. "Actually, they looked like daggers from your world."

"Yeah. I was going to mention that... those silver blades looked like modern daggers, with the single blade and the serrated edge on the other side. It reminded me of what we call a Bowie knife."

"Now, the question this discovery begs, is what exactly are we dealing with? Dark Elves, or someone who found knowledge on them?"

"Well," I say, reminding him. "I felt evil when I cast Identify in the area. It was vague, but it was there."

Sighing, he nods. "Which is why I don't think this was a human, but as I worry—a Dark Elf."

"Dad," Marissa says slowly, "we don't have much information about Dark Elves. You mentioned that they were powerful

Mages. Could it be they've stayed hidden for eons? We should be able to deal with one Dark Elf."

Targun shakes his head. "Do you know what those daggers did?"

We all three look at each other and shake our heads. Carmen says, "They used them to keep their victims pinned to the ground?"

"Yes, but there was another reason such daggers were used. They sucked the Magic out of their victim, transferring it to whoever used the daggers."

We all look at him in surprise, but then a thought occurs to me. "Why did they leave the daggers behind, then? Wouldn't they need to use them the next time? Not to mention that leaving such evidence behind would make us aware of them?"

"That's where I have concerns. Because before, though we had unexplained sacrificial type deaths, Magical folk murdered according to the exact same methods, there were no daggers left behind as evidence." Targum shudders. "Them leaving the daggers behind can mean only one thing."

Marrisa softly replies. "They feel confident."

"They feel they can leave their tools out, because they aren't afraid of repercussions. They must feel powerful enough to take on whoever may come after them." Her father presses the palms of his hands to his eyes, and then runs his hands through his hair. "Remember that I said that on all the worlds, the levels of Magus' have gone down over time? We are most likely dealing with someone powerful—and becoming more so, if they are sucking Magic out of people, and using it as their own."

Under my breath, I whisper, "Fuckling hell,"

"But," Targun says, slapping his hands together. "All is not lost. We have a powerful team going after this Dark Elf serial murderer."

I blink at him in surprise at that. "We have a team out after them already?"

"That we do," he says, but then points to Carmen, Marissa, and myself.

"What?!" Marissa shouts in shock.

"Us?" blurts out Carmen.

I don't answer, but look at him keenly. "You knew?"

Targun slowly nods.

"Knew… what?" Marissa asks with a frown, looking between her father and me.

"This wasn't the first body that was found impaled with those daggers. You had an inkling this might happen again, didn't you?"

"I did," he nods. "But until you brought those evil tools back here, I wasn't one hundred percent sure. No one else ever brought back a dagger for us to examine, since… well, they are silver. No Magical folk will touch them. You are the first to bring me one. Now that I have those five daggers, I will be talking to the Council about them in a secret meeting."

"What can the Council do?" Carmen asks.

"Nothing. Which is why I'm glad Kevin happened. Because, right now, Kevin, you are a powerful weapon that I intend to take advantage of. As of now, you are being placed directly under my personal authority. Anything you need, you get.

Period. Many Council members are powerful, but not all are Magical."

He pauses, then grins. "By the way, Kevin, your test results came back."

Frowning at that, I ask, "My test results?"

Nodding, he takes a piece of paper out of the pocket of his robe, and passes it to me. I look down, and see it's written in Elvish—which I can now read, thanks to all that information that's been stuffed into my head. Skimming through the first paragraph, I see it is essentially a note saying that I had been tested and had been assigned a Magical level.

I look up at him in amazement at the number indicated on the page.

"Are you shitting me?"

"Nope," he says with a big grin. "Congratulations, Kevin. You are the first level twenty mage in over 10,000 years."

Both Marissa and Carmen turn to look at me in amazement, mouths agape.

"Jesus H. Christ," Carmen whispers in awe.

Marissa is the one that says it best. "Fucking hell!"

"So, that's why I'm glad you're on our side, Kevin. Though now, I truly wish I knew what was in that damn vial! Because those vials have been given to many people over the years, though none have ever gotten even close to level fifteen, never mind level twenty!"

I swallow hard. Level twenty? I mean, Targun is level fifteen, and he seems incredibly powerful to me! "But you're powerful!"

"Yes, but Kevin, you are doing things I never would have thought of."

Confused, I look at him.

"You change spells—using them differently than what was originally intended. I would never have thought to use Identify to find out if I could sense my target's presence in the immediate area, when they'd left hours ago. You did. And you sensed this evil, as you say. That, to me, confirms that it was most likely a Dark Elf." He spreads his hands out between us and shrugs. "Now, we just need to figure out how to stop them."

CHAPTER FIFTEEN

"Your father can't be serious!" I tell Marissa.

We'd crashed in one of the spare rooms, which had an enormous bed. All three of us are on the bed, with me leaning against the backboard, Marissa sitting next to me, and Carmen laying down at our feet, looking at us.

"Apparently so. My Dad doesn't want the news getting out that this old enemy is coming back. The Council have used the Dark Elves as a boogie man, of sorts, for a long time. Imagine telling folks that they are real, and back? So, we are now on a secret mission; a mission known only to the Chief Councillor… and the three of us."

Hesitantly, I ask her, "What about Preeka?"

Carmen snorts at that. "She's a goblin. They are, if nothing else, loyal."

Sighing, Marissa leans into me and nods at Carmen's comment. "Preeka has been loyal to my family for ages. I was a young child when her mother, who also worked for us, passed away. Goblins will take your secrets with them to the grave."

I have noticed lately that, as we have been together longer and longer, Marissa is more comfortable having others around—but also being intimate, with those others watching. Well, it's only really Carmen, as she's been around us a lot, now that she's our partner. I see it as an excellent start to thawing that golden heart of hers against humans.

I won't claim to be the best example of a good human, but I'm not that bad, either. Putting my arms around her shoulders, I pull her tight into my side. Snuggling her nose into my neck, she turns to look up at me, a soft smile on her lips.

"Should I leave you two alone?" Carmen asks with a chuckle.

Marissa's head turns to regard Carmen, but instead of snapping at the woman, she blushes and shakes her head. "No, you're good to stay."

Carmen gets a surprised look on her face.

Let's be fair. I am sure I have the same stunned look on mine, too.

"All right," the blonde says and then, without warning, she lunges across the bed until she's propping her chin on my lower chest, her torso resting between my legs, which I'd quickly moved out of the way.

I start to open my mouth to tell Carmen to take it easy, but Marissa surprises me yet again—squeezing my hand and shaking her head at me. I lift an eyebrow questioningly, but instead of answering, my wife turns to Carmen.

"You're welcome to stay the night if you want."

Carmen, who is all but laying on me, jerks in surprise, so I feel her shock. Though, I am sure, she feels mine, as well, as certain unnamed parts of me make their opinion known. She turns to look at Marissa incredulously.

"Really?"

"Really," she tells Carmen with a smile. "Unless you don't want to be with us?"

Carmen doesn't reply right away, only stares deep into Marissa's eyes, looking for something. Something she must have seen, because the blonde suddenly scoots up so that her chest is pressed against mine, reaches out and grabs Marissa behind the head, bringing her close and kissing her on the lips. And this is not a sweet peck or a tentative brush of the lips, either. I can tell this is something they've done many times before, and which Carmen obviously had been aching to do again.

When they finally pull apart, I sit there mouth agape, eyes blinking stupidly as I look on in wonder. Both beauties turn to me, and they each have a massive grin on their faces.

"So," Marissa asks softly. "Have you ever had two women at the same time, Kevin?"

With a frown, I say, "Just once."

"And was it an unpleasant experience?"

"I was young and inexperienced... so let's just say it was a very awkward thing."

"Then, I guess we'll just have to show you how us Changelings do it," Carmen chuckles.

My wife's grin grows even bigger.

The fact that I have two beautiful women, each of whom with such markedly different personalities, in my bed... and they both want me... is mildly shocking, to say the least. I decide to say fuck it, though, and so lean down to kiss Carmen on the lips, half expecting Marissa to slap me, because she was only kidding.

Instead, the kiss lingers, until I have to pull away to catch my breath. I look at Marissa, beside me, and she's smiling at the two of us.

"You're all right with this?" I ask her.

Instead of answering me, she leans in and kisses me just as soundly as Carmen just had. For the next couple of hours, we show each other just how much we want to be together. To say that this threesome was much better than my first time with two girls, back when I was nineteen, would be a massive understatement. It's a no-brainer.

As Mike would say, that would almost be as obvious as asking, 'Is the ocean wet?'

* * *

LYING IN BED, with a beautiful woman to either side of me, I can't help but smile. Both are asleep. One thing I will have to thank Tallen for, the next time I see him, is all the damn stamina I now have because of his bite.

Hearing a ping in my head, with a mental nod, I acknowledge it. It's my communication stone, which is in the pocket of my pants, buried in the pile of clothes on the floor. Fortunately, unlike a cell phone, where you had to press a button to answer a call, communication stones have a telepathic range of ten feet—all you have to do, is simply think of taking the call.

"Hello?" I ask, though it's all in my head. I direct my thoughts, or internal speech, at the stone.

"Is this Kevin?" asks a high-pitched, tentative voice.

"Liia?" I ask, somewhat surprised.

I had touched my communication stone to hers, so that she would have a way to communicate with me. At the time, it had seemed like a good opportunity to learn how to do so—since when Carmen had given Liia her *number*, Carmen had made me take my comms stone out, too, so that I could learn how it was done. So now I had Liia's number as well.

"Listen, are you and those two beautiful women of yours still hunting for the silver dagger killer?"

"You mean my two partners? Yes, we are."

I don't tell her that we found out it was possibly Dark Elves, but her next words interrupt my thoughts.

The anger in Liia's voice comes through the channel clearly. *"We found another body."*

I suddenly sit up in bed, causing Marissa to growl in her sleep as the arm she'd thrown over my chest slumps into my lap. Carmen, on my other side, grumbles and rolls over, burying her face into the pillow.

"Where?"

"This is second-hand news, but I heard they found a body in one of the Elven enclaves up near Sacramento, California."

"Elven enclaves?" I ask, somewhat puzzled.

"Right, I forget you're human, and this is all new to you." She sighs, before continuing. *"So, throughout the world, there are a number of Elven enclaves. Elves normally tend to hide away from humans, or from any of the races, really. They gather in enclaves that are hidden using Magic. This one, apparently, is near Sacramento."*

From the knowledge in my head, I glean that the Elves don't live inside human cities here on Earth. They are very much a nature-based race, and prefer the outdoors. I was kind of shocked to learn that many Elves on Earth had a hand in various types of newer technologies—seeking to make 'green energy' a reality.

"All right, let me get the address from you."

"So you're looking for a place called Walnut Grove, it's south of Sacramento," Liia supplies.

"Do you have a contact for us?"

"Yes. Ask for their Elder. I will tell them that someone from M.A.G.I. is going to meet up with them. The Elder's name is Mido."

"All right, thanks, Liia. Why did you contact me first?"

"Honestly? I wasn't sure who to contact. Normally we would contact M.A.G.I. directly, but since I had your number, I thought I would give it a try. I tried to call Carmen, but got no answer."

"Yeah," I say with a nod, though she can't see me, *"she's asleep next to me."*

"Oh?" Liia says, and I can imagine her with a big grin on her face.

I can't help but chuckle out loud, causing Carmen to groan and look up at me. I point to the side of my head, hoping she understands that I'm taking a call. She does, since she nods and turns over, propping herself up on an elbow to look at me.

Carmen turning over like that jostles the bed, and Marissa wakes, peering up at me with tired eyes.

"Okay. Will you be there as well?" I ask her.

"No, I am just relaying the news. The Elves have already secured the area and set up a Magical shield to keep the body from decomposing."

That is another thing about Magic that I was surprised to learn. There is actually a spell that you can cast, that creates a sort of magic container—and whatever is inside it, does not decompose. The theory behind it, originally I supposed, was it was a spell used to keep food from going rotten quickly. Someone, likely out of necessity one time, found that using it on a dead body, also slowed the corpse's decomposition rate down to a tiny fraction of normal.

It doesn't work with things that are alive, though.

Which to me makes no fucking sense to me, since the reason a body decomposes, is because of bacteria, germs and such inside the body that... well, eat it up from inside. So why would such a spell work on those things, but not something bigger that was still alive?

"All right," I tell her. *"We will head out that way as soon as possible. Thanks, Liia."*

"You're welcome, human. Just find that killer!" she growls through the communication stone before she breaks the connection, which is an odd physical and mental disconnection.

Carmen is the first to ask, "What's up?"

"That was Liia," I tell her, looking down at her naked body. "She says they found another body... in an Elven Enclave near Sacramento."

"Shit!" Carmen sits up suddenly, having absolutely no shame in showing off her prodigious assets. "Did she say if it was Walnut Grove, or near Diablo Grande?"

"Liia said it was Walnut Grove."

"Damn. All right, so that would be Elder Mido. All right. I have never worked with Mido before, but I did work with her predecessor once, which was her mother. I guess we are taking another trip."

"Do we need a plane?" Marissa asks from next to me. She had sat up and is leaning back against the headboard, frowning at Carmen over my own naked body.

Shaking her head, Carmen tells her, "No. I have Sacramento in my PDA. We should be good, though we'll need to rent a car."

"I guess we should get ready, then," Marissa says, pulling her legs out from under the covers and jumping out of bed. Reaching down, she starts pawing through the pile of clothes on the floor.

"Or..." Carmen says in a tone that makes Marissa stop what she was doing and look back at us over her shoulder, one eyebrow raised.

"Or?"

"Or, we can enjoy a nice hot shower together,"

"How? My Dad owns the same showers as most people, and it's a cold one."

"Sure," Carmen says with a grin. "But that's here on Vraka. But what if we went to Earth?"

"Where on Earth would we go for a hot shower?"

Carmen shrugs, which does amazing things to her chest, and gives us a massive grin. "We could go to my place. We need to go to Earth, anyways."

"You have a place on Earth, that has hot running showers?" Marissa asks her, with a frown.

"Yep, it even has a tub big enough for all three of us."

I look between the two girls and their byplay. I'm staying out of it, for now, because I am curious what Marissa's reaction will be. I know she has welcomed Carmen intimately into our bed, but how far will she allow things?

Marissa doesn't answer, only bends down to find her clothes once more. After pulling on her panties and a shirt, she stops and looks at us. "What are you two waiting for? Hussle up. We need to get to your place, Carmen!"

I laugh, getting out of bed, and go to grab my clothes, as well. I guess I will need to go shopping and get something else to wear.

As if reading my mind, Carmen says, "Don't worry. I've got a change of clothes at my place that might even fit you—my last boyfriend was tall, like you. Unfortunately, he turned out to be a douchebag who I had to kick to the curb." She wrinkles her nose. "I told myself I would never date a Beast again, but apparently, I didn't learn my lesson the first three times. I have stuff that might fit you, too, Marissa. Though, your," and here she gazes appreciatively at Marissa's barely covered chest, "tits might prove a bit of an issue. I thought I had big ones, but babe... yours are massive."

Marissa laughs and blushes simultaneously, bright pink staining her cheeks and creeping up her cleavage from under her shirt.

Shaking my head and with a big grin, I get out of bed, and get dressed in my two-day-old and badly in need of a wash clothes. Yeah, definitely need to pack a change of clothing. Looks like we all need to start carrying around a bag with clothes, toiletries, and a few other necessities, I think.

But, then a spell comes to mind.

It might not have been meant to be used like this, but closing my eyes, I lay one hand over the clothes in my other hand and push Magic into the spell. The spell was called Cleanse. It was meant to be used to clean up a specified area, of dirt and such. Feeling the tingle on my hand holding my clothes, I open my eyes. All the dirt and grime that had been on my clothes is gone. I bring the sleeve up to my nose, and sniff it, expecting it to stink of rank body odor, but instead it smells fresh, as if freshly laundered. Though I can't identify which, it smells lightly of some flower or spice.

"How the hell did you do that?" Carmen blurts out from behind me.

I turn to her and grin. "I cast the Cleanse spell."

Carmen and Marissa turn to each other, shaking their heads. "Of course. Leave it to Kevin to use a janitor's spell to clean his clothes," Carmen says, rolling her eyes.

"Hey," I tell her with a laugh, "it worked."

"Fine," she says, throwing me her pile of clothing. "Do mine as well." But I see that she's grinning.

"And mine," Marissa says, laughing and tossing her clothes into the pile in my arms.

So, I do precisely that, casting Cleanse on their clothing.

"How come you just didn't do it yourselves?" I enquire as I button up my jeans.

"Because," Carmen says, lifting her arms and putting her arms through the sleeves of her shirt. "It's a level ten spell. I don't have close to the power needed for that."

I frown at this news. It was a level ten spell? The guy who came up with it must have been one hell of a janitor. I check the information I have for that spell but, other than it being a powerful spell requiring a lot of power, it doesn't tell me the level of the spell. Mind you. The spell was obviously meant to be used in a larger setting. It was originally intended to cleanse a site preparatory to a holy ordinance... whatever that was.

Once we are finished getting dressed, with me thinking about that spell the whole time, or other spells and possible uses for them, Carmen takes out her PDA, and there's suddenly a black Portal in the room before us.

"Oh, hold on a second," Marissa blurts out. "Let me tell my Dad what's going on."

She takes out her communication stone, closes her eyes, and in less than half-a-minute, opens them again and nods. "Done."

CHAPTER SIXTEEN

Once through the Portal, the second one in less than two hours, I look around.

We had stopped, as promised, at Carmen's place. She owns a house well back in the woods; it's a sprawling rancher in Florida's panhandle. And why not? She has a PDA and can travel to it easily enough. It was a nice enough place, actually.

It was many times bigger than my apartment. I think my little apartment had been, maybe, a thousand square feet. Carmen's place, I'm sure, is at least 8,000 square feet—it is massive. But it's also out in the middle of nowhere.

As promised, though, it not only has a shower with hot water, but also a huge jacuzzi tub. Though since we are now on the clock, so to speak, we only have time for a relatively quick shower—albeit with plenty of touching, teasing, and skinship—before we headed out again.

Our portal opens in Sacramento, where we pop out between two large buildings. I look around, having no idea what to expect; I had never been to Sacramento. Checking my phone, I see it is just past four in the afternoon.

"Downtown, Sacramento," Carmen supplies.

"Why right downtown?" Marissa asks her.

"Two reasons," she replies, holding up a finger. "One, it's close to a car rental—there's actually one just around the corner. And second," she says, holding up another finger, "I used to hang out at a club just down the road."

"Of course," I say with a laugh.

I can just imagine Carmen clubbing when she was younger. Hell, I can imagine her doing that now

"When was the last time you went to a club?" Marrisa asks, beating me to the question.

"Hmm…" Carmen frowns, thinking about it. "About three months ago?"

"Of course." Marissa chuckles. "I miss my concert days on Earth. Though, I have never been to a club simply to dance. The last one I went to, was for work."

"One of Tallen's places?" I ask, taking a stab in the dark.

"Yep," she replies with a grin.

Carmen says, "All right. Let's go get us a car and then we can head up to meet with Elder Mido."

We nod, following her out to the main street from further down the alley between the buildings. Once on the sidewalk on the main street, I watch the cars zipping down both sides of the street. Carmen turns to the left and strides down the sidewalk, with us trailing her.

I look around, curious, seeing as we are downtown, but aren't surrounded by massive high-rises. Sacramento still has plenty of buildings with six or eight stories, but nothing like the eighty story skyscrapers we'd seen in New York City.

At the far end of the block, I see there's a building with an oversized parking garage that must be eight stories tall. A huge LED sign on the side of the parking garage proclaims 'Car Rental' in red neon letters. With all the prominent brand name logos that surround the marquee, I'm guessing this is what they would call a rental hub?

Carmen walks in the ground floor entrance, and I notice there are multiple counters—each with a sign overhead announcing their respective company. Carmen heads directly to a certain counter without pausing. She stops in front of the clerk, who I see is a pretty, young staffer with long brown hair and blue eyes.

As we come up to it, the young woman behind the counter smiles at us. "How can I help you today?" she asks.

"Hello," Carmen says, looking down at the girl's name tag, "Lisa. We want to rent a vehicle for, say, two days—but with the possibility for extending the rental, if needs be?"

"Oh!" the girl says brightly, knowing she going to get a good commission with us. "What kind of car did you want rent? A midsize, SUV, or truck?"

"Hmm," Carmen murmurs, looking back at me.

I shrug. "I have no idea. I'm good with whatever."

"Well, you'll be the one driving it," Carmen says with a grin.

"Fair enough," I say with a laugh. "Then I won't mind an SUV or a truck."

"Well," Lisa offers. "The truck is about the same as an SUV, price-wise."

"Want to go with the truck? We are going up into the hills," I suggest to the two girls.

"Well, we have multiple trucks to choose from," Lisa says, tapping away at her keyboard while studying the monitor off to one side. "We have a Ford 150, a Ram 1500, or a Ram 2500." She tilts her head cutely to the side. "However, that last one is a bit more expensive. But," she grins, "it is red."

"Damn, you got me at red," I tell Lisa with a chuckle. "I assume we can afford it?" I turn to Carmen.

"Yep," she says, passing me a credit card. Taking it, I look down at it.

It's a visa credit card. The same one she had gotten filled, when she'd given Houmad that gold bar. It makes sense she would still have money on it. I mean, it was a massive amount of money. I never did ask her how much was left on it. And I wasn't about to ask her now, not in front of a stranger.

I nod and pass Lisa the credit card.

"I will need your driver's license," she says with a smile my way.

I nod again, taking my wallet out, and pass her my New York driver's license. She looks at it, bobs her head, and sets it on the counter in front of her next to the credit card. Within minutes, we have the keys to a nearly new quad-cab Dodge Ram truck, and after saying our thanks to Lisa, head to where she directed us—up the elevators to the fourth floor, down two aisle to the right, and to the gleaming vehicle parked in spot number 412. As stated, there is a massive Dodge Ram 2500 there, cherry red in color.

Grinning, I climb into the driver's seat and look around, familiarizing myself with the truck's controls. Marissa hops into the passenger seat, admiring the interior, and Carmen slides into the back seat after doing a walk around to make sure there are no scratches, dents, or marks that were missed on the forms. We might be Magical folk, she says, but she hates paying extra for stuff that she doesn't need to. I wasn't about to argue.

Once we are settled in, I punch in our destination in the dashboard's GPS map system. Once it's in, I see that it's going to be roughly a 30-minute drive, though I'm sure with traffic, it'll keep updating. Finally, as we leave the congested downtown behind, it says it will be a 45-minute drive.

* * *

"Right here, on the left," Carmen, who had been sitting in the back, says.

I look at where she's pointing from between us, and I see a small road leading off from the highway. It is essentially a dirt road; no gravel here. We'd been on Highway 5 for a while, but had eventually turned off it onto some two-lane county road that led us up towards Walnut Grove.

I mean, it wasn't in Walnut Grove itself, but just on the outskirts. We still had to pass through the town itself to get to our destination. When we got closer, Carmen had taken out her communication stone and had messaged Liia, asking for more details on the exact location.

"I thought you'd been up here before," Marissa asks.

Carmen nods. "Yes, I've been here before—but that was over ten years ago."

After turning down another dirt road, we drive for a good ten minutes before finally stopping. There's a gate in front of us, blocking the road. Carmen gets out and walks up to the gate. Before she gets there, someone appears in front of her —as if from out of the thin air.

The person is obviously not human, even I can tell that from here. The person is male, and one hundred percent Elven. He looks a lot like Luitta, the M.A.G.I. trainer who had tried to break me, by stuffing my head full of so much information. He had the same long blond hair, and slender, pointed ears. He is older, though, and somewhat taller.

Rather slim, he is wearing a one-piece white outfit that looks something like a robe—though not quite. Looking over the blondes shoulder at us, he asks Carmen something, to which she replies. His head snaps back to her, and I can clearly see the look of disbelief on his face.

He barks something at the blonde again, and I can see her face cloud up with anger from here. She barks back at the elf and he takes a step back. He takes a breath, obviously preparing to retort, but suddenly there's another Elf behind him, a female this time, who lays a hand on his shoulder. He jerks in surprise at the touch, and looks back over his shoulder to see who it is. When he sees who it is, his face closes off, all expression gone.

The newcomer nods to Carmen and says something. Carmen bows to her and nods, before coming back to the truck. In the meantime, I see the male Elf go to the gate, unlock it, and open it up, glowering at us. No... he's glaring at me, actually.

"Fucking asshole," Carmen growls, sliding into the back seat.

"What was that all about?" Marissa asks.

"That fucking Elf was going to deny us access to the murder site. When I told him that we three were partners and worked for M.A.G.I., he didn't believe me. He said M.A.G.I. didn't travel around with multiple partners. That was when I told him that I was with the human who had Magic." Carmen sighs. "Knowledge of you has reached all the races—they already know about you here. The fool was about to deny us again, until that other Elf showed up. That's Pirta; she's on the Elven Council. She vouched for us. Of course, that prick wasn't at all happy with that."

"Too bad," Marissa growls. "We have a job to do."

"That's what Pirta said," Carmen snorts, and suddenly she's grinning.

As we drive through the gate, I see Carmen in side mirror. She grins at the disgruntled Elf, waving to him as we go by.

"Don't agitate the locals," Marissa says, but she's laughing as she says it.

I follow the road, until I get to a point where even our truck can't continue. The road is so bad, that the truck felt like I was riding a bucking stallion as we lurched from one massive pothole to another. Pulling as far to the side as I safely can, I stop the truck and turn it off.

"I guess we walk from here," I say.

"Yep," Carmen agrees, getting out as well.

Marissa gets out and looks around curiously. "I guess we just follow the road on foot?"

"Yes," a voice says from beside me, making me jump nearly a foot into the air.

"Fucking hell!" I cry out in surprise.

The female Elf from earlier laughs at my shock. "I'm sorry about that, young man."

Turning to her, I finally get a closer look. I see that where before I'd thought she was a young blonde, now I see that she isn't. Her hair is so grey it is nearly white, and although her skin might be free of wrinkles, it has that ageless quality to it that screams experience and wisdom.

Elves are a long-lived race, with a lifespan reaching well into the hundreds of years—ancient compared to humans. A human might make it to a full century, if they are lucky. Elves generally lived between four hundred to five hundred years. The only race close to getting that kind of mileage from their mortal life were Vampires, at around three to four hundred years.

"Yes, we just head down the road. I'm sorry your human vehicle can't make it down the road, but we do that on purpose. No technology is allowed."

"What about our phones?" I ask, taking mine out and showing it to her.

"No, those are fine. We have those, as well. It's mostly the larger items that we do not allow—unless the Council warrants it's required. Phones are fine. Cars," and here she points to our large red rental, "are not."

"Fine by me," I tell her, nodding as I put my phone away. "Lead on, please."

She nods, smiles, and turns to Carmen. "It's been a long time, Carmen."

"It has," Carmen tells her, bowing. "it's been almost ten years, Pirta."

"That it has. And are you going to continue to be so formal with me?" Pirta asks her with a raised eyebrow.

"No," Carmen replies with a laugh. Walking up, she hugs the Elf, and even kisses her on the cheek. "I missed you."

"And I missed you as well, child. You know you are always welcome to our home?"

"I know, but... hmm. I left on bad terms."

"No," Pirta says, shaking her head. "You left Tommy on bad terms. My idiot of a son was the one who lost out, on someone amazing."

"Thanks, Prita," Carmen tells her, blushing.

I must have had a confused look on my face, along with Marissa, because Carmen laughs awkwardly. "Years ago, I came to live here with the Elves. I stayed with Prita and her family. She has a son, who is almost my age. We dated when I was here and, while I wanted to stay to make a more permanent attachment, he—shall we say—had other ideas. He was only interested in keeping me around as a bedmate... which I had no interest in."

I frown at her explanation. Wait. But, we are bedmates, aren't we? Or, does she expect more than a physical relationship? Not that I'll say no, of course.

Looking at the vivacious blonde, I can't help but smile and thank my lucky stars that not only is she our partner in this stressful and challenging job, but our partner in bed. Maybe I will have to marry her, too? I mean, according to what I'm hearing, most Magical races don't believe in monogamy.

My thoughts are interrupted by Prita. "Well, you don't have to worry about him. He moved to the Enclave up north. He's now in Manitoba, I hear. And married with three wives." She lifts a shoulder in a shrug. "He is doing well."

"Good," Carmen tells Prita, hugging her once more. "I'm glad to hear that Tommy settled down. Kids?"

Instead of answering, Prita grins at her.

"Nice!"

Prita's grin soon fades, though, and she sighs. "I assume you are here for the body?"

"Yes," Carmen tells her. "Please tell me it's not someone I knew?"

Shaking her head, Prita tells her. "No. It was an Elf who had moved here from Ilia, the Elven world. They moved here about six years ago. Come, let's go have tea before we take you to see the body. It's being protected from animals and decay."

"Sounds good. We got here as quickly as we could."

Prita looks at Marissa and me and smiles. "Yes. I am sure you did."

I look at Marissa. Shit. Do we smell like sex? I know we cleaned up in the shower, but we also took advantage of the fact that Carmen's huge shower could easily fit at least four people.

She shrugs and mouths. "No clue!"

CHAPTER SEVENTEEN

"What can you tell me about the body?" I ask Prita.

We'd finally made it to the Enclave, or village. There were houses everywhere you looked, but not normal houses like you might see in, say, a suburb of a large city. These were cozy homes, with large round doors and plenty of windows. They almost looked like hobbit houses, backing mostly into hillocks, except larger. The roofs all had grass growing on them, or was that moss?

We were in one of those huts, which I learned was Prita's home. She'd served us tea as soon as we'd settled down. The room beyond a short hall where we entered, was a combination of a kitchen and living space. There were two doors off to one side, leading to what I assumed were bedrooms. And another leading to a bathroom, since the door was open and I can see an honest to goodness white porcelain toilet bowl.

"Do you have a favorite tea, young man?" Pirta asks, turning to me.

"Hmm," I say, caught off guard.

"Or do you prefer coffee?"

"Coffee, please, if you have any."

With a smile, she nods. "I do. And you?" she asks, turning to Marissa with a question in her tone.

"Sorry," Carmen says with a blush. "This is our partner, Marissa Lalouton."

"As in THE Lalouton family, the daughter of Sir Targun Lalouton?"

"The same," she replies with a smile.

"How is your hard-headed father?"

With a laugh, Marissa replies, "He's good."

"Good to hear. What will you have to drink?"

"Do you have mint tea?"

"I do. Carmen?"

"Coffee for me, please," she answers her with her own smile.

"Very well. Come, sit. Find yourself a seat," she says, waving towards the living area, where there are two comfortable looking sofas.

We all nod and head to the indicated sofas, sitting down on the bigger one, which holds the three of us comfortably. Pirta goes to the kitchen area, pulling cups out of a cabinet, and begins to prepare the coffee using a French press. She has a big ass kettle on her potbelly stove that I see probably uses pellets to heat it, instead of coal or wood.

The place was definitely an eclectic mix of the old and new— or in this case, of Elven and Human influences. There was even a radio on the shelf. I look around, and yep, there's a light switch on the wall that must control the light on the ceiling. From my quick scan alone, I see the radio, the light switch, and the light. And I'm pretty sure that that potbelly stove isn't some Elven design. It looks like technology, human technology, is used freely here. Though, it does tend toward the organic, or green tech.

Once Pirta is done with the French Press, she comes back into the living room area with four mugs on a tray. She places the tray on the table between the sofas and passes us our hot drinks. Marissa's is a weak-looking tea, but I can smell the mint from here, while Carmen's coffee is black. Oh crap, I forgot to ask for cream, but I need not have worried—it seems Pirta put some in mine.

"I only put a little cream in. Did you wish some sugar, Kevin, was it?"

"Yes, ma'am, it's Kevin," I tell her respectfully. "I am good with just cream. How did you know my name?"

"Everyone knows of you." She grins at me. "The only human able to do Magic? And at quite a high level, if the rumors I hear are correct? Word is that you could even give Sir Targun a run for his money."

"Well," I say, blushing. "I'm not sure about that. He has decades of experience, where I am still learning."

She waves her hand dismissively. "You will gain experience, and learn over time. Though you humans count life so short, that I hope you get to learn as much as you can, before your time on this planet is done."

"Oh, Kevin should be around for a long time," Carmen tells her with a chuckle.

"Oh? Am I missing something?"

"Tallen bit him."

Pirta gets a confused look at that and then peers at me closely. "So he is under Tallen's influence?"

"Nope," she replies with a big grin. "He got the full transformation."

She tilts her head to the side, looking at me again with a frown on her ageless face. "But he still smells human; he doesn't smell like a Vampire."

"No, something happened when Tallen bit him. And, well... I'm sure Tallen didn't expect it either. But it seems Kevin has the physical benefits of a Vampire—strength, speed, vitality, and stamina—without turning into a full-fledged Vampire. He is an adopted member of the Royal family, as Tallen gave Kevin a medallion."

"Do you have it with you?" Pirta asks, looking at me with a raised eyebrow at this news.

I nod, taking the medallion out of my pocket. It is the size of a large silver dollar. When I extend it in my hand to show it to her, she leans forward to stare at it. A long moment goes by without her saying a word.

Finally, she nods and settles back into her sofa with a snort. "What is the world coming to? A human who can do Magic... who is apparently something other than a Vampire, but who still has been adopted by the Court's royalty."

The way she says it, though, doesn't set my hackles up, since it isn't said in anger or derision. It is more of a simple statement of fact. Her next words catch me off guard, though. "About fucking time."

"Excuse me?" I blurt out in surprise.

"It's about time a human was able to do Magic. We Magical folk need to do everything we can to bring you humans into our world. I'm with Tallen on that, at least. We desperately need humans—or at least the humans' technology. We cannot live apart in our own separate realities any longer." She looks down at her hands, clenched around her mug. "You humans, with your short lives, come up with items that just astound us and would make our lives so much easier."

"Like cell phones," Carmen tells her with a chuckle.

"Like cell phones," she says, laughing back, taking hers out from a hidden pocket and holding it up.

"Can I ask you a question, Young man?" Pirta turns to me with a curious gaze.

"Of course, Ma'am," I tell her with a nod.

She rolls her eyes. "First off, you don't call me Ma'am—please call me Pirta. I don't stand on formality. What are your intentions, now, as a powerful magus?"

With a puzzled look, I frown at her question. "My intentions?"

The ageless woman sits back on her sofa, contemplating me with a look that I can't fathom. Slowly, she takes a sip of her tea. "You are, from my understanding, a very powerful Magus. At least level ten, if not much higher, I hear. As such, you will be someone to observe and worth listening to. Compared to you, I am very low on the Magical scale. I'm only level five."

She takes another sip of her tea. "Forgive me for being so artless and blunt, but what are your intentions in the Magical world?"

"Honestly? I have no clue." I pause. "Until over a month ago, I was just a simple man working a job and trying to keep up with my bills—until I found I was dying from cancer." I shrug. "That's it. I was a nobody... nothing. But now, I can do Magic, and apparently am very powerful."

Marissa squeezes my leg in support.

"But I don't feel powerful," I continue after giving her a smile. "I still have to have my two partners here help me with all kinds of stuff."

"For now," Carmen says with a snort.

Three heads all turn her way.

"Kevin has been using spells differently than we do. He seems to think outside the box... perhaps because he never learned our—that is, Magical folk's—norms, when it comes to casting spells. Fortunately, he has the two of us," she says, waving a hand between herself and Marissa, "two great partners to keep him grounded and level-headed."

"Good," Pirta says with a nod. "And do you have a wife yet?"

"I do," I tell her with a smile. "I'm married to Marissa."

"I figured it was something like that. Though, I would not have thought it would be to Sir Targun's daughter. Automatic citizenship?"

"Yes," Marissa tells her. "It was that, or become the property of the Council."

Here, Pirta gets a sour expression on her ageless face. "Yes. They would not want someone so powerful, especially a human, running loose. I assume you are under the protection of this young lady's father?"

"Correct."

"Good," she says with a firm nod. "Your father is a smart man, Marissa. Now, let's get to the reason for your visit. The body."

"What can you tell us?" Carmen asks her.

"About a day ago, we found the body. The victim was an Elf, relatively new to our commune. He moved here about six years ago from the Elven home world. He was our pottery expert."

"How old was he?" Marissa asks.

"He was a little over two hundred years old—210, to be exact. Young, by our standards," she says with a sigh. "No one should die so young."

Jesus, two plus centuries is young? Then, again, they are Elves. I am sure if I lived to see nearly half a millennia, two centuries wouldn't even be half my life. Automatically translating these fantastic numbers to a human context, if most folks live a bit past eighty, forty years old would roughly be the halfway mark. So this person was not even middle aged, though they weren't a teenager anymore. That would put them, carrying through with my analogy, in their thirties—if they'd been a human.

I wonder how long I will live now, thanks to Tallen's bite?

"Do you have any idea who might have wanted to harm him?" Carmen asks.

"No clue. He was a very quiet and gentle Elf. Bromar had no enemies that I know of."

"Was anything found near the body?"

Here, a nervous look disturbs her ageless features before she schools them again to placid calm.

Carmen smiles gently and asks, "Let me guess... silver daggers?"

Pirta nods quickly, a flash of fear crossing her face. "Yes. You don't seem surprised, though?"

"It's not the first body we have found with the same, shall we say, method of death."

"Was it a human, who did the killings?" she asks Carmen.

"That we aren't sure about," Marissa says, adding "our team is currently investigating a few such heinous acts."

We had agreed that we would keep the entire Dark Elf thing quiet, so as not to panic the Magical folk. Targun had asked that we play it close to the vest, until it was confirmed—as in, until we see an actual Dark Elf.

"What is the world coming to that someone would be killed like this?" Pirta asks, but it's a rhetorical question, and she shakes her head.

"We aren't sure. But we are here to find out. Can you show us the body?" Carmen asks her softly.

"Yes. Of course," Pirta says, lifting her mug to take the last sip of her tea.

I do the same, and finish my coffee, with Carmen and Marissa following suit with their respective drinks.

"Come. The body is only ten minutes' walk from the commune. It's still on our land but, thank the Gods, it was found a ways away from our commune."

"What was a pottery expert doing so far from the commune?" I ask, puzzled by why a pottery expert might be so far from home.

"He was looking for dyes. He often went out and found new dyes to extract from the plants around here. When he did not return after two days, we sent out search parties. His body was found about ten minutes north of here. We immediately cast a spell to preserve the body and anything else around it."

That makes sense, I guess. I'm not a pottery expert, so take her explanation at face value.

"What about any witnesses?" Carmen asks her.

Pirta shakes her head. "Nothing. We didn't know anything was wrong until the second night, when someone mentioned that they needed a new water jug and asked where Bromar was, but no one had seen him all day. That's when we started actively looking for him, and could not find him anywhere in the commune. No one was home at his place, and it was all locked up."

For the next ten minutes, we head deeper into the forest, following a path until eventually Pirta turns off the dirt trail and heads deeper into the forest. I see that someone—or several folk, actually—had recently come this way, as the grass has ben beaten down by multiple sets of footsteps. But I also notice that the path we had walked along was relatively new, not like something you expect to see of a well-worn trail.

"Here we go," the elf says, pointing ahead with her finger.

I look up, gazing in the direction her finger points. At first, I don't see anything, but as we get closer, I finally notice that what I thought was a log on the ground, isn't dead wood, but a dead body. The Elf in question lies flat on his back, and I'm glad this isn't the first body I'd seen like this. Bromar's body is pinned to the ground—just like the other victims—with silver daggers staking out his hands and feet, with a fifth dagger plunged through his neck. Jesus.

"Fucking hell," Carmen mutters behind me.

CHAPTER EIGHTEEN

"Is it just me," Marissa says quietly in the clearing. "Or does this murder seem more brutal than the last one?"

I nod at her, because I have to agree. While we'd only seen the one body, it had been mangled and chewed on by the local wildlife, but hadn't been desecrated like this poor elf. Bromar hadn't just been killed in a sacrificial ritual, the murderer had first skinned him alive. I had thought the body had started to decompose, despite the elves' magic, because the skin was darker—but no, that darkness was blood all over the body.

Carmen approaches the body, but stops about three feet from it. I go to squat next to her and ask, "So?"

"The spell is keeping the body fresh for us. Let's see," she says, holding her hand out.

I sense the Magic gathering around her hand before it disperses. I can't tell what spell she just cast, but I know that each spell has a distinctive signature. This is one I don't recognize; then again, most Magic is still a new thing.

"I tried to cast a spell to see if I can pinpoint any Magical items, but get nothing." The blonde looks around and frowns. "Prita, can I undo the spell holding the body in stasis?"

"Here," the elf says, nodding. "I was the one who cast it, so let me just remove it."

She waves her hand and nods to Carmen, letting her know Stasis has been canceled. Carman nods, and moves closer to the body. I start to follow her, but as soon as the Stasis spell fades, the smell hits me. The odor of blood, that unmistakable coppery smell, and shit assault my nose. Not a surprise, really. I'm sure that when he died, his bowels released. I find it oddly comforting to know that Magical folk die just like we humans do—meaning it's not pretty.

Marissa had walked in a wide circle around the body to approach it from the other side, while Carmen and I stay on the body's left side. "Can you remove the daggers, Kevin?" Marissa asks.

"Sure."

I bend down and pull up all five daggers, tossing them off to the side and away from everyone.

"That's just freaky," Prita says, shaking her head.

"What? Me removing the daggers?" I ask her.

"Your hand grasping the hilt of the silver daggers, and not being affected by it—even though you now can do Magic," she replies with a nod.

I shrug at her. "It seems that, even with Magic inside me, I can still touch silver. I'm sure that Marissa's father will want to figure that one out."

With a knowing look and a nod, Pirta says, "I'm sure he will."

"Look at this," Marissa says, pointing to the corpse's neck.

I look, but don't know what I'm looking for.

Thankfully, she explains what she wants us to see. "The neck has bruising, compared to the rest of the body."

"Choked him to death—or at least until he lost consciousness?" Carmen asks her.

She nods and points to a couple of other marks on Bromar's neck. "From the marks, I would say the murderer used a scarf or something to choke him," she says, looking around the body, as if the scarf might have been left simply lying on the ground.

"Ah-ah!" she says, getting up quickly from her crouch and moving about fifteen feet from the body.

Nearly impossible to see in the grass is a darker spot of green. My wife bends down and brings up a dark green scarf, about six feet long, held carefully between her thumb and forefinger.

Prita adds. "That's the scarf that Bromar wore all the time. With the weather getting cooler, he probably wore it in the morning hours. That tells me he was here in the early morning hours, since it gets much warmer in the afternoon."

Marissa comes back with the scarf, holding it out to me. "Want to cast Identify on it?" she asks.

I nod, and hold a pile of the material in my hand. The scarf is very soft, though I can't tell what it's made of slightly, and slightly damp from the grass. I cast Identify and, in my mind's eye, the image of a male Elf appears. The Elf is rather young-looking and is smiling, with gentle, gray eyes. Part of my mind idly wonders—so that's what this skinless body looked like, before it was flayed. Then I also get a feeling of fear.

Looking around, and deciding to do what I did last time, I place both hands on the ground and cast Identify once more —but this time I pour enough Magic into the spell to encompass an area nearly a hundred feet in diameter. Suddenly, a wave of dizziness sends me to my knees—not from using Magic, but from the backlash of what I can only call vitriol, that comes through loud and clear.

The sheer amount of anger that floods back with what I sense, is astounding.

"Kevin!" Marissa cries out, her hand clutching my arm.

"Sorry," I say, swallowing back a mouthful of bile I hadn't noticed until now with a shudder.

"What happened?" Carmen snaps at me.

"I just cast Identify on the area, and whoever his killer is, they have A LOT of hatred."

"Towards Bromar?" Prita asks.

I turn towards her. "No. At life, in general. I get the feeling that whoever the killer is, they are all but consumed by this anger. It drives them—And I don't just mean they are bitter, but HATE—the vitriol overwhelmed me."

Prita stares at me with a concerned look. "How did you figure all that out?"

Carmen is the one to answer her. "Kevin figured out, that if he casts Identify on the area itself, he can get residual impressions of the area—which include, as you just saw, strong feelings and emotions," she says, waving at me.

Prita looks at me in amazement. "By the gods! I wish I was high enough level to cast that spell! That would be so handy to have."

"What is that?," Marissa asks, pointing back at the body.

We all look at what she's pointing to. It is a small pin, stuck to the body. We had missed it, since it was under a piece of torn clothing that had stuck to the victim's raw flesh. In case it is silver, I reach down and grab it. It is a small piece of jewelry.

About the size of a dime, on the back of the broach is a needle that you might use to pin it to your clothing, the front side being a silver disk with an image I'd not seen before—a stag outlined on it in a black silhouette.

"Fuck," Carmen swears.

"Shit," Marissa says at the same time.

I look up from the broach at all three women. Surprisingly, Prita's face reflects the strongest reaction to whatever this is. Though she hasn't said anything, her face is twisted up in a look of disgust and anger. No... not anger, fury.

"What is it?" I ask.

"That pin marks an ancient group who hate Magical folk. Humans. They call themselves the Stags. We have been fighting them for over three hundred years." The normally sweet and placid elf, turns her head to the side and spits. "The Stags, as far as we can figure out, are a small group of humans who know about us Magical folk. Fortunately, they are a very small group."

"The Stags?" Marissa mouths to me, with a quick shake of her head indicating that this is new to her, as well.

"As best we can figure," Pirta continues, "they only number around 50 or so. They never increase their numbers above that. They keep their numbers small and work in cells. We have been trying to eradicate them for years."

"So like terrorist cells?" I ask.

With an affirmative nod, she says, "They do work like your human terrorist cells that I have read about."

"I thought humans weren't supposed to know about the Magical world. The whole Article 1 thing?"

She shakes her head. "That's for the other worlds. Humans here know—or some do—that we exist. The Stags used to be a radical branch of the humans' Catholic church, but they got excommunicated, because they were considered too brutal— even by the churches standard. They made the Inquisition look like a group of choirboys."

I gape at her, wondering if she is kidding. But at the serious look she give me, I just shake my head and mutter, "Jesus."

How is it that this fringe group of anti-Magical humans, the Stags, are involved with Dark Elves? This doesn't make any sense. Just when I think we are making headway and some things become clearer, another turd floats to the surface and muddies the waters.

As if thinking the same thing, but not wanting to give anything away, Carmen turns to Pirta. "Can you tell us what dealings, if any, you have had with them lately?"

Prita gets a thoughtful look and finally shakes her head. "The last time our Commune had to deal with a cell of Stags was more than sixty years ago."

Carmen turns to me and gives me a knowing look, as if to say there is no way what we are dealing with here is the Stags.

I have to agree. The vitriol I felt through the spell was so intense, it was simply inhumane—something I doubt a human could feel and remain sane. This felt utterly... wrong. Like, the person who was giving off such feelings was not of this world. It was hard to explain, but the feeling I'd gotten was that this was not the work of a human.

To me, it felt like the murderer was almost alien.

"Well, I doubt we are going to get much else here," Carmen says, looking around, just in case we missed something.

"Truth," Marissa says and nods. "Kevin, did you want to cast Identify on the body itself?"

I look down at the body, and swallow nervously. "Yeah. I never thought of doing that, since we already have confirmation of who the victim is, but it's probably a good idea—in case something else comes up."

I go back and kneel next to the desecrated body. Steeling myself, I set my hand on the bloody area just above Bromar's flayed chest, and then I cast Identify. At first, I get nothing. It's almost as if it's foggy.

"It's foggy," I mumble out loud.

Marissa rubs my back, her hand warm. "Can you push more Magic into the spell?"

"Let me try," I say, and close my eyes. Except that, instead of casting Identify again—since I already have it running—I instead push much more Magic into the spell. It feels like I'm pushing something inside of me to the outside. I direct that power through my hand and into the spell.

With a suddenness that surprises me, I hear a shattering sound, as some sort of veil crashes down around us. I blink in the sudden darkness, looking around only to find the entire field we had been standing in has disappeared. Instead, there is just me and the body. But, this time, the body I see is still whole. I see Bromar as he looked before death—or before he'd been flayed.

"Hello?" I ask out loud, though I don't expect or get a response.

Getting up quickly, I turn in all directions, peering into the darkness. But there's nothing else here—nor is there anyone else here. The sky has disappeared, but I am able to see just fine, though the entire area is dark. The forest, too, is gone, and I am surrounded by darkness. Somehow, though, this small patch of the field where the body lies beside me, remains well lit.

Looking back down at the body, and I get another surprise. Bromar has his eyes open and is looking at me. I don't mean that the corpse's eyes are open, but that this person sees me— it feels like his eyes are following me. The body was alive somehow—that is, Bromar is alive and breathing. I know this, because his chest rises and falls with his breaths.

Tentatively, I ask, "Bromar?"

He sits up, looking confused. Peering into the darkness, he finally looks back at me. "I'm dead?"

"Hmm. Yes? How am I able to talk to you, if you're dead?"

He tilts his head to the side and studies me curiously. "You're human."

"Yeah," I tell him, affirming his statement with a cautious nod.

"Then you must be that human all the rumors are going around about." He looks around once more and asks the obvious question—the question that I would be asking, were I in his boots: "How did I die?"

"We aren't sure. Your body was found ten minutes away from the Commune."

"Ah," he says, nodding. "I was out looking for a new dye color."

"Do you remember anything about your death?"

He gets a confused look on his face. "No. I only remember leaving my house first thing in the morning. The sun had not even come up yet, was just peeking over the horizon, when I locked my door." He purses his lips, trying to remember. "I got to the field I had seen flowers in once, with the color I wanted to try replicating. I remember sitting down in the field, closing my eyes and feeling the sun on my face, wanting to enjoy its heat as the day started, and praying to my god." He stops. "Then, I woke up here."

Sighing, I nod. "Well, I'm sorry to say, Bromar, that you were foully murdered. A killer is on the loose, going around murdering Magical folk, using silver daggers," I tell him, deciding not to lie to him, even though he is dead.

Was I talking to his spirit? Can a magus speak to spirits? There was no information in my head about anything like that.

Bromar doesn't answer, simply breaths deeply, one hand absently digging in the dirt. Finally, he looks back up. "Will you avenge my death?"

"I will avenge all the deaths," I reply quickly, though I know it is little more than a platitude. I really do want to catch this murderer and see justice done. Because if what we are finding out is true—that it's really a Dark Elf or Dark Elves—we truly need to take them down.

"I will miss being among the living," he says quietly. "But I lived a good life, and now I can let my soul join my god."

"I'm sorry," I apologize lamely.

"For what?" he ask, looking up at me.

"That you died."

He shakes his head, wistful smile turning up the corner of his mouth. "It was not your fault, young man. May I ask your name, so that I might let my god know of you?"

"Kevin, Sir. Kevin Johnston."

"Well, Kevin... Kevin Johnston... Please find my killer and show them justice."

"I shall."

Looking around at the darkness surrounding us once more, he sighs again. "I guess it's time. I can feel the tug of my soul. Goodbye, Kevin Johnston. May the gods help you walk the path."

And just like that, I'm back in the field, with the girls clustered worriedly around me, the sun beating down, and Pirta looking at me expectantly. I shake my head to clear my thoughts, and look down at the body of Bromar, which hardly looks at all like what I had just seen in.... what? A dream state?

Marissa's hand on my back lifts, and she holds me by the chin, staring into my eyes. "Are you all right?"

I look up at her and nod. Quietly, I say, "Yes. But we need to talk later."

"Nothing?" Prita asks me.

Looking over at her, I remember that I'd cast Identify to see if I can get anything else from the body. The fact that I had, in fact, gotten more—though what it meant was beyond me —was something I was hesitant to share. I didn't want to give too much away.

"Nothing much—except to confirm what you deduced from his scarf, that he came here early in the morning."

Sighing, she nods. "I guess we should dispose of the body?"

"Yeah," Carmen tells her. "Did you wish to take care of it, or did you want us simply to get rid of Bromar's corpse?"

"No," she says sadly. "We shall take care of it. Come, I will take you back to your vehicle. Thank you for coming out all this way."

"You're welcome, Prita."

CHAPTER NINETEEN

"She's nice," I say in the truck, after pulling back onto the main road.

"She is," Carmen says with a tender smile. "I missed her."

"Are you going to tell us what you really saw?" Marissa asks.

I nod and explain to them what I experienced as we drive down the highway, following the GPS' directions back to the city. Once I'm done with my explanation, Carmen gives a low whistle, while Marissa grunts.

With hesitation in her tone, or perhaps it's incredulity, Carmen asks, "So, you're saying that this spell Identify let you talk to Bromar's ghost?"

"Seems so. Though… was it real?"

"Oh, it's real," Marissa says. I look at where she sits in the backseat in the mirror. Carmen had laughingly called 'shot-gun' the moment the red truck had come in sight, and Marissa had surrendered the front seat to the blonde, though not without a few choice words.

"How so?"

"There was a paper I once read in my Dad's library—when I was younger—about how there was a spell that allowed a magus to speak to the dead within a certain time frame. I would say that the spell that kept his body from rotting, also kept this Bromar person's soul there."

"Damn," Carmen tells her, her eyes wide. "And it was the Identify spell?"

She shakes her head. "No. That's what's odd. It wasn't so much a spell, as an ability."

"Wait. You're saying that Kevin is a spirit medium?" our companion barks out, eyebrows crawling into her hairline.

"It seems so. It seems that all this Magic and stuff that has happened to Kevin, allowed him to commune with the dead."

I shudder. "Hmm. I'm not so sure I want to be haunted by dead people—don't want them all begging for me to avenge their deaths," I grump.

Both girls laugh at me.

"You don't have to worry about constantly being pestered by ghosts. My understanding, is that you have control over it. Though, it's odd that it happened when you empowered Identify. Others have cast that spell before, and there has never been any talk about them seeing or communing with the dead."

"Great," I say, rolling my eyes. "Add one more oddity to my uniqueness."

"Well, whatever it is, I'm glad you got it." Carmen shakes her head. "Though it proved pretty much useless in this case, except to confirm that Bromar did leave early in the morning. He wasn't able to give you anything else?"

"No, but the other thing that I felt when I was with him, was that whoever the killer is—or the killers are—they have an inhuman amount of anger and resentment. And it wasn't directed at Bromar, specifically." I sigh. "It felt like this hatred was directed at anything living."

"Shit." Carmen closes her eyes and leans back in her seat. "We can assume there will be other bodies, then."

"Yep," Marissa is the one to reply. "I wish we had a solid lead or something."

For the rest of the trip, we all sit quiet, each of us absorbed with our own thoughts. Since we can use the Portals, we don't bother driving the vehicle all the way back downtown, stopping at the first rental place for the company we'd borrowed it from, and drop off the car. Once done with the paperwork and the truck is being driven to a carwash by some fresh-out-of-college face, we head around behind the building. Once there, Carmen brings out her PDA and casts the Portal.

She has more locations on her PDA, so we have been letting her cast the spell, though we— meaning Marissa and I—tag the location before we walk into the Portal. Once through this Portal, I look around, and am pleasantly surprised to see we are back at her house in Florida.

"There should be beer in the fridge," she says, going around to flip the lights on. "Grab me one, Kevin?"

"Me too, please," Marissa says, throwing herself onto one of Carmen's large, plush sofas.

Nodding, I go to the kitchen, open the fridge, and grab two bottles in one hand, snagging a third one with my other hand. I remove the beers' caps and drop them in the garbage before walking back into the living room. By the time I get there, Carmen has the lights she wanted on and, like Marissa, sprawls out on the sofa.

I pass the blonde a bottle and do the same for Marissa, noticing that they conveniently left a space between them for me to sit down. Sighing, I take a pull of my beer. "Now what?" I ask. "We have no clues."

"Good question," Carmen tells me. "We know that it's probably a Dark Elf... but that's it. But, the new clue, about the Stags, is concerning."

"How so?" Marissa asks her, looking across my lap at our partner.

"The Stags have been around for hundreds of years, right? Not being from Earth, you probably never heard of them." Carmen frowns. "Though the Stags are a small group, they have caused a lot of grief here on Earth for us Magical folk. We thought they had been stopped for good back in the 1960s, but it seems that we were wrong."

"Do we have any leads on where to find them?" I ask her.

"Nope," she says with a sour expression. "Like I said. We thought we'd gotten rid of them in the '60s."

"Like you thought the Dark Elves had been 'gotten rid of'?" I ask.

"Pretty much," she admits, her sour expression getting more pronounced.

"Would Tallen know anything?" I wonder.

"Hmm," Marissa says, thinking that one through. "He might? He has been around for much longer than even my father."

"I guess we are going to see him in the morning, then," Carmen says with a firm nod. Then she turns to study me with a pensive look. "I wonder why Kevin here, with Magic in him now, can do so much more than what we Magical folk can?" she asks quietly, looking from me to Marissa.

"I've wondered about that, too. It could be because Tallen bit him, but that wouldn't be unique, since we have Vampires who can do Magic and cast spells."

"Could it be his human nature?"

Marissa shrugs. "No clue. Since he is the first human ever to have Magic."

"Are you certain humans never had it?" I ask them both.

Carmen thinks about that one before answering. "Hmm. I mean, in all the histories we have, both oral and recorded," Carmen says, "there is no mention of humans possessing Magic. We have heard tons of stories about humans trying to beg, steal, or try to buy access to Magic—but with no success."

"How far back do your histories go?" I ask.

"Thousands of years, at least. My Dad has some stuff in his library that dates back more than three thousand years ago."

"Damn. But we humans have been around a lot longer than that."

Carmen nods. "True. And it might be that humans once possessed Magic. But what happened, that was the case? What caused humans to lose that Magic?"

I snort at that. "Our stupidity?"

The two girls laugh as much at the wry look on my face, as at my rejoinder.

"I don't think all humans could have been that stupid," Carmen says with a chuckle. "Even though many Magical folk would think otherwise. If you humans once possessed Magic, we should know about it, I would think."

"Well," I say, finishing my beer, "I guess tomorrow we'll go talk to Tallen. Anyone up to trying that large jacuzzi bathtub?"

Both girls grin at me, finishing off their own beers quickly. And before I can take more than two steps towards the bathroom, both of them are already making a beeline for it. I can't help but grin. Oh, this is going to be fun.

* * *

"KEVIN!" Tallen shouts, getting up from the table where he had been eating breakfast.

"Tallen," I greet him with a grin, returning the hug he gives me.

"To what do I owe the pleasure of your company?"

"We need some information, and we were hoping you could find some time for us?"

"Of course!" he says, waving for the three of us to sit down. "Go ahead and grab some breakfast. There's tons."

I nod and sit down, Carmen and Marissa flanking me on either side. Looking at the spread on the table, I can't help but grin. The table's been set with enough food for at least a dozen people. Once we have our plates filled, Tallen sits back with a cup of coffee in his hands.

Only then does he ask, "I assume this is related to M.A.G.I?"

"Yes," I tell him. "We are working on the silver dagger murders."

A flash of anger crosses his face. "Yes. I lost two good men to whoever is killing Magic folk."

I had talked to Targun about this, as he'd wanted to limit the number of people who knew about the Dark Elves. Fortunately, he'd approved—permitting me to tell the Vampire Count everything we knew—if I decided we needed Tallen's help.

With a significant look at all the staff standing comfortably at the edge of the room, I turn back to Tallen. "Can we talk in private?"

One eyebrow lifts and he looks at me for a moment. Then, he nods and, looking at the staff, declares, "Leave us."

His staff, without question, all immediately head out of the room, closing the door behind them.

I look back at Tallen. "Do you mind if I cast a spell?"

"Of course, go ahead," he says, puzzled.

I nod and cast Shield, encompassing the room itself. The spell would allow us to hear others outside, but anyone trying to listen in would get nothing—this spell was proof not just against someone pressing their ear to the door, but also against Magical or electronic eavesdroppers.

"You wish to ensure no one hear this conversation?" he asks, once the spell takes hold. Right, I remind myself, he's a Magus, too. He would know what spell I just did.

"For this, yes," I tell him, not going into it.

He slowly nods, sets his cup of coffee down on the table, sits back, and gazes at me.

"So, while investigating the killings, we found daggers that had an ancient script on them," I begin.

"Script?" he interrupts, puzzled.

I take out my phone and show him one of the photos of the daggers that clearly shows the flowing script on the dagger's hilt. He takes my phone and, staring intently down at the photo, his frown grows.

"What am I looking at?" he eventually asks, looking up from the phone at the three of us.

"Dark Elven script," Carmen says softly.

His gaze snaps to Carmen. "You jest?"

"No. This is real. One thing that Kevin can do, that we can't, is that he can use Identify to get a feel for the surrounding area he casts it in. When he cast Identify at the scene of one of the murders, he sensed evil. We took the silver daggers from that crime scene back to show the script on them to my father; He knew right away what it was. Combined with the feeling that Kevin got, Dad believes that it's a Dark Elf—or Dark Elves—doing this."

Carmen picks up when Marissa stops. "At a minimum, it's someone pretending to be a Dark Elf. Though, how would anyone know about the Dark Elves? Remember, the murder weapons are five silver daggers." She shivers. "One thing we learned from Sir Targun about those daggers? They suck the Magic out of their victims."

Tallen frowns at this, and opens his mouth to ask something, but then closes it again, his frown turning into a confused look. "But, they must have been able to touch silver—which I don't think even Dark Elves can do. Tell me more about this feeling you sensed."

This last is directed at me. "When I cast Identify, I can sense the emotions, or the feelings, of the killer—and they were unbelievably intense. What that felt like, to me, was nothing but pure evil."

Shaking his head, Tallen says, "That is something I will have to look into with you more at a later time. Based on the script and Kevin's feeling, your Dad, Marissa, feels that we might be dealing with the Dark Elves once more?"

"Unfortunately, yes."

"Gods," he says, breathing deeply. "I thought we'd never had to deal with them again. As Count, I am required to know our complete history—and this was a history of a really bad time for us Magical folk. We were essentially slaves to these Dark Elves. As you can imagine, I don't want to see that age return."

"Neither do we," Carmen says emphatically. "The history that Targun told us was not pretty, for any of the races."

"Do you have any leads?" he asks.

"Not much... What do you know about the Stags?" I ask him.

At my question, Tallen slams his fist into the table, causing the thick oak to crack from his powerful blow. "Are you saying those fuckers are involved, as well?"

"Possibly," I say, looking between the two girls. What the hell was all that emotion about from the normally reserved Tallen? "What can you tell us about them?"

"I can tell you that I thought we got rid of those fuckers back in the 1960s. I was part of the group that hunted them down, to a man. But you're saying they are back?"

"It seems so. We found this," I take out the silver broach with the stag on it and show it to him, "at the site of the most recent murder."

He looks at it closely, without touching it, even asking me to turn it over before growling and slumping back in his chair. "It seems the hunt is on, once more."

"I guess any clues you might have about the Stags would be over sixty years old?" Carmen asks him.

"Correct," he says, nodding. "But I might have someone who would know a bit more. Looks like we are going to be taking a small trip."

"Where to?" I ask, curious.

Turning to look at me, he smiles. "Lotri."

"Lotri?" Marissa asks. "Why the Fairy world?"

"Because that's where the Fairy who helped me track them down last time lives. She moved there after those battles to retire. It looks like we might need to call her out of retirement."

"You think she will?" I ask him, unsure.

"Pffft. I just need to tell her that the Stags are back, and she will sign up on the spot. Come, let's finish up here, and then we can head out."

I nod and dig into my food, which had gotten cold in our discussion. Something tells me it might be a while before I have time to sit and enjoy such a feast.

CHAPTER TWENTY

Once we finish eating, Tallen suggests we head out. According to his phone, it is already starting to get late where we are going. Apparently, they head to bed early, and he didn't want to get the Fairy he wanted to go see all upset for missing out on her beauty sleep.

I, on the other hand, didn't care! I was going to meet a fairy! Well, I'd met one before—two, actually, if you count Mavin's mother, too. But I'm curious what a Fairy from the Fairy world of Lotri looks like.

Once through the Portal, I look around curiously. Puzzled, I ask, "Are we still on Earth?"

Tallen turns to me and grins. "No. Welcome to the world of Lotri. The Fairy world."

"But," I say, looking around the place and seeing the same kind of trees, flowers, and bushes I might find on Earth. "It looks just like Earth!"

"Yes, well, thank our gods for that," Marissa says with a laugh.

Tallen is the one to give me a proper answer. "When our gods opened up these worlds to our races, we think they created these other worlds to be exact replicas of Earth. There are the same species of plants, animals, and such, in all the Magical worlds."

Knowing my voice sounds skeptical, because I was, I blurt out, "Wait? All eight of the other worlds out there look exactly like Earth?"

Carmen laughs at the look of sheer incredulity on my face. "I know. When I first found out about that, it surprised me too. But it's not just that Earth's plants, animals and such, were copied—but even the landmasses are the same."

I turn to her to see if she is pulling my leg. But I can see that she's not bullshitting me. My god, or I guess in this guess, I should be saying, 'my gods'. Apparently these gods hadn't just opened Portals to some new planet somewhere out in the middle of the galaxy; they'd created exact duplicates of the Earth.

Just how powerful were these gods? I remember hearing that after the gods granted their followers' prayers and opened the Portals, that they were much weakened. But I can't imagine the immense power it must take to duplicate a fucking planet! I'd want to nap for a few eons after that, too.

"Wow." Is all I say.

Marissa throws an arm around my shoulder. "Just go with it. We know now, as science from Earth has given us an inkling, just how much power it must have taken for that divine feat. Our ancestors simply thought that all habitable planets were like this." She pauses. "But, there is one planet that is different."

"Oh?" I ask, looking down at her.

Nodding, she says, "The world that the goblins wanted. They wanted something different—something darker. Also, if you look at the world of the Vampires, it's slightly darker as well. I'm sure their sun pushes out the same amount of energy, but the cloud cover is much more intense."

Tallen nods. "Because of that, the plants, trees, and such have all adapted. If you go to Vamir or Grog—the goblin world— they are the only ones you will see that have slight differences. But, even there, they still have pine trees and such. The flora and fauna have just evolved to live in the darker environments."

I shake my head in wonder.

"Who goes there!" shouts a shrill voice that comes from the woods. It had been so piercingly loud, that I could not tell if it was male or female.

Tallen turns towards the voice and lifts his hands up, palms out, to show they are empty. I see the girls do the same, Marissa removing her arm from around my shoulder. I follow suit and do the same.

"I come in peace. My name is Sir Tallen Voldermoten, the Count of Earth."

"Oh! Oh! Oh!" squeals a different voice.

The first voice yells from the trees. "Oh! oh! We need to, hmm... check something." And then, almost as an afterthought, the voice hollers out, "Your Majesty!"

"It's Count, you moron!" another high-pitched voice chimes in.

"You're the moron!" screams the voice. "You're the one who just asked a Count who they were!"

"That's because I don't know who he is!"

"You can just look at him, and see that he's a Count!"

"What are you talking about? You didn't know, either!" the voice screams.

"Hello?" Tallen calls out with a chuckle. "Can I meet your superiors?"

"Oh!" both voices cry out, surprised that we are still there. "Right away, Count!" shouts one of the voices.

Suddenly, a small Fairy comes zipping out of the trees, a bow — very tiny bow—in his hands, aimed at us. "Don't move. My partner is gone to get help."

The Fairy hovering before us is smaller than Mavin. I mean, of course, Mavin was small to start off with, being a Fairy. This little guy has the same wings as Mavin, though theirs are brighter in color than my Oreo-chomping friend. When I first met Mavin, I'd freaked out—thinking that he looked like a male version of Tinkerbell. But seeing this male Fairy, I have to admit that Mavin looked more... masculine? Manly? Does that even make sense?

This male Fairy looks really feminine, closer to being female, with long green hair braided in three tails that stretch down to his belt. Mavin's hair had been black. I only know the Fairy before us is a male, since he had no shirt on, with only the leather strap of his quiver across his chest. I see the fletching of his arrows sticking up over his tiny shoulder.

"We shall not move, little one," Tallen tells him in a placating voice, with a smile.

"Good," he says with a firm nod. Then the Fairy suddenly blurts out at Tallen, "Are you really the Count?"

"I am. I'm the Count of Earth. I would never lie about that, little one."

"My name is Lotmi."

Tallen bows to him, saying, "My apologies, Lotmi."

The little Fairy sketches a half bow in mid-air. "All good, your Highness."

"Sir Tallen is fine."

"Fine, Sir Tallen." His head whips around to look over his shoulder. "Oh, here they come."

Suddenly, from out of the forest comes another Fairy, followed by another that must be Lotmi's partner—looking rather nervous. Actually, he looks embarrassed. Almost identical to his partner, Lotmi, his hair is a bright red in color, and cropped short.

"I am terribly sorry, Sir Tallen," says the new Fairy.

Looking closer, I see that she's female. And slightly larger, by at least an inch, than the two males. With her long blond hair, she looks like an exact copy of what I imagine Tinkerbell would look like—right down to the damn outfit. Except that her dress, which goes down to her knees and is open at the arms, has tiny flowers all over it.

"It's all right. Protecting one's home is a good thing."

"Yes, well. These two morons here don't know protocol. Please allow me to apologize on behalf of my clan, the Lily Clan. My name is Riipa."

"Well, Riipa, apology accepted."

"Thank you, Count. Now, how can I be of service, Sir Tallen?"

"I'm here to see an old friend; she, too, is of the Lily Clan. I'm here to visit with Mirtha."

"Oh! You're here to see one of the Elders? Why didn't you just open with that?"

"Hmm. I never got that far?" he tells her with a raised eyebrow.

The female Fairy turns on her two counterparts, giving them a glare. They both shrink in on themselves. "We shall discuss this afterwards. Get back to your guard duty. After your shift, though, come see me."

"Yes, Leader," they each mumble, chastised.

Riipa turns back to us, bowing again. "Please follow me. But before we go, I will need the names of your friends."

"Ah, completely understandable. These are my friends, Marissa Lalouton, whose father is the Lead Councillor, Sir Targun Lalouton. And this is Carmen Milgrang, and Kevin Johnston. All three are from M.A.G.I." He smiles. "Kevin is also my adopted son."

At each introduction, Riipa had turned and bowed to one being introduced. But at the mention that I was Tallen's adopted son, her eyes open wide in amazement. Then, she's pointing her finger at me and shouting, "You're that human!"

"That he is," Tallen tells her with a smile. "Now, shall we head to go see Mirtha?"

"Of course," Riipa says, schooling her features and getting control of herself. Almost reluctantly, she looks away from me.

I didn't get a bow. Oh well.

But, as if remembering her manners, she spins in place quickly my way, and bows before turning back to Tallen. "If you will follow me, Sir Tallen?'

"Lead on, Leader," he tells her with a smile.

"Leader?" I whisper down at Marrisa.

But I guess I didn't whisper it low enough because Riipa turns to me with a giggle that is just about the cutest thing I've ever heard. "I am the Leader of my squad, which consists of twenty Fairies. Each Fairy squad has one Leader." Her mouth twists into a grimace. "The two morons you met earlier are my squad members. Above me is a Captain, who leads ten squads. Above them are Majors, who each have five Captains under them."

"What's above that?" I ask, curious.

"Above a Major, is a Captain Major. They are responsible for the ten majors under them." She frowns. "Captain Majors are the top rank in our army. Above them, is our Queen."

Interesting. So if I got the math right, each Captain Major had a total of 5,000 Fairies under his or her command? I wondered how many Captain Majors are there?

As if reading my mind, Riipa says proudly, "We have ten Major Captains. We are the strongest Fairy military."

Holy shit, that means there are over 50,000 Fairies in this Fairy military? That's mind-boggling. I mean, nothing compared to the size of my home country's military might— with over a million active-duty service members. But, these are Fairies we are talking about! Just how many Fairies live on this world? Hell, how many other races live here? I never really got details like that in the information overload I got dumped into my brain during training.

For the next ten minutes, we walk through the woods, with Riipa flying ahead of us, pointing out trees and plants as if they were new to us. She also, at times, would cry out a name, and a Fairy would pop out of a tree, or bush, bow to us, and then hide once more. How Riipa was able to find them all, I have no clue. Either it was Magic, or she knew all their hiding spots.

Eventually, we come to an open meadow, and I stop in my tracks. The clearing is large, open to the sky, with what I can only guess are hundreds of flying Fairies, zipping all over the place. I turn in place to take in the sight. The Fairies, if nothing else, are colorful—every hue of the rainbow streaks across the sky, with plenty of colors thrown in. Riipa had stopped and is staring at us with a big grin. I turn and look at the girls, and they each have their mouths open, as well.

Tallen laughs at our reaction and says, "I didn't want to say anything, because seeing a Fairy Village for the first time, is something else."

"There's so much color!" Marissa blurts out.

"Yes," he tells her with a chuckle. "My father once called it a Peacock of Color explosion."

"Come," Riipa says with her own giggle, "this way."

With a nod, Tallen follows her, a route through the Fairies suddenly opening up. The entire Village, I'm sure, is now looking at us. Everyone had stopped doing what they had been doing, to look at the newcomers. To say I was nervous, with hundreds of eyes on me, would be an understatement. There must have been over two hundred Fairies here.

Finally, we stop at a tree like many of the others, but when Riipa asks us to wait, I get a better look at the tree. It has a small door that is roughly at eye level to my six foot frame, with two small windows on either side.

Riipa cups her hands and yells out, "Elder Mirtha!"

"What?" A shout comes from inside the tree, through an open window beside the door.

"You have guests!"

"Don't care! Tell them to go away."

"Are you going to tell an old friend like me to go away like that?" Tallen shouts.

Without warning, the small door in the tree's trunk slams open, and out of it comes a small Fairy with gray hair, whose wings had probably seen better days. I also notice that she seems blind, as her eyes are clouded over with a white film.

"Tallen?" the small Fairy asks, disbelief clear in her voice.

"Hello, Mirtha." The Vampire chuckles. "It's been a long time."

"Tallen!" she cries, suddenly zipping faster than I can follow to slam into Tallen's chest; he reaches up and catches her with a laugh.

"My gods, it's been too long!" she cries into his chest in joy.

"That is has, Mirtha. But, I wish this was only a social visit, but it's not. Is there somewhere private we can chat?"

"Oh, by the Flower of Life," the old fairy sniffles, "it's still good to see you. At least I can still see you—if I'm up close.

"Still having issues with your vision?" Tallen asks her worriedly, looking down at her in his hands.

"Of course," she answers him with a snort. "I am nearly 300 years old; I should be dead."

"Oh hush," he tells her soothingly. "You're still young."

She laughs at Tallen's flattery and shakes her head. "You're just as much a flirt as your father."

"I am not," he tells her indignantly. "You take that back!"

"Yes, you are," both Carmen and Marissa say in unison.

He turns to glare at both of them. "I never flirted with either of you."

"Hmm. You flirted with me ages ago. But I'm sure you didn't flirt with Marissa here, because you knew her husband would kick your ass. Which—since you gave him the full Transformation—he can do even better."

With a sour expression, Tallen turns back to his old friend, who had been listening. "Wait, you gave him the full Transformation?" Mirtha asks him with a raised eyebrow. "So that would make him your adopted son?"

"Correct," Tallen tells her. "But it didn't work as intended."

"Oh? What happened?"

"This is Kevin. The human."

I'm pretty sure I heard the sound barrier being broken with how fast her head whipped around on her neck towards me. It's a wonder she didn't giver herself whiplash.

"Hi," I say lamely, lifting a hand and waving to her.

Suddenly, she zips out of Tallen's hands and is floating in front of my face, right in front of my nose. She is glaring at me—well, that is… she's glaring at my left ear.

"I missed your smell; I did not notice that you are human. How is it a human is here?" The question was not directed at me, but at Tallen.

"Are you telling me you have not heard the rumors?"

"What rumors," she growls. "I stay in my house, and expect if I'm not bothering folks, that they don't come bother me."

So, for the next five minutes, Tallen explains to her what had happened to me, from accidentally swallowing the contents of the mystical vial, to getting Magic and being trained, and now being employed by M.A.G.I.. Of course, Tallen can't leave the girls out, having to explain that Marissa is my wife and partner, with Carmen being my partner, as well.

By the end of it, she has a look of utter disbelief on her face, and is shaking her head in wonder. "What are the worlds coming to?!" she mutters. "And the last vial? Didn't your father," she asks the question of Marissa, "figure out how to recreate those vials?"

"Gods no," she replies with a laugh. "But, Kevin is under my father's protection, so no one can touch him."

Carmen snorts. "Not that they could, anyway. Kevin is at least a level ten Magus."

Mirtha turns back to me, getting right up in my face and studying me critically. "Hmm. Yes. I can feel power emanating from him. I assume you didn't come here, Tallen, to introduce me to this human, though?"

"No, I need your help."

"Oh?" The surprise is evident in her voice. Owlishly she blinks at the Vampire. "What kind of help can this old Fairy offer you?"

"Information. I need information on the Stags."

At the mention of the Stags, her face clouds over. "They are all dead," she whispers fiercely.

"Unfortunately, Mirtha. They aren't. We need information, and you were there when the Stags were taken down—or when we assumed they were."

Mirtha growls low under her breath, but because she was floating right in front of me, I'm sure I was the only one who heard her curse, "Mother fuckers."

CHAPTER TWENTY-ONE

"What was that?" Tallen asks, but I see he has a smirk on his face.

"Nothing," Mirtha tells him with a scowl. She turns around to look at her door, and then back at us. Nodding, the old Fairy says, "Come. Follow me."

With that, she turns around and flies away. Tallen looks at us and shrugs, then points to the small door in the tree. "Not like we can fit into her house."

"True," I say with a smile.

With Marissa and Carmen trailing me on either side, I keep up with Tallen, who follows Mirtha. After a couple of minutes of brisk walking, which I see is away from the Village, she finally stops in a smaller clearing. Here, I see, there are logs that have been cut lengthwise, and placed flat end facing up around a dead firepit.

Mirtha lands lightly on one of the logs and, pointing to the others, indicates we are to join her. Once we are sitting down, she looks at me. "Since you're a Magus young man. Care to call up the Shield spell?"

"Hmm. Sure," I say, nodding.

I place my hand on the ground and I cast Shield, making it large enough to encompass us and the logs. Once finished, I nod to her. "Done."

"Impressive. I have not seen anyone cast Shield that quickly before. Yes, I would say that level is inaccurate. I would have pegged you at least level twelve or so."

Tallen is the one to respond. "Well, if it helps, Kevin has not been fully tested yet. We figure his power is closer to level twenty, than level ten."

With a squawk of surprise Mirtha turns her milky gaze on Tallen, as if to see if he was bullshitting her. When he simply stares back at her, she shakes her head. "Now, about the Stags. You are sure they're back?" she asks him.

"Yes," he says with a sigh. "Have you heard of the silver dagger murders?"

"Yes," she says with a frown. "And you think they have something to do with it?"

"Kevin, show her," Tallen instructs.

I nod and take out the silver broach—the one with the stag etched in black on one side, and the pin on the other.

Mirtha flies over, a curious look on her face, but the moment she sees the design on it, she sputters in anger. "Shit. Where in the seven hells did you find that?" she hisses, glaring up at me.

"On the body of one of the victims that had been murdered."

"Hold it up for me?" she asks.

I do as she bids and hold up the broach. She flies over until she is hovering only inches from it and waves her hand over it. I'm careful to hold the broach steady, as I can't imagine how much damage the silver jewelry might do if it touches the old Fairy. As she closes her eyes and continues to pass her hand above its surface, I feel Magic stir the air.

She sighs. "It's real."

"What do you mean?" Tallen asks her.

"We found a stash of these, years ago, in a warehouse. We didn't know who was supposed to come get them, so we added a Tracer spell to the tokens." She drifts back a foot or two, wringing her hands together. "Actually, it was me who had cast the Tracer spell. So I know that that broach was one of the ones we found; it still has my Magical signature on it."

"We have Magical signatures?" I blurt out, surprised at that. And even as I say it, I know the answer.

But Mirtha turns to me and explains, as if I should know such a basic fact of life. 'Stupid human', I'm sure she's thinking. "Yes. Each time you cast a spell—especially a spell that lingers on an item—such as Trace, the person who cast the original spell can sense it; even after more than eighty years."

"Eighty years!" Carmen cries in amazement.

"That's right." She pauses, frowning. "Let's see... what year is it on Earth?"

"Hmm," I say, when everyone looks at me expectantly, "it's 2022."

"So, if I remember, I did those," Mirtha points to the pin in my hand, "around 1938. So... that would be, what?"

"Eighty-four years ago," Tallen supplies with a chuckle, shaking his head.

"Close enough," she tells him with a grin.

"So, we know then that this was one of that original batch you cast Trace on. But, what can you tell us about the Stags?" Tallen asks her.

Mirtha shakes her head sadly, and grunts. "Let's see. The Stags were a group of humans that probably came to light in the eighteenth century in Europe. It wasn't until the early twentieth century, though, after the First World War, that they really came into their own—though, they kept hidden." She shakes her head. "We only noticed them, because we noticed our people on Earth were disappearing in ever larger numbers—especially in the towns of London, Cambridge, and Manchester."

"In England, you mean?" I ask.

"Yes, in the United Kingdom. When we—and by we, I mean some of us Magical Folk—started looking into it, we stumbled upon them by accident. One of them was an idiot who was bragging in a pub that he'd just killed a Werewolf. The fool was even showing off its head, in wolf form. Some friends and I had been there for a drink, but I kept hidden, thanks to my Invisibility spell. But my friends, who were Elves and Changelings in human disguise, were there to see it with me."

"We were lucky that it was just a wolf he'd killed, and not a real Werewolf. But, he kept saying things about real Werewolves that most humans wouldn't know. Knowing that he must have met a Werewolf, we waited until he left and then followed him."

"Let me guess," Tallen says softly, frowning. "It was a trap?"

Mirtha nods emphatically. "It was a trap. And we almost walked right into it—which would have been our deaths. Fortunately, humans—no offense to Kevin, are morons."

"None taken," I tell her with a smile.

She smiles back at me and continues. "We walked into a trap with four humans, with no Magic except swords and knives —and not even silver ones. I'm sure they expected there to be only one of us, not nine of us."

"Nine of you?" Carmen asks, with a raised eyebrow.

"Yes," she replies with a grin. "We were out celebrating my fiftieth birthday, so it was a large party. It was only my third time on Earth." She smiles softly to herself, before shaking her head. "But, back to the story. In the process of capturing those four humans, we found out some interesting things. It seems that some humans did know about us—humans that we were not aware of. The 'Stags', as these humans called themselves, knew about us and had known about us for quite a long time. They also knew things about us that we thought humans had forgotten. But, apparently, not."

I have to admit. I was confused. "Okay, but what's so special about these Stags?"

Mirtha nods as if expecting the question. "The Stags are different, in that they are run by the government."

"What?!" Tallen cries in horror.

"Yes," she says, turning to him. "Back then, it seems the British government knew about us. I don't mean the entire government—but certainly some people high up in it. We learned they had files on many of us." She pauses. "Did your father, the Count, not know this at all?"

"Gods no!"

"Well, we were lucky that the moron had decided to brag in the pub that night, trying to lure out one of us Magical folk to their trap. I don't think they expected to have so many in one spot, though. We Magical folk tend to avoid humans whenever we could—Or we did back then. I hear it's slightly different, now."

She turns for confirmation of this rumor, to Carmen. "My cousin, Milta, Queen of the Fairies on Earth, told me that the Magical folk on Earth are much closer to humans these days?"

Wait, she's the Queen's cousin?

Tallen, though, is the one who answers. Nodding at her, he says, "That's pretty accurate. Many of us feel that we need to show ourselves to the humans, or to certain humans, so that we can gain access to their technology."

"That's what Milta said," Mirtha nods. "She said that we can either be left behind, or learn to use the humans to our advantage."

"Okay," Marissa says, "but what does that pin mean?"

"If you found this on a dead Magical folk, it means that we didn't kill all the Stags off. We worked for decades to eradicate them. We even assassinated some pretty powerful humans, to keep this all secret." She sighs. "If you found this now, though, it means we still have an issue."

I stare at her and wonder who, in the 1930s and the 1940s, had been assassinated, but nothing comes to mind. I'd sucked at history—never mind the history of another country. I'm sure that if I was British, I would be able to snap my fingers and yell 'Egad!' But… nope. That ain't happening here.

"What governments would be behind this, though? The British again?" Tallen asks.

"Where was this found? On Earth, I mean."

"It was found in the United States of America," Carmen supplies.

Sighing, Mirtha shakes her head. "So that means it might not be the Brits this time, but these Americans, as you call yourselves," she says, looking my way. "That must mean that some information must have been discovered, and now some human—or human organization—is using it to their advantage. What else can you tell me about these murders?"

We all three look at each other, and I wonder if we should tell her about the silver daggers with their ancient flowing script, and the fact that we think that Dark Elves are most likely involved.

"She needs to know," Tallen tells us.

"Are you sure?" Carmen asks him hesitantly.

"She needs to know," he repeats. "We need information, and I don't want her keeping anything back because of some deep-seated need for secrecy on her part."

"Know what?" Mirtha asks suspiciously, buzzing up close in front of one of us, and then the others, until she's glared at all three of us.

"Did you want to ask your Dad?" I ask Marissa.

"Sure," she says, nodding. My wife takes out her communication stone and closes her eyes.

"Know what, Tallen?" Mirtha hisses to her old friend.

Instead of answering, he holds up a finger and points at Marissa.

Mirtha looks over at Marissa and grimaces.

Finally, Marissa, after what must have been a couple of minutes, opens her eyes. "All right," she says, "I was able to convince him. He's not happy about it, but he understands. He's trying to keep the number of folks who know this information to an absolute minimum. But we need info as well, and he agreed to let us tell her."

"All right," Mirtha breathes slowly. "Now, care to explain what all the hush-hush is about?"

Tallen nods and takes a deep breath. "The so-called silver dagger murders actually used silver daggers to sacrificially murder a number of victims."

"My gods!" she cries out in horror.

"But it gets worse," he says, and I can see how hesitant he is— even with permission from Targun—to talk about this. "At a recent murder scene, the silver daggers were left behind— and these had an ancient script on them."

Now puzzled, Mirtha asks, "A script?"

"A Dark Elven script."

Mirtha stares at Tallen with a blank look. "Come again?"

"We think that the murders are done, either by someone who knew about the Dark Elves and is pretending to be them... or worse."

Mirtha replies with what I can only imagine is skepticism. "Worse... how? That the Dark Elves are back? But, those are the boogie-men we use to scare our kids with."

"Mirtha, you should know better than that. Wasn't your mother a scholar?"

"Yes, she was," Mirtha sniffs. "But I was more of the adventurous type. But seriously... Dark Elves?"

"Dark Elves," Carmen repeats. "And we found that Stag pin on a dead body that had been flayed, the corpse pinned to the ground through the hands, chest, and throat with silver daggers... silver daggers with Dark Elven script on the hilts."

"My gods," the old Fairy finally says, as if the pieces clicked together for her. "You think that these Dark Elves are using humans to gain something?"

"Something... or someone," Tallen tells her. "Which is why these three, as M.A.G.I. came to see me. And I thought you would have more information about the Stags than I did, and could give them something."

"Well," she says, deflating with a sigh. "There's not much I can tell you. The last time I saw that pin was back in 1938."

"Crap," Carmen says, sighing defeatedly.

"I might have something, though," Mirtha says slowly, almost hesitantly, thinking about something. "It's not much. But, I do remember one thing we found, that seemed odd at the time. On one of the bodies, during our hunt for the Stags, we had found a piece of paper that mentioned something about the city of Waterford."

She shakes her head. "But, we weren't sure what it meant, except that—at the time—getting to Waterford wasn't easy.

The Old Land was going through what the humans call The Great Depression. It was hard, even for us Magical folk there, so many of them moved to the Americas." She shrugs. "We never got a chance to follow up that lead."

"Waterford?" I ask, looking around, but everyone else is just as confused.

"Waterford, in Ireland."

"Oh! Ireland," I say, feeling stupid. But then again, I sucked at geography, or world geography.

"I guess we're going to Ireland," Tallen says out loud.

"We are?" I ask him with a raised eyebrow.

"You think I'm not going?" he asks me with his own raised eyebrow.

"But you're the Count," Marrisa reminds him.

"And your father is the Lead Councillor on the Galactic Council of Magical Folk. Does he stay home behind a desk all the time?"

Marissa scowls at that and mumbles. "No, which caused mom endless grief back when she was alive. Even to this day, he goes into hot spots."

"Precisely. So, as I said, we all are going to Ireland."

"Well, I'm too old for traveling," Mirtha sniffs. "So I shall wish you luck, and pray the gods watch over you. But, Tallen, if it really is the Dark Elves, will you be fine? They were a powerful race, if the stories were true."

He nods at Mirtha and says, "I think we should be all right. We have a secret weapon."

"We do?" I ask him.

He turns to me and grins, "We have you. A Magus the likes of which the world hasn't seen for eons."

"A possible level twenty Magus," I tell him, reminding him that I have yet to be fully tested and had gotten the results already from Targun.

He waves his hand dismissively. "Trust me. I know a powerful ally when I see one. And having fought you—and fought beside you—I know I'm right."

"Fine," I say with a sigh. "Ireland it is. Right, girls?"

Carmen snorts. "Men."

I look over at Marissa, and she is shaking her head. "What?"

"You men are all alike. Jumping straight into battle without a plan."

"Oh, we will plan," Tallen says, looking smug. "At my place, in Scotland, before we head over to Ireland."

"You have a place in Scotland?" Marissa asks, but then holds up her hand. "Never mind, I keep forgetting you're the Count."

With a big grin, he tells her. "Exactly!"

CHAPTER TWENTY-TWO

Looking around, I ask Tallen with skepticism in my voice, "This is your place in Scotland?"

"Yes? Why? What is wrong?" he asks me defensively.

"Oh, I don't know. Because it's a fucking castle on a hill!"

Tallen turns around to look up at the building I was pointing to accusingly. On the hill we had just Portaled beside sat a castle, like one I would see in movies. It was massive, much larger than Mike's parent's place—And they owned a frickin' mansion.

Tallen turns back, "What is it with you humans and your fascination with castles?"

Hearing a cough, Tallen turns around to see who had coughed, and it was Carmen.

"What?"

"It's not just humans, Tallen. I think your castle is fucking amazing!"

"I have to agree with Carmen," Marissa says with a chuckle. "I always wanted to live in a castle. Except my Dad thought they were impractical."

"Well, this is just a stopover," he growls. "Not my fault, I inherited it."

"Oh, I'm not dissing your castle, dude," I tell him with a laugh. "I love it."

Carmen next to me snorts.

"What?"

"Only you would call a Vampire Count, 'dude'."

I frown at her, but hearing a chuckle, I turn to Tallen, and see he's grinning cheekily.

"That's what I like about Kevin," he says. "He doesn't fawn over me. Hells, I've heard he doesn't act any different around your Dad."

"Am I supposed to?" I ask, starting to get worried, now.

"Gods, no!" Tallen laughs. "Don't change. Most people would be shaking in their boots, just being in the same room with this one's father," he explains, pointing at Marissa. "But it doesn't seem to affect you at all."

"Ah," I say, starting to understand. "I would say that's mostly because of Mike. His parents are rich, but thanks to him being my best friend, I grew up in the presence of rich and powerful people." I shrug. "I might not be rich, but I have dealt with them my whole life. To me, they're just people."

All three of them laugh, as Marissa comes up behind me and hugs me. "I'm so glad I met you—even if the circumstances were less than ideal."

"I'm glad as well, and not just because I got Magic," I tell her, turning my head to kiss her.

"What about me?" Carmen asks in a saucy voice.

I open my free arm, and she comes in as well. With a grin, I kiss her as well.

"And I see you have taken to our customs like a duck to water," Tallen says with a guffaw.

I grin at him and say, "When in Rome... as they say."

He frowns at me, but suddenly snaps his fingers. "Ah! The saying: 'When in Rome, do as the Romans do'." He chuckles. "Yes, I guess that it would be very apropos here."

"Now, let's go in and see this castle of yours," Marissa tells Tallen with a grin.

"We shan't be here long, but it will take me a few hours to make arrangements for us to get to Ireland."

"No one has Ireland in their Portal stone?" I ask, looking at the three of them.

Shaking their heads, Tallen is the one to answer. "I have never needed to visit it, until now. Most of the land I own on this side of the world, is in Scotland and Britain."

Once inside the castle, Tallen shouts out, "Hello, the home."

"Coming!" I hear shouting from another room.

Suddenly there's crashing noise, followed by swearing, and finally, a man emerges out of one of the doors.

The man is tall, wearing a butler's outfit. He's an older man, probably in his sixties. When he sees Tallen, his eyes open wide.

"Master!" he shouts.

He rushes over to Tallen and hugs him, Tallen hugging him back with a huge grin.

"How are things, Latus?"

"They are good, Master. It's been years since last you visited!"

"I know," Tallen says with a sigh. "And we aren't here long, I'm afraid. I am on my way to Ireland. My friends and I will need two rooms. One for myself, and one—preferably one with one of the larger beds—for my other three guests here."

"I can arrange that easily, Master," he replies, stepping back from Tallen and bowing.

"Stop that, Latus. These are friends. Good friends. You don't need to pretend around them."

Latus turns to Tallen and grins. "Very well, Master."

"And stop with the Master thing." Tallen scowls, rolling his eyes.

"You know I can't do that, young Master," Latus replies with an even bigger grin. "I have known you since you were a wee lad in diapers—but you are still the Master of this house."

"I'm also your Count," Tallen snaps at him with a glare.

"Yes, yes, a Count who I helped change the diapers of," Latus says with a laugh.

I look more closely at Latus. He's a Vampire? I would never have guessed. I know that everyone in the Magical world seems to keep mentioning how I 'smell' human. But does that mean they can smell other races as well?

Latus, as far as I could tell, looked human—if slightly pale from not getting enough sun. But, this is freaking Scotland—the whole country is probably vitamin D deficient. The old codger certainly didn't look like a Vampire. Then again, I frown as I look back at Tallen, if I hadn't known he was a Vampire, I might never have guessed it.

I only see him now as a *Vampire*, because I know that is what he is.

"Thanks for the reminder," Tallen tells him with a scowl, but then he brightens up. "Is Leenna here?"

"She is, Master," Latus answers with his own smile. "Do you wish to have her tonight?"

"Please. Let her know that I am here and, if she is available, please ask her if she would do me the honor. But, it's," and he looks down at his watch, "almost supper time. Please ask the kitchen staff to make something light for us. I don't want them to go overboard or anything."

"I will see what I can do, Master," Latus says, bowing low. "If you will excuse me? I shall go start with the necessary preparations. Will you need a driver?"

"Hmm. I was going to fly, but you know what? Driving might be nice. It will let me see the scenery, as I have never been to Ireland."

"Very well. Do you know where exactly you wish to go?"

"It's a place called... Waterford?"

"Very well, Master. I will let the driver know. Do you have a preference?"

"Hmm. Does Joey still work for me?"

"He does, Master. Did you wish him?"

"Yes. Let's go with him, if he is available. If I remember right, he's got family in central Ireland—might even be near Waterford."

"Very well. I shall inform him. Tomorrow at 9 AM?"

Tallen looks at us for confirmation, and I shrug my shoulders. "I think that's good?"

"Let's go with midmorning—say around ten o'clock."

Latus nods, bows, and heads out of the room.

"Let's go to the main room. We can discuss our plans there, about what we'll do once we get to Waterford."

We follow Tallen as he heads deeper into the castle, until we come to a set of double doors. Opening them, he leads us into a massive library, with wall-to-wall bookshelves that go from the floor all the way up to the ceiling, with hundreds of books in them. There's even one of those ladders-on-rails, to help you get that one book off the top shelf you have to grab, and a fire in an enormous fireplace, which crackles merrily.

Looking closely, I can see that it's all new logs—so it must have just been lit. The castle itself was cool inside, compared to late afternoon air, which had been rather muggy.

"My gods," Carmen says, looking at all the books. "Some of these books aren't even written by humans!"

Marissa is holding a large book in her hands, and it looks ancient. The massive thing is bound in luxurious red and blue leather, with a large painting on the cover of some mystical three-horned animal.

"Is this a copy of Elven philosopher Mitgra Lamnon's essays?" my wife asks, looking over at Tallen disbelievingly.

Coming over, he looks over the book. "Ah... that. It was a present from my father, when I turned eighteen. Do you like it? You can have it."

"Do I... Do I like it?" Marissa stutters, her mouth agape.

Curious, I ask, "Is it rare?"

"There are maybe nine copies left in existence! My father 'borrowed' a copy once..." Marissa snickers and does air quotes when she says 'borrowed', "from the Galactic Library on Ilia. The Elves didn't want to lend it to him, but my father wasn't in the mood, really, to ask nicely."

"Your Dad stole a book?" I gasp.

"Stole is such a harsh word. He only borrowed it. He returned it—eventually."

Tallen laughs. "If it's the incident, I think it is. Your Dad ended up 'borrowing' it for more than a decade. Though, I heard it was a good thing he did, since the part of the library that it had been housed in burned in a fire and more than two hundred irreplaceable books were severely damaged."

"Yep," she says with a grin. "And he still has it. The Galactic Library gifted it to him, on loan indefinitely, I believe is how they phrased it—as long as they could copy it."

Marissa takes the book and heads over to one of the large stuffed leather chairs in the room. Sitting down, she opens the book to its first page and begins to read it. I could tell we might as well not exist now, as far as she was concerned.

"What about you?" I ask Carmen

"Oh, I'm not much of a reader. I prefer watching television," she says with a grin. "The whole Netflix and chill thing."

Laughing, I grab her hand and pull her over to one of the sofas with me and we sit down, almost sinking into it and getting lost. Then, there's a knock on the door.

"Come in!" Tallen shouts, as the doors are pretty thick here— I'm sure they're at least two inches thick and probably constructed to withstand an invading army.

The door opens, and Latus enters the room with a large tray in his hands. "I prepared some coffee and tea, Master, and I asked the kitchen staff to prepare some food. They should be ready in about another twenty minutes or so."

"Thank you, Latus," Tallen tells him gratefully.

Latus nods and heads back out of the room, closing the doors behind him.

Getting up from the sofa, I walk to the table where the tray sits enticingly. I pour myself a cup of coffee and turn to look over my shoulder. "Anyone else want something?"

I take everyone's requests and prepare a tea for Marissa, black coffee for Tallen and Carmen, and coffee with cream for myself. Serving everyone their hot drinks, I head back to my seat.

"Now. We need to figure out where to go. So... Waterford. We will need to catch a ferry at Cairnryan. I know that much. Let's see," Tallen mutters, taking out his phone and tapping away for a bit. "The trip should take roughly ten hours, as we'll need to take the ferry across the Irish Sea to Belfast and then travel from there to Waterford. I'm sure Joey knows how to book it for us."

Marissa looks up from her book. "How long will it take us to get to the ferry?"

"Well, my castle is near Kirkintilloch," he says, and at my startled look, he laughs. "I didn't name the place. It should be roughly four hours to Cairnryan. But, I want to leave early with Joey, so we can sightsee some on the way from Belfast to Waterford. I know," he says, holding up a hand to stop Carmen from cracking a joke, "that we're working on a murder case, but I still like to enjoy life. I might live to be three hundred or so, but I still like to sightsee."

"Oh, I wasn't about to complain," I tell him with a smile. "I've never traveled across the ocean. I have traveled some in Canada, and my own section of the US. But, except for that jaunt via Portal with Carmen to North Africa, this is my first trip abroad."

"And I only visited big cities when I came to Earth to see concerts," Marissa says, not bothering to look up from her book.

"Then, it's settled. We shall eat supper, get a good night's sleep," he says with a smirk, winking at the three of us. "And then we can figure out what the hell this Stag business is all about."

Taking a sip of my coffee, I ask Tallen. "I meant to ask before —but things got a little hectic last time we spent some time with you. What was the full Transformation thing that you did to me supposed to do? How come it didn't work?"

Tallen takes a sip of his own coffee. He had moved to one of the large chairs, identical to the one that Marissa lounges in. Nodding, he scowls. "Yes. So... we Vampires have the ability to bite other races, and we feed off their stamina and their emotions. It's what sustains us, allowing us to live longer.

Normally that bite is just a shadow of what the Full Trans-formation, as we call it, is. We don't control humans or other races with our bite—it's more of a… connection. While I benefit from it, so do those who I bite."

"Like those big lugs you had working at the club," I tell him, remembering the massive security guards at his club.

"Those big lugs," he nods. "My bite, if freely accepted, will modify someone to be slightly like a Vampire. One example, as you noted, are the men I hire as security. They received more muscle, or enhanced muscles." He shrugs. "For some, it's speed; others, it's brainpower."

"The Full Transformation is different, though. It's a gift that only a Royal—such as a Count, or one of my line—can bestow. We aren't sure how it works, but it's only given by those who are Royalty. We figure it's an inherent part of our Magic, as a race. The Full Transformation allows us to take any race and, for all intents and purposes, turn them into full Vampires—as if they'd been born one."

He gets a sour look on his face. "Well, with you, something failed."

"So what am I, then?"

Tallen sighs. "Of that, we have no clue. In our history, and I went back and took a look, there has never been Vampire Royalty who tried giving the Full Transformation to a human. It has always been given, willingly, to one of the Magical races. And it always transforms them."

He shrugs. "You seem to have received many physical enhancements of the gift, but not an actual transformation. And I'm not sure if that's because I didn't ask your permis-sion first—that may be why the Magic failed—or there is something else going on." He tilts his head to the side, studying me. "Why? Are you having issues?"

"Not if you think being stronger, faster, and somehow feeling smarter, isn't an issue," I tell him with a snort.

"And you still have no desire for blood or others' emotions?"

"Nope."

"Damn," he says, shaking his head. "Then I have no clue what is going on. I am sorry I did that to you, without asking first."

"Well, I—for one—am thrilled with his extra stamina," Carmen chips in, a big grin on her face.

"I have to admit, that part of your gift has been fun," Marissa chimes in with a laugh.

"Well, tonight we shall feast and then, with a good night behind us—be it with sleep or without—we'll head to Waterford tomorrow."

"Sounds good," I say, lifting my cup in salute.

CHAPTER TWENTY-THREE

The next morning, I walk out of the castle, trying in vain to suppress the yawn that cracks my jaw unbidden.

"Tired?" Tallen asks me, but I see that he has bags under his eyes as well.

"Yeah," I tell him with a smile. "But it was well worth it."

"Good," he says with his own smile.

He yawns suddenly as well. "Guess that coffee for breakfast didn't help. Hope you don't mind that I had Latus bring you three breakfast in bed. I wasn't up to getting out of my own this morning."

"I'm sure," I tell him with a chuckle, knowing he'd had his own fun last night. "No problem," I tell him, nodding. "It was quite nice waking up to that. It felt like I was at some fancy hotel,"

"Sir?" I hear from behind us and, turning, see there's a short man standing there, with a full dark beard that flows down to his chest. His accent is a thick Scottish brogue—sounding more like 'Sair?

"Joey!" Tallen turns, with a big grin for the man dressed in a dark blue business suit.

"You asked fer me ta drive today, Sir?"

"If that's all right? We've known each other since you were a child, hell I knew your parents. Please call me Tallen."

"Of course, Sir," he says, bowing nervously. "Latus said you wanted to go to Waterford?"

"Yes. Will that be any trouble?"

"No. Traffic is pretty light. And we got the new limousine a couple of months back that your company sent over…"

Tallen had started to shake his head. "Nope. No limo. I want to use one of the SUVs. I'm not advertising the fact that I'm here."

"Hmm," Joey says, thinking it over. "Then, I'll hafta run back an' grab a different set o' keys. I'll be back in five minutes, Si —" he starts to say, but stops at Tallen's glare.

Joey bows, turns on his heel, and heads back into the large castles' front entrance. In seconds, he is gone.

Carmen asks, coming through the doorway and looking back over her shoulder at Joey, who she'd just passed. "Does Joey know about… well, what you are?"

Marissa is behind Carmen, eating an apple. She gives me a sweet smile and comes over to kiss me.

"No," Tallen replies to Carmen. "Most of the staff here just know that I am some rich, eccentric old man who likes to use a lot of his money on rejuvenation procedures." He smirks.

"Which is why he doesn't blink twice at my looking so young, even though I knew his parents."

I turn and stare at him in disbelief. "Are you serious?"

With a snort, he replies, "You'd be surprised what humans will believe."

Remembering all those magazines out there talking about Aliens, Monsters, and such around the world, I shake my head. "Oh trust me, I do," I mutter.

Hearing tires crunch the gravel, I turn as a black SUV pulls up in front of the castle. The vehicle has heavily tinted windows and, if I don't miss my guess, seems to be riding rather low.

"Bullet proof?" Carmen asks Tallen with a raised eyebrow, intrigued.

"And hermetically sealed," he tells her with a grin.

Marissa is the one who whistles in appreciation before I can. "Damn," she says, walking to the SUV. Before she can get to it, Joey pops out of the drivers' side and runs around to open the back passenger door on Marissa's side. He smiles at her as he holds open the door.

Marissa gets in, with Carmen right behind her.

Tallen looks my way, "Shall we?"

Nodding, I head to the car's door and look inside. The interior is a rich, dark leather, only slightly lighter than the car's exterior. But before I can get into the car, I hear a grunt of pain. Turning, I look over curiously at Tallen, who made the sound, and I get a shock. His eyes are wide, and he has his hand pressed to a red stain on his chest.

"Tallen!" I cry in shock.

Without warning, I'm pushed out of the way by Carmen, as she jumps out of the SUV and slaps her hand on the ground. I feel a burst of Magic, and suddenly around us and the vehicle, a Shield spell snaps into being.

And just in time, too, as I hear a shot smack into the Shield and then ricochet. As I was the only one stupidly standing next to the vehicle, staring at Tallen like an idiot as he slumped to one knee, I'm sure it had been aimed at me. If it wasn't for Carmen's Shield, I'm sure I would have been shot.

"Where is that coming from!" Marissa shouts.

"I'm not sure!" Carmen cries, pressing a hand to Tallen's chest, just above the wound, and casting Heal.

Joey, I see, had ducked to the ground and is looking around, dazed and not sure what to do. "Get inside the car now!" I yell at him.

The man turns to look at me, confused, until I point to the driver's seat. "Get in the fucking car. Or your head will be next!"

That makes him move. The man suddenly jumps up, ducks back around the car, and scrambles into the driver's seat. I go to Tallen and help into the back seat of the car, just in case Carmen's Shield falls, or somehow, whoever is shooting at us gets something through the Shield.

I hear another ping from a round hitting the Shield. I'm not sure how much Carmen's Shield can take. The thing about Shields, are that they expend Magical energy with each hit they repulse. The more powerful the Magus who casts it, the longer a Shield can last,--but even that has its limits. Hit a Shield enough times, and it will fail. And I'm pretty sure the kinetic force of a bullet smashing into the Shield will drain it faster than, say, a dagger hitting it.

As if Tallen had been reading my mind, he grunts, "We need to find that sniper fast, or the Shield will fail."

"On it," I tell him and, closing my eyes, I cast Identify. But instead of focusing on the immediate area, I cast it wide. Hells, I'm not even sure this will work, as I'm not using the spell anywhere close to how it's probably meant to be used. But when I feel the Magic leave me, it seems to flow out in a circular wave, emanating from me.

With my eyes closed, it is a decidedly odd feeling. It's like watching a burst of sound leave me, and then, as magical echoes return, I see in my mind's eye the placement of other living things around me. I feel strong life-forces close to me —which would be Carmen, Marissa, Joey, and Tallen. I also feel weaker life-forces behind me, back inside the castle, and I count four of them. But, then out a ways in front of the house, I sense others.

Some are small, the life forces of rodents and rabbits, and maybe even a fox. But, then, about a quarter-mile away, in the bushes, up in a tree, I sense a human life-force—or at least one from something big, that feels like one of us.

I hear another ricochet. Shit, so they are still shooting at us.

"Sniper, a quarter-mile from the front of the castle, at one o'clock, up in a tree," I call out, not opening my eyes and not pointing, in case the sniper can see me. I don't want to let them know we know where they are.

"Shit, we need to take them down. Maybe I can run fast enough to get to them," Marissa growls angrily.

Tallen tells her with a grunt of pain, "You would not make it ten paces."

"Well, we can't stay here. That Shield will go down in a minute. It's taking a beating with the kinetic force of those shots. It can take maybe... what? Another two or three shots?" And I know, even with my eyes closed, that Marissa's question is directed towards Carmen, who'd cast the spell.

"If that," she grunts. "I'm surprised it took this many shots already. I guess my Magic has gotten stronger."

"Well, we need to figure something fast," Marissa tells us, stating the obvious.

I still have my eyes closed; I'd been focusing on the life-force of the sniper. Can I get to them quickly enough? Tallen's bite had certainly given me great speed. But, would I be fast enough, running full out, to get there unscathed?

I doubted it. I'm sure I would get maybe twenty feet or so, and then would get a bullet to the head. I can't Portal to them, since I would need to have the location behind the sniper in my P.D.A. to open a Portal too. How am I going to cross the quarter-mile or so between us and the sniper without, literally, biting the bullet?

But then I grin, as another spell comes to mind—though, I doubt it was meant to be used like this. The spell is called Teleport, and it is meant to teleport something, small items, though, across short distances, of maybe twenty feet. I imagine some lazy Magus came up with it to snag the remote control or something from across the room.

But, here, I was thinking of using it to Teleport myself a good quarter mile or more, to just behind our target. Here is where I hope that where everyone thinks my being close to level twenty Magus would be handy because I will need to punch a lot of power into the spell to move myself.

With my eyes still closed, I focus on the target and where I want to land. I can feel that they are about twenty feet up in the air. So I don't want to pop up behind them since I would end up falling those twenty feet to my death, or more likely to a broken leg or sever ankle injury, at the least.

Gathering power, I push it into the Teleport spell, but I don't finish the casting. I keep pushing power into the spell, as I somehow know I will need it, to Teleport that far. When I think I have enough power, I finish my casting of Teleport and, with a displacement of air that even I can hear—a loud *crack* as air rushes to fill the space I just occupied—I shift.

With a suddenness that surprises me even though I had been expecting it, I move from one location to this new location, which was ten feet past my target, behind a large tree, where I can stay hidden. Moving slowly, so that I don't make any noise, I look around the trunk of my tree and up.

I don't see anything at first, but thanks to my hearing, I hear a puff of sound. Looking at the location the sound came from, I finally make out my target. It's a body covered in a camouflage suit. And then I make out the long barrel of the sniper's rifle. The sniper crouches in a shooting stand that had been attached to the tree.

I know they are alone, since my Identify had already found every life form in the area. Other than the four in the castle, that included Carmen, Marissa, Tallen, Joey, and our sniper here—not counting the hundreds of smaller life-forces of little animals, we were alone.

Deciding that I need to take this sniper down fast, I take a closer look at the tree. I could burn it up, but that would likely cause a lot of collateral damage, and... well, the last thing I want to do is start a forest fire on Tallen's property.

But, to be honest, I want our target alive. I want to find out who they are, and who they work for. Think, Kevin. What spells can you use here that might help? Wait... Can I Teleport not just myself, but my target?

With a thought, I use my communication stone to call Tallen.

"Kevin?" Tallen answers, and I can hear the confusion in his voice at me calling him during a firefight.

"Do you have a cell inside that castle?"

With a puzzled tone that comes through the call clearly, he asks, "A cell? Do you mean a jail cell?"

"Yeah. I have a plan."

"Well, not really. I'm sure the castle had them before, but the castle's interior was renovated about fifty years ago, and I had the dungeon modified into a wine cellar. Why, what's your plan? And where the fuck did you go, anyhow? We heard a small thunderclap, and then you were gone."

"Yeah, I used Teleport. I'm looking at my target. It's a person in camo-suit in a tree stand."

Even though I can't see him, I can imagine Tallen's mouth open in shock as he asks me, "Wait. You cast Teleport on... yourself?"

"Yeah. I'll explain later. But we need to do this fast."

"Can you teleport the target to my office?"

"I think so," I say, thought I'm not sure.

"Trust me. It has a Magical barrier. If you can send them there, they won't get out. Though, if they have weapons…"

"Well, I was going to Teleport them without their sniper rifle, but they might have a handgun or a knife."

"The knife we can deal with. A handgun might be harder."

Looking back up at my target, I check to see if they have a sidearm, and I notice a holster on their left hip.

"They have one I can see, but I can't tell if they have anything hidden."

"Teleport them, if you can, and then you will need to explain to me how the fuck you are doing it." He pauses. "We will deal with the rest, just let me tell the girls really fast."

"All right."

Thirty seconds later, he comes back. "Done. And by the way, Carmen says—and I quote—"that boy needs to show me his damn tricks."

Laughing internally, as I don't want our sniper to know I'm here, I tell him, "Hell, I didn't know I could do it, until I tried."

"Can you Teleport yourself and the target?"

With hesitation, I explain, "I don't know. It took a shit ton of power to Teleport myself behind the sniper. My plan was to jump up to them and touch them, casting Teleport to send them somewhere. I know your office, since you gave us the tour last night, but I'm not sure I can do it to myself as well."

"You know what? You get them into my office, and we can deal with the rest. Just let us know when you cast Teleport and we will rush into the castle."

"Sounds good; I will tell you when. Stay connected."

CHAPTER TWENTY-FOUR

Taking a deep breath, I pre-cast Teleport. Until I'd considered doing it, I didn't know I could. But it seems I can cast the spell, but hold back the final element of the incantation in my head—though it's not so much an incantation, as a set of rules that I need to follow. Which is odd, as I seem to be doing things that others can't do, or simply haven't tried?

Once I have put a shit ton of power into the spell, holding it just on the cusp of being cast, I gather myself. And then, before I chicken out, I rush out from behind my tree. As I do so, I also cast a second spell. I'd originally considered Fireball, but remember that minor issue of a big, uncontrolled fire in the middle of my friend's forest? Instead, I cast a minor spell called Boom.

It does precisely what it sounds like—creating a loud explosion of sound. I'm sure it made for one hell of a prank spell in whatever passed for a magic school amongst the Magical folk. But I'd cast it to the left of the sniper's tree.

The sniper's head snaps to the sound, and I take advantage of the distraction to rush forward. As soon as I get close enough to the sniper's tree, I flex my knees and jump. Normally, jumping twenty feet almost straight upwards would be impossible, but thanks to Tallen's Full Transformation—or whatever it was that he did to me—I was able to manage it. Barely.

But barely was good enough, as I just needed to touch my target. And I did.

When my hand slaps the sniper's foot, I unleash my Teleport spell, which had started to feel as if it was straining against my control, fighting its constraints. With a minor thunderclap as the air rushes in to fill the space where they had been, my target is gone. Since I had tasked the spell to shift my target only, and nothing that was with them or on them, as I fall back down towards the ground, I see a host of items fall with me to the ground or drop onto the small platform the sniper had crouched on.

The sniper rifle, the handgun, and hmm… shit, the sniper's clothing and other items. My feet hit the ground, and I look back up at the pile of stuff on the platform and then down at the stuff that fell around the base of the tree.

"Oops," I tell Tallen.

"Oops?" he asks, slightly out of breath.

I guess they are running from the car's protection with the Shield around it to his office.

"Yeah. Our target might be… uhh… naked."

Puzzled, he asks me. "Naked?"

"Yeah. My spell worked better than I intended. I made it so that my target Teleported where I wanted them to, but it seems I was too literal. Only the target got Teleported to your office, without anything they were holding... or wearing."

I hear nothing from him for a full ten seconds before he's starts laughing. "Are you telling me that you Teleported our target into my office, naked as a jaybird?"

"Pretty much," I tell him, and I can't help but chuckle.

"Oh, this should be interesting," he says, and I can imagine the predatory grin on his face that comes through clearly in his voice. Or, in this case, a Vampire's grin, which is worse.

Looking up at the mess of clothing and weapons, I frown, wondering if I should grab something. Deciding to play it safe, I grab the sniper rifle and the two handguns that I find in the pile of clothes on the platform. I don't find anything else, except for the clothing—not even a wallet.

I jog towards the castle in the distance. As I can run on my own, I don't bother using something so powerful as Teleport to get back to the castle's entrance. Once back at the vehicle, I find Joey there, standing there looking confused, his eyes wide.

"What the hell just happened?" he asks.

"Go ahead and put the car away for now," I tell him.

Looking at the weapons in my hands, he nods numbly. "Yes, Master."

I nod, not bothering to correct him, as he looks utterly confused. Jogging into the castle, I make for Tallen's office. When I get there, having expected them all to be clustered outside the door, I am surprised to find the door is open. I rush in, thinking the worse, but stop dead in my tracks.

Tallen, Carmen, and Marissa are staring down at a body on the floor—a dead body.

But it was the skin color of the body that made me stop in confusion. It wasn't any human skin color I had seen. The body has gray skin.

I frown, looking at the face. Whoever it had been—or whatever—was a male, if a male can be called beautiful. The male's gray skin almost has a silver sheen to it. He also has ears that taper back, exactly like an Elf's, and his eyes are closed.

"Is he dead?" I ask.

At my entrance, all three of my companions turn to look at me.

"No," Tallen says, and there's puzzlement in his voice. "But, we found whatever this is out cold on the floor. Did you knock him out first?"

"No," I say, shaking my head. "I merely touched his foot and Teleported him. I'll admit, I didn't expect him to be Teleported without his clothing. But it was rather convenient; I was able to send him without these," I say, holding up the sniper rifle and pistols.

"Damn," Carmen says in appreciation, taking the rifle from me. "These aren't cheap. It's a Barret M95, and it's got a decent suppressor. That's why we didn't hear the shots. It uses a .50 caliber BMG. No wonder my Shield was going down so quickly."

Tallen squats down next to the body, looking at it.

"You know what this is, don't you?"

I look down at the body once more, and take a guess, which is more a statement of the obvious.

"A Dark Elf?"

Nodding, he says, "A Dark Elf. I have never seen skin that color before."

"Which tells us that we really are dealing with Dark Elves," Carmen says with a frown.

Marissa asks us, "Can we wake him and ask him questions?"

"Let's see if we can wake him up," Tallen says. He pokes the naked body, hard.

The Dark Elf groans, but doesn't wake up.

Tallen looks up at me. "Care to try?"

"Sure," I say, not sure exactly what he expects me to do, but I bend down and slap the man on the face. I get with the same results—he groans but doesn't wake up. Deciding to be more forceful, I slap him harder.

That worked.

His eyes pop open, and that's when I see that his eyes are not like mine, or anyone I know, really. They're pure black. I mean, some of the goblins I have met have black eyes as well, but they also have red in them—usually because they are bloodshot. But this guy's eyes are pitch black, with no white sclera like a human, or any of the other races I have met.

When he sees us all surrounding him, he glares up at us. When his glare turns to me, though, he utters something in a language I can't understand: "Noma lomtia manchi. Noma me le maan."

I turn to Tallen, but he's frowning. "We don't speak that language," he tells the Dark Elf.

The Dark Elf sneers. "Of course you don't," he says in a deeply accented English. "I would not expect a fucking Vampire to speak the Tongue."

"The Tongue? You mean, Dark Elvish?" I ask him with a raised eyebrow.

At my mention of Dark Elvish, his head snaps back to me in shock.

"Yes," I tell him. "We know what you are. Care to explain why you were trying to kill us? With human guns?" I hold up the two handguns I had taken from him.

"May the Darkness take my soul," he shouts suddenly, springing up from the floor and rushing at me with his hands open to grab me.

But, just as quickly, I kick out. My boot catches him unexpectedly in the head, knocking him over backward like he'd bounced off a brick wall. But he's spry, and without pause, he turns his sudden backwards momentum into a flip. Like that, he's back on his feet, and growling at me.

"You shall not take me alive."

But then suddenly, he has vines all around him, vines that shoot out of the office's wooden floor—well, smashing through it more like.

He struggles, but it's pointless, as the vines have completely encased his legs and torso, binding his arms to his sides.

"No use struggling," Marissa tells him. "You won't be getting out of those."

He turns his head towards her and spits, but suddenly there's a Shield in front of her, causing the spittle to fall to the ground.

"You lowborn shall get nothing out of me," he says. Sneering and looking at me, he continues, "Why is this human even with you?"

Tallen snorts at the Dark Elf. "You might want to start talking, or I will let this human have you."

The Dark Elf looks closely at me, his intense gaze traveling up and down, and then he frowns. "You smell different," he says.

"What the fuck is it with all of you saying I smell funny?" I say, throwing my hands up in the air in annoyance. "It's not like I don't use the same soap the rest of you do."

Marissa chuckles and Carmen rolls her eyes.

"But, never mind that." I step into his personal space. "Why are you Dark Elves killing Magical folk?"

"You mean the lowborn?" he asks with that same arrogant sneer.

"Lowborn?" Carmen asks.

He turns to her, eyeing her up and down. "You would be a Changeling, and so is she," he says, nodding towards Marissa. "He is a Vampire... but you," and now he looks back at me, with a puzzled look on his grey face. "You smell somewhat like a human, but also... not"

He looks around the office. "How did you get me here without me noticing? That took a lot of skill. I did not hear you even come up behind me. Was that bang from you, used as a distraction? Which one of you knocked me out and brought me here?" Finally, he looks a little discomfited, "And why am I naked?"

Carmen, Marissa, and Tallen all turn towards me.

"What?"

"You're the one who did it. Care to explain to Mister Dark and Haughty here what you did?" Tallen says, though it's obvious he is struggling to hold back a laugh.

"Not really," I say with a shrug. "How did you find out we were looking for the Dark Elves?"

At my question, the Dark Elf's eyes go wide, showing me slight whites around the edges. Okay, I think, so their eyes aren't pure black, their pupils are just huge.

"Wait," my eyebrows climb into my hairline, "you didn't know we were after you?"

The Dark Elf doesn't answer. He simply stares at me, still shocked.

Sighing, I turn to my friends. "What now?"

"Well," Tallen says, tapping his chin thoughtfully. "We could torture him."

"I'm not so keen on that," Marissa says, disgust clear on her face. "No matter who or what he is."

Carmen beckons me over next to her with a smile. When I take a few steps back from our gray skinned captive, she beckons for me to lower my head. Putting her lips right up against my ear, she whispers a single word: "Coercion."

As soon as she says it, the spell comes to mind. And I can't help but snort. The spell Coercion is meant to be used on animals, to get them to do what you want. It supposedly wouldn't work for a magus on other sapient beings.

But, I was no normal magus. I wonder if I push enough power into the spell, if I can make it work on a person? It's worth a shot.

"You think so?"

"You've always got 'no' until you ask… only way to find out, is to try, right?" she says with a grin.

I look back at the Dark Elf, who stares back at me suspiciously. I also notice that Marissa and Tallen are giving me and Carmen the stink eye.

Shrugging, I nod. "What've we got to lose, right?"

I step back towards the Dark Elf, who tries to struggle and leans away from me, but he can't get far, as the vines bind him tight. As I get closer, he begins to struggle more and more. Just in case, I cast Shield in front of me.

At the casting of my spell, the Dark Elf's eyes snap up to my face—and if they were wide before, now they are panicked, and he has started to pant. He is terrified.

Better to do this quickly, I think, before he gives himself a heart attack. Bringing up my power, I push it into the Coercion spell, but I hold back the final element and let the Magic build. Once I have enough, which takes about a dozen seconds, I slap my hand against his cheek and cast the spell.

The spell flows through my arm and hand, but unlike other spells I have done, this one produces a concussive blast of sound that blows everything around us back, as if a massive gust of wind had suddenly come through a window, whipping the girls hair all about and sending papers and such flying.

The Dark Elf's eyes suddenly glaze over, his mouth going slack.

"Well," Tallen says in an impressed voice. "That seemed to work."

CHAPTER TWENTY-FIVE

"Did it work?" Marissa asks me, followed immediately with, "And if it did, care to explain what that was?"

Carmen is grinning like a Cheshire cat.

"Yep—at least I assume so. From the glazed look our friend here is giving us," I say, pointing to him, "it seems that Coercion can be used on other sapient beings; it just requires a hell of a lot more power than normal."

"Let's find out," Tallen says, walking up to the Dark Elf.

"What's your name?" he asks him.

The Dark Elf doesn't reply, simply keeps staring off into space.

Tallen scowls and looks at me, waving me forward towards the Dark Elf.

Nodding, as I have a feeling this is a spell where the caster is the one who has control, I ask the same question Tallen just asked the vine-bound Dark Elf.

"What is your name?"

"Ilo."

"Well, it seems to work," I tell the group. "What should I ask him?"

"Why was he trying to kill us?" Marissa says.

Nodding, I turn back to Ilo and ask him that question.

"My target, if they were to show up, was to kill them."

"Who was your target?"

"I was to kill the Count, Sir Tallen Voldermoten."

"How did you know he would be here?" I continue, before Tallen can ask me to ask that. Since I too am curious to know how they knew we would be here, at this castle, today.

"We didn't. We are watching all his properties. Wherever he shows his head, we are to take him out."

I look over at Tallen, seeing that he looks paler than usual— which is saying a lot, since he was already fair-complected as it was, being a Vampire.

"Why him?"

"To disrupt things on our world with the rest of the Magical lowborn.," he slowly mumbles.

I guess a side effect of the Coercion spell is a general lethargy.

"You call us lowborn? Why?" Tallen me to ask the dazed Dark Elf. I relay the question.

"Because you all are. We Dark Elves are the rightful owners of this world, and everyone else are lowborns. Humans are even lower—they are nothing more than animals."

"Well, I suppose I can guess how we humans would fare in your dark new future. But, why go after the other races?" I ask him.

"Because they have what was taken from us," Ilo responds.

"You Magical folk took something from them?" I ask, turning to Carmen, Marrisa, and Tallen.

They all give me blank looks, confused.

"I don't know what that could be. Hell, until a day ago, I didn't know Dark Elves still existed. The only time I'd even heard of them were in the closed histories—except in stories one tells to children to make them behave," Tallen states.

I look at Marissa and Carmen, and they both shake their heads, indicating they have no clue, either, about what Ilo is talking about.

Something that had been bothering me for a while—ever since learning what the Dark Elf Assassin's daggers could do —clicks. The pieces all come together. I blurt out, "You no longer have Magic!"

Everyone in the room jerks back in shock at my exclamation.

Ilo, because I guess I figured it out, and Tallen and the two girls because they had not even considered it.

"Wait," Tallen says, staring at Ilo, "ask him if that is the case."

"Your race can't do Magic?"

"We had Magic, until your fucking gods reduced us to what we now are. We are little better than filthy humans, now," he growls, and there is anger in his voice, despite the lethargic effect of the Coercion spell.

No, not anger… this is so far beyond anger. Calling this anger, would be like comparing a firecracker going off to a nuclear blast. This was in the realm of whatever lies several exponential degrees beyond hatred.

"What did our gods do?" Carmen is the one to ask what I had been about to query him about, but of course, he does answer her.

I repeat the question, as I had been doing; repeating the questions my friends had been throwing at Ilo.

"This was before I was born. This was done to us, during our fall from glory in our proper place as the rulers of this world." Sullen resentment burns in his black gaze. "We once ruled over all you lowborn races—until your gods took ours down, and reduced our might to little better than humans. But our day is coming. Once more, we shall be powerful and rule over all of you lowborn." His sullen gaze switches from my companions to me, "including you irritating humans."

"Shit," Tallen says, shaking his head in wonder. "I was never aware of this. I never knew our gods were directly responsible for the downfall of the Dark Elves. We assumed they had been all killed by the united Magical races when we'd had enough of their tyranny." He pauses. "Or so the closed histories say."

"Who else are you going after?" I ask, thinking that there is no way they are only going after the Count on Earth.

"I'm not familiar with my Elder's plans. I only followed my orders to fly here and do what I needed to do."

"How were you able to do it without Magic? To hide your different appearance."

Almost in a slur, he answers. "We have ways to use Magic still."

His accent was getting stronger and stronger, becoming difficult to understand.

I look at Tallen knowingly. "The daggers."

He nods. "Seems that while Magic was taken from them, they can still use it. I think that is how they are doing it. Using those daggers with the ancient script on them to drain Magic out of someone and place it into them."

"How are you able to use Magic still?" I ask, turning back to Ilo, at which I notice his head is tilted sideways.

"We use special daggers to remove Magic out of those who do not deserve it."

"Sounds like your assessment was spot on," Carmen tells me with a nod.

Tallen turns to Marrisa. "Can we get him to your father, Marissa? So he can hear these answers, and ask him questions?"

"I'm sure we...," she starts to say, but without warning, Ilo bites down hard, and I hear an audible *crunch*. His head suddenly falls forward, and blood starts dripping from his nose, eyes, and ears.

"Shit!" I curse, rushing forward to lay my hand on his neck to heal him, but I'm too late.

He's already dead, slumped over, only being held upright by the vines.

"Fuck!" Tallen screams in anger. "I had more questions for him!"

"So did I," I say, stepping back with a sigh. I shake my head. "So, what do we know?"

Tallen growls, turning to me. "That I was a target?"

"Yes. But something tells me that you aren't the only one. I have a feeling the Dark Elves are going after the more powerful members of each of the races here on Earth. It seems their activity has increased enough, of late, that we now know about them."

Carmen frowns. "Who else might be in their cross hairs?"

"Mavin's mother, the Queen!" Marrisa cries suddenly.

"Shit! Where is she?" I ask, turning to Tallen.

"She's here on Earth, in her own grove, I would assume. We need to get to her fast."

"But what about our mission in Waterford and the Stags?" Tallen points out. "Can we not simply contact her?"

Carmen starts shaking her head, adding, "She won't do anything if we try to send her a message. She's a royal Fairy —she will think she is safe within her Magic. But as we saw with our sniper here," she touches Tallen on the chest where he'd been shot, "you only survived because his shot missed your heart by inches."

Marissa nods, pointing out, "And we healed you within seconds, with the help of your regeneration."

"Yes, though it still hurts like a bitch," he says, rubbing his chest over the red-stained hole in his nice, expensive shirt with a sour expression.

I take out my communication stone and contact Mavin, as I don't have the Queen's contact info. I never thought to ask for it, and... well, she is a Queen.

"Hey, Kevin! What's up?" I hear the happy voice of Mavin in my head. Then he suddenly blurts out, "I didn't mean to eat all your cookies!"

"No worries, Mavin. Listen, where's your mom? I need to get in touch with her."

Even through the connection in my head, I can hear the confusion in his voice. "My mom? Why?"

"She might be in trouble. Hell, right now, a lot of leaders of the Magical folk on Earth might be in trouble. Can you call your mom and tell her she needs to keep her eyes open and her security alerted for, hmm..." I pause, trying to describe the threat they should be looking for, "people using sniper rifles or human-like weapons?"

"You mean non-Magical weapons?" he says, and I can picture the little Fairy hovering in the air, a confused look on his face.

"Exactly. I need you to contact your mom and tell her Kevin wants her to take all security precautions she can. We were just attacked in Scotland by someone using a sniper rifle. They shot Tallen."

"Oh, gods! Is he all right?!!"

"Yeah, they missed his heart by an inch, and we were able to cast Heal within seconds. I need you to contact your mom right away, and convince her just how important this is. Okay? Tell her that Tallen was almost assassinated."

"Who is trying to assassinate our leaders?"

"Hmm. Right now, that's on a need-to-know basis. But, if your mom needs to talk to someone, ask her to call Sir Targun, as I'm sure she has his contact info in her communication stone." Here I was taking a stab in the dark, but it made sense for Magical heads-of-state—or in this case, heads of races—to have the contact information for the Chief Councillor of the Galactic Council.

"Yeah," he quickly says, "that's standard with our leaders. All right. I will let her know. But Kevin, you need to tell me what is going on... when you can."

"No sweat, buddy, you will be one of the first ones I'll tell... when I can."

"Good," he says. "I will call my mom right now. Though please don't mention the cookies to her? Please! I was able to exchange credits and get twenty dollars American for you, so you can buy more."

With a snicker, I ask, "So you can eat them?"

"Well, duh!" he replies with a laugh, cutting the connection.

"All right," I say, looking at the folks watching me expectantly. "Mavin will contact his mother and tell her the severity of this threat. If she wants the details, she'll have to get them from Marissa's Dad."

"Good," Tallen says, nodding. "She's smart. She will know to contact the other Magical leaders here on Earth, and may even reach out to the other worlds. The question now is, are these Dark Elves only on Earth, or already on the other worlds?"

"From the way Ilo talked, I would assume it's only Earth. It seems it's only this planet that they want."

"So you think the other leaders, on the other worlds, are safe?" Marissa asks me.

With a sigh, I tell her, "I have no clue, really, but I can hope. In order to cross between the worlds, you need access to a PDA, right?"

"Yes, the only Magic that will let you travel between the worlds is your PDA and the Portal it opens."

"What happens, then, if everyone on Earth loses their PDA, or forgets a location in their Porting Device Assistant?"

"There are too many of us with the locations in our PDAs," Tallen says. "It would take the entirety of Magical beings on Earth to die off, for no one on Earth to be able to access the other worlds." He shrugs. "But, don't forget, the other worlds have people on them with PDAs who have the locations of places here on Earth, as well as locations of the other worlds in theirs."

"Well, that still leaves us with no clue as to where the hell this Dark Elf came from." I scowl down at the body. "But at least we now have confirmation that Dark Elves are real, and that they are behind the Silver Dagger murders. What do we do about the body?"

We all look down at the body of Ilo, who had slumped to the floor when the vines released him after his death.

"We could ask your Dad to take it?" Carmen asks Marissa.

"Hmm. Can't we just get rid of it?" she says with a frown.

"No," Tallen says, shaking his head. "We need to get a closer look at them. No one has seen a Dark Elf in a long ass time. I'm sure we can get some helpful information from a physical and Magical autopsy."

"Then that would mean my Dad," Marissa nods with a sigh.

"Let me call him and ask," I say to the room. At everyone's nod, I pull my comm stone out again, and I call Sir Targun.

"Kevin? Is everything all right?"

"Yes and no, Sir. So... hmm. How would you like to do an autopsy on a Dark Elf?"

"Ha ha ha, very funny," he says through the connection, though I hear he is far from amused.

"Well, then what should we do with the body we have here of a Dark Elf?"

"What!?!"

"We were attacked outside Tallen's castle, in Scotland. It seems Tallen was the target." I pause. "A Dark Elf assassin named Ilo tried to kill him this morning; the weapon used was a sniper rifle."

"You mean a Focus?"

"No. I mean a human sniper rifle."

With confusion in his voice, Targun asks, "How do you know, then, that they were a Dark Elf? And how in all the hells, do you know this Dark Elf's name?"

Ignoring his second question, I look down at the body and explain to Targun what the body looks like.

"Crap on a cracker! Where are you in Scotland, precisely?"

I look over at Tallen. "Targun is asking where your castle, is exactly?"

"Tell him I will open a Portal and come get him," Marissa says.

I relay what Marissa said, and Targun replies, "Good. Good. Give me thirty minutes or so. I need to grab some gear." He closes the connection, but not before I hear him shout, which I am sure he meant to do verbally: "Preeka!"

CHAPTER TWENTY-SIX

"Where's the body?"

I point behind me. We have moved away from the body, mainly to get away from the smell, as the body had released its bowels. Death isn't always clean.

Marissa had opened up a Portal and gone to get her father. He had come back through, with Preeka in tow. The little ugly goblin smiled up at me and waved.

I'd waved back at her—at least she's not glaring at me anymore.

Targun, for lack of a better word, runs to the body and throws himself down next to it, his hands hovering over it, almost afraid to touch it. Excitedly, he mumbles, "This is just incredible! They look exactly as the books I have describe them. Dusky gray skin, midnight black eyes, with dark hair, almost like tar!"

"Hmm. Is tar all that descriptive?" I ask no one in particular.

Targun turns and glares up at me.

Holding my hands up in surrender, I chuckle. "Fine. It's descriptive of hair."

He nods and turns back to the body, placing his hands on it. Suddenly, it's enshrined in a black cocoon of some sort.

"There," he stands. "I put the body in a statis pod. That should keep it from decaying. Preeka!" he shouts.

"Yes, Master?"

"I will need you to carry it for me... my old bones and all that," he says, waving her forward.

I'm about to say that there's no way that Preeka can carry the Dark Elf's body by herself, but I'm shocked to see just how strong goblins are. She scoots beside the black cocoon, propping it up on one side until she can slide a hand underneath it. Then, she lifts it over her head, like it weighs nothing.

I must have had a shocked look on my face, because Marissa comes over and hugs me, grinning up at me. She whispers, "Goblins are very strong, but also as they gain Magic for working for the other races, they physically change—getting stronger. Preeka has been working for my Dad for so long, that she is one of the most powerful goblins out there."

I shake my head and mutter, "Damn!"

"All right," Targun says, clapping his hands together and looking around to make sure he didn't miss anything. "I will let you know what I learn. If you find any more of these..." he points to the black cocoon encasing the Dark Elf. "You contact me right away. Okay? Here, take this."

He hands me a stone.

I look at the black stone. It's round, though much smaller than a communication stone or a PDA. "What's this?"

With a massive grin, he explains. "It's my own invention. That is what I call a tracker stone. It lets me open a Portal beside wherever that stone is."

I hear gasps all around, and notice Marissa, Carmen and Tallen all staring at Targun in shock.

"I assume that isn't a thing?" I ask, tapping my head. "I don't have any information on it."

"Nope," he says, his grin growing wider. "It's my own invention."

Marissa frowns. "Dad... Are you saying you invented a way to open a Portal to a location that someone doesn't have, as long as that stone is where they want to go?"

"Well," he says, turning to her, "it's not quite as easy as that. First, I had to create a new PDA to pair it with, as it needs to be on the same resonance as the target. Then, I had to create ten of those stones that are in tune with my new PDA." He winks. "It wasn't easy, let me tell you."

"My gods," Tallen says, awe in his voice. "This will change the way traveling will be done!"

Nodding firmly, Targun tells Tallen, "Yes. Which is why you all need to keep this to yourselves. If this gets out before I have fine tuned it, I will be inundated with calls."

"But you are okay with us using it?"

"Of course," he says, nodding my way. "That one," he points to the stone in my hand, "has been calibrated specifically to my PDA. If you get another body, I can open a Portal right to where you are."

"All right," I say, putting the stone away in my pocket. "I can do that. We are heading to Waterford to check it out and see if we can't find something more out about the Stags."

"Keep me posted." Targun grins. "I will be busy now with that," he says, pointing to Preeka and the black cocoon.

Taking out his PDA, there's suddenly a Portal in front of Preeka. Without waiting, she goes through it without being told.

Targun turns to us all. "You all be careful. These are new, dangerous times, and something tells me that we haven't seen the last of these Dark Elf assassins."

Sighing, Tallen is the one to respond. "I cannot disagree more. Something tells me something even bigger is afoot."

"Be safe," Targun repeats. Walking through the Portal, he and the black circle disappear.

"I guess we need to get going," Tallen points out uselessly. "Waterford awaits."

He takes out a cell phone and dials a number. "Joey? You still with us, my man? We are ready to go once more. Can you come around front with the car? Thanks."

Within minutes, it takes us that long to get back to the front entrance of the castle from Tallen's office, we reach the front door. Joey is waiting, and already has the back door of the big SUV open, ready for us to climb in.

"All good, sir?"

"All good," Tallen tells him. "We need to get to Waterford, as quickly as possible."

"I will get you to the ferry as fast as possible, Sir," the man nods.

"Just don't break too many laws," Carmen tells him with an impish grin.

"Law? Out here?" he snorts. "There isn't a cop 'round here for miles. We might come across one as get closer to Cairnryan, but that's it."

"Well, get us there quickly, and I promise you a bonus, next payday."

"Deal," Joey says with a big grin.

To say that Joey got us there quickly, would be an understatement. I'm pretty sure that he might need to replace the SUV's undercarriage, or at least check the wear on a tire or two. We crashed through so many potholes, I'm surprised the heavy vehicle didn't break an axle. But Joey got us to the ferry at Cairnryan as promised—fast.

That doesn't mean it was comfortable, though.

We arrived with nearly an hour to spare before departure. That gave us just enough time to hit up a T. F. Woodside & Co—a department store that advertised 'Menswear, Ladieswear, and Confections' in nearby Stranraer. I'm worried about losing Marissa and Carmen in the Ladieswear section, given how short we were on time, but they surprise me. The girls beat me back to the register with a cart full of clothes, toiletries, and three suitcases.

"Good idea," I nod at the suitcases over my armful of trousers, shirts, boxer briefs, socks, belt, and a jacket. Sometimes it's good to be married, I think—though I wisely keep that observation to myself.

Marissa smirks. "Figured you might not think of it. I grabbed you a toothbrush, too."

When we join Joey and Tallen on the ferry, each of us is pulling a travel bag across the deck behind us. Joey elects to stay with the car for the two plus hour trip. I'm feeling drained from our adventure earlier, so happily stretch out on one of the benches, my head in Marissa's lap. I fall asleep with her combing her fingers through my hair.

* * *

JOEY DROPS us off in downtown Waterford, and then takes off. He said he needed to refuel, but that if he hurried, he could catch the last ferry back to Scotland.

"Do you have any contacts here?" Carmen asks Tallen.

Shaking his head, Tallen tells her. "Not really. I have some in Belfast, but not in a smaller town like Waterford. Even in Scotland, most of my contacts are either in Glasgow or in Edinburgh—except for those who maintain the castle for me. Actually I have a cousin, third removed, who lives in Belfast." He frowns. "But, a small town like this? I don't bother. Though, now, if I find something here, I will make it a priority to ensure I have contacts all over."

"That's a lot of work," Marissa, tells him. "For so little return."

"Yes, but at least I will know what's happening in my own backyard."

"Fair," she tells him.

I snort quietly to myself. Tallen's lands in Scotland are four hours from the ferry—and now Ireland itself is his backyard? As they are talking, I look around. The houses here are old; I

mean, some are newer construction, but downtown Waterford is very much an older style.

"Ideas?" Carmen asks, from beside me. "What next?"

"Good question," Tallen says, coming up to join us while
looking around. "I don't know where to start."

"What about a Trace spell?"

"We'd need something to Trace with," Carmen says, shaking
her head, "but we don't have anything."

"Well, I have one of the handguns Ilo had," I say, lifting my
shirt and showing her the weapon tucked into my belt, then
just as quickly hiding it again. I don't want someone seeing
that I'm armed and calling the cops. The holster for it wasn't
a concealed carry, and I wasn't about to haul it around in the
thigh-rig the Dark Elf had for it—so this seemed the best
way to carry it. The second pistol we had left in Tallen's
office.

"Won't that just identify Ilo's location?" Carmen points out.
"Which, right now is not even on Earth?"

"Yes. But can't I modify the spell, so that it searches for a
person's race, and not the person themself?"

"That won't work," Tallen says. "You need to have blood for
that. And there is no blood on the gun, I assume?"

With a sour expression, I say, "No."

"What about DNA?" Marissa asks.

We all turn to her, each of us with our eyebrows raised.

"What?" she says, scowling at us. "I read books on Earth
sciences. If not blood, what about DNA—like from his skin

cells? I'm sure that if that was his gun, he had to have left some cells on it."

"Those glasses aren't just for looks?" Carmen teases her with a laugh.

Marissa snorts at Carmen, but there's no anger there, only laughter. And it's true. Those glasses definitely do it for me with Marissa. She looks so incredibly cute in them.

"Well," I say slowly, an idea coming to mind. "I might be able to work with that. Lets see," I say, putting my hand on the handgun's grip, but not letting it show. I focus on the spell I want. It's meant to be used to extract items from say, a rock, but maybe I can modify it to extract dead skin cells from the plastic checkered grip of the pistol?

I cast Extract, but instead of extracting a particular thing from a rock, I formulate the spell to extract the remains of what was once living. In this, since the weapon's grip is made of a sturdy plastic, the only once living things my spell should extract are skin cells from whomever had held it.

Without warning, in my mind's eye, I see an image—two images actually. One is of a human, and the other is an image of the Dark Elf. Does that mean the human is the one who sold him the weapon? I guess the second one would be Ilo.

"I think I've got it," I say, my eyes still closed, standing in the middle of the sidewalk. "I've identified two different types of skin cells. One is human, which I assume is from the human Ilo purchased the gun from. The other is our Dark Elf."

"Can you separate them, so that you don't go after Ilo's body?"

With my eyes still closed, I nod at Tallen's question. "Yes, I think so. The spell I am using is a modified version of

Extract. I was able to extract only two living things that had touched the weapon. Now, the trick is forcing the spell Find to use that to find a race, not the person."

"Kevin," Tallen says, and his tone makes me open my eyes. "You do understand that what you are doing has never even been attempted, or hell, never thought of, right?"

"I guess? I mean, the way you all use your Magic just seems so very... limited. I don't understand why you have never thought of using spells differently."

Sighing, Tallen says, "Because we aren't human. You humans have a knack for thinking, as you say, outside of the box. You all are about innovation and trying something new." He pinches the bridge of his nose. "It is one reason many of the other races are afraid of you humans. William has it right, in that we need to keep up with them—humans, that is—or we will be left behind."

Puzzled by his pessimism, I tell him, "How so? You have Portal's to travel with."

"Yes, but one day, your race will take to the stars. How many planets will you all discover? I don't think your race is up to space travel, across several galaxies anytime soon... but one day, you will be." He sighs. "And we Magical folk will be stuck on our eight planets, while you humans will have colonized... how many? How many humans will there be 500 years from now? I have seen some demographic data about humans in the year 500. It worked out to roughly 200 million humans across the entire planet." He arches an eyebrow. "How many of you are there now?"

As he's explaining this, I nod. "Well over 6 billion."

"Try more like 7.7 billion," Carmen snorts.

"While Magical folk number perhaps a little more than 10 million on all eight planets," Marissa offers.

"You see?" Tallen concludes, "We either work with you humans, or stay behind and live on our worlds, locked away from you."

"Sorry. I'm not interested in that," Carmen says. "I love my Magical roots, but I also love human things."

"Well, let's work on this problem first," Tallen says with a soft smile.

"Anything?" Marissa asks me.

I nod and cast Extract once more, but remove only the Dark Elf cells from the grip of the handgun. Focusing on this clump of cells, I cast Find, pushing much more Magic into it than I know the spell calls for. Suddenly, in my head, I have— somehow—the knowledge of what a Dark Elf *presence* is.

To say that it is a weird feeling would be a lie. It's almost like I'm a bloodhound, and can smell it. And there is evidence of that scent in this area. I end up sneezing.

"Are you all right?" Marissa asks me, concerned.

"Yeah," I tell her, rubbing my nose. "As odd as it sounds, I can now smell Dark Elf."

"Oh, nice! And?"

"And, let's just say that my nose detects a lot of them."

Tallen looks around carefully, concern on his face. "Shit."

CHAPTER TWENTY-SEVEN

"Like, how many?" Carmen asks nervously.

"I'm not sure, as this is new to me. I can tell you it's more than one, though."

"Close by?" Marissa asks, and she has her Focus out, which looks like a .357 Magnum. She has it tucked against her leg, with her body away from the road so no one can see it.

"Hard to tell," I admit, sneezing again. "I'm still getting the hang of this." I turn around, closing my eyes, trying to see if I can smell it more strongly in one particular direction. Sadly, no. It's all over the place.

"Can you cast Target on it?" Carmen suggests.

Opening my eyes, I look at her with a smile. "Oh, that might work." I do as she suggested, and I cast Target, but imagine it being for only one, not the multitude I smell. The problem with a scent, is that it doesn't tell me how long ago it was there. I could be smelling a Dark Elf who passed by here weeks ago, or one who came this way an hour ago.

How does a dog do it? Do they know the time frame? Does scent dissipate after a while at a calculable rate?

My thoughts are interrupted as suddenly, in my head, I get a heading—a single heading. I turn until I'm facing that direction. When facing it, I suddenly also get a distance marker. I don't point, in case we are being watched, but I quietly say, "There's one the direction I am facing, roughly five miles away."

"Five miles?" Tallen asks, taking his phone out.

I can see he has a map open on his phone. After tapping on it for a minute or so, he finally looks down at it and frowns. "If it's five miles from us, that would be either at the University Hospital or the Waterford Castle Hotel and Golf Resort."

"Damn, too bad Joey already left," Marissa says with a growl.

"We can hoof it. Though," Carmen says, looking up at the sky. "Did we want to wait until nightfall to check either of those places out?"

We all look at Tallen for feedback. He puts his chin in his hand, thinking about it. "I want to say yes; that way, we can go get a bite to eat and wait for the cover of darkness. But will they be there tonight?"

"I have one Dark Elf tagged." I shrug. "If they move, I should know it." I turn to Carmen with a frown. "Which, by the way, Target feels really... weird."

"Yes," Carmen says with a laugh, "It takes some getting used to. You have it now, so you can release the spell and call it up again when you need it. Maybe we can get some food, and you can cast it every hour or so to make sure our target hasn't moved?"

I look to Tallen for confirmation. This is his neck of the woods, so I defer to him. We might be here in our capacity as M.A.G.I. but I wasn't about to step beyond my comfort zone. Then again, these last couple of months have been nothing so far outside my freaking comfort zone, that I'm fairly certain I simply left it behind.

"I think that would be good. Let me phone Joey quickly and ask him what is a good local, quiet, place."

"Sounds good," I tell him.

Tallen already has his phone out, so he brings it up to his ear after dialing Joey's number. "Hey, Joey. No, I'm good. Listen. We need a local place to eat that is quiet and open late." He pauses, obviously listening. "Yeah. All right. I will try those. Thanks."

Putting away his phone, he looks back at us. "Joey suggested a small pub that his family owns near the water. Actually, that works out well, since he said it's on Outer Ring road—which is fairly close to either of our targets."

With Tallen—phone in hand—leading the way, we follow him. The five kilometer walk ends up taking us a good hour, but it was nice, and Tallen got to sightsee, just like he'd wanted to. I enjoy walking around and seeing the older buildings and homes. Having a beautiful woman hanging onto each arm makes the afternoon that much more pleasant.

Once on Outer Ring road, we finally find the pub that Joey had suggested. It is right next to a large mall with tons of parking. But, the place we want, is just beyond the shopping center parking lot, in a quaint building. Once there, we head inside. The place was two stories, but I can see that the upstairs must be living space, while the main floor is for the pub itself.

"Welcome!" I hear a female voice shout from the back of the room. "I'll be right out. Just grab a table. Doesn't matter where."

As indicated, we grab a table at the back of the room, well away from the door and the front window. We hadn't been sitting down for more than a minute, before an older woman in her sixties comes out of the back room—which I assume is the kitchen.

She stops at our table, and smiles. "Welcome to the Broom and Stick," she tells us in a thick Gaelic accent. "Are you the people that my nephew Joey said were coming by?"

"That we are," Tallen tells her with a charming smile. "I didn't know that Joey had such a beautiful aunt."

She turns to him and smiles but, but I see she's blushing as well. "Well. He said to make sure you are treated well. I understand you're the one who owns that castle where he works?"

"That I do. We are just here visiting the town, and we wanted something good to eat. He suggested your place."

"Of course he did," she says a snort. "Best place in town. Unless you want fast food—something like Subway, or KFC, which you can get in the mall," she says, waving back the way we had come, which included the parking lot of the mall. "Though the fastest thing about it is how quickly is races from yer gut to yer arse."

"No thanks," he tells her with a smile. "I much prefer real food."

"Well, that you will get here," she tells him with a smile.

"So what does the name Broom and Stick mean?"

She turns to Marissa, who had asked the question. "Ah," she says a laugh. "That would be from my mam. She believed in witches and such, 'an wanted to have it named after the supernatural. So when we were looking for a name, the hubby and I went with that."

"Nice," I tell her with a laugh.

"Now, can I start you all with a nice pint of ale?"

"I normally drink wine," Tallen says, but holds up his hand as she is about to say something. "But, if the ale is as good as you make the food out to be, I would be pleased to try one."

"And you three?" she asks with a raised eyebrow.

"I'm good with ale," I tell her with a smile.

"I'm down for ale," Marissa tells her with a grin.

"Ditto. Bring me two pints. I already know I will love the ale," Carman tells her with a chuckle.

"A woman after my own heart," she tells the blonde with a return chuckle.

She points to the table's end, next to the wall. "Menus are there. Pick what you want. But the special today is sea bass, with rice and steamed veggies, or Scotch Pie with gravy. The only thing we don't have today that's on the menu, is the cod or the salmon. The rest we have."

"What would you suggest?" Tallen asks her.

"I would go with the Scotch Pie. My husband made them, and he makes the best Scotch Pie in Waterford. Hell, he says the best in Ireland, but I think he is reaching for the stars with such boasting," she replies with a good-natured laugh.

"Then I am for the Scotch Pie," I tell her. Everyone else agrees.

"So, let me get you those Scotch Pies, but first, I will get you your pints after I put in the order."

"She seems nice," Carmen says out loud.

"Yes. Joey comes from a good family," Tallen says, nodding.

"How is it you have a castle in Scotland?" I ask him.

Tallen chuckles. "Because this is where I am from."

"What? But I thought you were from the USA?"

"Gods no," he says, laughing. "Remember, I am old. I said once that I am in my thirties, if you think about it in human terms. But that means that I am over two hundred years old."

Marissa giggles and taps under my chin, causing me to close my mouth.

"I used to live in Scotland," Tallen continues. "I was born there. That castle was once owned by my father. Though, the locals didn't know that. They just knew it was owned by some nobleman."

Carmen snorts. "I'm sure you own more than one castle here, then."

"Yes," he tells her with a grin. "I think I have nine castles around the world that I own? Three of them are in Scotland." He pauses. "Though I'm sure they are registered under false names and dummy corporations."

"Man," I say wistfully, "to own a castle."

Tallen looks at me contemplatively, and finally nods.

"I'm sure that can be arranged. You are, technically speaking, my foster son now. I think, as royalty, you need to have a castle of your own."

"Whoa!" I say, holding my hands up. "I wasn't asking for one, Tallen."

"I know," he replies with a laugh. "But we Royals, in the Magical world, have an image to uphold. And I can't have you appearing to be some poor destitute castoff, now. Can I? I will look into getting you a small castle when we get back. It might not be in Scotland, though."

"Dude. You seriously don't need to…" I begin, but Marissa's hand on my arm, cuts me off. I turn to her curiously.

"Kevin, let him. What we are talking about is not some human norm. What Tallen says is true. Since he bit you, and did the Full Transformation—or what he thought would be the Full Transformation—you are, in his eyes, his adopted son. And to the rest of the Magical world, you are as well."

Carmen smirks. "You are also human, who can do Magic. Not sure which claim to fame is more noteworthy."

With a frown, I turn back to Tallen. "What about your own children? Don't you have any sons or daughters?"

"I have none. I have not been so blessed—yet. But I am also still young. I am also missing something important."

Puzzled, I ask him. "You are?"

"A wife," he admits, just as our server comes back with a tray full of large glasses.

"Here we go," she says, setting the tray on the table and passing out five large glasses filled to the brim with a rich dark ale, foam touching the rims.

Carmen 'oohs' appropriately.

"Don't worry, I made sure to keep the foam to a minimum. None o' that shite here. Unless you're a tourist," she ends with a laugh. "I put in the order for the Scotch Pies. They should not take long."

Tallen looks up at her and smiles. "Thank you...?"

"Mary," she tells him with a smile and another blush.

"Thank you, Mary," Tallen returns her smile. "These are my friends, Kevin, Carmen, and Marissa."

Mary turns to everyone and nods. "Well. Welcome to Waterford. First time seeing Ireland? I assume with your accents, that you're American?"

"I am," I tell her with a smile.

Carmen replies, "Yep," with a grin.

"I'm from elsewhere," Marissa says with a smile, but doesn't go into it.

Nodding, Mary looks back at the kitchen, when she hears her name being called.

"Right. That would be the hubby asking for my help. Be back soon, folks."

"She seems nice," Carmen says, grabbing two of the tall glasses for herself and taking a sip from one of them.

"Oh, gods! This is so good!"

I take mine and bring it up to my lips, taking a sip. My eyes widen with pleasure. "Jesus, this stuff tastes so much better than that swill we call beer!"

"Doesn't it? I keep barrels of this stuff in my castle. I would say that this is probably Tennent's Lager." He frowns. "They are a bit newer. Unfortunately, some of the older breweries are no longer around."

"Clarify 'newer'?" Carmen asks with a raised eyebrow.

"Fine," he says with a laugh. "They have been around since something like 1880. There's another Irish brewery that has been around since the seventeen-hundreds, but their stuff is much harder to get. I do keep a keg or two of the good stuff, but it's in my cellar in California."

"Wait," Carmen says, turning to him quickly. "Is that the stuff you made me try two years ago at your party?"

Tallen doesn't reply, only nods while bringing his glass to his lips. With a grin, he takes his first sip.

Carmen sits back in her chair with a thoughtful look. "Damn. Now I need to try and get some, while we are here."

Mary breaks into our conversation by coming back. "Here we go," she says happily. "Four Scotch Pies with gravy."

She places a plate in front of me, and I look down. It's a small, flaky-crusted pie, the size of a personal chicken pot pie. It smells fantastic. I can see steam coming out of the slits in the pastry.

"Oh wow," Marissa says, sitting up. "That smells and looks amazing!"

"That's me own husband's recipe. Has been in the family for over a hundred years. As a bonus, he said to give you all this."

She takes another plate off her tray and sets it down in front of all of us, right in the middle of the table.

I look at her curiously. It's a deep cooking tray, with something that looks like cheese on top.

"It's called Scottish rumbledethumps. It's a mixture of fried up veggies with shredded cabbage, onions, sauteed and mixed with mashed potatoes, then it's baked with cheese on top until it's golden-colored like that."

"My gods," Tallen cries in delight. "I haven't had that since I was a kid!"

"Enjoy!" Mary says with a big smile and walks away.

"Dig in, folks," Tallen says, grabbing the spoon that was in the rumbledethumps and scooping himself out a large portion, placing it next to the Scotch Pie on his plate.

Once we have all served ourselves, we all dig in. Something tells me we will need the energy from all this food later tonight.

CHAPTER TWENTY-EIGHT

"You're sure they're in there?" Tallen asks me.

"Yeah. The target is in there. I can't pinpoint what floor or specific area, but I know they're in the hospital," I tell him, nodding at the building in question.

"Damn it!" Tallen curses in annoyance. "I had hoped they would be in the resort. There is a lot less security there. What would a Dark Elf be doing in a hospital?"

I don't bother answering as, frankly, I have no clue what a Dark Elf might be doing in a human hospital.

"Do you think they took over the hospital?" Carmen suggests.

"For what reason?" I ask, a puzzled look on my face.

"Maybe they need human doctors?" Marissa guesses.

Tallen nods, and says, "Only one way to find out."

"We go in," I say, nodding. "But should we wait until it's dark? We still have another hour or so of daylight."

"Makes sense. Unless you have some trick you can think of to get in there unnoticed while it's still light out?"

I shake my head at Tallen. "Not really."

"Let's see if we can use Hide, and move around to the back, through the bushes," Carmen says, pointing to the side of the hospital where it borders a small glade of trees.

Nodding, I cast Hide, knowing that the spell itself creates an effect such that if anyone who is lower than me in level, which should be everyone, would subtly be encouraged to look the other way. But, seeing as I am apparently above level fifteen, doesn't that mean even the girls and Tallen should end up looking away from me—as if hearing a noise or a distraction? I don't know exactly how it works—it's Magic.

Did I mention how much I fucking love Magic?

Once I feel the spell settle on me, I turn back to the girls, and find Carmen is shaking her head, as if trying to clear it of something. With a sour expression, she tells me, "Remind me to look away when you cast that spell. Gods, that felt weird." She presses one hand to her belly. "Watching you cast the spell and then being forced to look away wasn't much fun for my stomach."

"Tell me about it," Marissa says with the same level of sourness.

"I'm so used to being the stronger Magus," Tallen says emphatically. "That that was the oddest feelings."

With a grin and a shrug of my shoulders, I tell them, "If it's any help, I'm not used to being a Magus—weaker, stronger, or otherwise."

"A level fifteen plus Magus, to boot. At least you aren't letting it go to your head," Marissa says with a bigger grin. "Otherwise, I would have to kick your ass."

"I'm not sure you can anymore," Tallen tells her with a chuckle.

Marissa looks at me, eyes me up and down, and snorts. "You may be right. But I have the experience, and I fight dirty."

"Doesn't help if he has the speed," Carmen reminds her, "But," and now she is the one eyeing me up and down, "I'm sure the two of us can tag team him."

"You know I'm right here, right?"

Both girls turn to me, their grins even more prominent, causing Tallen to snort in laughter.

"Shall we, ladies?" he asks them.

Once we are on our way, I look around, making sure no one can see us. The interesting thing about a spell like Hide, is that it works on not just human's—and even Magical folk's—eyes, but also on electronic ones.

Anyone looking at the camera feed, or even viewing this recording, would be affected the same way. The Magic attached itself to the resulting images, and if someone were to look at the recording, they would not see us.

How? No freaking clue. It's Magic.

"Stop," I say suddenly, feeling as if something had walked over my grave. If I had a grave.

"What?" Tallen asks, turning to me.

"I just felt something wash over me. Almost like someone cast a Find spell."

"Shit. You think they're on to us?"

I stand still and slowly turn around, checking out our surroundings. There are some people walking around, but they are far from us and aren't looking our way.

Carmen closes her eyes and lifts her hand. I feel power being called up, and a spell being cast. With her eyes closed, she frowns.

"There's a spell here. It's not that we are being observed, it's that there is a barrier in place, though it is very weak. Our Hide, thanks to Kevin's level, is holding. But, that tells us that there should be more Magic traps or wards around the hospital."

"Okayyyy," Tallen intones slowly. "That's not normal. Something is going on in this hospital."

He turns to me. "Should we cast Shield on each other, just in case?"

"Hmm," I say, thinking it over. "What if it's someone powerful? We should let me cast the spell. At least the Shield will be the strongest we can use."

"That might be a good idea," Carmen tells me.

I nod, and cast the spell Shield four times, saving myself for last. Once I feel it settle on me, I nod to Tallen. "We are good."

"Damn," Tallen says with a snort. "I don't recall ever having a Shield this powerful on me before. I might have to hire you to cast it on a regular basis."

Grinning at him, I say, "Well, being a Count, you can probably afford my fees."

"Fees?" he asks, eyes narrowing dangerously.

"Need to make money somehow."

Tallen looks at me as if I just said something incredibly stupid. Turning to Marissa, he asks, "You haven't told him?"

Shrugging, but blushing, Marissa replies. "No. There was no reason to."

I look at her curiously.

Carmen snorts.

"What?" I ask, confused.

"Not the time," Marissa growls.

"When *is* a good time?" Carmen tells her.

Sighing, she nods. "Fair enough." She turns to me and looks up at me, almost nervously.

"You know how I lived in that apartment building by myself? It was cheap, but not super cheap?"

"Yeah." I frown. "Like how you lived, maybe not on the bottom floor, but not the top floor either?"

"Correct. Well, that was my personal choice. I could have lived on the bottom floor. That I didn't, was only because I didn't want to use my Dad's money."

"Wait. But, your Dad is the Magical equivalent of a government functionary, isn't he? They voted him onto the Galactic Council as the Lead Councillor?"

As I'm asking this, all three begin to shake their heads.

"Not quite. My Dad's position is given to the most powerful person in all the worlds. Lead Council members are more powerful than Kings or Queens... or a Count," she says, nodding towards Tallen.

I drag a hand down my face, not sure where this is going. I mumble, "All right..."

"In his capacity as Lead Councillor, my Dad is in on many big deals, from which he profits. And though my Dad's position has a slim possibility of being taken over by someone even more powerful than him, Lead Councillors are paid handsomely—so they aren't tempted to take bribes and such."

"There's someone more powerful than your Dad vying for his job?" I blurt out.

All three of them look at me without answering. Marissa hides a smile behind her hand, Carmen snickers, and Tallen rolls his eyes. Then it clicks into place.

"No fucking way," I say, shaking my head hard.

"Yes. Fucking way," Tallen says with a snort of humor. "You will most likely be tagged next year to be the next Lead Councillor."

"I don't want the position! But what does that have to do with money?"

"You know how my Dad lent you money to buy our apartment on Vraka?" Marissa asks.

"Yeah. He also got me a bigger signing bonus, as the first human in M.A.G.I."

"Did he ever mention my dowry?"

"What? No! But that's an antiquated system!"

"Maybe." Marissa shrugs. "But, it's how our world works. You humans might have done away with it, but we still have them, though it's mostly only in the Magical worlds. By marrying me, you get my dowry."

"All right. So that's… what? A couple thousand credits?"

She shakes her head.

"Tens of thousands of credits?"

"Try more like ten million credits."

I stare at her, my brain suddenly shutting off at the enormous number. Finally, I blurt out. "But… why?!"

"Because," she says with a shrug. "I've had lots of people try to date me, just hoping to get a shot at marrying me—all for that dowry. "

"Fucking pigs," I growl. "Men are idiots."

"Oh, it wasn't just men." Marissa shakes her head. "You forget we are not only not monogamous but also that marriage is supposed to be about two people in love, not just when that person is of the opposite sex."

"Wow," I say. "So what you're saying is, I'm not only powerful, but rich, too?"

"Yes," Carmen answers. "But, that's all right. We're here," she says, putting an arm around Marissa's shoulders, who I see doesn't glare at her but nods, as well, "to make sure you don't let it go to your head."

"Oh, to be young again," Tallen says wistfully.

"And what about you?" I ask him.

"What? Me marry you? No thanks," he says with a grin. He eyeballs me up and down. "You're not my type."

"Meaning, you don't have a vagina," Marissa stage whispers.

Carmen giggles.

Tallen grins at her. "Precisely. Now, shall we get on with our mission, and we can talk about your finances later?"

"Sure," I say, hesitantly. "Lead on"

Still in a daze at finding out that I am rich, I follow the three of them, taking the back spot in our group. Every now and again, Marissa would look over her shoulder at me and smile, and then shake her head. Carmen would lean in and whisper in my wife's ear, making her giggle, and then both of them would look back at me.

Tallen, on the other hand, just smiles and shakes his head.

My thoughts are interrupted as we come out of the woods next to the hospital. There's a side road here, that leads up to a docking bay. The doors are closed, though, and no one is around. Knowing we are good, we head over to the door, and try it. It's locked. Tallen puts his hand against the doorknob, and I feel him cast a spell. The door *snicks*, unlocking with Magic.

Once we are inside, I look around to find we are in a docking bay filled with pallets of stuff wrapped in plastic, or stacked in boxes. It seems there is a bit of everything, here, from medical appliances to cleaning supplies.

"Where?" Tallen asks me.

I close my eyes, and concentrate. I'd found that if I kept my eyes open, my Target spell lost some of its strength, making it harder to understand what my spell was telling me. I'm sure I can focus, with my eyes open, but this makes it easier to pin point our target. I point my upward, towards the back of the hospital.

"What floor?"

I frown and focus on that, trying to imagine the height of each floor in a three-dimensional construct in my mind's eye. After adjusting this estimate a time or two, I finally come up with a rough number.

"They are on either the third or the fourth floor. I'm not sure which. But it's in the back of this wing of the hospital."

"Over here," Carmen calls out.

I open my eyes and look over to where her voice came from. She is at a desk and is looking at something on the wall.

It's a map of the hospital wing we are in—the east wing. Looking at the schematic for the third and fourth floors, we eventually rule out the third floor, since it is labeled MRI and Radiology. The fourth floor is more of what it might be. It's labeled as being a Palliative Care ward.

"You sure they won't be hiding there?" Tallen says, tapping the area on the map.

Carmen frowns. "Not sure if they can be around radiology equipment like an MRI. I know that it affects us Magical folk, but I'm not sure how it would affect them. It's not deadly, but it does make us nauseous."

"Guess only one way to find out," I say shrugging.

"Fourth floor it is," Carmen agrees, taking point heading to the back of the building where, according to the map, there is a stairwell leading upwards.

Just as Carmen is about to push open the door to the stairwell, I bark out. "Stop!"

Carmen freezes, her hand scant inches from the door, and looks back at me curiously. I can sense Magic on the door. Tallen quickly steps forward to study the door, while Carmen steps back and does the same.

She holds up one hand with a hiss. "It's a fucking Sigil."

"Which one?" Tallen asks her quickly.

Carmen closes her eyes again, and frowns, her hand still up, palm out. Finally, she snaps her eyes open, and they are wide with fear. "Fucking hell; it's an Explosion Sigil. And a big one, too! It would have taken out this entire section of the building—but it's only triggered if another Magus touches the door."

"How the hell did a Dark Elf cast that spell? Sigils take a shit ton of Magic. I should know. I have them all over my club."

"Yes, we know," Carmen says, reminding me of when I'd found one simply going down the stairs into his club—though I did disable that one, almost without thinking.

"Can you disable it?" Marissa asks Carmen nervously.

"Not that one; it's on the other side of the door, so I can't touch the Sigil."

"Ideas?" Tallen asks us.

"Take the elevator?" I suggest.

With a sour expression, Tallen growls, "Not much choice."

"Elevators it is," Marissa says with a sigh. "Gods, I hate elevators."

"You seemed fine before," I tell her.

"That's because I didn't want to seem weak in front of you. But I hate those things. I have no problem what-so-ever with stairs... lots and lots of stairs."

Going up to her, I hug her. "I don't think you are weak."

Looking up at me, she smiles. "Thanks, Kevin. Now, let's get this over with."

I nod to Carmen, and she takes point again.

CHAPTER TWENTY-NINE

Once in the elevators, I drop Hide, since we didn't someone to walk into us and have them freak out, not being able to see us. We are lucky, in that given the late hour, there aren't many people around. We have the elevator to ourselves, heading to the fourth floor.

"Here we go," Carmen states, once the doors open on the floor we want.

Carmen holds up a hand before we step out and whispers, "Sigil."

"Seriously?" Tallen whispers as well, his tone echoing his annoyance.

"Seriously. Though now that I know to look for them, I found this one easily enough. It's one I have used before, so I know its signature. It's a Warning Sigil, meant to let someone know when another Magus has entered into their area.

"How the fuck are Dark Elves using so much Magic, for a race that had it taken away from them!" Tallen growls.

"Have Magical folk had a lot of people go missing over the years?" I ask.

All three of my Magical friends frown at the question, but it's Carmen who supplies the answer. "Well... Yes. There are always missing people reports coming into M.A.G.I. We typically assume they are just those who got into trouble with humans, or one of the other factions. We might be Magical folk, but we aren't like you humans. We have our differences, and battles are still a common way to solve disputes—to take it out back, so to speak, and figure things out."

"So it stands to reason, that some of those missing Magical folk may have been taken to have their Magic siphoned from them."

"Fucking hell," Marissa says in horror. "I remember seeing in the annual report from last year, that we had over 3,000 missing people reports—from every race."

"How many of those were on Earth?"

Thinking about it, her head tilting slightly with her intent focus, she says, "Hmm. Maybe a third of those?"

"So, in other words, over 1,000 Magical folk. If we assume that half of those beings were killed by Dark Elves to siphon their Magic, that's over 500 souls gone."

"Can we take care of this first, and talk about that afterwards?" Marissa says. "I might need to write a report about this."

"What, that we know about Dark Elves?" I ask her with a raised eyebrow.

"Oh shit...Right," she growls.

"Can you get rid of it?" Tallen asks Carmen.

"Yeah. Whoever placed this one was shitty at it. See," she points to the inside of the elevator door. Where the door opened, there was a space, and just slightly back from the wall, facing the elevators, is the Sigil. But it looks odd; it doesn't match what I have in my head.

"What am I missing?" I ask, not sure what it is, but I know that it's wrong.

"The trailing end of that line," Carmen says, "it should have gone upwards, not down. That was a waste of Magic, since now, it's slowly leaking. Meaning they must have to keep replenishing it. The only reason I caught it, was that leakage."

She slowly reaches a finger between the elevator doors and into the mechanism, easing her finger towards the broken line. Now that I know what I am looking for, I see the sudden flash of power and the Sigil disappear in a puff of white smoke.

"There," she says, rubbing her finger clean on her clothing.

"Are there any others?" Tallen asks, looking around.

Carmen closes her eyes and slowly turns around in place. Finally, she shakes her head. "No. If their Sigils are all created like this, we should be good to find them."

"Well, the one before this was hidden," I point out.

With a sour expression, Carmen frowns at me. "Then we better be on our toes."

"Great," I say with a chuckle. "At least we have my Shield up."

"And we might need it. Now, shall we go before someone wonders why we are holding up the elevator?" Marissa says, grabbing my hand and dragging me out of the elevator.

Once out, I look around, and see what looks like your typical hospital ward, with a nurses' station and a waiting room. There is currently no one there, though. It was late, so the lights have been turned down. All was quiet.

"Nothing," Tallen quietly informs us.

"I guess…" I start to say, but without warning, there is a loud gunshot, and Tallen, who had been standing next to me, goes flying backward, as if propelled.

"Shots fired!" Marissa shouts.

I throw myself away from where the shot came from, and just in time, too. I feel my Shield get clipped, sending me sprawling in a tumbling mass of arms and legs. But then I'm safe, behind a wall.

Carmen and Marissa had both done the same thing, jumping into action, they'd thrown themselves sideways, one to either side of the hall. Marissa had jumped to the same side that I had, and my getting clipped with what I assume was a shot from whatever gun had been fired, threw me sideways into her.

We end up in a tangle, with her on top of me.

"Sorry," Marissa cries. Getting off of me, she suddenly has her Focus in hand and aimed upwards, as she flattens herself against the wall. Quickly, she peeks around the corner, but then snaps her head back.

A shot goes right through where her head had been and slams into a wheelchair behind us, causing the chair to spin in place.

"Shit," she growls.

"Keep your heads back," Tallen informs us pointlessly. He is lying sideways, half behind the nurses' station and grunting in pain. "Fucking hell, that hurts!"

I check him over quickly, and there is no blood, thank the gods. His Shield held.

"You got hit?

"No, my head bounced off the floor when I fell. Thank the gods your Shield held up," he growls. "Why do they always shoot me first?!"

"Because of your good looks?" Carmen offers.

"Ha ha, very funny," he growls again, rubbing the back of his head, where I assume he'd smacked it against the floor or the wall.

"Did anyone see who the shooter was?" I ask, knowing they know I'm asking if it was a human or a Dark Elf.

"I did," Carmen says. "Kevin, are you all right?"

"Yeah," I grouse, "I got hit, but my Shield saved me. Though, I can tell it's now at a third of its strength." I also noticed that, without thinking, I had called up my Focus. I now have a dagger in my hand as black as midnight.

"Man, how powerful is that Shield of yours? If I had cast it, that attack would have slammed through mine," Marissa tells me.

"Don't care," Carmen pipes in. "I'm just glad Kevin cast it and not you."

Tallen interrupts our musings, "Questions can come later. We need to take that sniper out."

"Ideas?" I ask.

He snaps his head out to peek around the corner, but just as with Marissa, he barely manages to get his head back just in time, before a shot slams into the corner he is hiding behind, causing drywall and paint to fly off in a pattern of destruction.

"Crap," he growls. "I didn't get to see anything except the muzzle flash."

"Well, at least we know they aren't using a Focus," Carmen says.

It's true. While Focuses can fire off Magical bullets, they don't have a muzzle flash. That tells us that the person shooting at us is firing a conventional human weapon. But what it doesn't tell us, is if the person pulling the trigger is a human or a Dark Elf.

I wish there was a way to see them without exposing our faces. I look around, hoping to see one of those big mirrors up on the walls—the ones you use to see around a corner, so you don't run into someone coming the other way. But I guess the shooter had the same idea, as the mirror only ten feet behind me shatters into a thousand pieces as another shot rings out.

Shit, guess that idea is out.

Tallen looks at me and holds up his communication stone. I frown but take mine out, and he calls me.

"Wanted to say this quietly, in case they have good hearing. We need to get around them. I think I might be able to Teleport behind them. I got a quick look, and all I caught was a rifle sticking out and them hidden behind the desk. But, behind them is a room. I assume it's the nurse's break room. The door was open. I might be able to Teleport there."

"Isn't the distance too far for you?" I ask him.

Nodding and sighing through the connection, he tells me, "Yes. But, what other choices do we have?"

"What if I Teleport you?"

"How are you going to do that? You haven't seen the place."

"No, but I can jump across the space to your side and look. I still have my shield up."

"You know if you do that, your girls will kick your ass for taking the chance."

"Yes, but right now, we're sitting ducks. I'm sure the rest of the hospital heard the shots. I'm pretty confident that the cops will be here soon."

Nodding, he scowls and says, "Right. So our time is limited."

"What I can do, is recast Shield and jump across. But the shooter might suspect something is up, so we need to do it quickly. Can you knock them out? We need them alive, I assume?"

"Oh, don't worry," he says with a massive grin. "You get me behind them, and I will keep them alive enough for us to get information out of them, be they human or Dark Elf."

"What are you two talking about?" Marissa, next to me asks me suspiciously.

"A way to take the shooter out," I tell her.

"Kevin," she tells me slowly, "If…"

I hold my hand to stop her. "Do you have any other ideas? The cops will be here soon."

She stares at me and growls. "Fine. But if you get hurt, I will not be happy."

"Trust me, if I get hurt, I won't be happy either," I tell her, grabbing her hand and squeezing it.

"What's the plan?" she asks me.

I shake my head. "We are keeping it hush-hush, in case they can hear us."

"Well, if they can, they now know something is up."

"Yes," I tell her with a smile, "but not what."

"Fine. Be careful," she says.

I look across the hall, and Carmen is glaring at me. Shit. Are both of them upset with me? We are sitting ducks here. We need to do something, and right now, it seems—something quick and drastic. Releasing Shield on myself, I recast it—although this time, I hold it longer, adding even more power to it. When I finally release the casting, I feel it settle over me like a cold sheet of water.

I nod at Tallen. "I think I'm ready."

"All right. As soon as you Teleport me, I will make sure to take out our target—but keep them alive."

I stand up, getting ready to jump across, but I know that won't be enough. I move back, until I am a dozen or so feet down the hallway we had been in, the shooter just around the corner. As quick as I can, I sprint forward and dash across the hallway, turning my head to look down the hallway to where the shooter is.

And I get it! I also see a couple of things in the one or two seconds it takes me to fly across the space. I had thrown myself at the last second across the intervening space.

I saw the shooter, who, thanks to the gray skin, told me it was a Dark Elf. I also see that he has some kind of sniper rifle. Actually, in those microseconds, I see it's the same kind of rifle as Ilo had. I also see the nurse's station, and behind that is the room Tallen was talking about.

Then, I feel my Shield being clipped not once, but four times. Shit, did they go full auto?

The shots aren't completely stopped by my Shield. It deflects them, but as I find out, it only stopped three of them. The fourth shot smashes through my weakened Shield and slams into my upper left leg, which was one of the last parts of me exposed, as my upper body was already past the wall.

The pain is excruciating, but we have to do this quickly. As soon as I hit the floor, my hand is already reaching towards Tallen. And though the pain threatens to disrupt my spell, I cast Teleport and send Tallen behind the sniper. My fingers are suddenly no longer touching Tallen's outstretched hand.

CHAPTER THIRTY

"Shit," Carmen growls, pressing her hand into my bleeding leg.

I feel a wash of warmth, with her hands showing a slight green glow around them, as she casts Heal on me.

"Is he all right?" Marissa cries in worry.

"Yeah," Carmen tells her. "He got hit in the upper leg. Thank the gods the bullet hit a meaty area and didn't shred a major blood vessel."

"Still fucking hurts," I grunt out.

"I'm sure it does. Maybe next time that means you won't do something stupid," she tells me.

I simply stare at her and don't answer.

"Who am I kidding?" she says, shaking her head and causing her blond hair to fly around her. "Of course you will keep doing stupid shit."

"Got her," Tallen cries from down the hallway.

Carmen lifts her hands away from my leg and, with her help, I stand up. Marissa peeks around the corner, and I guess it's safe, because she rushes across to our side. Once there, she slaps me, hard, on the chest.

"Don't you dare do that again," she snarls, but then hugs me to take the sting out of her words.

"You know I can't promise that. Just as I'm sure you can't promise me you won't do something foolish to save us, Marissa. We needed to take them out. Fast." Hopping on my one good leg, unsure how well the other will bear my weight, I accept her assistance as she tucks my arm around her shoulders. "We should see what Tallen captured."

"Grrr," she says but hugs me hard from the side and half assists, half drags me over to Tallen. Once there, and sure that I can stand on my own, she kneels down beside our Vampire friend.

Carmen come up beside me and hugs me, as well. She whispers in my ear, "She truly cares for you. Please be more careful. And I care for you, too. So... be careful for the two of us, okay?"

"I'll try," I tell her softly, smiling down at her.

"Good," she says, hugging me close again before stepping away and squatting next to Marissa, who kneels over the body.

"I thought you took them alive?" I ask, leaning against the nearest wall.

It takes a body several minutes to get rid of phantom pain and aches after a healing. I know that within minutes, I will be fine. Unfortunately, the memory of that pain—even as it fades—doesn't go away. It's a reminder that I'm mortal.

"She's just out cold. Though she will have a massive headache when she wakes up."

"She?" I ask, looking down at the sniper.

Yep. The sniper was female, based on the pillowy lumps I see spilling from her jacket. She may not have been as big as my girls, but she would still had plenty of cleavage to show in the right outfit. She was wearing a doctor's smock and a white jacket, over light blue scrubs. The most obvious difference between her and a human doctor, was her dark gray skin and hair so black it is almost purple. I'm sure if I pulled back her eyelids to check her pupils, they would be totally black.

"Did you bite her?" Carmen asks him.

With a snort, he turns to her and says, "No. I punched her in the back of the head."

"Ah," I say with a chuckle. "Then, yes. She will wake up with a massive headache. But, just in case..." I lean down and cast Sleep on her. Her features, which were tight with pain—even out cold—ease and her body relaxes.

Then, low in the background, we all hear the sirens. "Shit," we all four say in unison.

"Let's grab her, and we can Portal to my castle."

"You didn't want to take her straight to my Dad?" Marissa asks, pointing down at our hostage.

Tallen thinks that one through and finally nods. "That might be best. He might have a better idea on what to ask her."

"Right," I say. I start to bend down and grab the body of our hostage, but stop and grunt in pain as my thigh seizes up.

"Yeah, you're not fully healed... yet. It will take at least another ten or fifteen minutes before you are good as new," Carmen tells me. "You won't be carrying her. One of us can. The last thing we need is for you to fuck up the healing I just did."

"I've got her," Marissa says, grabbing the body like it weighs nothing and tossing it over her shoulder.

With our hostage over Marissa's shoulder, I nod and cast Portal, opening one to Targun's place—or at least to the entrance hall. Once the Portal is steady, Carmen, Tallen and Marissa stride through it, with me following behind them. I'm just in time to hear shouting down the hallway, but as whoever it is can't see the Portal, unless they are a Magical being, I walk through and cancel the spell as soon as I can.

I look around, and see we've come out in the entrance to Targun's place. The place is massive—I'm pretty sure the vaulted ceilings are at least twelve feet, if not more. But the luxury of it is what takes my breath away. Why did I never notice that before? Even this entrance hall, now that I take a closer look at it, is expensive as hell.

Hearing a screech, my head whips around, and I see that it's Preeka.

She stares at us in shock.

"Hey, Preeka," Marissa tells her, shifting the weight on her shoulder slightly. "Is my Dad home?"

Preeka turns her gaze to Marissa and nods dumbly. "He eating."

"Can you tell him we have something for him?"

The goblin looks at Marissa suspiciously, but when her eyes fall on the Dark Elf, she squeaks in surprise. And just like that, she's gone, with a displacement of air that I actually hear pop this time. Abruptly, we hear shouting from another part of the castle. Followed by running feet.

"Preeka says you have something alive that is gray-skinned!" Targun shouts, running into the front entrance where we are.

Marissa answers for the group. "We got a live one, Dad. Kevin cast Sleep on her, so she will be out for hours."

"Her?" he asks, both eyebrows stretching towards his hairline.

The old Magus comes closer to his daughter and lifts up the head, which lays against Marissa's back, and looks at the face.

"Damn," he says, shaking his head in awe.

"Were you able to learn anything from the other Elf's body?" Tallen asks him.

Targun turns to him and grins. "Oh, hells yes. Come. Bring her in. I have a cell in my lab we can put her in. She won't get away."

We follow Targun into his lab, which I see is just as messy as before. Preeka is already there, popping from table to table, picking items up, looking at them, and either throwing them back down on the table or popping away with them. I assume she is cleaning up, storing them somewhere.

"Over here," Targun tells his daughter, pointing to the back wall, where there stands a large cage.

Marrisa nods, goes to the cage, opens the door, and then places the female Dark Elf on the metal cot that is in there.

Once done, she walks out, and her Dad closes the door of the cage, muttering something with his hand over the lock mechanism. I expect to hear the *snick* of a lock clicking shut, but instead there's an angry buzzing sound, right at the threshold of my hearing, but then it fades.

"Don't touch the bars," Targun orders, turning back to us with a grin, "unless you want a pain that can be, as I have heard it described, quite agonizing." His grin is infectious. "Now, care to explain what happened?"

So, for the next ten minutes, we explain to him about our trip out to Waterford. We also explain that many other leaders of the Magical folk might be in danger, and that we had sent Mavin a message to give to his mom.

"You... ahh..." I tell him, rubbing the back of my neck. "You might get a call from Mavin's mom. I told Mavin that she should come to you, if she wanted any details."

"Smart," he says, nodding. "I should have started reaching out to the ones I trust already. Preeka!" he shouts suddenly.

I notice that Tallen is the only one to jump out of the four of us. Guess I'm getting used to it.

"Master?" she says, appearing suddenly down by his feet.

He looks down at her. "I need paper and a pen. I need to write a couple of messages to some of Earth's leaders in the Magical world. Can you grab those things, and hire me eight goblin messengers?"

She nods and is gone again.

"Eight?" Tallen asks him curiously.

"Yes. I need to make this official. Messages will be sent to the leaders on Earth of the Fairies, Werewolves, Elves, Beast,

Dwarven, Changeling, and Centaurs. I am sending one to you as well, Tallen, as an official notice. Oh, I guess I will also need to send one, as a courtesy, to the goblin leader on Earth."

"Wait!" Tallen blurts out. "You're going to reveal to everyone that Dark Elves are real?"

Sighing, Targun nods. "I have no choice. This is big. We can't fight against them and still hide them from everyone else. I will send out an official notice that they are real. I have already notified the Council of Magical Folks."

I can't help myself. I'm shocked to hear the name of the races that he had called out. "Centaurs are real?"

Carmen lays a hand on my arm with a smile. "Later. I will tell you about them."

"Please," I tell her, nodding quickly.

My god! Centaurs?

"Master," Preeka says, making me look over.

"Ah, you got nine? Smart girl. You knew I would also need to contact the goblin Leader on Earth?"

Preeka grins and nods, which I'm sure if I had seen three months ago would have scared the crap out of me. But now, I have gotten used to her looks.

"Let me get these letters out," he says, heading to a table and shoving a pile of stuff in his way aside, making half of it fall to the ground. Preeka is there instantly, grabbing items, disappearing, reappearing, and grabbing more things until the floor is cleared. All the while, we stay quiet, watching Targun write away furiously.

Fifteen minutes of us just looking around the room or lifting up random items to try and identify them, and Targun says finally. "And... done. Preeka?"

Preeka appears next to him on the table, with her hands out. Targun hands her nine scrolls that had been rolled up and tied with a golden string. The information in my head supplies that the scrolls can only be opened by the person they are meant for.

How, you ask? Magic, of course. Man, I love Magic.

"Make sure you get them to the Leaders promptly. Oh, and make sure that one of the messengers isn't Polto. I need him for another task later."

"It will be done, Master," she says and is gone.

Targun turns to us, clapping his hands together. "Shall we go wake up our guest?"

We all turn to the cage and make our way to the back of the room. The Dark Elf is still unconscious, as I had not canceled my Sleep spell.

Once we are all there, Targun turns to me. "Please go ahead and cancel Sleep."

I nod and do as instructed, releasing the spell.

Suddenly, we hear a groan, and we all look into the cage at the waking Dark Elf. She bolts upright, groans again in pain, and puts her hand to the back of her head.

I frown at Tallen. "How hard did you hit her?"

"Pretty hard. I wanted to knock her out quickly," he shrugs, "and I have never fought a Dark Elf. I had no clue how much force it would take to knock her out. Besides," he says with a smirk, "if I had killed her, it would only have been just retribution for shooting me."

"Well, she didn't shoot you—she shot me. That other Dark Elf shot you."

Shrugging again, he says, "Potato, tomato."

"Hmm. Not sure you're using that expression correctly," Carmen tells him with a laugh.

"Shit!" I hiss, snapping my fingers. "Suicide tooth."

Targun suddenly turns quickly back to the cage and waves his hand. I feel Magic flow from him into the cage. Unexpectedly, the Dark Elf begins to gag, and then coughs something out. Something white skips across the floor of the cage —a white tooth, with some blood on it.

The woman's expression turns even more gray, as the tooth bounces on the floor. She suddenly rushes to grab the tooth —which I assume has some kind of poison in it—but without warning, it lifts off the ground and zips across the cage into Targun's fingers. He looks at the tooth curiously and then tosses it over his shoulder, where it bounces off a table and hits the floor before stopping against a pile of books.

The Dark Elf turns to us, following the path of the tooth she had just failed to recover. On seeing us, her eyes widen in shock.

"Hi," I tell her with a grin.

She reaches for something behind her, but her hand stops there.

"Are you looking for this?" Marissa asks her, holding up a very human-looking Glock pistol.

Shit, I never thought of checking her for weapons. The same way, I didn't think of taking her suicide tooth out earlier. I should have done so right off the bat, especially since we lost the last Dark Elf that way.

The Dark Elf glares at my wife, and if looks could kill, Marissa would be dead.

"You shall get nothing out of me," she says in perfect American English.

Targun snorts at her comment, making her glance his way before transferring her glare to him.

"I'm afraid you don't know who I am," he tells her with a smile. "I am the Lead Councillor of the Galactic Council of Magical Folks. Do you know what that means?"

At his statement, the Dark Elf's visage turns white, her eyes widen so much, that I see the white of her sclera instead of the pure black of her large pupils.

"Ah, so you do know what that means," he says with a chuckle. "Shall we start with some questions?"

CHAPTER THIRTY-ONE

The Dark Elf snaps her mouth shut, which had opened in surprise, and she glares even harder at Targun.

"Why don't we start with something simple," he tells her. "What is your name?"

She doesn't answer him, only continues to glare.

Preeka returns, standing on the table next to me, and hands me something. Looking down, I see it's a piece of candy in a wrapper. I'm surprisingly touched by her simple gift.

I look at the goblin, smile, and whisper, "Thanks."

Maybe she's warming up to me? I see Marissa give me a thumbs up; she looks impressed. The brunette comes over beside me and whispers. "It looks like Preeka's taking a liking to you. That's from her personal stash of candies."

Turning to Preeka, I give her another smile and bend down to whisper in her ear. "Thanks a bunch, Preeka. I love candy. And cookies."

As I was closer to her than normal, I expected her to smell like... I don't know, something nasty, I guess. But all I got was the scent of patchouli.

"You have cookies?" she blurts out quietly, not interrupting Targun.

"Not with me, not right now. But next time, I promise to bring you some Oreos from my place."

Hearing coughing, I turn, and Targun is glaring at the two of us. We both blush and zip our mouths. Targun turns back to the Dark Elf, but I feel a tug on my shirt. Looking down at Preeka, she is smiling with her crooked teeth and nodding happily. I can't help but grin back at her and nod as well, as if we now share a great secret.

"Again," Targun asks our prisoner, "what is your name?"

Again, no answer except that glare.

Sighing, Targun heads to one of the tables and begins to rummage through it, with all of us— including the Dark Elf —looking on curiously. Though, her features also show some uncertainty.

"A-ha! Thought I had one left," he cries happily.

He returns, holding up an item in his hand. We all look at it, but it looks like nothing more than a shiny, black pebble to me. I arch my brows at Marissa, Carmen and Tallen, hoping to get an idea of what they know about it, but they look to be just as much in the dark as I am.

"What is it?" Marissa asks her Dad.

He grins. "It's a Truth Rock."

"A... what?" Tallen asks, looking more confused than ever.

"A Truth Rock," Targun repeats.

"Dad," Marissa says, exhaling. "Naming something a second time doesn't mean we will understand any better what it is."

His grin turning into a scowl, he grunts, "It's a rock that forces someone to tell the truth."

"We got that much from the name," she tells her Dad, rolling her eyes. "But what exactly IS it?"

"Gods above, below, and in-between... Your generation nowadays. Don't you know old Magic when you hear it?"

"Dad," she says, pinching the bridge of her nose. "Did you invent that?"

"Yes?"

"Did you ever give it out to anyone before this?"

"What? No. It was my own invention."

"And did you register it with the Council?"

"What? Of course not! It's mine."

"And so, how could we be expected to know about it, if you invented it but never registered it so that others can make or use them?"

He opens his mouth to retort, but then shuts it with a snap. "Oh."

"Right... Oh. So other than the name, which gives us an idea of what it *might* do, what—in sufficient detail to explain the effect properly—does it do?"

"It was something that I invented about a hundred years ago. It has a Truth spell stored in it, but also a Bind spell—so that whoever I used it on, the spell stays active until I cancel it."

"How does it work?" I ask. "Do you make them swallow it?"

"Gods, no. That's barbaric," he says, scowling at me. "I just hit them with it."

"How do you do that?" Carmen asks before I can ask.

"Like this," he says, and with the stone in his hand, he flicks his fingers, and the black pebble zips through the bars to hit the Dark Elf in the stomach, causing her to startle in surprise. It went so fast, that I barely saw it. And whereas I'd expected the stone to bounce off her, it instead somehow gets absorbed—right through her smock and scrubs.

"That's how," he says. "It only takes a minute or two for it to work."

"Why a couple of minutes?" Tallen asks, intrigued.

"The spell is special in that it gets absorbed by the body of your victim... err, sorry... your target. Once inside the target's body, it goes to the brainstem. Once there, it latches onto the spinal column. Only then, does the spell go off."

As Targun explains how it works, the Dark Elf gets a look of horror on her face, her hand scrambling at the back of her neck, as if she can feel the thing moving around under her skin. And for all I know, she just might.

"What did you do to me?" she cries in horror.

"Oh, don't worry," Targun tells her with a smile. "You won't feel any pain as it moves into place. I made sure that little oversight got fixed—with this version."

"You had a version that the target could feel the stone traveling through otherwise healthy, solid muscle?" Tallen says with a laugh.

"Yes," he says with a sour expression. "I finally decided to modify it, after some trials."

I stare at my father-in-law, hoping it wasn't tested on normal targets. Then again, I'm not sure I would want such a terrible thing tested on unwilling targets, either.

"What did you do to me?" the Dark Elf growls again, looking at Targun with pure vitriol spilling from her dark gaze.

"Nothing... yet." He returns her glares with a smile. "In a moment, though, you will be telling me all your secrets."

She stares at him as if to gauge how truthful he is. She must see something in his face, as suddenly she stands up from the metal bed and rushes the bars of the cage. But I get a shock, and so does she, when she suddenly stops feet away from them. I assume she was trying to hurt herself, as she had tilted her head forward, so as to slam it into the bars, but instead of her forehead crashing into the metal, she is stopped in her tracks, her body frozen in place before she can even so much as reach out to touch the cage's metal bars.

She struggles, but to no avail. She's stuck fast.

"That's the stone's doing?" Carmen asks out loud what we are all wondering.

Targun turns to her and grins. "No. That's the bars. I can't have my prisoners hurting themselves, can I? The bars of the cage power a spell that stops them from doing exactly that. No matter what she tries to do to hurt herself, she won't succeed. Though," he scowls, tapping one finger against his lips, "I never thought of a tooth with poison inside. I might need to modify the cage's spell."

"Now," he says, turning back the Dark Elf. "Shall we try this again?"

She doesn't answer, but her glare this time, though filled with hate, includes a first hint of fear.

"What is your name?"

I can see she's struggling not to open her mouth, but finally, almost out of breath, she says, "Balina Montromina."

"Ah, a wonderful name. Good," he says, looking around.

"What are you looking for, Dad?"

"Something to take notes on," he replies.

"Or, we can simply record it," she tells him with a snort, holding up her human smartphone.

"Fine," he says, waving his hand dismissively at her, but then stops and peers at the smart phone. "Actually. That might just work. I will need a copy, I guess, for the Council members."

"Fine," she says, pointing her phone's camera at her Dad and the prisoner, this Balina Montromina.

"Ask her what her name is again, so that we can get it on the video."

He nods and turns towards Balina, who is now staring at Targun in a panic.

"What is your name?" Targun asks her again, and with that look of panic still on her face, she tells him her name once more, with Marissa catching it on video this time.

"What is the reason you are attacking us?"

Balina frowns. "We aren't attacking you."

"Let me rephrase, then. Why have the Dark Elves returned?"

"We never left."

"Why are you attacking Magical folk?"

"Mostly for their Magic."

Grunting in annoyance, he looks back at us. "Any ideas for questions? This is getting us nowhere fast."

We offer some suggestions, with Balina looking on gloomily, knowing she can't help but answer them.

Once he has a good number of questions to ask, Targun turns back to our prisoner. "What do the Dark Elves want with the people of Earth?"

"We are the rightful owners of this world," she declares. "Not humans. Not you Magical abnormalities. Us. The only race that the Gods favored."

"Hmm… Didn't your god get killed by our gods, and you had your Magic taken away?"

At this question, Balina gets a shocked look on her face. "Yes. We know. Apparently, the last Dark Elf we spoke with was very open with his concerns."

Her face clouds over at that, but she growls. "You lowborn were never meant to rule this world. This Earth—as the humans call it—was gifted to us by our God."

"Is that what they told you?" I ask out loud.

Balina turns to me, and even though she isn't compelled to answer me, but I guess the question touches a nerve, because she sneers at me. "I'm not sure why a human is here, but this world was given to us by our god—a gift to his children."

"And what about the other gods? And their *children,* as you call them? Are you saying that all the other gods that these

Magical folk believe in, the world was never given to them to enjoy?"

"They were meant to be our slaves. That is what our God told us. We are the true inheritors of this world."

"Wow, talk about fucking conceited," Tallen says with a snort of derision.

"Why are you now coming forth? We have not heard from or about you Dark Elves in eons," Targun asks—one of the questions we had postulated.

Balina turns to him and glares, but has she has no choice but to answer him. "Because humans are getting too greedy, and their sciences will take them to the stars. And with them, go our chance to take over this world."

"Wait, you're saying that the humans' scientific advances are the reason you all are coming forth? Then why are you attacking us Magical folk?" Targun asks her with a frown.

"Because we need to make it look like it was the humans who did it, so that you would go to war with them."

"Fucking hell," I breathe in shock. "The Dark Elves are hoping to get us to go after each other, until we are weak."

"How many are you?" Marissa asks suddenly.

It wasn't one of the questions we'd discussed, but her Dad nods to Marissa, and turns and asks Balina that question.

"We are over four million strong."

At that number, we all turn to stare at each other, stunned into silence at the unbelievable number that she just told us.

"How?! Where are you all hiding?"

"We are hiding below ground. And for those of us who have Magic stones, we can disguise ourselves to be among the humans."

"Is that why you are dressed like that," Targun asks her, waving a hand at her doctor's outfit. "And what is a Magic stone?"

"A Magic stone is a stone that has been imbued with Magic, given to us by our Elders before we go on missions. I'm dressed this way, as I live in the human world. I am a trained doctor. The physiology of humans, and most Magical folks, is not far from our own. So this way, I am learning to be a healer for my race."

"Magic stones? You mean after you kill one of the Magical folk, you draw their Magic out using those silver daggers, and it's then placed inside a stone and given to you?" Targun growls in a menacing voice.

Balina either doesn't see his menacing look, or doesn't care. "Of course," she says with a snort. "To us, you are nothing more than cattle."

Targun lifts his hand, but his daughter slaps it down. "No, Dad. We need her alive."

The Magus spins on her, and there is anger burning in his eyes, but slowly it abates until he nods. Straightening his shoulders, Targun takes a deep breath.

"Come. We need to discuss this. She will be safe here; she can't hurt herself. But, just in case…" Targun waves his hand and, without warning, Balina slumps to the ground, fast asleep thanks to the Sleep spell he just cast.

I notice that her head doesn't hit the ground. I guess the cage's Magic precludes accidents that might hurt her, too.

CHAPTER THIRTY-TWO

"What are we going to do?" Carmen asks everyone seated around the table.

We had left the laboratory, and Targun had yelled for Preeka. He'd asked to have dinner served in the main dining room and she had nodded before disappearing. By the time we got to the dining room, she was there setting plates. Soon, we had a pleasant meal served to us

Sighing and sitting back in his chair, Targun answers her. "No clue. This is unexpected. I had figured we would be dealing with a couple of thousand Dark Elves, at most. Not a conceited, diabolical race that number over four million. How in the gods' many names did they hide for so long?"

"As she said, underground," Marissa replies with a snort. "But, Dad, the better question to ask, is how long have they been killing our people? And how involved are they in human affairs? You heard what she said—she is a doctor. Which means that she must have gone to school at a human university, for which she needed to have the appropriate background and schooling, such as what the humans call High School, and all that." She shakes her head. "The real concern is, how have they been living among humans this entire time, and yet we never knew?"

Carmen is the one to ask the obvious question. "But that would mean they have been around for eons, directing the humans. I know we Magical folk once did. But how come we never ran into them before this? And why now?"

Preeka places a glass in front of me, which I see has beer in it. I smile down at her and whisper softly, so as not to interrupt the conversation, "Thanks." She smiles at me with her broken teeth and disappears, reappearing with another glass with red wine in it, this time in front of Carmen, who smiles down at her, patting the little goblin on the head.

"Well, she mentioned that they were trying to make humans look like the bad guys. I can understand now why there has been such an increase in humans finding out about us," Targun says, taking a sip of his own drink. "That's disconcerting, to say the least."

"If they have money, we humans will do a lot for it." I frown. "Even sell out our own race, I'm not happy to say… but it's true. There are some really skanky people out there who would sell their own mothers for drugs or money to buy drugs."

Everyone around the table nods, which doesn't give me the greatest vote of confidence in how my race is perceived. "We need to figure a way to stop them."

Sighing, Carmen nods. "Do you think she's telling the truth about their numbers?"

"Well, she said there were over four million Dark Elves while under that spell," Marissa points out.

"Yes. But what if that is just what she believes, because that's what she was told?"

Targun regards her. "You think their numbers may be lower, and they are lying to their own agents who go out, to inflate their numbers?"

"Well, I'm not sure they meant their agents to get captured, but… maybe?" she says, sounding unsure herself.

"Misinformation," I supply the word.

"Misinformation?" Targun asks, looking over at me.

"What have we learned about these Dark Elves?" I summarize what we know: "They look at us all as cattle. We are nothing better than animals to them, and they want to enslave us all. The one we have said that there are over four million of them. As a member of the Council, what would you do, if you faced an enemy over four million strong?"

"Well," he says, frowning and his head tilted sideways in thought. "We would be slow and cautious. We would not jump in."

"So, if the Dark Elves came out openly, in the human world, the Council would most likely take a hands-off, cautious approach?"

He doesn't answer right away, but his eyes get wide. "Bloody hell. If we knew such 'facts' were misinformation, we would not." He presses his palms to his eyes, shaking his head. "If that even is what this is."

"Then, I guess we know our next mission," I point out.

Sighing, he nods. I'm sure Targun didn't get to where he is based on his Magic alone, but on smarts, too. Though, based on what I am finding out, power plays an enormous role in securing and keeping that Lead Councillor chair.

"We need to find out first if that number is accurate, Dad."

"I know. But how do we do that? Balina can answer only what she knows," he tells her, flipping a thumb over his shoulder at the laboratory beyond, where our guest sleeps.

"As Kevin was saying. We know our next mission. We need to find out."

"Where do we start, though? We don't know where to start."

"Well," Marissa begins, "we know that she's a doctor in the human world. And I mean, a real doctor, as in she spent years in school and trained in some medical program. But that must mean she got into medical school based on false records." She pauses. "Or do you think they are living as humans to gain their entire education?"

"Like a sleeper cell?" I ask.

"Sleeper cell?" Tallen repeats, I'm certain he isn't familiar with the term, based on his puzzled frown.

"A sleeper cell is a secretive group of either spies or terrorists —though I would put these Dark Elves in a higher group, as their aim is to enslave the all the races on Earth—who remain inactive within an ignorant population, and only act when ordered to."

Tallen nods. "But how does their organization or masters communicate with them?"

"Usually by secret orders. I mean, it would make sense if Belina was in a sleeper cell, that she might not have information on anything other than her own cell."

"Then how do we get information from her if she doesn't have it?"

"She might not," I admit. "But maybe something she has will give us a lead we can follow up on."

"You want to go check out her apartment," Marissa says with a sudden grin.

I point to her grin. "Bingo."

"So, I guess after supper, we need to have another chat with our prisoner and find out where she lived," Marissa says, nodding to herself before digging into her meal, knowing we now had a mission.

"I guess I can't do an autopsy on her?" Targun asks with a sigh.

"No!" we all shout at him.

Marissa softens the clamor by laying a hand on his arm and patting it affectionately. "You can do your autopsies on any other dead Dark Elves we bring you, Dad."

At that, he brightens up. "Oh, good!"

* * *

"So, is this the place?" I ask, checking the address on the paper we have and the place itself.

Whoever this Dark Elf was, she was wealthy. The house was massive, with lots of windows, but it was also dark. It is late at night, probably just past three in the morning.

"It sure looks like, while she might hate you humans," Carmen says with a snort, "she didn't mind using your money."

"Do you think she lives alone?" I ask.

Tallen points out. "She said she did in our questioning of her."

"Well, let's go see what we can find. I find it hard to believe that she worked solo, but she said she was alone here in Ireland."

I nod at Carmen, and we all head deeper into the bushes, coming out around the back of the large home. From there, we can see the large patio doors. The only light I can see on is the one over the stove.

Hearing the barking of a dog, we all freeze in our tracks, until Tallen whispers, "It's four houses down. I doubt it's barking because of us."

We all nod and keep going. The good thing is, with the light over the back door off, no one will see us. I go to the door, and with my hand barely touching it, I cast Disarm. With a *click*, the door unlocks.

I go to open it, but Carmen grabs my hand. I look at her quizzically. "Alarms," she whispers.

"I cast Disarm."

"Doesn't matter," she shakes her head. "Disarm only unlocks; it doesn't take care of the alarms. Cast Hide."

"Really? Hide works against laser detectors or whatever alarms use?"

She grins and nods. "One hundred percent."

"Though it won't work against pressure plates," Tallen adds.

I look at him and arch an eyebrow when I see how he is blushing, with a scowl on his face. "From experience?" I ask.

"You could say that," he admits, but doesn't go into details, and I don't ask. This is not the time, nor the place, but that is one story I will need to remember to ask him about. It sounds rather interesting.

"So, what works for pressure plates?"

"A fairy," they all answer at the same time.

Right, a Fairy. Wings. Flying. But Mavin isn't here with us. Maybe we should look at adding a Fairy partner? I can probably pay them in Oreo cookies, I think with a grin.

I cast Hide, as instructed, and then stand at the doorframe and look inside, trying to see if there's anything I should be worried about. But nothing jumps out at me. Then, something else comes to mind.

Hide is a spell that hides me from visual, auditory, olfactory, and even heat, pressure and something like six other senses. I wonder if I can cast it but reverse it? Or have it do the opposite? No spell comes to mind that does that. There is no opposite spell to Hide. It's not like Heat and Cold. Or Water and Dry.

What if I want the opposite of what the spell hides, that instead brings hidden things to light? Can I do it? Maybe I will call it Reveal?

Lifting my hand, I call up power into it, and force the spell to do what I want. I imagine it in my head as a spell that acts like a radar, bringing anything hidden out in the open. I feel the Magic leave me, and it slams into the house, almost like a sound wave that you can't just hear, but can also feel.

"What the fuck was that?" hisses Carmen.

Marissa and Tallen had both glared at me when I'd released my spell.

I blush and admit, "I cast a spell that I just came up with. I'm calling it Reveal. It should uncover anything that was hidden."

"Kevin," Tallen slowly utters, staring at me hard. "Are you saying you just created a spell that will blow away whatever a Hide spell was cast on?"

"Uhh... Yes?" I say it slowly, feeling like a kid getting caught doing something he isn't supposed to.

I glance over at Marissa, and she has her eyes closed and is taking deep breaths, muttering what sounds suspiciously like numbers under her breath. Then I look over at Carmen, and she is just grinning and shaking her head at me.

"What?" I ask, not sure if I did something wrong.

Had I broken some unwritten rule of Magic? There's no information in my head saying I broke any rules. So why are they freaking out?

"Kevin," Tallen starts but closes his mouth. Finally, he turns to the girls. "I have no idea how to explain to him what he just did. Care to try?"

"I'll try," Marissa says, opening her eyes. She comes right up to me and peers up at me through her glasses, chest to chest. "Kevin... Do you have any idea what you just did?"

"I had an idea that I thought of and then turned that idea into a spell that seemed to... make sense?"

"No. What you did was you, on a whim, created a spell—The first new spell in over three thousand years, if not more. The last spell that was created from an idea, was the spell for Hide. That spell was a game-changer for us Magical folk. It's the spell we all learn at a young age—for many of us, it's our first spell. It's one of those *you need to know* spells."

In shock, I hiss, "What? But how? There are so many uses for Magic!"

Tallen puts his hand to his face and scrubs it, hard. Between his fingers, he mumbles, "Kevin, are you saying that you have other ideas for new spells?"

"Sure. Doesn't everyone who learns Magic just itch to create a new spell once they know they can harness Magic?"

"No," all three of them say at the same time, in the same forceful tone.

I frown at the three Magical folk. "Seriously?"

"Seriously," Marissa says, shaking her head.

"Damn. I'm glad you're my foster son," Tallen says, followed by with a chuckle.

"And that he's on our side," Carmen adds with a grunt.

Marissa looks at me and waves me through the doorway, but not before she says. "We need to talk after this."

Worriedly I tell her, "Hmm... Ok?"

Looking back into the house, I try to see if I can see anything that was previously hidden now showing, but I only see the same room as before. But just as I'm about to go over the door's threshold, I look down and something catches my eye.

I stop dead in my tracks, with my foot still in the air, about to walk into the home. Just inside the patio door's track, I see something that wasn't there before, though it's still faint. It's a tiny Sigil.

"Sigil," I say, pointing down.

And it's a good thing I noticed it before anyone stepped over it. It's the Sigil for Fire. If anyone had stepped over it, the Sigil would have thrown up a flame as high as me, engulfing whoever stepped over it and burning them to a crisp within seconds. At least that is how the Fire Sigil was supposed to work, according to the information in my head.

CHAPTER THIRTY-THREE

"Shit, that would have stung," Tallen says, putting his hand to his chest, remembering having been shot less than two days ago.

"Can you disarm it? Like you did that Sigil above the stairs at Tallen's club?" Carmen asks me, peeking around me to examine the Fire Sigil.

"I think so?" I say, squatting down and studying the Fire Sigil.

They had hidden it using a Hide spell. If I had walked over it, a large flame would have burst out of that Sigil and instantly fried me, or more likely baked me—from the outside, in.

I remember that when I'd been in the club, just putting my finger next to the Sigil and slowly pushing power into it to overload it had worked. But, as I'm staring down at the Sigil, I look up—and I'm glad I did.

Above my head, in the same track that the Sigil was in, there's another Sigil. I point upwards. "Someone's anal."

All three look up, and Tallen snorts. "Jesus. Is that a Frozen Sigil?"

Carmen growls, "Yes. So in other words, if you had stepped over the threshold, you would have been burned to a crisp and your crispy body would have been flash frozen."

"That's morbid!" Marissa says, shaking her head. "And a bit of overkill, don't you think?"

I bend down and slowly place my fingertip as close to the Fire Sigil as I can without triggering it. I push power to the tip of my finger, and then express that power beyond my fingertip into the Sigil itself. The Sigil disappears in an explosion of light motes.

Standing up, I reach up to do the same thing with the Frozen Sigil, but Tallen suddenly snatches my hand and pulls it down, stopping me. I turn to him with a questioning look.

He snorts and points to the inside of the doorframe, about waist-high. There's another Sigil. This time, it's a Stun Sigil. If I had come close to it, it would have gone off and stunned me. At best, it would have knocked me out, flat on my ass. I shudder, these traps not only would have burned me to a crisp and then Frozen me solid, but I would have been stunned, so that I would not have felt any of it.

"Fucking hell," I breathe.

"Whoever put these here, they really were paranoid about ensuring they were protected," Carmen whistles.

"That's a lot of Magic," Carmen points out what we missed. "Whoever this Belina person is, she must have had a lot of stored Magic. These Sigils might be low-level ones, but they still use a lot of power to initiate."

"Do you think there will be more inside?" I ask my friends.

"Oh, hells yeah," Tallen mutters. "Undoubtedly."

Carmen growls in frustration. "How do we get rid of all of them? Kevin can reveal them, but we have to find and disarm each of them, else we might trigger one and maybe explode this entire house."

"Can we... I don't know, overload them all at once?" I ask, looking at each of them separately.

All I get in return are stunned looks.

Nervously, I ask, "What?" at their looks.

"It's only a theory," Tallen says slowly, staring hard at me. "But the theory is, if you push enough power into an area, you can overload Sigils within that area. It's like what you do with each one individually, but on a massive scale. It would require A LOT of Magic."

Marissa looks at me, pursing her lips with a contemplative look. "He might be able to do it."

"What?! But that's a metric shit ton of power," Carmen states.

"Remember," she tells her. "Kevin is supposed to be several levels higher than even my father. If anyone has the power to prove the area overload hypothesis, it would be him." She flicks a thumb my way.

"That's still a massive amount of power," Tallen warns me. "You might be out of it for a bit."

"Well, it's either that, or we probably walk into one large booby trap," I remind him.

Carmen shares, "We can all do Magic. If Kevin is out of it, and unable to use Magic for a bit until he regains some power, we should be fine. We might not be at his level, but Marissa was at the top of her Academy class, and I was at the top of mine. And," here she turns to Tallen and gives him a wink, "we have a Count with us, who I've heard is never a slouch in the Magic Department."

Hesitantly, Tallen nods. "If you think we can handle it, if something comes up."

They all turn towards me.

"How will you do it?" Carmen asks, raising an eyebrow and looking at me curiously.

"Well. I would need to overload the Sigils with power, but won't be able to touch or even see them." I squat down, propping my chin on my hands and thinking it through. "How can I do it without touching them? The only thing that comes to mind, is to cast a massive Circle around myself—including the whole house within it. Once done, I would then flood the Circle with Magic, until it fries the Sigils wherever they are."

I pause, looking up. "Do you think that might work?" I ask, unsure now of this plan.

"Don't look at me," Tallen says, holding up his hands. "I'm not even sure if you could even cast a Circle that large."

"Well, let's find out then," I say, standing and taking a deep, if nervous, breath.

I open my arms wide, palms down, and close my eyes. I imagine in my head a Circle that encompasses the entire property. Once I have it firmly in my head, I cast Circle and push Magic into it.

I hear a gasp beside me, but I don't open my eyes. "What?" I ask uneasily.

"Nothing," Marissa says breathlessly. "I simply never saw so much power invested in a Circle spell before."

"Well, hang on tight. That was just the Circle. Now, I need to flood the area with Magic to overload all the Sigils."

With my eyes still closed and my arms out, I begin to feed more power into the Circle. At first, it's a slow trickle, but then, without warning, it's as if a floodgate opens, and Magic pours from me. In my mind's eye, I imagine the power as a stream, bright blue in color for some reason, pouring out of me into the Circle spell. The stream is so intense, that a throbbing pain starts to build back behind my eyes.

To say wielding that much power was heady, is a gross understatement. I can feel my skin tingling. I can feel my eyes, which remain squeezed shut, jerking around in their sockets, as if trying to view all this power at once. Then, I hear an explosion.

"It's working!" Carmen cries excitedly, clapping her hands.

"Fucking hell!" Tallen says, after three more explosions. "It's actually working. He's overloading the Sigils one by one."

After the tenth explosion, Marissa whispers in awe. "My Gods. The amount of Magic you're putting out, Kevin, is unheard of! I don't think even my Dad could do even half so much."

Then, abruptly, it's done. I hear another four explosions, but something tells me that nothing else remains. With the Circle, I don't sense any Magic that isn't my own.

"Done," I say, cutting off the stream of Magic flowing into the Circle. Without warning, an intense wave of dizziness washes over me and I almost fall on my ass. Fortunately, everyone is there to catch me.

"Whoa there!" Tallen cries, grabbing my left arm, while Carmen—who had been on my other side—grabs my right.

Marissa rushes up to me and grabs my face with both of her hands, looking deep into my eyes. "Your eyes are still swimming with power! How are you feeling?"

I start to say that I'm fine, but then a massive migraine hits, and it feels like an ice pick is being driven through my skull. And I still feel dizzy. "I... hmm... should sit down, I think."

With everyone's help, I slowly lower myself to the ground, onto my hands and knees, my head hanging down and facing the open doorway. Marissa stays right with me, lowering herself to the ground as I wobble there on my hands and knees. Tallen keeps a firm hand on my shoulder to steady me, and Carmen rubs my back.

With concern in her voice, Marissa asks me, "How's your power levels inside you?"

I close my eyes, which seems to help with the spinning a bit. "It seems all right. But I can feel I'm depleted. I'm not completely out of Magic, but I can only do maybe four or five lower-level spells—or one large spell."

Tallen snorts. "Leave it to you, to be able to do what you just did, and then brush up on 'four or five lower-level spells' for dessert. Level fifteen, my ass. I would peg you at level twenty or higher."

"Should we tell him?" Carmen asks Marissa.

"I don't think your Dad would mind," Marissa says with a sigh. "The indicators are there that Kevin is quite powerful and it will get out. It will get out sooner or later."

"Am I missing somethning?" Tallen asks curiously, looking between all of us.

"So Kevin is level 20," Marissa says finally, having thought about it a couple of seconds.

"Fucking hell!" Tallen blurts in shock, but then shakes his head. "Why does that not surprise me with Kevin."

"But, you need to keep it hush hush for now," I tell him. "We aren't sure what will happen if it gets out."

"Fine. I can do that. But, to know that my foster son is so powerful is kind of good to know," he tells me with a grin. But, then he gets back to our mission. "How many Sigils do you think he got?" Tallen muses.

"I counted twenty-two," Carmen supplies.

"I counted the same." Marrisa confirms Carmen's number.

"How the fuck did that Dark Elf have the power for… what? Twenty-five freaking Sigils?" Tallen wonders, shaking his head in disbelief.

"What I want to know," I tell them, my head still hanging low, "is what they are hiding here, that needed that many Sigils' protection?"

Carmen points to the open doorway, "Guess we are about to find out. Who wants to go first?"

"Since Kevin just used up—what was the measure you used, Carmen? —a 'metric shit ton' of Magic, and I still have his

Shield on me, I will go," Tallen offers. Hearing no one else volunteer, he nods and slowly walks through the doorway.

We're all cringing inside, I'm sure. But, when he's inside and nothing happens, I slowly get to my feet with the help of Marissa and Carmen. I'm still dizzy, but we need to get this done—since we have no clue who might show up; or if anyone will show. Hells, we aren't even sure if Balina was working alone.

Once inside the house, I look around. It's your typical, modern-day, incredibly expensive McMansion. There's one whole wall that is entirely windows, from floor to ceiling. The place screams money.

"Talk about rich," Carmen whistles appreciatively.

"Stop!" Tallen cries suddenly, making us all stop in our tracks and look at him.

He points up to the corner of the room. We look, and I see there's a camera there.

"It's good," I say, nodding. "I felt them in my Circle, so I disabled them."

"Could have warned me," he says with a sour expression.

"Sorry," I tell him with a weak laugh. "I was trying not to throw up."

"All good." He pauses. "All the alarms have been disabled in here?"

"Pretty much." I remind everyone of the reason we are here. "I guess we just need to look for clues, now."

"Right," Carmen says, heading deeper into the house.

I head towards the kitchen, with Tallen and Marissa each taking another part of the house. For the next hour, we search the house from top to bottom. Even going as far as to check up in the crawl space in the roof.

Then, I hear a shout from another section of the house. It is Marissa.

"Found something!" she calls out excitedly.

Wriggling out of the crawl space and dropping to the floor, I jump up and push closed the trap door that leads to the crawl space beneath the roof, making my way back into the house to where Marissa waits with her discovery—which would be the master bedroom.

Marissa is there, and she holds something up with a big grin.

"Is that a fucking PDA?" Tallen asks her, disbelief in his tone.

"Yup. Now you tell me, how the hell did they get a PDA?" she asks him with a raised eyebrow.

"They shouldn't! It's tagged to each individual user, and it's a bureaucratic nightmare of a process to get one. Hells, your average person doesn't own one. Usually only a powerful Magus or those who work for the Council have one. Or if you're rich enough."

"Do you think they stole that one?" Carmen supplies.

"How hard can it be? I mean, they gave me one," I tell her.

She turns to me and snorts. "That's because you are part of M.A.G.I. Trust me. No one gets a PDA that easily. Hell, even after I graduated, I couldn't get one. I had to wait until six months after my training was done and I'd joined M.A.G.I. and only when my trainer felt I was ready for one."

"Same here," Marissa says. "I had to wait almost a year."

We all turn to Tallen. He grins and then shrugs. "I'm royalty. We get one when we are young. I think I got mine when I was... ten?"

"Fucking hell," Marissa says, shaking her head, but she's grinning. "Leave it to Royalty to get all the best perks."

"That still doesn't explain why a PDA is here, though," I point out. "Can we access it?"

They all shake their heads. "No, since each PDA is tagged to an individual, only the person who owns it can access it."

"Hmm," I say, looking at the PDA in Marissa's hand. "I wonder if Mike and Jim can access it."

"What?" Tallen says in surprise.

"Oh right," I tell him, grinning in embarrassment. "I wasn't supposed to let that cat out of the bag. But I think we can trust you. As long as you promise to keep it hush-hush."

"I swear to the gods I will, but what the hell do you mean? Isn't Mike your human friend?"

"Yeah. He and Jim figured out how to access a PDA's energy and could actually get information from one. It's incredibly technical, so I'm not sure how it works, but if they could discern the number of tagged locations on my PDA, I wonder if they could get locations off of that," I say, pointing to the PDA in question.

"Only one way to find out," he says, grinning suddenly.

"I guess we are going to see your buddy Mike again," Marissa says, pocketing the PDA.

"I should call him," I tell them. "To warn him we are on our way."

CHAPTER THIRTY-FOUR

"Mike," I tell my best friend. "Thanks for seeing us on such short notice."

"It sounded urgent," he says, rubbing the sleep out of his eyes. "Anything for you, Kevin. You know that."

"Still. It's three in the morning. Hope I didn't wake your parents."

Mike waves his head. "Nah. They are dead to the world. Mom had her nightcap, and Dad had a busy day."

"Where's Jim?" I ask.

"Right here," he says from behind us. "I just got here. Mike said it was urgent?"

"Yeah. Can we go inside? I don't want to discuss this where stray ears can hear us."

Mike doesn't answer me, only nods and waves us inside. Once the front door closes behind us, with me, Marissa,

Carmen, and Tallen standing in the front hall, we all follow him.

"I assume you want to go to my lab?" Mike says, turning to look back at me over his shoulder.

I nod and say, "Yeah. We wanted to know if you can check a PDA for me."

"One of those stones?" Mike asks, stopping suddenly and grinning.

"Yes?" I ask nervously at his enthusiasm.

"Hot damn!" Jim cries behind us.

I turn to him. "Am I missing something?"

"We had some breakthroughs after you left, thanks to Targun. Dude, that man is scary as hell," Jim says, shaking his head.

"Your ladies I know, but who is your friend?" Mike asks, nodding towards Tallen.

"This is Sir Tallen Voldermoten, the Count of the Vampires on Earth."

Mike turns to look Tallen up and down critically, but he nods. "As in Count Dracula?"

Tallen chuckles. "Not like that. But I am a ruler of Magical folk here."

"Wait," Mike says, holding up a hand, "as in the King of the Vampires?"

Tallen rolls his eyes. "No. As in the Count of the Vampires," he tells him.

"Damn," Mike says, looking at me, eyebrows jumping. "You're moving on up in the Magical world."

"You don't know the half of it," I say with a sigh, but I don't go into details about how I might be powerful enough one day to be on the Council—more powerful than Tallen himself, politically.

I had not explained very much to Jim, Mike and his parents about the Council and the worlds. They knew some and had guessed even more, but Targun said we had to be careful that we only stretched and did not break Article 1 completely, even on Earth. Because they were working on a project that was under the direct purview of Targun, we were able to bend the rules some.

"Well," Mike says, waving us to follow him again. "We can discuss that later. For now, let's get to the lab and see if we can help you."

Nodding, we all follow him.

Marissa leans in and whispers. "I wonder what they found."

I whisper back, chuckling. "Knowing Mike and Jim, it's probably something that your Dad will need to get involved with again, since it will be so damn dangerous—either magically or politically."

"Here we go," Mike says, turning through a set of doors and flipping on the overhead lights in a large room with loads of electronic equipment that I am sure cost millions.

"Now, what is it you need?" Mike asks, getting right to the reason the four of us popped up on his doorstep at three in the morning.

I nod to Marissa, who takes out the PDA we'd found at the Dark Elf's home. We had surmised that all those traps might be there simply to protect that stone.

"Can you tell us the locations that it has stored in it?"

Mike frowns, but comes over and picks up the PDA, first making sure it was all right with Marissa for him to take it. At her nod, he holds it gingerly up close to study it.

"Well," he says, with a frown, "this might be a good test. One of the breakthroughs that Jim had, was separating the energy signatures. Once we were able to do that, I was able to write a Python script that extracted the data and allowed us to extrapolate a location."

Mike pauses, handing the PDA back to Marissa. "Did you know that the location shifts constantly?"

With a frown, I ask him, "It does?"

"It only makes sense," Jim chimes in. "We are always moving. The planets are spinning, orbiting around their suns... hell, the entire universe is in constant motion. Something has to account for that. We aren't sure how yet, but that stone," he says, pointing to the PDA in Mike's hand, "seems to account for it all. It's like a gigantic processor, but a Magical one." He grins. "So, while the location you Portal to... is that the right term?"

At our nod, he continues.

"When you Portal to a location, to you, it's just that—a single location, say, like your house. But the location—relative to you—is always moving. If it didn't compute it and account for the differentials, you would end up opening a Portal into space, most likely. That PDA of yours somehow does all that Magically, and it tracks the rotation of the planets, the moons, the suns, or the whatever, to keep that location active. We think it sets a Magical marker of some kind that enables it to do so."

"Damn," Tallen says softly. "I never looked at Portals that way."

"Well, that was our breakthrough—the energy signature. Your Dad," and here Mike turns to Marissa and gives her a nod, "left us a simple stone, with a single location in it. He said it was your place, Kevin, on this planet called Vraka. Which, by the way, is still freaking amazing—but I digress. With that single stored entry, we were able to figure out the location of where this planet is in space."

"You did what?!" Marissa asks, mouth agape in shock.

"Yep," Mike says, going over to a computer that he sits inf front of and begins tapping away at a keyboard. "Let's see… according to this, the planet Vraka is rotating around a sun that is roughly one hundred and twenty million light-years from here. The location is just a bunch of numbers to us, but I guess to those living there, it's Vraka, and its sun."

"Damn. Well, can you tell us how many locations are on that?" I ask, pointing to Marissa and the PDA she has in her hand.

"Let's see," Jim says, holding his hand out to Marissa.

Almost reluctantly, she hands it to him. I can't blame her. Against all the rules that had been drilled into her, she was handing a piece of Magic off to a human. But still, she gives it to him, and he nods his thanks to her.

Jim takes the PDA and goes to a heavy steel tray full of equipment that seems to have a hundred lasers aimed towards it. Placing the PDA on a black plate in the center of this array, he steps away. Stepping over to the machine next to it, he presses a bunch of buttons, and the stone is bathed in a red glare by five pulsing lasers.

Mike taps away on his keyboard. "Light optimal," he says.

"Lasers one and three seem to be fluctuating, increasing power slightly," Jim says, reading a dial on his own machine and turning a knob slightly. I don't see a change in the color of the laser lights, but somehow, I can tell more power is being pushed into them.

"Energy signature found!" Mike says excitedly. But then he frowns.

"What is it?" I ask him worriedly.

"There are only two signatures."

"So only two locations?"

He nods. "Each location saved to a PDA has a signature. That one, it seems, has only two. The one that Targun gave us now has two on it as well—the one he provided us for your place and now a registration for here, since he wanted to make sure that if we ever somehow got it to work without magic, that I could get back."

"Have you tried using it?" Tallen asks curiously.

"Fuck no," Mike says with a chuckle. "I've been very careful not to use it. While we can open a stable Portal. Neither of us have had the balls to walk through it."

"Hold up," I say, raising a hand to stop him. "Did you just say you were able to create a Portal—a stable Portal?"

"Yeah!" he replies with a massive grin. "We figured out what the problem was before. Unlike last time, where the Portal seemed to be glitchy and unstable, we were able to stabilize it —and all it took was adding in some sound."

"Sound?" I ask, puzzled.

"Yes. It seems that one of the things that Jim discovered, was that in order to make the Portal stable, we needed to add a specific frequency—an energy wave of a specific amplitude and cycle—so... a sound. That sound is what makes the Portal stable. We had Targun come and cast a Portal for us and we tested it. It's a sound well beyond the human spectrum, though, one we can't hear."

Jim snorts. "It's so off the charts, I doubt any animal or creature can hear it. Even bats."

"Damn," Tallen says, shaking his head. "I'm glad these two are your friends."

"Same here," I say with a chuckle.

"What can you tell me of the two locations of that PDA? Can you pinpoint the locations?"

"Sure," Mike says, tapping away at his keyboard again. "Jim. Can you add lasers six and seven, and increase the power by twenty-five percent?"

"On it," he says, and stands up to go and adjust something next to the cluster of lasers. Suddenly, two new beams lash out against the rock.

"Now... let's see," Mike says, tapping away again. "One seems to be located in Scotland. But the other... that one makes no sense."

"Why?" Tallen asks him quickly.

Mike looks up and, with the confused look still pinching his brows together, he says. "Because it's underground. Roughly five miles down in the Earth's crust."

We all look at each other at that.

"No way," Tallen whispers, awe in his voice.

"You don't think it's that easy do you?" I ask him.

"What?" Mike asks.

I haven't told Mike about the Dark Elves. That's something I'm not sure I can tell him without getting into trouble.

"We are after some bad people," Marissa chimes in, saving me. "We wonder now, if that's where they are hiding."

Mike looks back down at his screen with a frown, the puzzled look still on his face. "But that's five miles underground. The deepest borehole ever drilled, if I remember, was something like seven miles deep?"

"7.5 miles," Jim adds. "And it took them over twenty years to drill down that far."

"Right," Mike says, and he looks up at me. "And you're saying that someone lives down there? Five miles down?"

"I'm not saying that," I tell him, pointing to the PDA stone bathed in laser light. "That thing is telling you. That is, if your tech is right?"

"Oh, our tech is right. Wow… just, wow."

I look at Tallen, Carmen and Marissa.

"It would explain why we have never seen them or caught wind of them for so long," Carmen says.

"That it would," Tallen says with a sigh. "I'm still curious how they got that PDA and were able to activate it."

"Insider?" I suggest.

Shaking his head, Tallen speculates. "I doubt it. They seem to have an almost instinctive hatred for those of us they call 'lowborn', so I doubt they would be working with one of the Magical folk."

Mike and Jim, through all this, had been switching their gaze back and forth between each of us, trying to follow the conversation. I can tell that they are each getting more and more confused. I look at Marissa and tilt my head at my friends. She turns and sees their confusion.

Coming up to me, she whispers. "Your call. This is your show."

"And your Dad?" I whisper.

"Pfft. My Dad will follow your lead in this."

I take a deep breath and blow it out, nodding slowly. I hate hiding things from my two best friends. "So," I speak up, "the people we are after? They're killers. They've been murdering Magical folk for who knows how long, siphoning off their Magic using enchanted silver daggers. We are after them. That PDA," I say, pointing the stone we'd found at the Dark Elf's place, "Was in the house of one of the people we were after. It was incredibly well protected—so well that the safeguards in place almost killed me several times over."

Mike and Jim both blanch.

"I think all that protection was there to protect that stone, and the location stored in it."

Mike frowns. "Wait. Aren't we humans, the Magical folks' enemy?"

"We thought so, but it seems we now face an even bigger threat," Tallen says, seeing where I was going with this.

One thing about my Vampire friend—he isn't stupid. He catches on fast. I think he knows I will be letting my friends in on this secret. He is helping me ease them into it. I mean, I'd already introduced them to the Magical world, full of Changelings and Vampires and Faeries. That was a shocker all by itself. How much of a difference does it make to add Dark Elves to the mix of fantastical races?

"Who are they?" Mike asks, looking at us all suspiciously.

I look around, and Marissa, Carmen, and Tallen all nod at me, agreeing with my plan to let them in on the secret.

"Dark Elves," I say quietly.

Both Mike and Jim's eyes go wide.

"Bloody fucking hell! Drow exist, too?! Are you shitting us?" Jim sputters.

I'm shocked at his outburst, this being the most expressive I have ever heard him get. "I wish I was," I say with a sigh. "It would make things so much easier."

CHAPTER THIRTY-FIVE

"The big question now is: Can you open a Portal to that location?" I ask Mike in a serious tone.

Mike looks nervous. "I can open a Portal, Sure. But we haven't tested someone going through it."

"Well, I guess we are about to find out if it works," I tell him with a crooked smile, albeit a shaky one.

"Kevin..." he starts to say.

I shake my head. "We have no choice. Trust me; this is big. We need to confirm some information about these Dark Elves, and that," I say, pointing to the PDA once more, "is the only way to do it."

"But you're risking your life with my tech. I trust it, sure. But asking you to trust it is... different."

"Mike. How long have we been friends?" I ask him.

"Pretty damn long," he says with a sigh.

"And I trust you and Jim as much as I trust anyone in this world—though I now have to include my two beautiful partners in that. I trust you with my life. If you say you trust your tech, then I trust it as well."

"Kevin?" Jim says.

I turn to him.

"I'm not saying this to convince you otherwise, but we don't know what will happen if you go through that Portal. All the numbers indicate it should work, but we have not tested it."

"Then how can we test it?" Marissa asks.

Jim turns to her and frowns. I know the frown is directed at the question, not her asking it. "We can toss inanimate objects through it—maybe even something tied to a string and then pull it back through." He pauses. "But the only way to test it properly, is for someone to go through it."

"Either way, you need to conduct tests," Carmen indicates.

Jim now gets a sour expression. "Yes," he says slowly.

"Then, let us test it. We need to know what is at that location. Right now, unknown numbers of Magical folk on Earth are being killed to harvest their Magic by these Dark Elves. We need to stop them."

"Fine," Mike says. "But I'm testing it."

"What?" I blurt out in surprise.

"No way!" Marrisa says, shaking her head.

"Are you nuts?" Tallen burst out.

I notice that Carmen is the only one who hadn't said anything. She was looking at Mike intriguingly.

"You just want to go through a Portal," she tells him.

Mike turns to her and grins. "My tech. My choice."

Jim coughs, and Mike rolls his eyes before amending his statement: "Our tech. Our choice."

Jim grins and nods at that.

I look from Carmen to Marissa, and then to Tallen. Our Vampire friend wears a sour expression, while Marissa simply glares at Mike and Jim. Carmen, on the other hand, is smiling.

Seeing the smile, I ask her, "What?"

"Mike and Jim are very much like you, aren't they?"

I frown at her comment. "What do you mean?"

"You don't care much about danger—you three are very much alike. You seem to do things with Magic we Magical folk have never considered. And now they are doing the same, but with human technology."

Mike and Jim each give me curious looks, raising their eyebrows at Carmen's comment.

Shrugging, and feeling uncomfortable since it's true, I slowly nod. "It's not that I don't care about danger. I just don't think about it."

Jim, with a massive grin, says, "Sounds like the time Mike tested an explosive round for his Dad's company that was meant for a truck-sized weapon. Mike wanted to make a shoulder-fired version of it."

"What happened?" Tallen asks.

Mike scowls. "I broke my collarbone."

"And bruised his face," I add.

"And broke his nose," Jim adds.

"Oh shit... I had forgotten that part," I say with a chuckle. "What about the time you tried to wire up that security system with lasers three years ago?" I remind Jim.

"Hey, it was supposed to work! It worked in the Star Wars movies."

Mike rolls his eyes. "That was a movie. This was real life."

"Well... it almost worked," Jim mumbles, blushing.

"True. Until the lasers you used almost burned down the house," Mike tells him with a laugh. "God, my Dad was so upset with you about that one."

"Not as much as your mom," I remind him. "Jim ended up torching all the rose bushes in her garden."

"Anyhow," Carmen interjects before things got even more awkward. "I'm afraid you can't be the guinea pig for this, guys. If we were to allow a human to use a PDA Portal—even if just for testing purposes—I don't think that even Marissa's Dad would be able to keep us out of going to jail for it."

"Right," Tallen agrees. "So we will be the ones to test it. You fire it up, and we will test it. Though, I would rather not test it right off the bat by going into the belly of the beast, so to speak. Can you test it using say, Kevin's PDA stone, first?"

Mike and Jim look at each other, and reluctantly nod. "Fine. Yes. We can use any PDA now. We can test Kevin's. Where did you want to test it to?"

I take my PDA out of my pocket and hand it to him. "Well. I have Tallen's castle in Scotland registered on it—we can test that. If anything odd happens, I can call from there and Tallen can come get me. I assume that works?" I ask Tallen.

"Works for me," he says, nodding in agreement.

"Who said you were going to be the one testing it?" Marissa growls at me.

"Well, I'm the obvious…" I start to say, but she's already shaking her head.

"You just used up a metric shit ton of Magic, Carmen called it. I think you should rest for a while and regain that power, I'm sure we'll need it when we go wherever that PDA from the Dark Elf sends us and we need to fight."

Knowing she's right but hating it, I slowly nod. "Fine," I grumble. "But I still think I should be the one to go."

"I should go," Tallen says. "It is my castle."

"Jesus. Do all of you have a death wish?" Mike mutters. "We haven't tested it!"

Tallen turns to him and nods. "If Kevin trusts your tech, then I will trust it as well. I haven't known Kevin long, but I trust him with my life."

"You trust him that much?" Mike asks him.

"I do. Kevin is my foster son."

"He's your… What!?!?" Mike yells in surprise, turning to me for confirmation.

I rub the back of my neck. "Things… happened. And now I'm technically a Vampire. Though it didn't quite go as planned and… I'm still human. But anyhow, because of that, I am part of the Royal family, and his foster son."

Mike turns to look at Tallen and then back at me. Several times, back and forth, and then he gets a look on his face I have seen too many times. It's a calculating look.

"No, I can't bite you," I tell him.

"Shit," he says with a scowl. Looking over, as expected, I see that Jim had the same look on his face.

Jesus, these two, I think with a laugh.

"Fine," Mike mumbles. "But I won't stop trying to join your Magic club."

"I don't expect you to," I tell him with a laugh.

Sighing, he looks at Jim. "All right. Take his PDA, and let's test it with that."

Sighing as well, Jim takes my PDA back to his work area. First though, he turns off the seven lasers pulsing against the Dark Elf PDA. Once the lasers stop, he swaps out the PDA Marrisa had given him to identify, out for mine, placing it down in the same spot.

Jim fiddles with a few buttons, and the lasers are back on, all seven this time—instead of the original five.

Mike starts to tap away at his keyboard. "Okay, I think I've got it. You have multiple signatures on this one, but I am seeing one that is here on Earth, in… Scotland?"

I confirm, "that would be it."

"All right, here we go," Mike says. "Jim. Increase the power incrementally this time. Make sure the resonance numbers don't go into the red."

"Power increasing ten percent at a time. Dilation is good. Power is stable. Sonics are spot on, within an acceptable range of 0.04 percent."

"Good. Increase tachyon particle rate by two."

Tallen asks with a frown. "Tachyon particles? Aren't those still theoretical?"

Mike turns to him and grins. "Yes. According to most scientists out there."

"But yet you and Jim figured it out?" I ask him with a chuckle.

"Company secret," he tells me, holding up finger to his lips with a massive grin.

I can't help but laugh. Leave it to Jim and Mike to figure something like that out. These two are too smart for our world—the human world, that is. I'm glad I am bringing them into the Magical one. I have a feeling that Mike, Jim, and Mikes' parents' companies will be a tremendous boon to the Magical worlds.

"Portal in three, two, and one," Mike says, as the hum of power in the room increases.

Suddenly, in a clear area off to the side, where my PDA had been pointing, a Portal opens up black as midnight, though it seems to be slightly distorted. The Portal at first shows signs of being unstable.

"Increase power by 15 percent," Mike tells Jim.

Jim nods. "Power increased by 15 percent."

That does it. The Portal, which had glitching along the edges with bursts of static, snaps into existence stable and clean.

"We have Portal!" Mike shouts ecstatically.

"Mike looks down at his monitor and says excitedly, "Portal reading steady at 98 percent. The connection to the other location is solid. No interference to speak of. It worked!"

"Now to test it," Carmen says with a deep breath.

Before anyone can go to it, though, Mike jumps out of his chair and darts across the space between where he had been sitting and the Portal. He jumps through before any of us, even with our faster speeds, can catch him. He caught us all flat footed as he disappears through the Portal.

"Mike!" I shout in a panic.

"What the hell!" Tallen says, but though he was closer and faster than me, even he wasn't able to snatch Mike back before he jumped into the black Portal. He'd nearly caught hold of Mike's shoulder but missed by an inch as suddenly, Mike disappears from the room.

We all stand around, stunned by what just happened, staring dumbly at the Portal.

Hearing a heavy sigh beside me, I turn to look, and it is Marissa.

She turns to me, shaking her head. "He's just like you, isn't he?"

"What? I'm not that impulsive!"

Tallen turns to me from where he stands in front of the Portal and snorts, but says nothing.

"I'm not that impulsive!" I repeat.

Carmen comes up to me and pats me on the arm. "Sure, Kevin. Keep telling yourself that."

I look over at Jim, and see he's staring at the Portal which Mike had just jumped into. He's already halfway out of his seat.

"You fucker," I tell him. "You were about to jump as well, weren't you?"

Jim jerks in surprise, easing back in his seat with a guilty look. "I have no idea what you are talking about."

"Jesus," Marissa says with a laugh. "Both of them are just as bad as you."

I'm about to respond to that accusation, but Mike suddenly reappears with a massive grin on his face. "It worked!" he shouts triumphantly.

"You know you just broke, I have no idea how many Magical rules, right?" I tell him with a scowl.

"Oh, it was worth it!" he says with a massive grin.

"It worked?" Tallen asks him quickly.

"I assume it worked. I brought up my cell phone and was able to use a map app to confirm that I was in Scotland, right in front of this massive castle." He turns to Tallen. "You own that?"

"Yes, that's one of my castles."

Mike doesn't say anything, but finally, slowly, he asks. "And just how many castles do you own?"

"Here on Earth? Nine? Ten? I always forget. I also have a small one on the Vampire world of Vamir, but it's more of a keep than a full castle."

Almost in an awed tone, Mike asks him, "Just how rich are you?"

"Hmm… Not sure. I never really thought about wealth like that. But," he sighs, "I'm a Count, so I suppose I should look into that some day." He shrugs. "I'm probably the richest Magical person on Earth."

"Focus." I cough into my hand. "So it works?"

"Yes," Mike says, blushing.

"You know that was probably the stupidest thing you've ever done, right?" I tell him. ""Worse even than that time you tried asking the entire Varsity squad of cheerleaders to the Prom."

Mike turns to me and grins. "Yes. But I'm not about to apologize."

Shaking my head but grinning at him. "Oh, I wasn't going to ask you to say sorry. But, if you ever do that again, I swear I will beat the shit out of you myself. You nearly gave me a fucking heart attack."

He scowls at that and looks me up and down. With Magic, I have added some impressive mass to my frame and even grew an inch or two. Gods, I love Magic!

"Why couldn't you have stayed skinny, like when we were kids?"

"Because if that was the case, you would not have had me as your wingman to guide you unerringly to the promised land when we were in college," I tell him with a laugh.

"Should we swap out the PDAs and try that underground location?" Tallen suggests, interrupting our banter.

Mike nods, getting serious. "Right. Let's change it up. It should only take us another couple of minutes to bring that one up and open another Portal. Jim, slowly bring the power down and turn off the lasers, swap out the stones, and we will repeat the same steps with the other PDA."

"On it," he says.

Within minutes, as predicted by Mike, we have a new Portal open.

"Ready," Mike says, nodding towards the new Portal.

CHAPTER THIRTY-SIX

"All signs show it's stable," Jim says, looking up from his own monitors.

"Levels are good across the board for me as well," Mike pipes up.

The Portal looks the same as every other Portal I have cast; the only difference being that this one leads into enemy— according to their instruments—territory.

"How do you feel?" Marissa asks me.

"You mean how am I for power?" I ask, giving her a smile.

She's standing right beside me, in front of the new Portal.

"Yeah," she says with a smile.

"Good. I can tell I've recovered some of my reserve. I should be good for whatever we run into."

"We hope," Tallen says.

Rapping my knuckles on the wood of a nearby desk , I nod, "We hope."

"Are you sure you don't want us to come?" Mike chips in.

"No!" we all shout at him.

"Fine," he grouses, looking down at his monitor and pressing a button. "Portal appears to be stable. All parameters good."

"Mike," I tell him softly. "Trust me. As much as I would kill to have you and Jim at my side, this is too dangerous. Even for us, it's incredibly dangerous."

"I know," he mopes. "I just hate seeing you go on these adventures and being left behind."

"I know."

"We got everything we need?" Tallen asks.

"Probably not," Carmen says with a snort.

Tallen grins at her. "Well, we will improvise, if need be. Though, make sure each of you have your PDAs handy, in case we need to cast a Portal to get out quickly." He turns to me. "Kevin, can you cast Shield on each of us again, or would that take too much of your remaining reserves?"

"No, I'm good for that," I tell him. Doing as directed, I cast Shield on each of us.

Once done, Tallen nods and looks at Mike. "As soon as we are through, close the Portal. I would rather us get out some other way, than have the enemy rush a Portal I have no control over."

"Smart," Mike tells him, pressing a button. "I will close the Portal as soon as the last of you are through. I don't want to get overrun in here." He frowns, looking around at the laboratory. "I never even considered bringing weapons in here, in case of something like that. We will have to reconsider proper security measures, I think."

"Good idea," I tell him. "Just don't use silver bullets."

"Oh, trust me. I know what silver does to Magical beings." Mike says with a chuckle. "But my Dad is working on a weapon for a Merc contractor, that would be perfect for here. It shoots liquid at such a high-velocity that it will shred anything, including a Magical being."

Tallen lifts an eyebrow. "Handgun, or shoulder fired?"

"Eventually, both," Mike tells him with a grin. "But for now, it's mostly in the larger format because we have yet to miniaturize the components. We are trying to micro size them."

"That gives you an idea?" I ask Tallen, hearing something in his tone.

"Yes. If it can shoot liquid. I wonder if such a weapon could deliver, say, doses of drugs that would knock someone out—even a Changeling in their Bear form, or a Beast in Bear form?"

"Oh, nice!" Mike says, pulling his phone out and tapping away on it.

I look at Mike with a question.

"I just emailed the researcher working on it to see if that would be a viable drug delivery means. Can you imagine being able to knock someone out from hundreds of feet away using this tech?"

Tallen turns to me. "This is why we need to be part of the human world. We'll be left behind with technology that soon will be indistinguishable from Magic."

"Shall we get this over with?" Carmen says out loud. "We are just stalling, here."

"Yes," Tallen says with a sigh. "I am stalling. I might be a Count, but that doesn't mean I love jumping into the unknown, especially when we know it is into danger."

"Then why are we?" Marissa asks the obvious question.

"Because who else will?" he tells her. "And how else will we confirm or deny the intelligence we already gathered?" He snorts. "You three are the most powerful M.A.G.I. agents out there. Hell, with Kevin on our team, we are the most powerful team in all of the known worlds."

"Not to be too cliché, but we're doing this because we are the only ones who can. I would love to have William with us and his expertise, but we will have to make do without him."

"William's expertise?" I inquire.

I knew William, the Count of Vamir, though I didn't know him well. He was someone we'd helped once, who wanted to study human technology at university here on Earth. The issue that brought him to our attention, was that his sister had tried to get rid of him, claiming he'd gone feral. It was nothing more than a power grab, though, by his twin sister. They both were qualified to get a seat on the Council of Magical Folk, but she'd wanted it so badly that she tried to get William arrested by M.A.G.I. like us for going feral. I preferred to think she hadn't hoped we'd simply take him out.

Her plan didn't go as intended, though. Now, he was a friend of mine, studying Engineering at some Ivy League University in the United States—Cornell, I think. His sister ended up in hot water with Marissa's Dad, the Lead Councillor for the vaunted Magical Council she'd tried to kill to get onto.

Nodding, Tallen explains. "William is an expert in Magical combat. He is so good at it, that he should be teaching it. Instead, he wants to learn Earth tech."

"Damn," I say, looking at Tallen intrigued. "I will need to talk to him about that next time I see him."

"But first, let's get this mission over and done with."

"Should we tell my Dad what we are doing?" Marissa adds.

"Will he let us go if we do?" Tallen asks her.

She scowls. "Right. No, he would want us to take things slow."

"Then… no." Tallen smiles. "I think this is one of those cases where it is better to ask for forgiveness than permission."

"Mike," I say, glancing at him. "You still talk to Targun much?"

"Yes. I have his cell number. Though we typically text one another; he only sees them when he pops up on Earth."

"Hmm. I guess a communication stone would not work for you, since you can't trigger it with Magic."

"No," he says, frowning. "But, if I had one of those, I might be able to power it up from here, with Jim's help."

"No!" Carmen, Tallen, and Marissa suddenly blurt out.

"Sorry," Carmen tells Mike. "It's just that us handing you a communication stone would get us in all kinds of hot water. You've already had access to that," she says, pointing to the Portal that still thrums with power. "I doubt the Council would take kindly to you having access to a communication stone, as well."

"I get it," he says with a sigh. "I'm grateful to even know that this Magical world exists. Still freaky to know that my best friend who I grew up with is considered a powerful Magus. The most powerful one out there to boot."

"Portal is showing instability," Jim interrupts our musings.

"Right," Tallen says. "I'm surprised you have been able to keep it open this long. Even a Magus would be hard-pressed to keep one open for several minutes." He shakes his head. "This technology might change many things—even on the other worlds, if we can make it work there, too."

"Oh, trust me. Jim and I will make it work. Though, Kevin that reminds me. When you get back, I need you to sign some paperwork."

"Paperwork? For what?"

"For the patents on this stuff. While I can patent it on Earth, it's tech that humans won't see for a long time—but for the other worlds, Targun says we need to run everything through you."

I stare at him in surprise. "You want me to own the patents for this stuff?" I say, waving my hand around at his contraption and the Portal that it had opened.

"Either that, or the tech will get out, and someone else will benefit from it. It was Targun's idea—in fact, he insisted on it... something about a Form 3? Never mind; we can worry about that later. Now, let's get you all through that Portal, as I am seeing signs of instability now, as well." Mikes taps out a command on his keyboard and then call out, "Jim, increase power by fifteen percent."

Jim nods and turns a knob, and I can feel the thrumming of power increase slightly in the room.

"Done. It's stable again, though I'm not sure for how long."

"You're recording the numbers for later analysis?"

"Everything is being recorded," Jim nods in agreement.

"Now," Mike says with a grin, turning back to us. "Get out of my lab."

Laughing, I salute him. "Yes, sir!"

Tallen turns to me. "I'll go first."

"Sounds good to me," I tell him with a nod. "I will go last."

"No, I will go last," Carmen says, poking me in the chest. "We need you front and center in case the fit hits the shan."

"The order will be me, Marissa, Kevin, and then Carmen," Tallen orders.

Carmen and Marissa both nod.

"Here we go," Tallen says, taking a deep breath and walking into the Portal. He disappears.

Marissa does the same, but before she passes through the Portal, she calls up her Focus and has her handgun in her hand.

Before following my wife, I turn quickly to Mike. "Text Targun to let him know that we are going into what we think is a large habitat for Dark Elves. Let him know the location, and that we will keep him posted."

"Sounds good. Now move your ass before the Portal collapses."

I nod to him and jump through the Portal. On the other side, it's pitch black. I freeze, then feel Carmen pushing me out of the way with a curse. "Whoa!" I hiss, stumbling forward.

"Here," Marissa says from somewhere close, putting a hand over my eyes.

A flash of light blinds me. Blinking the spots from my eyes, I open them, and am shocked that I can see.

"Was that a See spell?" I ask, looking down at her.

"Yes. It's pitch black in here." She snorts. "Tallen busted his nose walking into the wall."

"Which smarts, by the way," he says, rubbing his nose, which I see is slightly red.

"Next time," Carmen grumps, "make sure you don't clog up the exit."

Look around, I see the Portal had opened before a cave wall. Where we had come out, there was only four feet between the Portal and the wall. I guess it was pitch black when Tallen had come through; he'd kept on walking and had face-planted into the wall.

The cave we are in is large. Probably with about a twenty-foot-high ceiling, and plenty of those rock formations that drip down. Stalagmites, or something like that? These are surprisingly colorful, with a mix of blues, reds, and browns.

The room itself was probably several thousand square feet. It is damp, and I can hear water dripping into a pool. But it's also hot—hot and muggy. Within seconds, all my pores have opened and I'm sweating profusely.

I cast Cool on myself, almost without thinking, and suddenly feel much cooler. The rest of my party looks at me with raised eyebrows. "What?" I say. "It's hot."

"Pass me some of that," Marissa says with a grin, damp hair already clinging to her face.

"If you're handing out Cool spells, count me in," Carmen says with a big grin.

I look over at Tallen, and he snorts. "As if I am going to say no to not sweating like a pig."

Once everyone has Cool cast on them, we look around. Not that we are laissez-faire about it. Marissa still has her Focus out, and Carmen has hers on her back, in its sniper rifle form. Tallen is holding a dark staff in his hands.

Once done casting the Cool spells, I call out my Focus and decide on a staff as well. I was still learning how to use my Focus. So far, I'd been able to turn it into daggers and a sword. Once the staff was in my hand, I glance at it. It feels like metal, though I know it isn't. It's Magic! God, I love Magic. The staff is as tall as me and well balanced, as if custom made for my hand—which, technically speaking, is true, since it was my Magic that called it up.

In the distance, we hear sounds—voices, though indistinct. We can't tell what language it is, or even if the speaker is male or female.

Tallen points to a rock formation, and we all rush to hide behind it, and I cast Hide just in time. Through one of the openings in the cave walls, a group of Dark Elves comes through, torches held high to see.

The torches are the old kind, made from black pitch-soaked cloth, and smoky.

There are six Dark Elves. No, make that seven. In the middle of them is another Dark Elf, but she is led by one of the others by a thick chain. She is hunched over because of the heavy chains. It wasn't until I noticed her chains, that the jingling noise I had been hearing made sense.

The male Dark Elf behind her growls something at her in a tongue I don't understand. She doesn't reply, and he shoves her—hard—causing her to falls forward onto her hands and knees. One of the other men kicks her in the side, all the while yelling at her, yanking her up by the chains and shaking her.

I hear low growls from beside me. Looking over, both Carmen and Marissa have their teeth bared, glaring at the abusers with hatred in their eyes. Sighing, because I know we don't really have a choice about this—as even I can't watch someone being abused like that—I touch the girls' arms and nod to them. Tallen nods to me, as well, indicating he under-stands we are going to rescue this prisoner.

And, to be honest, maybe we can get some good intel from her.

CHAPTER THIRTY-SEVEN

We wait until they come closer, before jumping out to ambush them. Carmen had stayed back, so that she could put her sniper rifle to good use.

I rush out, with Tallen right behind me, leaping into the middle of the group of Dark Elves.

Carmen takes out two of them with her rifle. Their heads suddenly exploding in a shower of gore, brain matter and bone blasting out of the back of their heads as the Magical bullets from Carmen's focus empties their craniums.

Not to be left out, Marissa has her focus, which looks like a .357 Magnum, in hand, and it barks twice. She shoots one through the heart, but her other target had jumped back in shock, and she only clips him in the shoulder. I turn my attention to my own foe, confident that Marissa will finish him off.

I had jumped at the one in the lead, whirling it around before slashing my staff forward without thinking, smacking my target in the head, then sweeping the back of his legs, to bring him down hard. He wasn't going out without a fight, though. Suddenly, he has a dagger in his hand and somehow uses it to parry the heavy downward blow of my staff, which I'd slammed down to crush his head. With only his dagger, he stops it—redirecting my strike so that the tip of my staff crashes into the cave's floor, instead.

Within seconds he's back up on his feet and, dagger in hand, he takes a probing swing—as if trying to find me. They can't see! The torches had most likely played havoc with their dark vision. Now, as the two who had been carrying them had been taken out by Carmen, the torches had sputtered out upon hitting the wet floor.

I jump back, clearing a good ten feet, thanks to my enhanced strength and speed. Once out of melee range from my target and his dagger, I change my Focus into a handgun. Now resembling a Glock, I bring it up and, while my target is still swinging his blade haphazardly back and forth, I shoot him in the forehead.

Turning to our last target, I see them go down, Tallen's staff literally taking the Dark Elf's head off. Tallen had swung for the fences, his staff removing his target's head from its shoulders at the neck. The seventh Dark Elf—the prisoner—is huddled down on the ground in a fetal position, her arms covering her head.

"That was easy," Carmen says, her Focus back on her back.

Hearing the blonde's voice, the prisoner lifts her head up in surprise, looking at us—or trying to. I'm sure to her everything is pitch black.

"You speak English?" she calls out. Her English is heavily accented, almost like hearing someone from Ukraine or another of those Eastern European countries.

We all look down at her, intrigued.

"Please don't kill me, humans!"

"Hmm," I say, looking at everyone else.

Marissa is the one to go to the prisoner. "We aren't going to kill you, as long as you give us the information we need."

The prisoner looks at where Marissa's voice is coming from, as I doubt she can see without some ambient light to relieve the pitch black.

I come closer, and she must have heard something, since her head snaps my way, her eyes darting left and right, though generally in my direction. "It's all right," I tell her softly. "I'm going to make it so that you can see us, but I need to touch your face to do so. Is that all right?"

She might be a Dark Elf, who are currently enemy number one, but she was still a woman. And I'd promised long ago always to respect women.

She looks confused at my question, but slowly nods.

I step forward, finally getting a closer look at her. She looks similar to Balina, the Dark Elf we'd captured at the hospital: Hair dark as midnight, with eyes pretty much the same. The prisoner's eyes are so wide in fear, however, that I can clearly see their white sclera. She was also really cute.

I guess there are notable differences in how their race looks. Whereas Balina's features seemed chiseled and haughty, all hard edges and angles, hers are softer, with high cheekbones on a slightly rounded face. I'm surprised to see her body is not slim and toned like Balina's, either. Hers is curvy.

She has a pair that, even in the rags she is in, I can see are on par with Marissa's and Carmen's stacked assets. Damn. Certain parts of me note—all south of my belt, I might add— complain how all that amazing cleavage will go to waste, if we have to kill her after.

I place my hand on her forehead, slowly lowering my palm until I am covering her eyes, though even at my gentle touch, she flinches. I cast See on her. Suddenly, she blinks, looking from one of us to the others. Her eyes open even wider at seeing not just me, a human, but a Vampire and two Changelings. Both have their tails and ears out, though I'm not sure when they had done so. But neither of my girls are in their human form.

"Who... who are you?" she asks slowly, almost in a whisper.

"We will ask the questions," Carmen tells her. "Who are you?"

She nods quickly and swallows, peering fearfully back at Carmen, her large pupils rimmed with white. "They call me Li."

"Li?" I ask her. "Just... Li?"

She turns to me quickly and shakes her head. "Li Olnon."

"Well, Li Olnon," Marissa chimes in. "Answer our questions, and we won't have to kill you."

Li nods quickly.

"Now," Marissa asks her, "why are you in chains?"

Li looks down quickly at the chains on her wrists, and her lips thin, her brows pulling down angrily. "Because I am being taken to my death. Or I was, until you..." and she waves a hand at the dead bodies around her. "Rescued me, I guess. Though it seems I have been spared, only to be killed soon afterwards," she finishes with a sigh.

"Why were you being taken to your death?" I ask, now really curious.

She turns, looking up at me. "Because I am an outcast amongst my people."

"Li," Carmen says, snapping her fingers. "If you are going to give us cryptic answers like that, we won't have a reason to keep you alive."

"Right," she says, her accent somehow getting more pronounced in her fear.

She mumbles something under her breath, but even though I catch her words with my enhanced hearing, it's not in a language I know.

"In the human tongue," Carmen growls at her.

"Sorry," Li says, nodding quickly. "I was calling myself an idiot for answering your questions like that. The reason I am an outcast," she says, licking her lips, "is that I think we should be working with the Top-Siders. Because of my heretical thoughts and ideas, I am being sent to my death."

"Top-Siders?" I ask, puzzled by the term.

She nods at me. "Yes. Top-Siders. Those who live on the surface of this world."

To ensure we are on the same wavelength, I clarify, "You mean humans?"

Li shakes her head. "No. All Top-Siders—including those who hide among the humans. The… the Magical folk, as they call themselves, like you three," she says, nodding to Carmen, Marissa, and Tallen.

Then she turns to me and frowns. "But, you did Magic. You're not a human, then, like I thought. What are you?"

"Different," I tell Li with a smile.

She frowns at my cryptic answer, but doesn't push.

"Now, Li, where are we?" Carmen asks her.

She turns to Carmen and doesn't answer right away but finally nods. "I am already dead to my people. You are near one of our cities. Well, we are still on its outskirts. They were bringing me to the killing pit."

"Killing pit?" Marissa asks her.

"Essentially, a hole in the ground that seems to never end. They throw the condemned into it, and they plummet to their deaths."

"That's fucking barbaric!" cries Marissa in shock.

"Hold up," Tallen says, holding a hand up. "You said you were being sent to your death because you thought that your people should work with us Top-Siders? I thought all Dark Elves wanted us 'lowborn' dead after draining our Magic from us?"

Li gets a bitter look on her face. "Not all of us. Some of us— the younger generation—want nothing more than to get out of the dark to go topside and live among you Top-Siders. But the Elders teach us differently. They teach us that we, as Dark Elves, are the master race, meant to rule over all the other races."

With a sneer, Marissa asks her, "And you disagree?"

She turns to Marissa and nods quickly. "Some of us do not wish to be masters of anything. We simply want to live on the surface, to feel the sun on our faces. By the Gods, I would love to feel the sun on my face. I have never felt it."

"You have never left the depths?" I ask her.

Li shakes her head. "No. Most of us live and die down here without ever coming to the surface... never seeing the sun or even the stars at night. We have stories about how wonderful it is. But... but that's all they are to us... Stories."

"Li," I ask her slowly. "How many of your people think like you?"

"Many," she says with a sigh. "I am the sixth person this cycle in my city alone being sent to their deaths."

"And this happens in all the cities? How many cities are there down here?"

She shrugs. "At last count, I heard there were over two hundred darkside cities. My city," and she points the way she and her group of guards had come from, "contains over two thousand souls, though we are just a small city."

"What's the biggest city?" Tallen asks her quickly.

"That would be Lamkar, the capital. It has over a million people. But, it's also one of only a few cities that hold so many. It's a journey of tens of days to get there through tunnels—and there are the beasts of the underdark to contend with."

"This might change our plans," I tell everyone, and they all nod.

"What plans?" Li asks me suspiciously.

I turn to her, wondering if I should answer her question. To be honest, she's our prisoner, and I have no clue what will become of her. Either she answers all our questions, or we will have to kill her. And right now, I would hate to kill her.

But she is still the enemy. Knowing that she might not live much longer, I decide to tell her. "We came here to get intel about your race, as we have had violent dealings with them, as you say, Top-Side. We came here with the intent to see if we could stop you. Your race, or some of your race, are killing Magical folk using silver daggers—draining the Magic out of those they kill."

Li nods and sighs. "We'd heard that the Dark Guards were doing that."

"The Dark Guards?" Carmen asks her.

"The Dark Guards are an arm of our King and Queen. They are the ones who work Top-Side, faithfully carrying out the vision of the Kings and Queens for thousands of years: hiding from the Top-Siders and stealing their Magic and whatever else we can. All so that, one day, the Kings and Queens will rule over all of this world, cutting the other worlds off from this one, the mother world."

"And your thoughts on this vision?" Marissa asks her softly.

"My thoughts?" she says, and again bitterness creeps in. "My thoughts don't matter since I'm a small voice in a large group. I only wish to see the sun and stars that I have heard about in the stories. I want to live my life the way I want to— without poisoning the future with hate. What does it matter that we lost our heritage? If you read between the lines when our stories are shared, it is clear we reaped the deadly caps of the mushrooms we sowed."

She shakes her head bitterly. "I know that the stories say the other gods fought our god, because they couldn't bear knowing he was right and they were wrong, but he lost and paid with his own life for this supposed truth, and our people lost their ability to do Magic because of it."

"I am not stupid enough to think that was what happened, though. I see how our leaders are—backstabbers all, ever cutting deals in the background, slicing their own mother's throats for a leg up."

In the silence that follows, I ask a question that has been bothering me. "How is it you can speak English, if you have never been topside," I ask her.

"We learn it, in case we need to go Top-Side one day. We all learn English, after our mother tongue. Some of us also learn other languages. I know my own language, but also English, Polish, Ukrainian, and Russian. These are countries on the Top-Side that I would love to see one day, but..." and the bitterness resurfaces, "I shall always be stuck down here, miles below the warmth of the sun. The only way I ever could, would be if I joined the Dark Guards—but I have no desire to kill those who have done nothing to me."

"Are there many others like you? With similar thoughts?" I inquire.

She nods quickly. "Yes. But, if we talk about it too openly... this happens." She waves down at her body to indicate the state she is in: in rags, bound in chains.

I turn to Carmen, Marissa, and Tallen. "Guys. This changes things."

Tallen sighs and nods. "Yes. Things just got more complicated. We might need to go back and talk to Marissa's Dad about this."

"Yeah. This is well above my pay grade," Carmen adds.

"Take me with you!" Li suddenly shouts, getting up off the ground quickly, standing and bowing low at the waist. "Please, don't leave me here to die at my people's hand for believing we should live in peace!"

CHAPTER THIRTY-EIGHT

I look back at Li, who is sitting down once more, and staring around at everything and everywhere, but at us. We had moved a dozen feet away to discuss her predicament.

"So, what should we do?" I ask my companions.

"I know what you want to do," Carmen says, giving me a grin and bouncing her eyebrows at me. "She's cute. I saw you checking out her curves."

"She is a beauty," I tell her with a smile. "But that's not a valid reason."

"I don't know," Marissa says, looking back at Li as well. "She is pretty—in a dark, mysterious kind of way. And she has a smoking hot body."

"But she's a Dark Elf," Tallen points out.

"But she's a Dark Elf," Marissa agrees, nodding.

"What will your Dad say?" I ask Marissa, hoping for some insight.

"Other than freak out at having another Dark Elf in his house?"

Quickly, I add, "I don't want him to dissect her."

She shakes her head. "No. He wouldn't do that, but to be able to converse with one—without having to force the words from her lips with magic? To gain insight to the mind of a Dark Elf?"

"Invaluable," Tallen says, looking at Li in a different light. "Hell, if he won't take her in and ward her, I will—just to gain that information. I don't think the Dark Elves are going away anytime soon. If anything, we are in for a long war against them."

"That was my thought, as well," I tell him, nodding. "We need intel. We came for intel. And Jesus H. Christ. We have the best Intel we can get—a person who has lived down there, who just so happens to speak English amongst other languages—well… human languages—sorry."

"We could always just pop in and surprise her old man," Carmen says with a big grin. "We brought him an uncooperative prisoner before—he'll freak if we bring him a Dark Elf willing to talk to him."

"Oh gods, he would have a fit," Tallen says with a chuckle. "We might give him a heart attack."

"Can't Kevin just say she's his ward?" Carmen suggests. "He's now the most powerful M.A.G.I. agent but also a royal of the Vampire Court on Earth, and I'm sure we can find other things. Oh, and let's not forget he's probably the highest level Magus now in existence—higher than Marissa's Dad."

"Yeah," Marissa says slowly. "But some of that hasn't been confirmed yet. Have you told anyone else about making Kevin your foster son, Tallen, by biting him?"

Tallen has the grace to blush at that and rubs the back of his neck. "Not really. It's still kind of embarrassing, to say I did it how I did. It wasn't an official request, as would normally be done between consenting adults. I… uhh… more or less, just took a chance. It worked out, but… hmm…."

"So that means no," Carmen says, grinning at him.

"What other options do we have?" I ask.

"I could take her under my care," Tallen mutters slowly, frowning. "But that would mean I would have to bite her and, to be honest? Doing what I did to Kevin—the Full Transformation—took a lot out of me. I doubt I can do a full one again for at least another year."

"Same for us, too," Marrisa says, waving to herself and Carmen. "Biting her would do nothing more than leave teeth marks and maybe an infectious wound."

"So that leaves your Dad," I say with a final nod. "Let's take her to your Dad's, then. Though we'll need to make sure no one else sees her. Otherwise, I don't think even your Dad, powerful as he is on the Council, could explain it away."

"Gods no," Tallen says, swiftly shaking his head. "It would cause chaos."

Turning back to Li, we all head towards her. She looks back up at us, and there's a nervous tic on her face, but also dread.

"Don't worry," I tell her softly with a smile. "We aren't going to kill you. But we need to have you stay with someone who can protect you. First, though, let's get those chains off."

She slowly nods and stands up. Once I'm in front of her, I grab her wrists gently and, with both of my hands on the metal cuffs that are bolted to the chains, I cast Break. Suddenly the cuffs fall to the ground, with the chains still attached. I bend down and do the same thing to the manacles attached to her ankles. Within seconds, she has no chains on her. The rags I can't do anything about.

"Actually. I need to hide your heritage... if you're all right with that?"

Nervously, she nods at me. "Hmm. Sure?"

Now that I'm closer to her, I see she is about the same height as Marissa—meaning she was rather short. Carmen is the taller of the two by several inches.

"What's your idea?" Marissa asks.

"I'm going to cast Illusion on her. I'm going to make her look like a Changeling, in cat form."

"Oh," she says with a grin, "that's a good idea. If someone sees her, they won't see through the Illusion spell, since you're such a high level."

"Bingo. Or at least, that is the idea."

Placing my hand on Li's head, with my eyes closed, I cast Illusion. In my mind, I think of the effect I want to achieve. I want her to look similar to Marissa, so I go with the same skin tone as my wife, though I keep the dark hair. I make her hair longer, too, as long as Carmen's. Li's hair had been fairly short, and even I can tell is in need of a desperate wash.

Once done, I remove my hand and open my eyes to look down at her. She's still cute, with lighter skin, but that mysterious dark allure she had as a Dark Elf is now gone. Which is fine, since that's what we were trying to hide.

Li frowns. "I don't feel any different."

"You won't," I tell her with a smile. "The spell is meant to hide you visually. If someone was to try to grab your tail, though, their hand would just pass through it. The spell is meant to look for stuff like that, though. If you were to try to grab your own tail, it would swish out of the way."

"Tail?" she blurts out, suddenly trying to look behind her, turning around in circles. She squeaks when she sees her tail behind her, which is a light gray in color, with darker spots. And just as I had said it would, when she tries to grab it, her tail swishes away from her grasping hand—almost like her tail had simply twitched.

"That is amazing!" she says in awe.

I look over, and Carmen, Marissa and Tallen are all grinning at her antics.

"Well, I guess we should get this over with," I say. "Marissa, care to open a Portal to your Dad's place?"

Nodding, she takes out her PDA, but then I blurt out. "Wait. I need to add this location to mine," I say, taking my stone out.

Everyone nods and takes out their own stone, to add this location to it. While I know Mike has the stone, and can redo what he did, I would rather have the location myself. Once we are all done adding the location, Marissa looks around to confirm we are ready, and then casts Portal.

When the Portal appears, Li gasps in wonder.

Carmen doesn't pause but heads directly into the Portal, followed by Tallen. I turn to Li and offer her my hand.

"Will it hurt?" she asks nervously.

"Not at all," I tell her with a comforting smile. "It will feel like walking under a cold shower, but without getting wet."

She nods nervously but takes my hand.

Once I think she's ready, I walk towards the Portal, with Marissa trailing behind us, as she was the one who had cast it. Once through the Portal, Li, beside me, gasps.

I look back down at her. "You get used to it after the fourth or fifth time," I tell her with a grin.

I hear a squawk of surprise, and looking up, see it's Preeka.

"Hey, Preeka," I tell her with a smile. "We're here to see your Master."

"What she!?!" the goblin shouts, pointing a finger excitedly in a jabbing motion at Li next to me.

"What?" I ask her, puzzled.

Wait, can Preeka see through my Illusion spell?

"What she!" she repeats more forcefully.

"Ah, I thought my alarm went off," I hear a gruff voice say.

Looking up, I see Targun come through the door into his front foyer. Preeka suddenly disappears from where she had been squatting on the floor, reappearing on Targun's right shoulder. She bends down and whispers something quickly into his ear.

He frowns and looks over at Li, who—at least to us—looks like a fair-skinned Changeling with dark hair, two tufted ears, and spots on her shoulders and tail. "Kevin," he says slowly, not looking at me, but frowning still at Li. "Preeka says that this person is not who she appears to be. Care to explain?"

"Yeah," I rub the back of my neck, "that was me. I have her under an Illusion spell so no one can see who she is."

"All right. What's so important about her, that you had to hide her?"

"Oh, shit!" he blurts out, staring at Marissa in horror. "You didn't bring your mother here, did you?"

"No, Dad," Marissa tells him, rolling her eyes. "I didn't bring mom here."

"Is there anyone else here?" I ask Targun, looking around.

He turns to me and, still frowning, shakes his head. "No one, other than myself and the normal staff of goblins. Preeka and... I think Keeno is here, as well?" he says, looking at Preeka for confirmation.

She nods.

"So yes. Just the three of us. What's this all about?" he asks, looking between the four, or rather the five of us, though his gaze keeps jumping back nervously to Li.

"Dad, promise not to freak out?" Marissa asks him nervously.

He looks at her hard and slowly nods. "I swear not to freak out."

She looks at me and nods, and I cancel the Illusion spell on Li.

To say that Targun's eyes widen in surprise would be an understatement. I'm pretty sure he forgot how to speak, because his mouth just opens and closes—no sound escaping his lips—several times in a row.

Finally, he rushes to his front door and, placing a hand on it, he casts a powerful spell, one strong enough that I can feel it from here. This spell is different, though. It was a trigger, that caused a held spell to suddenly encompass the entire house. Once the spell stops, he turns to me, nervously licking his lips.

"Did you just bring me another Dark Elf?"

"Yes," I tell him with a smile. "But she's under my protection."

He nods and looks at Li, who stands there nervously, looking at Targun. She looks beautiful with her gray skin, black eyes, and dark hair. The rags she wears looked like shit, but even those, she was able to make look good on her, in a wild kind of way.

"And you are willing to answer my questions, without my having to resort to magic?" he asks, suddenly sceptical.

She looks at me for permission to answer, and I nod.

"Yes. My people live deep underground. Kevin, was it? He rescued me, as I was being sent to my death."

"Wait, you haven't even introduced yourself?" Targun asks me in an incredulous tone.

"Ahh…" I say, blushing at my mistake. "We were kind of in a hurry."

Sighing, Targun shakes his head. Pointing to me, he says, "this is Kevin, and that's my daughter, Marissa, who is married to Kevin. And that's Carmen, who isn't… yet," he says, giving me a wink.

At that, both girls gasps in surprise.

"The lanky fellow here is Tallen. He's a Vampire Count and, I guess, technically, Kevin's foster father. This is Preeka, my house goblin, and I'm Targun. I'm also the lead Councillor on the Council of Galactic Folk."

"I'm Li Olnon," she says nervously, bowing from the waist.

"And a Dark Elf," Targun adds.

"And a Dark Elf," she says, nodding.

Targun turns to me, and he's grinning. "You brought me a Dark Elf?"

"Dad!" snaps Marissa at her father. "We didn't bring you a toy. She's a living person."

"Right. Right," he says, nodding quickly. "My apologies, Li Olnon, for my inappropriate behavior. I assume there was a reason you brought her here to me?"

"I did," I tell him. "Li has tons of intel on the lower cities of the Dark Elves."

"What lower cities?"

We explain to him what has been happening to us the past day and a half or so. And by the end of our tale, his eyes are even wider than when he'd first seen Li.

"Oh shit," he says softly. "We need to plan."

This is the end of Book 2 of M.A.G.I. Hunters

ABOUT THE AUTHOR

I am an older-than-dirt gamer. I started gaming when old school BBS' were a thing, playing Pit Fighter and Trade Wars. I remember buying my first PC when I was 14 years old; it was a RadioShack Tandy PC. Paid a ton for it.

When the internet became available, I was on the early (well, not THAT early) bandwagon.

My venture into online games started with Ultima Online. Then I got into the beta for Everquest. THAT was my addiction. I eventually convinced my partner at the time, to try the game since it seemed to be "taking you away from me almost every evening". And that is how my now wife became a gamer girl. We raided for years, and made some fantastic friends, who we still talk to on Facebook. Then came Everquest 2. Yet more addiction. I have tried WoW, many times. While the game was good, I just never got into it. Sorry WoW Players.

Since then, I have played tons of games that have come out, from online games to stand-alone ones. I have so many titles on Steam that one would think I would not run out of stuff to play, right? Yeah. If you look at my most played games in Steam, it would have to be in order: Elder Scrolls Online (over 900 hours), Ark Survival Evolved (over 500 hours), and Everquest 2 on Steam. But that doesn't take into account before I had it on Steam, so add another 2000 hours to that!

My love and passion for reading started at a young age. The first book I read for the sheer pleasure of it as a child was Lord of the Rings at the age of 12. From then on, it became an expensive habit. I have been reading Science Fiction and Fantasy ever since.

I am also a fan of Anime and Manga. Yeah, I know. How much more geek can I add to this? Oh, oh, you just wait. I was more into ichii and harem there. But also, more fantasy-based ones. I never did watch Yu-Gi-Oh or such. I did love comedy ones. Years ago, I remember introducing my older kids to Ranma ½. Yeah, I wasn't a good dad.

About three years ago, I was introduced to LitRPG and GameLit, and well, HaremLit. And I have not gone back. I have bought and read so many books on Kindle. I won't mention the numbers. I have wanted to write a book from a pretty young age, since I had lots of imagination and ideas. But I was always under the impression you needed a large publisher. I was wrong. Instead, I decided to put my thoughts to paper, as it were, and this started my new career as an author.

WHERE TO FIND ME

https://www.facebook.com/groups/LitRPG.books

https://www.facebook.com/groups/LitRPGGroup

You can also find me on Twitter @ https://twitter.com/DLevesqueauthor

CHAPTER 1- ELEMENTAL SUMMONER

"Alexander, I need you to go back there and fix that leak in the bathroom," yells my manager from behind the counter as I walk into the store.

Fuck, I hate it when he calls me by my full name. While my given name might be Alexander, I prefer Alex. And why the Hell am I fixing a leak? I'm a clerk. Ever since I told him my father was a renovation expert before he passed away from cancer, he's decided that somehow his skills had been passed down to me.

"Joshua," I tell him patiently. "You know that I tried to fix it last week, and it didn't work. Man, you need to call a plumber."

"I don't have that kind of money!" Joshua says with a grimace as I walk up to him. "Can you look at it please?" he begs me.

Technically, I don't start for another hour. I came in early to get away from the quiet at home, and the empty fridge. My mother, bless her soul, works 70-hour weeks at the hospital as a nurse. I barely get to see her. But this week has been worse than usual. She never even got a chance to do her weekly grocery run, and I'm not allowed to do it for her since I only pick up junk food.

I had come into work early to grab a drink and a pre-made sandwich and start reading one of the new fantasy books that one of the authors I follow had put out.

I say with a sigh, "Sure. But the sandwich is free."

"Deal!" he shouts to my retreating back. "But only if you can fix it." I stop, turn around and simply look at him. "Fine! It's free," he says gloomily.

I grab a drink and one of the pre-made egg salad sandwiches out of the cooler and head to the back of the store through a door that says 'staff only' on it.

Once on the other side, I open the drink, take a sip, and put it on the staff table. Beside the table are a couple of old torn up leather chairs that are a weird shade of putrid green but are comfortable as fuck, even with the duct tape that's there to keep the tears from getting bigger. I open the package for the sandwich and I devour the first half and set it next to the drink.

I place my bag on the chair and taking my sweatshirt off, sigh, and head to the bathroom in the back. The leak in question is coming from the water pipe, thank God, and not the sewer pipe.

Once I get to the bathroom, I pause to look at myself in the mirror that's above the sink, next to the toilet. God, I look like shit. I'm only 26, but I am already starting to let myself go and I look much older. The tire around my waist has gotten bigger, and my work shirt has gotten visibly tighter.

The goatee I started growing two years ago is still there, but you would think I only started it last month. It looks so pathetic. I am sure a 12-year-old could grow a better one. But I keep it there, hoping it will somehow miraculously explode in growth one day miraculously. My receding hairline isn't helping either. Nor do my eyes that are puffy from lack of sleep. I was up all night playing my addiction; the online game I had been playing for the last three years. To me, it was an escape from my shitty life. In it, I could pretend to be Juxar, the wizard.

I give myself a wan smile in the mirror and bend down and look at the pipe. There is a bucket underneath it to catch the dripping water that is leaking from the joint. Last time I had tried to use some kind of plumbing tape, but it didn't help, I guess. I look around, and I see Joshua's store toolbox sitting next to the wall.

I open it and look to see if the monkey wrench is there. Yep. I turn off the main water to the sink, I remove the offending cable pipe and look at it. The white plumber's tape is still there, but it's useful as shit. Fuck, why the Hell Joshua doesn't simply call a plumber is beyond me. The guy keeps saying he doesn't have money, but he does. He owns fourteen of these stores. This one so happens to be the one closest to his house, which is why he comes to work here.

Using my nail, I remove the white tape and grab a fresh roll of it from the toolbox. Maybe I had put it on wrong? I mean, *is* there a wrong way? I slowly wrap more tape around the pipe and then look at my handy work when I'm done. It looks like it's on differently. Maybe the angle you use when you do it makes a difference? Shrugging, I put the pipe back together and use the monkey wrench to make sure it's on tightly, but not enough to crack the breakable plastic ring surrounding it.

I turn on the main water slowly, and watch to see if there are any drips. Although, last time there weren't any either, so I might not find out 'til next week that yet again, the pipe is leaking.

I watch it for five minutes, with my mind admittedly going back to the Quest I did last night, which is the reason I am so tired today, and I don't see any leaking.

I had found a Questline that no one else had found. I even checked the wiki to make sure—nothing on the site about it. So I ended up staying up late to finish it before anyone else could, taking down details about it, so I could write up a walkthrough about it later for the wiki and stamp my name on the page.

I wash my hands clean from the germs I am sure are all over the place in here, using liberal amounts of soap and hot water until they are red and almost raw from the scrubbing. At least I know this bathroom gets cleaned weekly, as I am the one who does it. Once I'm done, I head back to my food that's waiting for me at the staff table. I sit down and finish the other half of my sandwich and my drink, and take my book out of my bag.

Ah, come to me, oh words of wisdom. I glance at my watch, I have forty minutes before I need to start my shift. Sweet, I think to myself. I open the book to my bookmark, which is a hot Elf girl that is mostly naked, other than the bikini she is wearing. Yeah, I know. What would a fantasy Elf girl be doing wearing a bikini? Who cares!

To make sure I don't get too engrossed in my book and lose time, I take my smartphone out and set the alarm for five minutes before my shift starts. Joshua hates leaving late to go home to supper with his kids and wife.

* * *

I get pulled out of my book with a shock and stare at my phone like it is something evil. Fuck, I had just gotten to a good part of the story. As much as I want to stay and read it, I know Joshua. He docks me an hour's pay if I am even a minute late. I learned that the hard way when I started working for him five years ago after dropping out of college. That's right, five years. That's part of the reason I am able to work the evening shift instead of the night shift. I have the seniority, and also Joshua likes me, even though he keeps saying I could do so much better with my life than work for him. I just shake my head and tell him I am doing exactly what I want to be doing.

The day staff hate working with Joshua. The night staff, well, Joshua's older brother has dibs on that shift. I put my garbage in the waste container next to the table, throwing my bottle into the blue recycle bin that I knew Joshua's brother will end up dumping into the wastebasket anyhow. I get up and stretch, stiff from sitting down without moving for so long, and place my bookmark into my book, before putting the book inside my bag. I walk over to the set of four lockers, I set my bag in one of them and close the door, placing my thumbprint on it to lock it.

One thing that Joshua was willing to splurge on was these lockers. He said he got them at a discount, but the staff didn't care since they were so damn cool. No keys, no combination to remember. Just your thumbprint, I think with a grin.

Heading to the front of the store, I walk through the door and stop dead in my tracks. There is a man in front of the counter, but he isn't buying shit. He has a gun in his hand, and it's pointed at Joshua. The man has a ski mask over his face, and he suddenly turns towards me, with the handgun tracking my way.

"Whoa, whoa!" I shout at him, putting my hands up.

This isn't my first robbery in five years, but looking at Joshua, I can see he is white as a ghost. Working the day shift, he has never been robbed before. "Listen, if you want the cash, we can give you the cash. All right? It's cool, man. Just my boss there, he will open the till and pass you the money. Good?" I tell him in a calm voice.

"What the fuck, man," the robber says, turning the gun back towards Joshua. "I asked you if you was alone, and you said yes. You fucking lied to me, you fucking asshole," he tells Joshua, waving the gun back and forth threateningly.

"Whoa, whoa!" I shout again, focusing his attention back on me, which unfortunately also means the gun is now facing my way again.

"He didn't know," I lied. "I came in through the back door and had been reading a book in the back room. Normally I would come in through the front door about this time, for my shift," I tell him in a soft and calm voice, even though my heart is in my throat from having a gun aimed at me.

"You's lying," he says, taking a step towards me, but I stand my ground. "You probably already called the fucking cops," the robber shouts in what I can now see is a panic. His eyes have gotten bigger, and his breathing has gotten quicker. Shit, is this guy jacked up on something?

"No, seriously, dude. I didn't call the cops. Listen, let my boss get you the cash from the till, and then you can go. We promise not to call the police, all right?" I tell him, unsure of what he will do. Most robbers at night are pretty well either drunk or nervous. This guy is going into full-blown panic mode.

Suddenly, I hear a scream from the doorway. I turn, and there is an old lady who must have just walked through the door and seen us being robbed at gunpoint. Instead of acting like a normal person and backing out quietly, she screamed. Really?

Shockingly, I hear a loud explosion, and something slams into my forehead that fucking hurts worse than the time I got a marble in the forehead from a slingshot when I was 11. And that is the last thing I remember before everything goes black.

Get your copy here!
Elemental Summoner 1